IN A FEVERED LAND

A NOVEL BY

IRENE SANDELL

Double Mountain
Press

Dedication

To the memory of my father, William Leslie (Bill)
Robinson.
All things in life, the good and the bad, were made better
when they were shared with him.

Book I
EMORY
1928

Chapter 1

The sun was dropping fast through the twisted mesquites. Two figures ran single file, squatted low, with their arms held high to shield their faces against the thorny branches barely visible before them in the fading light.

"Come on, Lon!" the leader pleaded in a half whisper. "I got to find it again before it gets too dark. Come on!"

"You're going to get us both killed out here," the follower whispered back. He dodged quickly as a branch swished, barely missing his face. "Watch it, Emory!"

"Will you just come on!"

They broke into a clearing and stopped to catch their breath, sucking in great mouthfuls of air.

"Old Handley catches us down here, he'll shoot us. You know that," Lon. the follower, whispered between deep breaths.

"Shh! Keep your voice down. It'll carry along the river." Emory searched quickly side to side. "There!" He pointed to a twisted mesquite stump with a washed out hole at its base.

The two crossed the clearing in an awkward crouch and dropped to their knees by the stump. Emory reached full head and shoulders back into the washout. A tale-tell clink broke the silence. He withdrew his hand and held up a jug. "What'd I tell you, cousin?" He shook the jug to test its volume. It sounded full. "Ha, ha! What'd I tell you?"

"It'll probably kill us both." Lon responded. "Ratch Handley never did anything right in his whole life. What makes you think he can make whiskey?"

"Hell! Old Ratch drinks it night and day, and he ain't dead. Now, come on, you said you'd drink it, if I could find it." He scrambled to his feet. "Let's get out of here before Ratch shows up."

They moved slower this time, each picking his way carefully through the brush in the thickening darkness. Emory cradled the jug like a baby in his arms. It made a metallic sloshing sound as he walked.

"You sure your folks won't be back till tomorrow?" Lon whispered after they were well away from the clearing.

"It's sale day. They won't be back. I swear, Lon, you worry too damn much." Emory held up the jug and patted it gently. "This is going to be great!"

The boys reached a plowed field thick with brittle brown cotton plants freshly stripped of their white produce and slowed their steps in the loose sand. They followed the furrow more from memory than from sight. The black outline of the barn was barely visible against the coming darkness. Neither one spoke again until they were in the barn with the door swung shut. Emory lit a coal oil lamp, and they dropped exhausted on a stack of hay bundles and caught their breath.

"This is the damnedest idea you've ever talked me into!" Lon wiped his sweat soaked hair back from his eyes.

"Yep."

The boys stared at the jug between them and started to laugh the nervous laugh of adrenaline-fed fear and excitement.

"Old Ratch will be fit to be tied when he finds this jug gone."

"Hell, he'll never know the difference. He's drunk most of the time, and crazy the rest." Emory produced two tin cups from behind the tack box. "Come on, pour up."

Lon filled both cups and sat the jug down carefully. Both boys stared at the liquor with some sense of ceremony. "Tell me again now, why we're doing this."

"Cause it's time." Emory voice sounded reverent. They picked up the cups in unison and brought them to their lips.

"Lord! This stuff is awful!" Lon stammered after the first swallow. The kerosene smell of the liquor filled his mouth and nostrils.

"Damn straight!" Emory managed. Both boys gasped for breath, but both kept drinking.

Emory drained his cup first and reached to refill it. He wiped the back of his hand across his mouth and shivered involuntarily, but after a moment he put the cup to his lips again.

Lon watched his cousin's determined actions. His own cup was still half full. He braced himself for another swallow. "Maybe if we went to the house and got some crackers or something." Deep in his chest, the liquor burned like fire.

"Man, you're pitiful!" Emory sounded out of breath. "Them old boys by the river don't eat crackers when they're drinking. They just drink. Now shut up. I think I feel something."

Lon raised his cup again. His lips were going numb. "Jeremy should be here for this." he said. His jaw muscles seemed to lock when he tried to speak.

"Hell, he's off out there in the oil fields with a girl under each arm and a jug in each hand. This is too damn tame for him."

Both boys giggled at the scene they imagined. "Anyway, he won't be lordin' it over us about being greenhorns no more when he hears about this."

Lon nodded thoughtful agreement and forced himself to drain the cup. He couldn't let Emory get too far ahead of him. "You think he's telling the truth about those oil field jobs? Six dollars a day? Do you believe that?"

"Hell no! You can't believe nothing Jer says." Emory reached to fill his cup again.

Lon watched with a mild sense of dread. Emory sure wasn't slacking off on this. He studied the cup in his own hand, stalling off his next swallow. "Then where'd he get all that money he showed us?"

"Who knows? Stole it maybe. Or maybe somebody paid him. But not no six dollars a day."

"Just the same, I'd still like to go out and see for myself." Lon gulped down a swallow and reached to poured more whiskey. "Like Jer said, I don't want to hang around here till I'm a dried up old man."

"Your pa ain't going to hear of you running off to no oil field. No more than mine would." Emory wiped his hand across his mouth in a disgusted motion. "You're wastin' time asking. You can read all them books on far off places all you want, and it don't matter a hill of beans. You're gonna be a farmer, same as me."

"I'm not! Not till I go look around a bit. And you ought to come too." Lon held up his cup in a kind of salute.

"Not a chance." Emory shook his head and busied himself pouring more moonshine.

"Well, we sure as hell don't want to end up like this; working like mules all day with nothing to show for it and laying up by the river at night drinking Ratch's moonshine for excitement." Lon jammed his hand down into the bib pocket on his overalls and pulled out a wad of bills. "Ya see this? This is a year's work Emory. A whole damn year! Seventeen dollars! I been busting my ass all year, and all I got to show for it is seventeen dollars! Cotton brought four cents a pound, for God's sake!"

"So you're going to just waltz in there and tell Uncle Henry that you're leaving?"

"I am." Lon took a big swallow. The kerosene taste was gone, replaced by an oily residue on his tongue.

"That's just the whiskey talking, cousin." Emory looked into his cup and pursed his lips. "This stuff works after all."

"No, it ain't the whiskey. I'm going. I'm going tomorrow." Lon waved the fist full of money. "This tears it! I'm through with farming!"

"Hell, cuz, you can't do nothin' without me. You'll just get off out there and get yourself killed or something."

"I'm going," Lon stuffed the money back in his overalls. His mouth felt strange as he formed the words. His cousin was looking fuzzy in the low lamp light. Lon slumped against the hay bale behind him and tried to run his tongue over his lips. They were gone.

Emory sat very straight and wiped his mouth with a deliberate motion like he was afraid he would miss. "I've got to admit, though; Jer's story about them girls caught my interest." When he leaned forward to refill his cup, his aim was unsteady. Some of the liquor spilled out on the hay, but he took no notice. "Now I would like to see that. Something besides all these prissy-ass girls we got around here with their legs crossed."

Lon gave his cousin an unsteady sidelong glance. "Shoot! All you think about is prissy-ass girls. Split your head open and there wouldn't be nothing else in there." He rubbed at his nose. It was numb to his touch. "If you ever did get hold of one, you'd likely faint."

"That's a damn lie! I'd know what to do!" Emory half rose to one knee, poised for a fight.

Lon struggled to focus on his cousin's face. It was flushed red, and his eyes were glassy and wild. "Come on, Emory. Don't get all riled up. You better slow down on that stuff." The barn walls seemed to waver. Lon blinked his eyes to clear them. He looked down at the cup in his hand. It seemed miles away. "Whew Lordy! I've had enough." He shook his head, and his insides rolled over in his gut. "I'm going home." He struggled to his feet.

"Home! You can't quit now." Emory shook the jug. It sounded almost empty. "You're a damn sissy, boy! You can't hold your liquor. I've never felt better in my life!"

Lon rocked from heel to toe trying to get his balance. "I doubt that."

"You won't tell your Pa nothing! You're a damn coward, always talking about leaving!" Emory swung wildly out at his legs. Lon dodged the blow and steadied himself against a railing.

"Hey man, cut it out!"

Emory swung awkwardly again, and Lon grabbed his fist. "Stop it, Emory! I ain't going to fight you. You're acting crazy!"

Emory jerked away and lost his balance. He sprawled back across the hay bales stirring up a swirl of dust and straw, grabbed outward at the wall behind him, but did not attempt to get up. "You ain't leaving! You ain't going to do nothing!"

"We've had enough, cousin. I'm going home."

Lon let himself out of the barn. He could hear Emory cussing him halfway across the field to his house. But it didn't matter. He'd get over it. Lon concentrated on the windmill tower ahead of him in the moonlight and putting one unsteady foot in front of the other.

There was no light showing in the house. Pa had already gone to bed like he had figured. He stopped by the windmill tank and stuck his head full into the water, letting the chill shock him awake. Then he slumped down on the cool metal edge of the water tank to collect himself. A full moon illuminated the field of empty cotton stalks stretched out before him. It was as close to light as the moon could make it. Old Ratch would be down by the river running his hounds tonight, he thought. And hopefully too busy to count his jugs.

He could see his open bedroom window clearly, just like he'd left it. Cautiously he climbed in and paused to listen, but his father didn't stir. Lon smiled at his cleverness and fell across the bed. He was asleep before his head hit the pillow.

***

He was awakened by the sound of the screen door squeaking on its hinges and slapping shut. Lon jumped at the sound and tried to raise his head before the blinding headache stopped him. He lay motionless, moaning in sleep-fogged agony and listened to his father make three false starts at turning the Model T's engine over before it caught. Then the engine sound receded.

Lord, it must be late. Why hadn't Pa gotten him up already? Sunlight was streaming in the window. It must be mid-morning. Sunday. It was Sunday, and Pa had gone to church.

Guilt pulled him out of bed, and he balanced his throbbing head against the jar of walking. He was going to have some tall explaining to do. He looked down at his rumpled clothes and dirt caked shoes. He was a mess. Nope, Pa had already figured it out.

"Oh, Lord." He steadied himself against the door frame. Another one of Emory's bright ideas. Stealing Ratch Handley's moonshine. What a stupid way to die. Old Ratch would have shot them for sure if he had happened up. Lon smiled a little and shook his head slightly. He was immediately sorry. He sank down at the kitchen table and sampled the coffee Pa had left in the pot. It was barely warm, but strong. That was what he needed.

Out the back door morning sun covered everything in a blinding glow. Lon squinted against the glare and cradled his forehead in one hand. Lord A Mercy! This is not worth it. I'll never make a drinking man.

***

He was cleaned up and fairly presentable by the time he heard the Model T coming back. Lon looked out from the shadow of the front porch and watched the boil of red dust turn at the corner of the upper field and came toward him. Pa brought the car to a rattling stop and cut its wheels crazily to the right, like he was tying it off.

Lon watched in amusement. He always half expected his father to yell "Whoa" when he stopped that contraption. Henry Prather never had trusted that automobile. He drove it like he was riding an unbroken horse-- wide open as if to let the machine know who was boss. His car was a symbol of some past success in farming. The reward from a better year when prices were high and the rains more opportune.

Henry gave his son a long gaze out the front wind shield, then climbed out. There was always a gently amused look in his pa's eyes that belied the seriousness of his expression otherwise. Times had been both fat and lean to Henry Prather, and he wasn't much surprised by either one.

"You water the stock?" was his only greeting.

"Yes, sir. Sorry I didn't make it up for church, Pa. I..."

"No need to explain."

Yep, he knew. Lon felt his queasy stomach do a slow roll.

"Bo Sills was talking after the service today. Price may go even lower than four cents. We may have got off light." Henry stepped up on the porch and started into the house.

Lon watched his father pass and then followed him in. The slap of the screen door cracked behind him as his eyes adjusted to the darker interior of the room. He dropped into a hide-bottomed chair by the door, glad to be off his feet.

"It don't seem fair, after all that work."

"Fair ain't got nothing to do with it." Henry appeared in the doorway from the kitchen and studied his son slumped in the chair. "I don't hold with this laying out all night, son. You may think you're almost grown, but if you're going to pull your weight around here, I'll not stand for that kind of life."

"We were just having some fun, Pa. I don't plan to make a habit of it."

Henry disappeared into the kitchen again. Lon followed him and leaned against the door jamb. He watched his father measure several heaping spoonfuls of coffee into a pot on the stove and stoop to stir the smoldering morning fire. The flames jumped to life, and Henry added a chunk of mesquite wood. Then, apparently satisfied with his efforts, he straightened and reached behind him on the shelf for two cups. Lon had watched this ritual a hundred times before --Pa and his coffee, boiled and straight. No problem was ever so great, his father didn't think a cup of coffee would help.

"So," Lon took a deep breath. "What are we going to do, now?"

"We'll get by. 28's just been a bad year. The market will come back. We won't make nothing, but we ain't lost nothing."

"Lost nothing! Pa, how can you say that. All that work!"

Henry turned and regarded his son, confused at the anger in his voice. "We're doing all right. We don't owe nobody, and between this farm of mine and the one your mother left us, we'll make out."

"But Mother's place won't bring a dime. Ratch Handley never plants a crop. You know that."

Henry shrugged his shoulders.

"Why do you put up with him, Pa? The man never does a lick of work, never turns his hand..."

"You seemed to like his whiskey right enough."

Lon stopped short and fumbled for something to say. "That was just a crazy stunt, Pa. It don't mean nothing." His voice trailed off under his father's hard gaze.

"Ratch is my problem, Lon. I'll take that responsibility."

"Your problem? Our problem, Pa. I work here, too, and I see that we aren't making it."

"Well, farming's never been no way to get rich, boy.

You ought to know that, by now."

Lon dropped the subject. He had never understood his father's reasons for allowing Ratch Handley and his large family to live on Lon's mother's place year after year while the land lay barren. Henry Prather worked from dawn to dark in any kind of weather, but he let his tenant lay up and sleep all day and run hounds along the river all night, without even a word of reproach that Lon knew of. It didn't make sense. None of this did. All this work and so little return.

The hiss of the boiling coffee caught their attention. Henry tossed in a dash of cold water to settle the grounds and carefully tipped the pot to allow the top liquid to pour out.

Lon reached for the cup his father offered, but he did not drink. He watched for a moment as Henry sat down at the kitchen table and took a sip. "Then, I don't want any more, Pa. I'm leaving."

Henry looked up quickly. "Now just where do you figure you'd go?"

"I've been talking to Jeremy Randell. He says he has a job out West in the oil fields making good money. If I go out there, Jer says I can go right to work..."

"Hell fire, boy! You know that Jeremy Randell. You can't put any store by what he says. There ain't nothing to it."

"They're paying six dollars a day starting out, Pa. Six dollars!"

Henry was silent, but his look was dark and anxious.

"Didn't you ever just want to go, Pa? Just light out?" Lon's voice was shaky with emotion. If only his father would understand.

"I don't hold with that kind of foolishness, son." Henry

11

sat hunkered over his coffee cup. "Chasing out across the country after some wild idea."

Lon stood silent and listened, as he had so many times before.

"There ain't no sense to it. You've got all a man needs right here. Two parcels of the best cotton land here a'bouts."

Lon started to speak, but his father's voice cut him off.

"I swear, boy. First it's some high-toned idea you want to go to boarding school or something, and now this." Henry shook his head. "You're sixteen years old now and a full grown man. It's time you took hold of life. It don't do for folks like us to dream too big." Henry paused to get a breath. "Now, I'll hear no more of these fool ideas, you hear?"

Lon smiled slightly and slumped his shoulders. It was no use to try and explain.

Henry pushed his cup away and stood up. "Now, let's see to them hogs. Looks like they will be our only moneymaker this year." He adjusted his hat and headed out the back screen door into the bright patch of sun-bleached yard.

Lon followed slowly. His father was still talking, calling over his shoulder as he walked. Something about the work to be done. But Lon didn't hear. His mind was racing over the things he might have said. He knew what he had to do.

***

Late that night, after he could hear his father's even breathing in the next room, Lon gathered a change of clothes in a bundle and slipped out into the autumn night. He paused by the corner of the house to adjust to the light of a moon so bright he cast a shadow across the yard. Something touched his sleeve, and a hot wire of fright jolted his body. In a reflex motion, he wheeled around ready to strike out with his free hand.

"Hold it, there! Don't take my head off!" Emory whispered.

Lon made out his cousin's toothy grin. "What the hell are you doing...!" Lon's heart was hammering in his chest.

"Me? Hell, let's talk about you. I ain't the one sneaking off into the night like a chicken thief."

"Shh..." Lon grabbed his arm and dragged Emory toward the road, out of earshot from the house. They squatted by the fence. "I figured you'd still be laid out in the barn, bad as you were last night. What are you doing?"

"So, you was just gonna light out without me. Just go."

"You aren't interested in going, remember," Lon shot back. He looked around at the house, half expecting his father to step out on the porch. "What do you want?"

Emory held up his hand to reveal a bundle tied in an extra shirt. "I can't let you go off by yourself, now can I."

"I ain't coming back, Emory. Not for a long time. Maybe never."

"Well, that's all right with me."

Lon studied his cousin's face in the moonlight. "What happened to you? You're all scratched up."

Emory brought his hand up quickly to the long set of scratches on his cheek. "Some of them mesquite thorns got me last night. That's all. Are we going or not?"

"What made you change your mind all of a sudden?"

"Hell, I can change my mind if I want to!" Emory looked away, back toward the house. "Come on, let's go! I can't abide a man who's all talk."

Lon hesitated only a moment. It would be good to have

some company.

"Well, come on!"

They ran until they reached the corner of the upper field, then slowed to a walk to catch their breath. Lon glanced back only once. Emory kept his head down, eyes on his path, but he looked back often. By sun-up they had crossed the Brazos and flagged down a ride on a bus to Abilene. Already the land they passed was strange and new.

Chapter 2

The Red Line bus between Abilene and El Paso slid to a stop before a flimsy frame building huddled by the highway. Slumped in the first seat behind the driver, Lon Prather snapped awake as his head fell forward with the braking motion. For a second he could not think where he was. He squinted out into the blackness beyond the bus window and then back at his cousin beside him. Emory Campbell was still asleep crumpled over like a rag doll in the cramped seat.

The driver pushed the door lever back and motioned with a turn of his head. "Pyote, Texas, boys. Rise and shine." He disappeared out the bus door.

"Come on, Emory," Lon whispered so as not to disturb the other passengers. He gave his cousin a poke in the ribs. Emory jerked awake and jumped to his feet. He gazed wildly around and then focused blurry eyes on his cousin and nodded shakily.

Both boys studied the building in quick looks out the bus window as they gathered their gear. By the time they got outside, the driver was finished unloading a stack of canvas mail bags from the roof. He jumped down from the railing and dusted his hands.

"You can get a cup of coffee in there." The driver nodded toward the building. "Curly's open. Mail-run to Wink will be in here about sun-up."

"Much obliged," Lon mumbled, but his heart wasn't in it. It felt more like the driver was abandoning them than doing them a favor.

The bus sputtered, and the man climbed back in and gunned the engine to keep it running. No one else on board had stirred. The other passengers were taking advantage of the last minutes before sunrise to sleep. It was still a long way to El Paso.

"Good luck, boys!" The driver called as the bus pulled away into the black distance.

Lon turned to look at his cousin in the dim light over the cafe sign. Emory was still rubbing sleep from his eyes, his wadded bundle hugged to his chest like a small child.

"Come on, let's get some coffee." Lon suggested. Emory followed him, mumbling under his breath.

The building looked even smaller on the inside than it did from the road. A scrawny man behind the counter seemed crowded in the narrow work space. The place was nearly empty, except for the three of them and one other man sleeping slouched in a chair, his hat over his eyes. They ordered breakfast and ate in silence. It was too early for conversation.

Sounds of motion drifted in from the predawn darkness outside, occasionally at first, and then more frequently as dawn approached. The familiar jingle of harnesses on mules and the muffled creak of wagon wheels suggested great activity, but no one came in to disturb their vigil. The two boys, now wide awake, fidgeted on their counter stools.

"What do you reckon will happen when they find we're gone?" Emory asked.

Lon shrugged. "Nothing, I guess. There's nothing they can do."

"Will they come looking for us, you reckon?"

"No. Pa won't come. And neither will Uncle Willis. We haven't done anything wrong, you know. We just left, that's all."

Emory jerked as though Lon had struck him. Lon looked around at his cousin and saw a strange look in his eyes. "What's the matter, Emory?"

"Nothing!" He thumped the counter. "More coffee!"

"Is something wrong?"

"No! Hell, no. I'm just tired of waiting, that's all."

A loud engine noise intruded on their conversation. Outside a car door slammed, and heavy boots struck the wooden walk. The boys looked toward the door as a barrel-chested man in a wide-brimmed hat swung the screen open and set one foot inside. He cradled a sawed-off shotgun in his arms, one hand on the trigger. "Any of you boys going to Wink?"

The sleeping man arose without a word and made for the door, but Lon and Emory were caught off guard by the gruff question. They sat dumfounded for several seconds, staring at the gun.

Ah, yes sir, we are!" Lon finally responded.

"Well, we're leaving." The man turned on his heels and disappeared from sight.

Emory's stare had shifted from the gun to his cousin when Lon answered the man. Now Lon glanced at Emory and saw his eyes wide with a look of doubt and confusion that mirrored the way he felt himself. Then as rapidly as it came the indecision was gone, replaced by grins that spread across their faces, and they were up.

"Here goes nothin'." Emory giggled.

Scrambling for their caps and bags, they followed the man out.

An open touring car, motor coughing, waited out front almost hidden under sacks of mail a little man was strapping to the fenders and running boards. The boys clambered into the back seat as the man with the gun indicated, and the car shot off straight north across the desert. Lon and Emory sat wedged in the back seat next to the fellow from the cafe, a bronze-skinned mountain of a man Lon figured to be an Indian, although he had never seen one up this close. While they bounced and jostled with every bump, the Indian sat silent and solid, arms folded, and stared straight ahead seemingly unaffected by the rough trip. In the front seat next to the driver was the man with the shot gun. He rode with one foot braced against the dashboard and a firm grip on the side bar of the car. In his other hand, cradled against the outstretched arm, rested the gun. The driver, a slight wiry man who could barely see over the front of the car, drove wide open, slowing up only at sudden unexpected intervals. The little man obviously could make out some sort of road. Guard, Indian, or driver never spoke.

Stretching away from the car lay desert terrain; flat sandy miles broken by sage and cactus only now becoming visible as the morning sun edged over the eastern horizon. They followed a low caliche ridge that zigzagged crazily. Here the car could apparently find hard ground. Along the way they passed a spotty stream of cars, trucks and wagons carrying every manner of goods from machinery to groceries. Wagons pulled by mule teams of six or eight hauled the heavy loads. One driver had misjudged the ridge, and his wagon sat mired in the sand to its axles. The mule skinners were busy shouting and cracking whips as the mules from two combined teams strained to free the load. Lon and Emory studied the scene with interest as they flashed passed, but the others in the car never gave it a glance.

As the wagons disappeared in their dust, Lon looked around at his cousin. Emory, trying to hang on to his cap and anticipate the next bump, had fixed his gaze on the way ahead. He looks like Uncle Willis, Lon thought. He had never noticed it before, but Emory had that same square jaw that all the Campbells had. He has no business on this journey, and his confusion showed in his eyes. Emory was born to be a farmer. He never should have let him tag along.

Lon took a deep breath of the desert air. As for himself, he felt free for the first time in his life. If he'd had any second thoughts about running off to the end of the earth, they had all disappeared with the leaving. Emory could go home if he wanted.

The sun climbed higher and bleached earth and sky to a blended shade of tan. Sweat trickled down the center of his back and soaked Lon's shirt only to be cooled and dried almost instantly in the breeze whipped up by the car. Sand stirred by their passing powdered the passengers like talc. Wedged in between the Indian and Emory, Lon concentrated on holding his balance and bracing for the jerky turns and dips. It felt rather like a bronc ride, he thought, and he smiled at his hapless predicament.

Two hours into the trip Lon caught sight of a hazy smear against the skyline. Scattered wooden derricks came into view and a heavy sulfur smell engulfed them. A deep rumbling growl could be heard from somewhere like a great wounded beast. As they drew closer, the whole landscape seemed to be alive with small fires, the flames high off the ground on long pipes that looked like so many great candles. A filmy layer of smoke covered everything. Surveying the scene, Lon remembered the fire and brimstone descriptions of hell he had so often heard Jeremy Randell's father expound from the pulpit back home, and the hair on the back of his neck twitched in a confusion of anticipation and fear.

The car roared past a row of oilfield equipment and careened on to what passed for a town street. Abruptly they were surrounded by cars, trucks, and wagons of every type, chugging along in both directions between rows of haphazardly constructed buildings; some tents, some lumber, some a combination of both.

The car skidded to a stop under a sign declaring CLUB CAFE and the three men climbed out without exchanging a word. The Indian gathered his gear and disappeared into the crowd. The driver began to unload bags of mail, and the man with the gun swung several sacks over his shoulder and carried them into the building. Lon and Emory picked up their belongings and stepped to the wooden sidewalk. They stared with bewilderment up and down the street before them. Noise was constant between engines and shouts of mule skinners, and over the din the sound of hammers added to evidence of progress. Board walks on both sides of the street were crammed with men shouldering along in an endless stream. Somewhere a piano could be heard occasionally.

The door behind them burst open, and the shotgun man reappeared for more mail sacks. He brushed past them briskly. "Give me a hand here," he ordered, and Lon and Emory jumped forward to take a bundle as he tossed them their way. They followed him in, struggling to carry the bulky sacks and their own gear at the same time. Several people looked up as they entered. The mail guard pointed toward a stack of bundles to one side of the door. "Much obliged, boys."

They mumbled some response, but the guard never glanced back. Instead, he joined a group at the far end of the room.

The boys sat down at the counter and were still gazing around in open-faced awe when the guard looked back at them and called out.

"You boys looking for work?"

"Yes, sir. Ah, well, that is we're looking for a man who promised us a job," Lon volunteered.

"We're looking for a fellow named Jer Randall," Emory put in.

"Don't know him, but that don't mean much in this town. Who does he work for?"

"We don't know."

A chuckle rippled through the group. "Well, good luck finding him, boys," and the man turned back to his coffee.

Lon and Emory looked at one another as the foolishness of their search finally struck them. Finding Jer was going to present a problem.

"Did Jer ever say where he was working, Lon?"

"Just Wink. That's all he said." Lon studied the blank look on Emory's face. What could he say? He hadn't expected this many people. They sat in silence for a few moments trying to take in their situation.

"Well, we'll just ask around, and if he don't turn up soon, we'll just find another job," Lon announced.

"Right!" Emory agreed, but his voice didn't sound so sure.

"Come on, let's get out of here."

The boys slipped out as quietly as possible. They worked their way through the crowd on the walkway to the corner of what passed for a street crossing and surveyed their surroundings again. Then, caught by the motion of the crowd, they let themselves be swept along as they gazed about in amazement. The doorways along the street revealed something new at every turn. Pool halls, domino halls, cafes, rooming houses, gambling houses, dance halls, bootleg joints with an occasional dry goods or grocery store mixed in stood door to door on both sides of the main street for two or three blocks. The mixture of smells and noises was endless.

Suddenly a screen door in front of them exploded outward. Two men came flying past and landed in the dirt street. Curses and shouts boiled up as the crowd parted, and a circle formed around the men. As quickly as they landed the two men were up and crouched for attack. Then in a flash, they tore at one another with swinging blows. Lon recognized one of the men as the big Indian who had ridden over from Pyote with them. He looked even bigger now. The man he fought was almost as tall, a huge bear of a fellow in oil-stained overalls. He was doing all the cussing while the Indian was doing most of the fighting, and the force of the blows the Indian struck made a jolting thud as they landed. Trapped in the crowd with a front row view, the boys dodged and cringed with the other onlookers as blood and sweat spattered the ground and air inside the circle. The blows flew both ways, but the Indian was clearly winning. Suddenly a third man from the crowd was in the circle. He clenched both fist together and swung a hard blow to the back of the big Indian's head. The Indian staggered but did not go down. Both men took advantage of the moment's hesitation and tackled the Indian with all their strength. They went at him like animals, and the big man, now outnumbered, thrashed about trying to free his arms. Men pressed in on all sides yelling encouragement and insults enthusiastically, and a couple of other fights broke out on the edge of the circle. One of the men had the Indian's arms half pinned, while the other worked him over. It was horrible to watch, and yet Lon and Emory could not look away. Just then a man from the crowd jumped on the back of one of the Indian's attackers. He was a little fellow, Lon noted. Too little to be messing with these men. But his size did not seem to slow him down. The little man yelled at the top of his lungs and gouged at the eyes of his target. The man he jumped screamed in pain and staggered back unable to shake off his burden, and this gave the Indian time to recover. The Indian shook his head to clear his vision and regained his footing. He let out a rumbling yell that managed to drown out even the crowd noise for a moment as he grabbed his remaining foe with one great hand and slung him across the circle like a piece of kindling. The man sprawled flat in the dirt, made a weak effort to get up, and then he seemed to think better of it and lay still. The big Indian then turned on the other fellow still stumbling about struggling with the little man wrapped around his head and shoulders. It was hard to tell any of the men apart any more, they were so covered in dirt. It would have been a comical sight, Lon thought, if their intentions had not been so serious.

Abruptly an explosion split the air next to Lon's ear that almost took him to his knees, and he turned to see the barrel of a sawed-off shot gun still pointed skyward. The crowd went silent and the Indian stopped in mid swing.

"That will do, boys," The man from the mail run said calmly.

"Ah, come on, Jack, where's your sense of fun?" Someone shouted from the crowd. A chuckle rippled through the throng, and people began to move away.

"You boys can cool off in jail," Jack ordered, "Get going." He brandished the shotgun skyward. "Clear the way there!"

The exhausted men slapped dirt from their clothes, retrieved their hats, and followed the lawman's order rather meekly for four fellows who had been trying to kill one another a few minutes before. The void caused by the fight filled with people again, and the street noise returned. Lon and Emory looked around, confused as to what to do next. Then like two twigs trapped in a spring flood, they moved on with the crowd.

Weaving through more traffic than they had ever seen in one place, they crossed the street after a time and found the sidewalk on the other side was just as crowded as the one they had left. They tried to stay together, but it was not easy in the crush. Lon was beginning to have serious doubts about the wisdom of the whole sightseeing tour. The thought crossed his mind that it would be a sorry way to die, being stomped by this mob of people before they even found Jeremy. Emory led the way which was no help, Lon considered, because his cousin was as lost as he was.

"Maybe we better go back," he yelled over the crowd.

"Go back where?" Emory shouted. And the good sense of that question caught Lon without an answer. They moved on in silence.

As they shouldered their way along, a ragtime tune belched from one doorway they passed. Emory stopped and stared up the narrow stairway to the second floor of one of the more substantial buildings on the street.

"You boys looking for some entertainment?" The man who spoke was just inside the doorway. Emory flinched at the sound of his voice because he had not noticed him before. The man laughed big and exposed a gleaming gold tooth. "You boys look like you need some action. Come on up. It's ten cents a dance with the prettiest girls in town." He started up the stairs.

"Come on Lon, let's go check this out." Emory was grinning ear to ear.

The two boys studied the doorway. "When are we going to find Jeremy?" Lon asked with only half-hearted effort.

"Aw, hell, come on. He's working. He probably won't be in for hours. Let's go see." Emory pulled Lon sleeve and after a moment's hesitation, they both went up the stairs.

The large room they found covered the entire second floor of the building. Around the walls were wooden chairs with eight or ten girls scattered through them. Two couples were on the floor doing a lively step to the music they had heard from the street. When Lon and Emory emerged in the doorway, all the girls perked up from they relaxed positions and smiled.

"Ten cents a dance, minimum of five," a gruff voiced old woman growled at them through a swirl of tobacco smoke.

"Give'em a dollar Lon. I'll pay you back." Emory was busy looking the girls over. Lon fished in his pocket and produced the dollar. The old woman took his money and showed him a slight smile, more of a smirk really. "Take your pick, son. It's a slow afternoon."

They did just that. The girls were fairly pretty, some of them about as shy as the boys were. To be diplomatic, Lon decided he would dance with a different girl each time. Emory followed his lead after the first song, and as soon as the girls caught on, they relaxed, knowing they were going to make some share of the money.

If there was one thing both boys loved it was dancing. Lon and Emory's shyness must have been refreshing for the girls. It was obvious they were avoiding the other two customers who appeared to be well soaked in gin. The sunlight through the windows played in the dust the dancers kicked up from the floor boards. Slim waisted and giggly, the girls were much like those back home except they made a little more free with their bodies, Lon thought. They snuggled close and pressed their breasts into his chest. He couldn't complain, mind you, but it was different. It made him sort of uncomfortable at first, but the girls seemed to think that was funny. Whatever the reason, he and Emory got the undivided attention of a roomful of woman, and that was worth the money right there. The first dollar went fast, and the second. Somewhere in there they had a soda water, compliments of the house. It was a fine afternoon.

Other men began to drift up the stairs. The day shift was getting off from the fields. That would mean that Jeremy might be around somewhere. Lon tried to get Emory's attention to leave, but Emory had honed in on one of the girls, and he waved him off.

"Come on, Emory," Lon insisted, "Jeremy's bound to be in town by now and, if we're going to find him tonight, we got to go."

Emory followed him to the door muttering all the way. The girl tagged along.

26

"Ya'll come on back again, ya hear. My name is Matty," she called over the music.

"Ya'll come back." She gave them each a kiss on the cheek that left a rosy smear and then watched them descend the stairs. When they got to the bottom, both boys looked back, but she was gone. They stopped on the landing to breath deeply out of the smoke and heat upstairs.

Emory studied the doorway over head. "Hell, get the name of this place. I'm coming back. Did you see where she let me put my hands?" He held his hands out to Lon like there was something to see in them. "Lord, I thought I was going to pass out!" Then noticing Lon grinning at him, he added, "What the hell are you staring at?"

"You got lip paint on your face," Lon pointed at Emory's cheek.

"Well, so do you!" Emory countered as he rubbed at the stain.

Lon wiped at his own cheek and glanced around to see if anyone was looking. "Come on, let's get out of here.

The street was as crowded as before, maybe more so. They studied their options and chose a direction. Emory gave the dance hall a soulful backward glance.

Fiddle music filtered passed. Lon looked toward the sound to find an old black man standing, back to the wall, playing a jig. Lon struggled to maintain his place on the walk as the crowd streamed passed. The old man's clothes were shabby and in disarray. He played with his eyes closed and his head tilted to one side almost off balance, and Lon realized the man was blind. Next to the fiddler stood a young black boy, no more than ten or twelve, Lon guessed, holding out a tin cup.

He spied Lon watching. "Penny, mister, penny for the music?"

Lon studied his small face and sharp black eyes. He rummaged in his pocket and found a stray dime that the dancers had missed, which he dropped in the cup.

"Thank you kindly, sir." The child grinned broadly, and at the sound of his voice the old man smiled and nodded, also. The boy quickly scooped the change up in his thin hand and dropped it into a pouch hanging around his neck, tucked inside his shirt.

Emory pulled at Lon's sleeve. "Come on, man. We don't have money to spare. What the hell are you doing?"

Lon watched the child without answering. The tune ended, and the old man reached a trembling hand toward the boy. He found the child's shoulder, and the pair shuffled away into the crowd.

Emory grabbed Lon's arm and pulled him toward the street. "Man, you're a soft touch."

Lon laughed in reply, but before he could say more, something else caught their attention. Emory slapped Lon on the shoulder. "Hey! Look yonder!"

Lon followed Emory's outstretched arm. Coming passed them was a Model T carrying three men, and one of them, his shock of red hair making him easy to pick out, was Jeremy Randall.

Chapter 3

"**H**ey, Jer!" Emory yelled, but his voice was drowned out by the street noise. Emory took a few steps and jumped on the running board as the car passed. There was a flash of confusion until Jer recognized his old friend, but by the time the driver had the car stopped, the two boys were laughing and slapping one another on the back in celebration. Lon, with some thought for their possessions, watched the whole proceedings from the curb. The car moved on with traffic as Emory and Jer walked back laughing and jostling one another like bear cubs.

"Howdy, Lon!" The two shook hands. "I was about to give you boys up."

"Well, we thought we'd come see if what you been telling us is true," Lon said.

"Oh, it is, man, it truly is." Jer spread his arms as if to show off the whole town.

One thing about Jer Randall, he always gave the impression he was in personal charge of his situation. Farm folk back in Krayly Creek might view Preacher Randall's boy as wild and sinful, but the other boys never saw it that way. To them Jer was excitement, the one who dared to do all the things the others longed to try, but were too timid. Lon and Emory had admired Jer Randall's reckless ways most of their life. And they had copied him ever chance they could, from practicing his cuss words down in the barn where no one could hear, to trying to chew tobacco like him without throwing up. Jeremy Randall certainly had some admirable qualities. He could make a licking from the teacher, look like a breeze when every other boy knew the Mr. Grayson was strong as an ox, and the whipping hurt like hell. But Jer would never let on. Not even the time he got caught roping the outhouse and pulling it over while old Grayson was in it. Lon thought the teacher was going to beat old Jer to death over that one. Then Preacher Randall got hold of his son, and it looked like Jer was a goner for sure. But Jer never let them see he was hurting. You had to admire that. Now, standing here in the street like he owned the place, he looked as cocksure as ever.

Jer slid his hat back on his mop of unruly red hair. "You boys are in for some fine times! Just stick with me. Where's your gear?"

"This is it," Emory indicated, holding up his sack.

"Well, come on, you can stay with me and my crew for now. We're boarding in a cot house at the edge of town. It ain't much, but the landlord won't mind two more."

The three struck out down the street dodging cars, wagons, and pedestrians.

"When did you get in?"

"This morning. We didn't know how to find you. You never told us your company."

"I guess that's right," Jer grinned. "It's McGuire Drilling. Have you been looking all day?"

30

"Not exactly," Emory confessed with a sly grin. They told Jer about the dance.

"Taxi dancers! You boys sure don't waste no time!" Jeremy laughed. "You got to be careful though. Them dance hall girls is dangerous. You'll wind up married to one of them. I'll take a whore anytime, myself. They don't expect nothing but the money. Them dime-a-dance girls are just waiting for some sucker to come along to get hitched."

"Not me," Emory laughed. "I just got here."

"Don't look at me. Emory's the one who got lucky!" Lon threw up his hands, and Jeremy tossed his head back and laughed.

They paused at a crossing to let a truck pass.

"Is it always this busy around here?"

"Most times. The work shifts run around the clock so the town is open just about all the time."

"What's that God-awful roar I keep hearing," Emory asked.

"That's a blowout. Gets your attention, don't it? A well got away from somebody and caught fire out at the east edge of town." Jer was walking so fast, Lon and Emory were almost running to keep up.

"Is that sort of thing dangerous?" Lon asked.

"Hell yes! There's enough gas out there to blow all of this to Kingdom Come. They've been trying to cap it for two days."

"Yeah, we been smelling it all day," Emory said.

Jer gave a hearty laugh, "That ain't the blow out. That's just the smell of the oil patch. You'll get use to it pretty quick. I don't even notice it anymore."

Lon and Emory exchanged a doubtful look as they hustled along.

"What about those jobs you talked about?" Lon asked.

"My boss is hiring. I don't know what's open, but if he don't need you there's plenty more work around." Jer stopped abruptly in front of a low timber shanty and opened the door. "This is it."

Lon and Emory took their attention off Jer for a minute and looked where he pointed. They stepped into a small room with bunks around the walls. A wood stove dominated the center of the room.

"We got running water and a crapper out back," Jer explained. "Twenty-five cents a night or day, whichever you'll be sleeping. It ain't fancy, like I said, but it's certain."

"Looks fine to me," the boys agreed. They were catching their breath now after the wild walk over and trying to not look too confused.

"You can pay the man when he comes around and lock your gear up with mine for right now."

The boys nodded not knowing what else to do.

"Now!" Jer slapped his hands together like some big decision had been reached. "You hungry?" he asked.

Their faces brightened. It had been a long day since breakfast.

"Let's go. We can catch my crew at the cafe." They struck out again into the twilight.

"How did your folks take to the idea of you boys leaving?" Jer asked. He cut his eyes around at them to watch their reaction to the question.

Lon and Emory answered with a quick glance at one another and Jer nodded.

"So you just walked off, too, huh? My old man and me had one too many fights over my way of living. I wanted to be where something was happening!" He winked in a knowing way.

Lon and Emory had carefully avoided mention of Jer's father. Everybody knew they had parted with bad feelings. The wild ways of Preacher Randall's boy had been the major gossip around Kraly Creek more than once over the years. His disappearance to the oil fields and his reappearance now and then had only confirmed in the minds of the community the burden the Reverend had borne so long.

"I don't never want to see the business end of a cotton hoe again, boys. All that preaching made my old man crazy. Thinks farming is noble work of the Lord!" There was bitterness in Jer's tone. "Noble enough, I guess, for them Bible thumpers, but not for me. Old Jer Randall has got some living to do!"

Yeah!" Emory chimed in rubbing his hands together. "Now, let's get to it!"

Jer threw his head back and laughed his laugh that took in a whole street, and the boys laughed with him.

The inside of the cafe was crowded now with oil field workmen and the accompanying smell of work stained clothing and tobacco smoke. Jer located his group in the back and led the way through the tables.

"Boys, I want you to meet some old friends of mine here, Emory Campbell and Lon Prather. Fellows, this here is Mason Poe and Friday Smith."

Each man nodded slightly to acknowledge the newcomers. The one called Friday appeared tall even seated at the table. A tuft of sandy hair shading his eyes and his smile was open and friendly. The other fellow, Mason Poe, was a little knot of a man with a guarded watchful look instead of a smile. His hair and eyes were black and a jagged purple scar ran from his left temple to his jaw line. The two motioned for the newcomers to pull up a chair.

"These boys here are from back home. They're looking for work and some of the good life."

"All right! My kind of folks." Friday said with a laugh.

"They're going to stay with us for a while till they get settled." Jer said.

"Fine, glad to have you. Long as you don't snore no worse than Mason, here." Friday gave his companion a playful shove.

The little man bristled, and the look he shot at Friday should have warned him off. Lon caught the glint of Mason's eyes and marked him down as a man not to mess with, but Friday didn't seem to notice.

"We call this man Friday," Jer confided as he slapped Friday on the shoulder. "because he won't tell us what his real name is. He swears it's too awful. We tagged him Friday because that's the day he hired in."

"Yeah," Mason growled in a dry tone. "Some day we're gonna get old Friday drunk enough to tell his real name."

Jer and Friday laughed loudly but the anger in Mason's voice made Lon and Emory uneasy. Mason seemed to be sizing them up, putting on a show of force for their benefit.

The waitress arrived, and they all turned their attention to her. Food was ordered, and Lon and Emory fell to it with enthusiasm. It had been a long day since Pyote.

Pushing away his plate, Jeremy announced, "Well, now boys, how are we gonna welcome our new friends here? Anyone got any ideas?"

"Well," Friday spoke up, "Maybe just one or two."

"Then let's get out of here." Jer lead the way out. As they reached the door, the man from the mail run met them coming in. This time he sported no shotgun.

"Evening, boys." The man's eyes cut over to Lon and Emory. "Are these the folks you were looking for?"

"Yes sir."

"Huh." He studied the group for a second. "You boys step easy tonight now."

"Right Jack, you got it." Jer spoke in mock seriousness. Everyone laughed except Lon and Emory.

"Who is that fellow?" Lon asked after they were out on the street.

"Name's Jack Williams. He's kind of the law around here, what there is of it," Jer told them. "He seemed to know you."

"Yes sir!" Mason mimicked in a high-pitched voice, and Friday snickered.

"He was guarding the mail in the car we came in on today, but we didn't get his name."

"Yeah, Jack's sorta closed mouthed. Takes himself a little too serious sometimes. He pushes the toughs around a little while he's not bootlegging. They say he's got a piece of every gin joint in town. Don't pay no attention to him. He won't bother us. Come on Mas, where'd you park?"

The five piled into the car, and Mason took the wheel. Jer reached in the back and produced a gallon jug. He opened it and took a long pull before passing the jug to the driver. Friday was next. He wiped his mouth in satisfaction and passed the jug to Lon. Without any hesitation Lon imitated the others, threw back his head, and swallowed a mouthful of the clear liquid. It was no different from before. The acid reek of kerosene filled his throat. He shook his head, and while he was blinking his eyes to clear his vision, Emory grabbed the jug eagerly from his hands and followed suit.

"Lord Almighty! That's worse than Ratch's moonshine!" Lon whispered as he recovered his voice.

The other boys erupted in peals of laughter.

"Don't tell me you boys have been sampling that swill." Jer laughed even harder.

"It gets smoother as you go along," Friday offered.

"Now hold it boys," Mason spoke up. "Jer, you didn't tell us these boys were greenhorns." There was more than a trace of sarcasm in his voice.

"They can hold their own. Right boys?" Jer came their defense.

"Right! Give me that jug," Lon ordered. He turned it up again, trying to appear confident. The searing liquid ripped down his throat the same as the first shot, but this time he felt it in his arms and legs. He passed the jug to Emory.

Mason brought the car to a stop in the darkness, and they concentrated on drinking. By the time the jug had passed around several times, all five boys were feeling no pain. Everything seemed funny. Lon watched Emory trying to negotiate the jug to his lips and remembered he had intended to avoid this stuff. The faces of the others were reeling before him.

"Now, let's get over to Sadie's," Jer ordered. "We're going to show you boys something that beats them taxi dancers all to hell."

The car began to move, and the motion turned everything upside down in Lon's head. Sights and sounds faded in and out.

"We're going to get you boys laid tonight," Friday announced to Lon and Emory. "I bet'cha that's gonna be a first too, ain't it, Jer."

Jer's response and the laughter that followed were a

jumble of words roaring in Lon's ears. He neither knew or cared what was said.

The car jerked to a stop before a collection of shacks. They scrambled out of the car by the glow of the light over the door of the closest building.

"Straighten up now, boys." Jer pulled Lon and Emory out of the car and slapped their caps on their heads. "Sober up some, cause you don't want to miss nothing."

"How much money you got on you?" Friday asked.

"Not much," Lon managed to say.

"What are you supposed to do in here?" Emory asked. Jer, Mas, and Friday roared with laughter.

"Don't worry, boys. Sadie's girls will show you what to do. All you got to do is come up with the two dollars," Jer instructed.

"Naw, I don't believe so." The group went quiet and Lon realized it was Emory talking. "You boys go on, I believe I'll..." He looked pale and sick all of a sudden.

The door to the shack opened. Jer grabbed Emory by the collar and dragged him forward. "Come on here, boy. This will give you a whole new outlook. I promise you that."

Lon's first reaction was to the paint on the face of the woman at the door. She wore even more than the old woman at the dance hall. The rouge on her cheeks looked like bruises and her eyes were hooded with paint.

"Evening, boys." The woman's voice was low and raspy. She opened the door and stepped aside. Inside the brightly lit room were five or six girls dressed in flimsy silk lounge pajamas. The veil of smoke in the room made their faces hard to make out. Or was it the moonshine?

"We're looking for a little entertainment here tonight," Jer announced. "Especially these two fellows here, if you get my meaning, Sadie." He was still holding Emory by the collar.

"A couple of ripe ones," the woman chuckled. She motioned, and two girls moved toward them. One approached Lon and threaded her arm through his. The strong smell of toilet water filled his nostrils. Between the cheap fragrance and the moonshine, his head reeled again. The girl led him out through a side doorway and up some narrow stairs. He could hear Emory and the second girl behind them. Laughter and encouragement drifted up from Jer and the others, but Lon was oblivious to it. His sight and balance were numbed by the liquor, but his pulse quickened with the touch of the girl's hand on his.

The girl did not speak, which was just as well because he couldn't have found any words anyway. He strained to focus his eyes through the moonshine and the dim light in the cramped little room where she took him. She motioned for him to sit, and he did, abruptly. The bed springs squeaked, and he jumped slightly. The girl looked up from her work of undressing and smiled. "Relax, lover boy. I'll take care of you," she said in a tone that sounded much too old for a girl of her years. "Just get out of those clothes and I'll do the rest."

Lon fumbled with his buttons like a small child until she came to help him. The closeness of her nude body made him dizzy. This was more like a dream than reality. Then she touched him expertly, and her fingers felt cool on his skin. Lon's awkwardness gave way to an exhilaration that far surpassed all those secret dreams he'd ever conjured up. So this was how it really was. The girl pushed him gently back on the pillow as her hands glided across his chest and down over his abdomen. His muscles twitched involuntarily and the girl laughed deep in her throat.

Chapter 4

The next thing Lon knew, the morning sun was across his face forcing his eyes open. How he had gotten out of that whore house and back to town, he had no idea. He could vaguely remember being slumped in the back seat of the car next to Emory, and later being half dragged to this cot. Now, as he tried to move his head, a lightning bolt crashed behind his eyes. Slowly, as if he had never moved before, Lon turned his head to see what was left of Emory Campbell doubled over the side of the next bunk. Other cots around the walls were occupied, but Lon recognized no one. He struggled to stand, then gave up and slumped back on the bed. "Emory...,Emory!"

"What?" came a pitiful reply.

"Where is everybody?"

"How the hell should I know. I thought I was dead till you called my name."

"No such luck."

"Pipe down over there!" a sleepy voice mumbled from across the room.

Lon strained his eyes toward the sound, and then remembering what Jer had said about people sleeping in shifts, he lowered his voice to a whisper and leaned over Emory. "Come on let's get out of here and find some food." He pulled his cousin up by the collar, and they staggered out the door.

"Man, don't mention food to me." Emory's voice was weak.

Lon straightened as they hit the bright sunlight on the porch. He squinted against the glare and looked at his cousin. "You look terrible."

"Me? You ought to see yourself." Emory staggered as Lon let go of his collar.

"We've got to shape up and find a job today." Lon tried to smooth his hair back and readjusted his cap. "Let's find some coffee anyway and figure out what to do." He dug in his pockets seeking change and came up with a crumpled piece of paper with a scribbled message from Jer.

Go see Red McGuire and tell him I sent you.

See you tonight. Jer

Lon showed the note to Emory, and the boys started toward town, tucking in shirt tails and shaking their heads to clear the cobwebs.

After a little breakfast Lon felt better. Emory refused to eat, but he downed three cups of coffee. By the time they left the cafe, they were almost solid looking again. Following the waitress's directions a block north, they found McGuire Drilling and asked for Red.

"Yeah, Jer told me about you," answered a burly man whose hair did justice to his name. "He says you boys are good workers."

"Yes sir," both boys chorused.

"Only trouble is I've only got one roughneck spot open.

You'll have to decide who gets it."

The two boys were silent for a moment, taking in his offer and considering what to do. This was a situation they had not thought of. The possibility of being separated had not come up in all their planning, but they could not afford to pass up work.

"Let's flip for it," Emory suggested.

Lon produced a coin.

"Heads," Emory called.

"Heads it is. You got it," Lon grinned.

"You sure about this?"

"Go ahead, I'll be fine."

Emory signed for the job.

"You start tomorrow morning," Red announced to Emory. "You'll be out with Jer, Friday, and Mason. The boys will tell you what you need." Turning to Lon, the man continued. "Sorry I can't take you on right now, but there's several outfits hiring. Just ask over at the Club Cafe and you can use my name. If I hear of an opening I'll let your cousin, here, know."

The boys shook hands with Emory's new boss and left. Back on the street, they stopped to consider their situation. There was an embarrassing silence between the wild excitement in Emory's eyes and the blank confusion in Lon's.

"Listen, Lon, I feel bad about this," Emory started.

"Naw, now, Emory, it isn't your doing. You have to take what you can." Lon assured him. "Anyway, at least one of us is working now. We aren't going to starve." They both laughed. "I'll be alright. Mr. McGuire said there are other folks hiring.

I'll just ask around. Let's go back to the cafe, like he said."

The cafe, like the street outside, was filled to overflow again today, but it wasn't hard to pick out the man they were seeking. Claude Jamison studied them with a solemn gaze while Lon explained what they wanted. Then the big man grinned and offered a giant handshake.

"Yeah, I'm pretty sure I can help you boys out. There's all kinds of folks in here day and night. I know most of the drilling company men by name. Hugh Sullivan is hiring, I think. He'll be in here around six o'clock. Why don't you just have a seat and make yourself comfortable here and I'll let you know when he comes in."

They ordered food, more confident now that they would not run out of money.. After they finished and had mopped their plates with Claude's hot biscuits, they sat back with satisfaction to survey the room. Lon watched Emory's face as he craned his neck to see the strange mix of people in the crowded cafe. There was so much to take in.

"Well, cousin," Lon laughed. "What do you think so far?"

Emory grinned broadly. "I've got no complaints. How about you?"

"Why did you come, Emory?" Lon asked after a bit.

Emory grunted a laugh at the question. "Why did you?"

"No, I mean, you were so dead set against this idea. Why'd you change your mind?"

"Well, hell! Can't a fellow change his mind" Emory's voice took on a defensive edge that Lon had not expected. "It don't matter now anyhow. I came didn't I? I can't have you wandering off like a lost hog rooting up fences. You ain't the only one that wants to see a few things before he gets buried behind a mule!"

There was no response to be made to that. Lon drank

his coffee. Emory fidgeted with his fork and surveyed the room like he was having a private argument with himself. "Say listen," he ventured after a bit. "If you need to wait around here, I was thinking..."

"Yeah, no need of both of us sitting here."

"I think I'll go back out to the house and try to find an empty cot. I'm feeling a little ragged."

"No," Lon said too quickly. "Go on, I'll catch you later. No telling how long this is going to take."

"You okay?" Emory asked catching the tone in Lon's voice.

"Sure, no problem." Lon watched his cousin hurry away as if he were escaping. He shook his head. Emory never sees anyone's problems but his own.

Lon settled back on his counter stool after Emory left and waited. As he watched people flow in and out of the café doorway, loneliness began to settle over him. Maybe this whole trip wasn't such a good idea after all. Maybe Emory had a right to be angry. It was a damn fool scheme. But he couldn't go back and face his father yet.

The cafe owner returned. "How 'bout another cup of coffee?"

"Sounds good."

The big man poured him a cup. "How do you like it?"

"Straight," Lon answered, "Boiled and straight."

Claude looked up from pouring," Pardon?"

"Hmm? Oh, just straight black will be fine."

The afternoon slipped by, and the evening crowd started to drift in. Lon shifted his weight on the stool. This was taking forever it seemed, and probably it would all come to nothing. But since he had no other ideas at the moment, he waited.

Three men came in that caught Lon's eye. They were

just in from a job, he concluded by their sweat stained work clothes. Claude greeted the group and served coffee all around. He talked to the oldest looking man as the others listened, and then all eyes turned on Lon. Claude left the group and came over.

"That fellow I told you about is right over there," Claude pointed over his shoulder with a thumb. "He says he'll talk to you. Name's Hugh Sullivan."

"Thank you, sir." Lon got up and walked around the counter. As he did, he got a sensation that his knees were knocking.

"Howdy," Lon managed a strong voice.

"Howdy."

"I understand you might be hiring roughnecks?"

"Might be."

"Well, I'm looking for a job, and I'd be obliged if you would give me a chance."

"You ever worked a drilling rig before?"

"No, sir."

"What makes you think you can do it?"

"Well, sir, I learn quick, and I ain't afraid of hard work."

The gray-haired man studied him in silence. All the time, the two men seated at the table never took their eyes off Lon. Lon stood his ground and stared back.

You've got the job." The man said abruptly. He stood up and extended his hand. "Hugh Sullivan."

"Lon Prather." Lon broke out in a wide grin and shook the hand enthusiastically.

"Pay is six dollars a day for a twelve hour shift. You'll work seven days a week, and I don't allow no drinking in my crew. First time you show up hung over will be your last day. Is that clear?"

"Yes, sir," Lon agreed, remembering his revelry from the night before. His head still didn't feel completely clear.

"Be here before sun-up tomorrow morning, and we'll pick you up."

"Yes sir, thank you." Lon shook the man's hand again. "I'll be here."

"You got work gloves?" Sullivan asked as he gripped his hand.

"Gloves?" Lon stumbled over the word, surprised at the question. "No sir, I don't."

"There's a Jew fellow down the block there." Hugh Sullivan pointed toward the street. "Go down there, and he'll fix you up. You're going to need a good pair."

"Yes, sir," Lon responded. "Much obliged," he added.

"Dawn tomorrow," Sullivan repeated and then sat back down.

Lon left the cafe with a feeling he was floating across the room. A job! Just like that! Six dollars a day! He stood on the walk and surveyed the crowd milling passed him and felt like shouting to the world. Emory was asleep. He had no place to go. He turned and started up the street too excited to stand still. The dry good store window Mr. Sullivan had mentioned caught his attention with a sign proclaiming, "All Your Needs in Work Clothes." Well, why not? He had a job, didn't he?

Inside the store, a small man greeted him in an accent Lon did not recognize. "Good afternoon, sir."

"Howdy. I need a pair of good work gloves."

"Those we have." The man walked down the aisle to a stack of gloves. "Let's see, what size? Hmm, large, maybe, extra large, I think. Here we are."

Lon slipped the heavy glove on his hand. The leather smelled good. He squeezed his fist to test the fit.

"That's good, I think. How much do I owe you?"

"That will be fifty cents."

Lon handed over the money.

"You're new in town, aren't you?" The little man peered at him over his spectacles.

"Yes sir, just got here yesterday." Lon was delighted to find someone with whom to share his news. "I just got a job as a roughneck for Hugh Sullivan, starting tomorrow!"

"Ah, Hugh Sullivan, I know him. He's a good man. You're a lucky fellow!"

Lon grinned broadly.

"Listen, you need some good work clothes or shoes for the new job?"

"Naw, I'm fine."

"How about a hat? You're going to need a good hat out in this sun, you know." The little man eyed Lon's touring cap.

Lon hesitated. He would dearly love a hat. His cap was for a kid. A working man needed a good hat. "How much?"

"Three dollars. The best money can buy."

Lon considered his dwindling cash reserve. "Naw, I'll wait. Thank you though. I'll be in another time."

"Listen, I know Hugh Sullivan. His credit is good with me. You work for Sullivan, your credit is good, too. You take the hat and you can pay me when you get your first paycheck." The little man studied the boy's face as he spoke.

"No, I'll wait, thank you. I'll wait."

The shopkeeper laughed. "You're a smart fellow. You're going to do fine. Never start out in debt." He offered his hand. "My name is Morris."

"Lon Prather. Glad to meet you, Mr. Morris."

"Just Morris, that's not my last name. No one can pronounce my last name so good, so I don't use it."

"OK, Morris."

"Listen, young man, I tell you what. I got a strong safe here. You get that first pay check, you put it in my safe, huh?"

Lon nodded, "I might just do that."

"Yes, you think about it. Good luck."

Lon left the store with the gloves in his hand. Money in a safe. The thought was almost overwhelming. Enough money to put in a safe? He stretched his shoulders back and took a deep breath. Somehow the sulfur smell in the air was not as bad any more.

Chapter 5

Lon slept very little, if any, between his own excitement and the antics of Jer and Emory and their crew. They tried their best to talk Lon into a little more celebration for the new jobs, but Lon begged off.

"I wouldn't work for no son-of-a-bitch who tried to tell me what to do on my own time," Jer bragged. "Me and Red McGuire get along fine. He minds his own damn business. Hugh Sullivan is a real hard-nose."

"Well, I'm going to find out tomorrow," Lon laughed him off. "Meanwhile I don't want to get fired before I get started, so count me out."

About midnight Lon was awakened by their return. Jer, Mason and Friday were feeling no pain again and laughing about Emory insisting that they take him back to Sadie's. Emory was past talking, himself. They poured him into bed, and finally all settled down.

Lon tossed fitfully for awhile, afraid he would over sleep. Then some time before dawn, he gave up trying and slipped out into the darkness. There were a few lights around, but for the most part it was the quietest he had seen the town since he arrived. All the stores were dark, and only a few domino halls and boot-leg joints showed any signs of life. Lon walked the several blocks to the cafe quickly, as if his hurry might hasten the start of the day, but when he reached his destination, all was quietly locked up.

A shuffling sound in the narrow alley between the buildings caught Lon's attention. He stiffened and listened intently. The sound came again, and Lon stepped cautiously to the corner, squinting into the darkness. A slight motion caught his eye. It was the Negro boy Lon had seen with the blind fiddler. The child was intent on his task of picking through the garbage from the cafe and did not realize he was being watched at first. He sorted through the food scraps and placed what he selected in a burlap sack.

Suddenly, the boy sensed someone was watching. His head jerked up, and his eyes were wild and white with fear, but he stood frozen in his place. Lon thought of a startled deer he had surprised once by the creek back home.

Lon raised his hands to signal that he meant no danger, and in a flash the boy shot past him and away into the darkness. Lon listened to his bare feet padding in the sandy street.

"You must have found work," a gruff voice broke the silence. Lon jumped and turned to find the man with the sawed-off shotgun.

"Yes, sir," he recovered his voice. "I start this morning."

Who you working for?"

"Hugh Sullivan."

The man nodded his recognition of the name.

"Lon Prather is my name," Lon extended his hand.

"Jack Williams," the gruff voice responded.

"We just keep bumping into each other." Lon smiled. "Don't you ever sleep?"

The man laughed slightly. "Not much. We had another knifing last night. I had to sign the coroner's report."

"Who was it?"

"Some drifter, I guess. Probably got in a scrape over a card game."

"Does that happen often around here?"

"Regular as clockwork, kid. This is a tough place. You never know what you are going to see."

Lon thought of the boy in the alley and nodded.

Their conversation was interrupted by the sound of an approaching car. It was Sullivan and the other two men.

"Glad to see you made it," Sully greeted Lon. "Morning, Jack. You have a little trouble last night?"

"Same old stuff, Sully." Jack lifted his hat and scratched his head. "I got some other boys over at the jail that might interest you, though."

"Don't tell me Rowdy and Moses have been at it again!" Sully said.

"Yep, they put on a pretty good show day before yesterday." Jack Williams let out a deep rumbling laugh. "I kept'em out of circulation, but I figured you would be looking for them this morning. I'll let'em out if you want to go their fine."

Sully turned to the short barrel-chested man beside him. "Charlie, go get'em, and let's get some breakfast down'em," Sully growled.

"Happens ever time they have a few days off," Charlie muttered as he and Jack disappeared into the predawn darkness.

The lights came on in the cafe behind them, and Claude opened the door. "How 'bout some breakfast, this morning?'

"Fire'em up," Sully directed. He led the way in. "This here is Sherman Caldwell." Sully introduced a gangly fellow not much older than Lon. Sherman grinned broadly and stuck out his hand.

"The rest of the crew will be here shortly," Sully added. "Soon as Charlie bails them out."

Sherman giggled.

"That damn Indian loves to fight better than anybody I ever knew," Sully growled.

"Yeah, but Rowdy starts'em. Moses just finishes'em," Sherman said.

"Well, I'll get'em back on the job and put an end to this fighting for a while."

"Did you say an Indian?" Lon asked, but before he could say more, the man Sullivan had called Charlie got back with his charges in tow. They were the two men from the street fight. The big Indian, looking all slump-shouldered and tame, following meekly behind Charlie. The other fellow, the wiry little pine knot of a man who had jumped in to help, looked as feisty as ever. Both could have used a good bath, Lon thought, and both were watching Sully to see what his next move would be. But Sully ignored their condition and went on like nothing had happened.

"Boys, I want you to meet our new hand, Lon Prather," Sully said. "Son, this is Moses Longhand and that ornery little bastard there is Rowdy Chapman."

The two men nodded.

"And this here is Charlie Brady," Hugh Sullivan slapped the short barrel-chested man on the shoulder. "He's the driller of this outfit and knows everything you need to know about a rotary rig. Right, Charlie?"

The man nodded lightly with a hint of a smile.

"I want you to stick with Charlie here and do whatever he tells you."

Lon nodded in agreement. Out of the corner of his eye, he watched Rowdy and Moses, downing cups of coffee and trying to shape them selves up a little at the next table, but the other men ignored them completely.

"You ever see a rig before, kid?" Charlie asked.

Lon admitted he had not.

"That's OK. Charlie is an old hand at training boll weevils. Right, Sherman?"

"Right," Sherman answered.

"That's what you are, isn't it?" He continued. "Trying to get away from cotton farming? Sherman was a boll weevil last year."

Lon laughed, "Naw, boll weevils didn't run me out of farming, but just about everything else did. I guess the name fits. I just decided I wanted to get paid for a change."

"Well then, we better let you get started." Sully suggested. "Time's a wasting." He turned his attention back to Rowdy and Moses. "You boys ready to quit fighting and start working?"

"Any time you say." Rowdy growled and Moses nodded.

They piled into Sully's car and struck out across open ground. Except for a wild criss-cross of ruts, there was no road that Lon could make out. As the car bucked through the sand hills, he studied the landscape. There was no caliche ridge to follow out here. They were passing other well sites, some sporting tanks, giving evidence that oil had been found. The early morning haze was lighted by the fires spewing from long pipes above the ground that Lon had noticed on his way into Wink.

"They're burning off gas," Charlie shouted over the engine's roar when he noticed Lon studying the scene. "The stuff is dangerous if it builds up around a well. Catches fire."

A large camp site came into view on their right. Tents and shacks of a large population were scattered about, and smoke curled from cooking fires in the early morning sun. Dust hung over a large pen filled with mules milling and stamping, as men worked among them. The cracking of whips and shrill whistles and shouts of the men carried above the noise of the car as they passed.

"Ragtown, muleskinner camp," Charlie shouted. "They do all our heavy work around here. Dig slush pits, bring in lumber sills for derricks, haul water for the boilers. A fellow is supposed to be finishing our slush pit this morning."

Sully turned the old car off the rutted path to the left. Almost at once, Lon felt the car sink and skid to the right.

"Hell fire! I hit this damn sand pit every time!" Sully shouted.

"This one or some other one," Charlie shouted back with a laugh.

The crew piled out and took positions around the car with a precision that suggested they had pushed the car before.

"Come on, kid, this can be your first lesson in oil drilling," Sherman grinned. "Always carry enough passengers to push you out when you get stuck!"

A few good heaves and a couple of boards that Rowdy produced out of the back to go under the rear tires did the trick, and they were loose.

"This happen a lot?" Lon shouted when they were moving again.

"Kid, it's a good ride when it only happens once a trip," Charlie shouted back.

The wooden tower of a rig came into view. Lon studied it intently as the car jolted to a stop. It was an imposing sight, standing silent and lonely on the flat plain. Off to the right below the giant wooden beams of the derrick, a man waved his arm in greeting. He was driving a team of mules hooked up to a dredge.

"That's Cabel Norris," Charlie informed Lon. "He guarded the rig for us last night. Never passes up a chance to make a few bucks, that kid. Looks like he's finished with the pit."

Hugh Sullivan walked over to talk to the muleskinner. Lon watched the man bring the mules to a stop and wipe his forehead with his shirt sleeve as he waited for Sully to come to him. He looked no older than Lon.

"Cabel's from that camp we passed back there." Charlie said. "He's a hard worker. Came in here last year with nothing but the shirt on his back. Now he has his own team of mules. I hear he won' em in a poker game."

The crew began to scatter over the rig to their various jobs. Lines were checked and the boilers fired. Charlie took Lon up the ramp to the derrick floor to survey the rig.

"This is called the rotary table," he indicated a large flat disk in the center of the derrick floor. "This is where it all takes place. We're going to spud in now. Just have a seat over there on the lazy bench and watch for a while."

Lon followed Charlie's directions and watched as the men began to move the heavy pipe around. Few words were exchanged, only hand signals. There were no wasted motions. Rowdy waved a ready signal from the boilers, Charlie pulled a couple of levers, and the rig came to life. The noise was almost deafening at first. Lon squinted his eyes and locked his jaw as the roar engulfed him. The rest of the crew didn't seem to notice as they watched the drill stem intently. In time, Charlie threw a switch, and the roar stopped. The crew replaced the short section of pipe with a full length joint. Lon looked up and saw Moses, balanced in the tower overhead, gracefully shift the long pipe into position. The new pipe was locked down and drilling continued.

Charlie came over to Lon. "OK," he shouted over the roar, "We're down. What do you think?"

"I think she's noisy!" Lon shouted back.

"Music to my ears, kid," Charlie responded. "You'll get use to it. It's a good sound. Means everything is working smooth. Come on, I'll walk over the rig with you."

Charlie explained the whole operation from boiler pressure to drilling mud as they walked. By the time they made the round, Lon had a fair idea of the rig and what his job would be. They walked out past the slush pit, away from the noise. Mud and water were already beginning to spew into the pit, bringing up the secrets from the rock layers below.

"It's okay to smoke out here." Charlie rolled a smoke expertly and offered his sack of makings. Lon took it and rolled one for himself, proud of the fact he could do it so well. He and Emory had practiced by the hour back home, curling the fragile paper just so and shaking out just the right amount of tobacco. It felt good to know how to do something right in a place were he had so much to learn.

Lon studied the man beside him as Charlie stuffed the sack of makings back in his shirt pocket. His hands were stubby and rough with dark lines around the nails and knuckles that looked like permanent stain. He had a solid thick build that suggested great strength and a no nonsense manner about him, but his eyes had a glint to them that looked like he was about to laugh. Lon had liked him right off and had a notion Charlie would teach him a lot if he listened. Charlie Brady was in his element around a derrick, you could tell that.

"How long does all this take?" Lon asked after he lit his smoke.

"It depends, but we'll probably run about a month to six weeks. By then we'll know if we've got anything or not."

"You fellows all look like you've worked together for awhile."

"Yeah, except for Sherman, we go back a ways. Sully is an old cable tool driller. I've been his tool dresser for years. Moses was a roustabout and Rowdy worked the boiler. When rotary rigs came in Sully switched over, and we came with him."

"What's Sully's job now?"

"He's out scouting more locations most of the time. When we finish here, wet or dry, we'll move on to another site." Charlie grinned broadly. "By then you'll probably know what the hell you're doing out here."

"You think so?"

"Sure. Do you think you got any of this, so far?"

Lon grinned and shrugged his shoulders.

"Well, let's go see." Charlie said.

They ground out their smokes and headed back to the drilling floor. Lon spent the rest of the day taking orders and scrambling up and down ladders. The crew seemed to take a good-natured view of his presence. By the end of the day he felt he had covered every inch of the rig, tower and all. When the night crew drove up, nobody had to call him twice to get in the car. All the same he didn't look any more tired then Rowdy and Moses, he thought. On the ride back to town Lon could hear the throb of the rotary engine ringing in his head.

Chapter 6

Lon hardly talked to Emory in the days that followed. They were still sharing the same cot house, but Jer and his crew seemed never to slow down, and Emory was right in with them. Emory was hypnotized by Jeremy and his easy talk. Lon kept his thoughts to himself, but he was getting disgusted with his cousin. Emory picked up Jer's language in no time, and his fumbling efforts at cussing became rich with added oilfield vigor. He also turned up in a hat like Jer's, a black felt fedora with the brim turned down all the way around. He was sparing no effort to be like Jeremy, and Jer was making the most of the attention by out drinking, out cussing, and out talking anyone around. Late night confusion and the jeers Lon was drawing for not joining in were making the living arrangements pretty cramped.

"You ought to try a little of this stuff, Lon." Emory waved a bottle in his face. "It helps after a long day. You'll sleep like a baby."

"Sleep is not one of my problems. Staying awake is," Lon laughed him off. "How can you make it out and work twelve hours with that stuff in your head?"

You get used to it," Emory bragged.

"Hell, this stuff will grow hair on your chest, boy. Make a man out of you," Jer added.

Lon just smiled, "Yeah, I know. An old man."

Within a month, Charlie invited Lon to move in with the crew and split the rent on a house they shared, and Lon welcomed the chance. The rift between him and Emory grew wider every time he declined a pull at the jug. The night Lon moved out Emory didn't even stick around to say good-bye. He and Jer went out on the town again, while Lon gathered his meager gear and walked away.

***

After his first month, Lon treated himself to a two dollar steak dinner at Claude's and new khaki work clothes at Morris' store. He had never had so much money to spend. The crew teased him about his new prosperity.

"Kid, if I didn't know better, I'd swear you look like a real oil man," Charlie announced.

Even Moses, who treated conversation as a condition to be avoided, commented on Lon's new hat. It was a Stetson with a modified western brim, Morris had explained. Sully wore one, and Lon thought it made him look like a man to be taken seriously. You could tell a lot about a man by the hat he chose.

Moses gave him an approving nod when he saw it. "It won't set right till you get a little sweat on the band," the big solemn man said.

Since Moses rarely spoke at all, anything he said was usually listened to by all the men. Rowdy did most of Moses talking for him, Lon had observed. The two men were as much of a pair as Sully and Charlie, and when he looked at them, Lon remembered the street fight and how Rowdy had jumped in to help. Rowdy was a firebrand with a quick temper and a sharp tongue. Sully and Charlie were the only two people Rowdy seemed to defer to. The men had worked out a carefully balanced working arrangement, Lon decided, that gave them all some space yet formed a team. He and Sherman were the heirs to their wisdom. By some lucky stroke, they had been sized up and chosen worthy of the trouble it was taking to teach them the oil business. For Sherman's and Lon's part, they were to keep their mouths shut and their ears open. It was a comfortable arrangement.

Fiddle music drifted into the cafe from the street outside. Lon listened over the conversation for a moment and then got up from the table.

"Where you going, boy? They'll be bringing out that steak of yours here in a minute." Charlie asked.

"I'll be right back." Lon motioned the others to go on with their banter. "I want to see somebody."

He stepped out into the autumn evening and scanned the street. Cars along the curb obstructed his view, but the music was coming from the far sidewalk. He crossed over. The old man was there, back to the wall, playing to the crowd that filed past, oblivious to him. Lon pushed closer, and there was the kid, stern-faced, holding his cup before him like a shield. The child's sharp eyes spied Lon watching and studied him with a silent stare as he drew nearer.

Lon squatted down before the boy and tipped his hat. "Howdy."

The boy's eyes blinked slightly, surprised at this man's attention. "Penny, mister?" He recovered his voice.

Lon reached into his shirt pocket and produced a couple of dollars clasped between two fingers. He stuffed the bills into the cup without taking his eyes from the boy and then waited for a reaction.

The child grabbed the bills in his fist like he expected the man to reconsider and take the money back.

Lon rose and turned to leave.

"Hey, mister!"

Lon looked back at the child.

"What's your name, mister?"

"Prather. What's yours?"

"Penn." The boy smiled, finally, and stuffed the money in his leather pouch as Lon crossed the street

"What was that all about?" Charlie asked when Lon got back to the table.

"I had to go see a friend."

Chapter 7

As the weeks went by Lon began to feel like a seasoned roughneck. The throb of the rotary ceased to crash in his head, but it still stayed with him all through the night like the rhythm of his pulse. The crew continued to call him kid, and playing jokes on him was their main diversion, but he was fitting in. Each day the bit probed ever deeper into the shale and sand beneath their feet. Time was measured by the drilling log and the length of pipe added to their string. The drill bit wore down quickly in the rock and had to be replaced. This meant every joint of pipe had to be pulled from the hole and broken off. A new bit was put on and then joint by joint, the pipe had to be restrung. It was a noisy exhausting job.

One evening after this process they ran over their shift, and it was dark by the time they got away from the well. When Sully picked them up the whole crew was dragging. The ride into town was unusually quiet as Sully struggled with the steering wheel, negotiating the sand dunes in their path.

Hugh Sullivan was a quiet man. He chose his words carefully and spoke in a deep voice laced with an Arkansas drawl. Lon watched him carefully when he was around, and he had decided he was a man to be admired. His face was creased with brown leathery wrinkles around his eyes from years outdoors, and his hair was bleached to silver. It was hard to guess his age. His frame was slim and ramrod straight, young in a way, but his manner suggested age and wisdom. The rest of the crew seemed relaxed in their banter with one another and at ease when Sully was present. But when he spoke, they stopped their conversation and listened, Lon noticed. Sully handled the special attention with total indifference, and his unassuming manner made him likeable at the same time his quiet ways made him distant and a little mysterious. Sully knew the oil business. That was clear. He had seen it all from Spindletop to Burkburnett, Charlie said, but he knew more than that. He knew people and how to pick them. He chose his crew by instinct as much as anything, and usually he was right. Lon felt very honored that he had been chosen to join this group.

"That core sample we took Wednesday looks promising," Lon heard Sully say to Charlie.

"Yeah, the cuttings are right. I think we're in the same formation as the Owens #1." Charlie rubbed his brow with his handkerchief.

"If we are, then we ought to know something within the week for sure."

You got that other job ready to go?"

"Just about. We're signing the papers next week. Only problem I'm having is finding a rig building crew. Everybody's busy."

"Well, I'll be ready when you are, but right now I just

want something to eat."

The cafe was crowded as usual. The crew found a spot in the back, and Lon was making his way toward the table with only food on his mind when he collided with Mason Poe, weaving through the tables.

"Hey, Mason, how you doing?" Lon recognized Jer's friend.

"What the hell!" Mason's eyes were glassy and mean.

"It's me, Lon. Where's Emory? Is he in here tonight?" He put his hand on Mason's shoulder to steady him.

Mason slapped it away. "Watch it, you son-of-a-bitch!" The words were slurred. Mason was stumbling drunk.

"Sorry, man," Lon raised his hands open palms out. "Say, is Emory here?"

"Hell, no, he's over at that whore house making a damn fool of himself." Mason's voice rose above the din of the cafe, and heads began to turn. Suddenly Mason's mood changed, and he grabbed Lon around the neck. "Come on, buddy. I've got a jug out in the car. Let's go check it out."

Lon pulled away. It took some muscle. Mason was strong for his size. "No, I don't believe so, Mas. I've got to get something to eat. I'll see you later. Tell Jer and Emory hello."

"What's the matter? You too damn good to drink with me anymore?" Mason shouted. "Too God damned high mighty!"

"Say listen, man, you're in bad shape. You better get out of here before you get thrown out." Lon was biting the words off a he headed Mason toward the door.

Mason stumbled onto the walk still mumbling to himself.

"I'll see you, Mason. Go home and sober up," Lon

called after him.

"Friend of yours?" Charlie asked with a grin when Lon got back to the table.

They ate heartily and set back to savor the meal.

"Well, boys," Rowdy announced as he wielded a toothpick. "I'm going to go home and sleep the sleep of the just tonight."

"Sounds good to me," Charlie agreed. They paid and left, stopping on the front walk to stretch their tired backs and survey the street. As they started across to the car Lon caught a glimpse of someone standing at the corner of the building in the shadow.

"Hey, Prather!"

Lon stopped and turned to see Mason glaring at him. Beside him were two men Lon had not seen before.

"I don't much care for getting pushed out of places, boy! I think you and me have a score to settle."

"Now, Mason, I didn't exactly push you out. You're drunk. I was just trying to keep you from getting thrown out."

"Well, why don't you come on over here and see how drunk I am now? That is, if you can get permission from your bodyguards there."

Lon looked around at the crew. They stood silently watching to see how he handled this.

"I'd like to oblige you, Mason, but you're in no condition..."

Suddenly Mason lunged forward attempting to knock him off balance, but Lon dodged and shoved his attacker to the ground. Mason staggered to his feet in the dusty street and glared at Lon. A flash of metal came out of his boot, and the little man charged again. The blade scraped Lon's sleeve as he pushed Mason aside, and the sickening gleam of the knife stood the hair on his neck on end. Mason made a low growling sound in his throat as he recovered his balance. The sliver of metal glistened as he crouched to attack once more. Lon's eyes were riveted on the blade dancing before him in small circles as Mason closed in. Panic washed over him. He felt naked, his gut exposed to the blade that he was powerless to stop. But as he stared a rage burst in his brain, and his fear was gone, replaced by a will to survive. In a split second, as Mason slashed the air between them, Lon grabbed wildly at the arm behind the knife. He sank his fingers into the muscles of Mason's taunt forearm and brought it down across his knee again and again as Mason floundered in the air like a rag doll. Gradually Mason's grip was loosened and the knife slipped into the dirt. As if in slow motion Lon watched the knife fall, then he turned his anger on his attacker, lifting the little man off the ground with the force of his blows. Mason made a pretense of fighting, but he stood no chance against Lon's rage.

The two men in the shadows made a move to join the fight, but like a shot, Rowdy and Moses were in their faces. "Since your friend started this, we'll just let him finish it, if that's alright with you boys." Rowdy counseled. They studied their options and backed off.

Charlie and Sherman pulled Lon off Mason who was now gasping for breath and struggling to shield himself.

"That's enough," Charlie spoke sharply to Lon, who was still coiled like a spring ready to throw another punch. "You don't want to kill this bastard."

Lon froze in mid swing. He stared at the pitiful being on the ground before him as Mason wiped mud and blood from his mouth.

"You get him home!" Lon directed Mason's

companions, "Sober him up." He turned and plucked the knife from the mud and jammed it into the porch post at the edge of the street snapping, the blade off at the hilt. Lon tossed the knife handle on Mason's chest. The two men stared at one another for a moment, then Lon turned in disgust and walked away.

The crew was silent as they drove home. Lon could feel them glance at him now and then, but no one spoke. When the car stopped at the house, Charlie looked over at his young charge.

"Man, I'll tell you. I ain't never going to call you kid again." He broke into a big grin and the other men started to laugh.

"Yeah!" Rowdy slapped Lon on the shoulder. "I'll tell you what. You ever get mad at me, you just let me know early. I'm going to stay out of your way!" The little man doubled over laughing.

Lon realized he had won some sort of honor in the eyes of his crew. Proven himself. But the memory of his anger left him with only a hollow feeling. When he had seen the knife coming Lon knew in his own mind he would have killed Mason if Charlie hadn't pulled him away. Raw anger left a metal taste in his mouth that locked his jaw. And this new knowledge about himself weighed heavy.

Chapter 8

On the way out to the rig the next morning no one mentioned the fight, but they talked around the edges.

Morning sport," Sully greeted Lon.

Lon pretended not to notice the remark. He tried to keep his gloves on as much as possible so they couldn't see the blood red bruises on his knuckles. He was grateful for the noise on the rig that drowned out any chance for conversation. He kept his head down and stayed busy.

They marked steady drilling time for the next four days and went through the duties of their jobs with a familiar rhythm. On the afternoon of the fifth day the derrick floor shuddered and a wild groan belched up from the hole.

"Hell fire, what is it now!" Sully exploded.

"I'm afraid I already know," Charlie shouted back.

Rowdy shut down the engine, and everyone stared at the drill table.

"Back it off, Rowdy," Charlie shouted with a wave of his hand.

The engine came to life again as the pipe began to come

out of the well. One by one the crew broke the joints off and stacked them in the rack inside the derrick tower. When the last joint came up it was missing half the bit.

Charlie unscrewed what was left of it and studied the break. It had sheared off just below the joint which meant there was still a sizable piece in the hole.

"Not much to get hold of down there" Charlie said. He handed the twisted metal to Sully. "It's probably buried up in the wall."

Lon and the rest stood watching the proceedings as the two top men talked the situation over.

"Well, boys, looks like we got a little fishing trip on our hands today." Sully said. "Rowdy, you got any suggestions?"

"Looks to me like you're going to need a span grab or some kind of scoop to get that bit out," the little man said.

"Yeah, you're probably right. Take my car and get whatever you think we need. Take the others with you. No sense in all of us sitting this out. We won't mark any more drilling time today. Send the equipment out with the night crew, and we'll see you in the morning."

"How long does this fishing business take?" Lon asked Rowdy on the way back to town.

"Hard to say," Rowdy answered. Lon noted that Rowdy's tone had changed toward him. All the reserve was gone from his voice. Lon flexed his sore knuckles inside his glove.

"Sometimes it can take days to fish something out, sometimes a week." Rowdy let the possibility of unemployment sink in for a moment. "Charlie and Sully know their business, though. If it can be fished out they'll get it."

"And if it can't?"

"They'll try to drill it out. It'll make a mess down there, but they'll seal up the wall as best they can and just keep going. I've seen them have to abandon a well, but that's rare."

"Meanwhile," Sherman leaned forward from the back seat and shouted over the car engine. "We've got us a few hours off!"

"Moses grinned and nodded. "Let's go to the cock fights tonight. We got time."

You're on, my friend," Rowdy agreed. "You ever seen a cockfight, Lon?"

"No, don't believe I have."

"That's fine for these old men, Lon, but I got a better plan for us," Sherman put in. "The town is throwing a big dance tonight, and some of those muleskinner's daughters can look pretty good. What do you say?"

"Now that sounds more my speed." Lon broke into a wide grin.

"Yeah, that's okay. You young fellows go blow your money. Me and Moses are going to go make a little."

"Tell you what, Sherman," Lon said. "I need to go look up my cousin first. I haven't seen him since I moved out. Let me meet you over there."

"Want me to go with you?" Sherman offered.

Lon knew he was remembering the fight. "No, no problem. This is my cousin, you know."

Lon got cleaned up and walked over to Emory's place. It was a hazy afternoon. He could still just see through the evening glow. Sounds seemed magnifies by the crisp December air. Lon made a mental note to himself to check with Morris about a heavier jacket. He could tell he might be needing one before long.

When he got to the house Emory's crew had not come

in yet, but he had figured to be early. He sat down in a cane bottom chair by the front door to wait and turned his collar up against the evening chill. He'd give them half an hour, and if they didn't show he'd just go find Sherman at the dance. He pulled a rolled-up dime western out of his back pocket and settled back to read by the porch light. By the time Emory and his crew drove up, Lon was so engrossed in his book he didn't hear the car at first, but the slam of the car door caught his attention.

Mas had been driving. He came around the car with his gaze fixed on Lon, sporting a bandage over his right eye. Lon ignored him but stood up to meet his cousin.

Before Emory could speak Jeremy broke in. "Well, if it isn't our two-fisted friend."

It's okay, boys," Mas muttered. "We're safe. He doesn't have his bodyguards with him."

The group chuckled. Lon locked his jaw and stiffened as he shot Mas a squinted stare. Mason looked away quickly and made for the door. The rest of the crew, except Jeremy and Emory followed him in the house. Emory neither spoke or smiled.

"What the hell is the matter with you?" Jeremy spit out his words. "I try to treat you like a friend, and you turn around and almost beat old Mason to a pulp."

"Listen, man, he picked that fight, not me, and he pulled a knife." Lon shot back in anger.

"Yeah, well, that's not how I heard it." Jeremy spoke through gritted teeth.

"Believe whatever you want." Lon responded. He looked at Emory and started to walk away, but Emory moved to follow him. His face was pale with fear.

"Knife! Mas didn't say nothing about a knife. Are you okay?"

"You coming, Emory?" Jeremy shouted as he started for the door.

Emory stayed by Lon. "Wait a minute, Jer."

"I said, are you coming?" Jer repeated.

"Naw, go on. I'll catch you later." Emory said.

Lon began to walk away, and Emory followed. "Hey man, wait up, will you?"

Lon stopped and turned to his cousin. "Are you going to take their side, too?" He spit the words out.

"Hey, I'm here ain't I?" Emory stared Lon straight in the eye. Listen, I mean, you have your faults old buddy, but you're no damn liar. If you say Mason pulled a knife, he did."

Lon relaxed.

"Besides," Emory said with a laugh. "It would take something like that to get you mad enough to do that kind of damage. You really beat the shit out of him!"

Lon didn't laugh, and Emory saw the pain in his eyes.

"Let's just forget it. I just came to see how you're doing."

Yeah, sure," Emory swallowed his smile. "Well, I'm great. How about you?"

"Fine" The two boys stood in silence.

"Listen," Lon finally spoke. "Let's go get something to eat, and we can catch up on things."

"Great, if you don't mind my work clothes. I don't think I'll go back right now, if you know what I mean."

Lon finally laughed. "Yeah, good idea."

"What are you doing so clean anyway? Don't you work for a living anymore?"

Lon explained about the broken drill bit and how he had lucked into a few hours off, as they walked to the cafe.

"Sounds good. Maybe I need to wrangle one of those

broken bits for our rig." They laughed, and the strain they had felt at first melted away.

After they were settled at a table Lon studied his cousin.

"Hey, man, I miss you," Lon said.

"Yeah, I haven't had anybody to tell me to straighten up since you left," Emory responded.

"How are those guys treating you?" Lon asked.

"Aw, alright, I guess. They're crazy. Man, I've drunk more whiskey in the last three months than I could have believed existed!"

"You better lay off that rotgut. You can't tell where it's from or what's in it." Lon cautioned.

"See, there you go." Emory pointed an accusing finger. "My conscience."

Lon smiled and shook his head. They ordered and sat back to wait for their food. "So, I also hear you've been visiting Sadie's a little."

Emory went serious. "Who said that?"

"That's what Mason told me that night of the fight while we were still talking. What's the matter?"

"That's none of Mason's damn business!" Emory shot back. "None of yours either!"

"Hey, man, I didn't mean anything. What's going on?"
"Nothin'!"

They sat in silence for a bit while the waitress brought their plates. It was starting again, Lon thought. Just about every conversation he had attempted with Emory since they got here turned into a shouting match.

"Have you written your folks?" he asked after a bit.

"No!' Emory shot back. "Have you?"

"Not yet, but I was thinking..."

"Leave well enough alone, Lon," Emory interrupted.

"Don't go telling 'em where we are. It'll just upset things."

"I just don't want them to worry."

"Well, leave me out of your writing. I don't have nothin' to say to any of them!"

Lon stared dumfounded at his outburst. Emory realized he was making a scene and calmed down as he glanced around the room.

Lon concentrated on his meal.

"So," Emory changed the subject after a bit. "How about you? What are you up to?"

Lon shrugged his shoulders. "Working. Not time for much else, I guess. You saving any money?"

"Me? Hell no." Emory was smiling again. "Spending every dime. What about you?"

"A little. This Jew fellow with the Dry Goods store. He's got a safe over there. I've been putting a little in there each week. My room and eats don't take much, and I don't need much walking around money."

"Don't need it! Man, you are something. You need to cut loose and live a little old buddy. Go back over to that dime-a dance place or something. Last week Jer, Friday, Mason, and me spent our entire paychecks that very night. The trouble with you is you don't know how to live. You might as well be back on the farm!"

"Not quite. I never made any six dollars a day on the farm.

"Well, it don't do you no good if you're too damn tight to spend it."

"Or too dumb to save it!"

The two boys stared at one another across the gulf of thoughts that separated them. Emory stabbed at his food and looked around the room. Anywhere but at Lon.

"Look, I've got to go." He shoved his plate away. "I

need a drink. I'll see you around."

"Look, I'm sorry, Emory..."

"I ain't going back, Lon. I ain't going!"

"What's goin'on, Emory? What about your farm? Don't you think...?"

"Look, don't you lecture me! You were the one who just had to come off out here. I don't see you going back!"

Lon studied his cousin's face, twisted in anger. "Well, then, I guess that's your choice, Emory."

"Damn right, it is! And don't be writing no letters for me. I don't need your help!"

Lon held his hands up as a sign of resignation.

Emory tossed some money on the table and stormed out of the cafe and off into the night.

Lon sank back into the booth and made no effort to stop him. He watched his cousin go with a deep pain in his gut. He had always felt responsible for Emory. Even when they were little, Lon remembered watching out for him. They were like brothers in that way, always together. Emory just never stopped to think.

"Oh, to hell with it," he muttered under his breath. "He's as old as me and big enough to make his own mistakes." He left to find Sherman at the dance

***

The town hall building was ablaze with lights. All the windows and doors were wide open, and the fiddle music filled the dark street outside. Lon paused at the doorway to buy a ticket and get his hand stamped.

"Thank you, sir. The money is for a good cause," a middle-aged lady confided in him.

"What are you buying?" Lon asked as he strained his eyes over the crowd looking for Sherman.

"A fire truck!" The woman announced proudly. "We've almost got enough."

"Well, that's good, ma'am." Lon smiled and moved away into the crowd. The floor was cleared of all furniture. Chairs and tables were pushed against the walls, and people were perched on every flat surface to stay out of the way of the dancers. Couples whirled and turned to the strains of the "Blue Skirt Waltz" as Lon made his way along the edge of the dance floor.

"Hey, Lon, over here," Lon looked up to see Sherman waving him forward. He pushed past several couples and came face to face with his friend.

"Where you been, boy?" Sherman shouted over the music. "Times's a wasting here. Ladies, I want you to meet my friend. This here is Lon Prather. Lon this is Betty." The girl giggled and extended her hand. "And this little thing here is...,"

"Lucy," the girl volunteered.

"Lucy, that's right. Lon meet Lucy. I've been telling these ladies all about you. Now don't you let me down."

The music stopped, and a loud voice shouted." Gentlemen choose your partners for the Texas Star!"

"Hey, that's our song, folks," Sherman yelled. Lon took Lucy's hand and they joined the dancers.

The first song ended and another began, but the two couples never left the floor. They danced and laughed and traded partners as the time slipped away. Lon felt light again. His fight with Mason and his meeting with Emory were far away. It was good to let go.

"Your friend tells me you are new here," the girl said. They had stepped outside to cool off and catch their breath, while the band took a break. Sherman and Betty had disappeared into the darkness behind some parked cars, but Lon could still hear their voices from time to time.

"Yeah, pretty new, I guess. A few months." Lon smiled, "It seems longer, though. Seems like I've been here forever."

"You got a smoke?"

"Huh? Ah, yeah sure," Lon fumbled for his tobacco and papers.

"Where you from?" the girl continued while he rolled her a smoke.

"Up northeast of here, north of Abilene." Lon started to lick the paper edge with his tongue, but stopped and grinned sheepishly. The girl giggled and took the smoke expertly from his hand, ran her tongue along the edge, and popped it between her pursed lips. Lon stared speechless. Lucy fluttered her eye lashes and muttered over the cigarette.

Light me, sweetie."

Lon jumped into action and produced a match that he struck across the bottom of his shoe several times and held it up to the girl. Lucy puffed at the smoke in earnest, then took it delicately between two fingers and blew the smoke out in a long breath that was probably intended to be sexy. She turned a wide-eyed gaze to Lon who had been watching the entire performance.

He recovered his voice. "And you, where are you from?"

The girl laughed again. "Everywhere. My daddy is a muleskinner. We've lived all over. Anywhere there's oil, and they need mule teams. She lowered her eyes and leaned toward Lon's chest. "You know if my daddy was to catch us out here, he'd probably kill us both."

"Why?" Lon's eyes got larger and he resisted the urge to glance over his shoulder. Laughter, a giggle, and scuffling sounds erupted from the darkness. Sherman was apparently having more fun than he was.

"Oh, you know," the girl giggled. "A handsome man like you taking me outside and giving me a smoke and all."

"Is he here now? Your father?"

"He's around somewhere, but don't worry. He and my brothers are probably busy out at the car. They brought a jug. Do you have a jug tonight?"

"No, no, I'm sorry," Lon raised his hands palms out and took the opportunity to glance quickly around in the darkness.

"Oh, that's too bad." Lucy pouted and then just as quickly changed the subject. "Where all have you lived?"

"I've never lived any place but Kraly Creek. Never been anywhere but here. Is it fun moving around all the time?" Lon asked. He lit a smoke for himself and tried to look relaxed.

"Not much. We never have a real place, you know. You got a real home, a house back in Kraly Creek?"

"Yeah, that is my daddy does."

"Why did you come out here?"

"Oh, I don't know, adventure I guess. I wanted to see something different. I was always reading about other places. I just wanted to see for myself, you know."

"I guess so. I haven't stayed anywhere long enough to get much schooling, but I think if I had my own place, I'd never want to leave it." As she spoke Lucy pressed her body close. "Never."

The music started again, and Lon was glad. The conversation was getting too complicated, and it was hard not to keep looking over his shoulder. "Hey, you ready to go again?"

Sherman and Betty emerged from the darkness flushed and slightly rumpled. Lucy stuck out her bottom lip ever so slightly. "Sure, I guess so."

They danced every dance. That suited Lon fine. He liked dancing, and it avoided conversation. All too soon the band played "Home Sweet Home" and closed down.

"You girls got a way home?" Sherman asked.

"Our daddy's here somewhere."

The four of them looked over the crowd as it poured out into the street. There was an awkward silence.

"Well, we better go find our folks."

"Thank you for the evening," Lon said.

"Any time," Lucy fluttered her eyelashes again. "And next time don't be so shy now." Lon felt his ears get red.

"Yeah, thank you, ladies." Sherman agreed. "They have these dances pretty regular. Maybe we'll see you again."

"Maybe so." The girls chorused as they disappeared into the crowd. Lon strained his eyes to catch a glimpse of their father expecting a seven foot giant, but he lost sight of the girls and turned back to Sherman.

"Man!" Sherman slapped Lon on the back. "Alright! But next time we've got to get a jug before we come. Now, what did I tell you?"

"You sure did, my friend. Except for a few anxious moments there, I had a fine time." He explained about the girls' father, and Sherman roared with delight.

"Well, now, sport. You didn't have to worry. I've seen you in action. I'm sure you could have handled the whole family."

"Just the same, I'll choose my own partners from now on, I believe."

"Lon, my friend, you've got to lighten up. Life is short."

"You're the second person to tell me that tonight."

"Well, it's true. I mean, I hand you a fine looking little honey with a weakness for big manly chests and you complain."

"You're right," Lon said. "You did good. I haven't enjoyed myself this much since I got to Wink. How about me buying you some bacon and eggs just to show there's no hard feelings."

"Hard feelings! In a pig's eye, boy. Show your gratitude!"

"Alright, you're on. Then we better get in home. Tomorrow is going to come early."

"Yeah," Sherman taunted, "And those flying feet of yours are going to drag in the morning!"

"Who, me? Man, dancing doesn't tire me out. That's the nicest kind of resting. Now you, I'll probably be carrying you all day tomorrow.

"Come on, let's eat. I'm starved."

Claude's was almost empty. A few people came in with the same idea as Lon and Sherman. The boys ordered breakfast and joked with the waitress. Their good mood from the dance carried over. Out on the corner of his eye, Sherman saw a friend come in and hailed him over to their table. It was the muleskinner Lon had seen that first day at the well site.

"Come on over and join us," Sherman invited. "Cabel, this here is Lon Prather, one of my crew. Lon, Cabel Norris."

The boys shook hands.

"I remember you from my first day," Lon told Cabel. "You dug the slush pit for our well."

"Yeah, that's right. How's that well doing?"

"We're down right now," Sherman explained. "Sully and Charlie are on a little fishing trip."

Cabel raised his eyebrows. "I see! Well, maybe they'll catch something pretty quick."

"Yeah, maybe, anyway, in the meantime," Sherman slapped Lon on the shoulder. "Old Lon and me here took advantage of the time off and went to the dance tonight."

"I see. I wondered what you working men were doing out at this hour."

"Did you go to the dance?" Lon asked.

"Me? No, I've been playing a little poker this evening," Cabel confided, "I'd rather spend my time at something that makes a profit."

"For you maybe," Sherman said, "But I've never had much luck at poker."

"Oh, I wouldn't say luck, now." Cabel shrugged his shoulders. "It takes a little skill along with it."

"You must be pretty good," Lon said.

The other two laughed.

"Yeah, pretty good," Cabel agreed. "I've won a few hands. Did all right tonight, I'd say." He produced a roll of bills from his pocket and flipped through it. Lon stared in amazement.

"Who were you playing?" Sherman asked.

"A table full of roughnecks who don't know better than to mix liquor and cards," Cabel confided. "It was easy pickins', my friends."

"Lord, man what are you going to do with all that, start a bank?"

"Maybe," Cabel laughed, "Someday. Right now it's going in Morris's safe first thing in the morning." He looked at Lon. "I've seen you in there, haven't I? You're doing business with Morris, too."

Lon nodded, "A little, but nothing compared to you, I guess."

"Still, it's a smart man that saves his money," Cabel declared. "Maybe we could do a little business sometime."

Lon laughed, "If you mean poker, I'm out. I've never played much. I'm not in your league."

"No, I was talking business. Oil leases," Cabel said. "There's still some good gambles not leased. Maybe we could invest together sometime."

"Maybe," Lon answered. The idea of investing his savings hadn't occurred to him before.

"I'll keep you boys in mind," Cabel said.

They finished their breakfast and said good night. Lon and Sherman tried to slip in without waking the others, but it wouldn't have mattered. Sully and Charlie were still at the well, and Rowdy and Moses were making so much noise with their snores, busting down the door wouldn't have raised anyone. Apparently cock fights took a lot out of them.

Chapter 9

As they approached the rig the next morning, the long faces of the night crew told the story. No luck. Charlie and Sully were still huddled over the rotary table as if their presence might be enough to pluck the broken bit from the hole. The two men, bleary eyed from their night-long vigil greeted Rowdy with a shake of their heads.

"Anything?" Rowdy questioned.

"We moved it a little, I think," Charlie said. "Broke it loose from the side, maybe."

"If we can maneuver it enough to set some casing down around it, we've got it, but its hard to judge," Sully added.

Rowdy chuckled deep in his throat. "That pipe don't read as easy as the old cable did, does it?"

The tired men smiled slightly.

"Let me and Moses have a go at it, and you two take a break," Rowdy suggested. The four men traded places, and Charlie and Sully slumped on the lazy bench grateful for the respite.

"How can you tell anything about it that far down?" Lon questioned.

"You can feel the vibration on the drill rod." Charlie informed the two young crew members. "With a cable tool rig the vibration was easier to read. This rod isn't as clear."

"What did you get hold of it with?" Sherman asked.

"We've got a scoop on there, now." Sully said. "I'm pretty sure we can pick it up, but it's angled. Won't come up, and the casing can't drop down. Maybe Rowdy and Moses can get it."

"I need a little coffee, myself." Charlie spoke up. He stretched his back and walked over to the tool shed. The four men each took a cup to cut the morning chill.

"How's your cousin?" Sully asked Lon.

Lon looked up from his coffee cup in surprise. "Fine. He's doing alright."

I figured you'd hunt him up since you had a little free time," Sully explained.

Lon hesitated not knowing what to say next.

"You tell your cousin that I'm going to have a job open next week. He's welcome if he wants it."

Lon smiled. "I'll sure tell him. Thank you."

"No need to thank me. One of the night crew gave me notice last night, and I thought maybe you two boys might want to get together again."

"I'll sure talk to him."

"Let me know soon as you can. Now if you boys will excuse me, I'm going to stretch out on that cot over there and get some rest. Charlie?"

"Right, I'm going to the car. You boys stay handy and help Rowdy if he asks."

Lon was excited. The prospect of working with Emory, and more important, getting him away from Jer and his influence was the solution to everything. He spent the rest of the morning planning how he would talk Emory into taking the job.

If curse words could have raised that bit, the well would have been cleared in no time. Rowdy waxed creative in his curses as the morning wore on, and when he became exhausted Moses took over. The rhythm of their profanity took on the feel of an incantation almost, but to no avail. Suddenly the two men fell silent as the casing slipped a little.

"Easy now, easy," Rowdy whispered.

"I felt it," Moses reported. His hand rested lightly on the drill rod.

Rowdy jumped to the switch and the pipe began to rise out of the hole. "Look alive, boys!" he shouted.

The crew jumped into action and the long process of pulling the pipe began. Sherman took Moses' place in the tower to guide the pipe and, Sully and Charlie reappeared wide awake and eager. When the last joint came up the crew broke loose. Whooping and back slapping broke the tension of the long ordeal as they looked at the grimy piece of twisted metal that caused all the trouble.

"Put that in your collection, Rowdy," Charlie shouted as he handed over the broken bit.

Rowdy nodded and scooped up the part.

"Now boys, let's get back to business, here," Sully shouted. "We should know about this well by morning."

The rig came to life, and the crew guided the pipe joint by joint back into the earth. The crews didn't leave after their next shift. They hung around out by their car talking among themselves. A man drove up in a model T truck and strolled to the derrick floor. He had the rolling gait of a cowman in his walk, Lon noted.

"That's the owner of this god-forsaken piece of real estate," Sherman informed Lon as they watched the man approach. "He's already got four wells and he's looking to add another this morning."

The crew stood back as the core sample was taken. Sully and Charlie did the honors, but when the sample came up it was dry. They had missed the oil sand. They had a dry hole.

Lon couldn't believe it. No maybe. No try again. It was over. The man studied the sample for a few minutes and then shrugged his shoulders. He shook hands with Sully and Charlie, and then turned and walked down the ramp, never looking back.

Hugh Sullivan turned to his crew. "That's it. We missed. Let's plug her up and get moving."

The rest of the men went to work, but Lon hung back, frozen in his disbelief. After all this work and time, it was dry?

"Come on man," Sherman slapped him on the shoulder. "Let's get cracking. Quicker we move this thing, the quicker we get some time off."

"Well, my boy," Charlie caught Lon's eye, "Now you've got your first dry hole under your belt."

"How do you know?' Lon managed to ask. "Maybe we just need to go deeper."

"No, it's dry. We hit bedrock. That's the layer under the oil sand. We know that from the other wells that have made. The oil isn't under here. It pinches off somewhere between here and that well a mile away over there. This one is dry.

Lon still stared in disbelief.

"Don't take it personal, now. You'll see more dry holes

than good ones if you stay in this business. Now get moving. We've got another well to drill.

Chapter 10

They spent the rest of the week breaking down the rig. Sully had not been able to find a full crew of rig builders, but a couple of men showed up who knew what to do. Lon and the rest of the drilling crew filled in and the rig came down. Cabel Norris hauled the heavy sills and equipment to the new site. A cold north wind lashed at the men as they worked and Lon turned up the collar of his new work jacket.

"We may get a little snow out of this one," Rowdy ventured.

Lon looked up to see Sully approach. "Well boys, this is about wound up. The rig foreman tells me him and his boys can get this thing ready in a day or two. That will give us time to check over our machinery. Meantime, let's break off early today, and I'll treat you to dinner tonight."

"Sounds good to me!" Rowdy announced.

"What are we celebrating? Lon asked.

"Where you been, man? It's Christmas Eve!" Sully slapped Lon on the shoulder. "Come on, I can smell that dressing down at Claude's right now."

Late that night Lon sat down to write his father. He'd meant to before now, but somehow he'd let it slip. He stared at the card trying to decide what to write. Nothing came to him. Finally he began:

Hope you are well. Me and Emory are both working. Tell Aunt Martha howdy. Merry Christmas.

Lon

He sat back in satisfaction. Turning the card over, he studied the picture on the other side. It was a street view of Wink at its busiest. Maybe Pa would enjoy seeing where he was. He added his address so his father could write him back and headed to bed. Tomorrow he would look Emory up and tell him about the job offer. And he just wouldn't mention the letter.

***

Lon found Emory easily enough on Christmas afternoon. Sherman and Charlie drove him out to Sadie's. He kept thinking to himself he needed to get there early enough to catch Emory before he started drinking, but it was a waste of time.

"Is Emory Campbell out here?" he asked the woman who held the door open just a crack.

"Who wants to know?" The woman's voice was low and raspy, just audible above the music and voices inside.

"I'm his cousin. I need to see him."

The woman moved back and motioned across the room. Lon stepped in squinting into the light.

"Well if it ain't Lon Prather!" Lon recognized Jeremy's booming voice. "Come on in old buddy!"

"Howdy Lon!" Emory shouted. He was standing to one side of the room, his arm around a wisp of a girl in a flimsy cotton dressing gown. Lon surveyed the group and recognized Friday Smith and Mason through the smoky haze.

"Come on in here, boy. No hard feelings. Right, Mason?" Jeremy declared. He moved to put his arm around Lon's shoulder. "Tell your friends to come on in and join our celebration. We hit it big today."

Emory yelled, "How about that Lon, old buddy. That bitchin' well blew in at 10,000 barrels a day. Here, have a drink on me."

Lon braced himself against Jer's enthusiastic hug and smiled. "Well, I guess you boys are feeling alright. It came in today?"

"Better than Santa Claus!" Jeremy announced and the group laughed. He passed a glass to Charlie and Sherman, and the three men tossed down a shot of whiskey.

Jeremy wiped the back of his hand across his mouth. "I heard you boys came up dry again." There was a glint of mockery in his eye.

"Yeah, I'm afraid so," Charlie said.

"Well," Jeremy spread his arms with a drunken flourish, "That's how it goes, you know. Better luck next time." He raised his glass in salute. "You boys looking for a little Christmas entertainment tonight?"

Lon laughed, "Well really I was looking for you boys. I need to talk to Emory." He looked over at his cousin who was giving all of his attention to the girl at his side.

"Hey Emory!" Jeremy shouted, "Pay attention, boy. Your cousin wants to talk to you."

Emory turned bleary eyes on Lon as he snuggled against the girl. Her gaze was now fastened on Lon with a look of more than mild interest. Emory looked down at her, then followed her inviting look to his cousin.

"What do you want?" Emory asked.

"I want to talk a little business, that's all," Lon said.

"Business," Jer interrupted, "He must be wanting to cut in on our luck today, Emory." The group laughed.

Emory shook his head drunkenly. "Naw, I'm too drunk to talk serious tonight. Catch me tomorrow. I'm busy. Right?" He turned to the girl.

She kissed him and nuzzled his ear, but all the while she had never taken her piercing gaze off Lon.

Lon looked away, uncomfortable with her forwardness. The girl pulled Emory toward the door. "Nice to meet you, Lon. You come back some time, now, you hear?" She and Emory disappeared through a doorway toward the stairs.

Jer handed the bottle around. "You boys are welcome to stick around."

Lon looked at Charlie and Sherman. They were both smiling sheepishly. "What do you say?" Lon asked.

"We ain't in no hurry, I guess. We have the day off tomorrow," Charlie reasoned.

"Yeah," Sherman agreed, as he studied the other girls. "I mean, we're here and all."

Lon laughed and raised his glass. "Merry Christmas, boys."

Across the room through the laughter and motion Lon caught sight of Mason. He sat hunched over on a bar stool seemingly unconscious of the party going on around him. His black eyes were only slits in his face next to the purple scar, and he was studying Lon with a stare that reminded Lon of a crouched animal. Lon stared back for only a second before the view was blocked by the dancers.

***

"Quit my job! Man, are you crazy? Why?"

"I thought it would be good for us to be together again. Hugh Sullivan is a good man to work for, Emory."

"Well, so is Red McGuire!"

Lon and Emory were talking over coffee at Claude's the next morning, clearing the moonshine from their brains from the night before.

"It was just a thought." Lon shrugged his shoulders.

"Yeah, I'll bet! Just a thought to get me under your watchful eye! Listen, cousin." Emory spit the words out. "I don't need nobody to take care of me. Why would I want to work for a man who tells me how to live my life!"

"Maybe you could use some telling!" Lon shot back. "You can't keep up with Jer, Emory. Drinking all night, working all day. It'll get you before long."

"I knew that was it! You want to step in and run my life! Look, Lon. I'm fine. I've got a good job, good friends. Stay out of my life!"

He rose to leave but turned back to point a finger at Lon. "And listen, cousin, stay the hell away from my woman!"

Lon started to respond, confused at the last remark.

"I saw the way you were looking at her last night. Stay away!" He turned and disappeared out the door, slamming it behind him.

Lon watched him go, a mixture of anger and sadness boiling up in his throat.

"Hey, what's happening, old buddy?" Sherman slapped him on the shoulder.

Lon turned quickly and then relaxed.

"Well, did you have any luck?" Sherman asked.

Lon laughed softly. "No, but I just got put in my place pretty good, though."

"Well, you tried. If Emory can't see what's happening to him, there's nothing you can do."

Lon shrugged his shoulders.

"You want to shoot a little pool?" Sherman suggested.

"You're on." Lon slid out of the booth. "We better make the most of it, because we'll be back out in the cold tomorrow."

Chapter 11

They went back on the job early the next morning, checking over the cables and boiler equipment. Lon watched the rig builders with interest. It was almost like magic the way they raised the huge timbers and bolted them down. The dry hole was forgotten, and excitement was building for the new site. The off-setting well was looking good, and the crew was anxious to get started.

Cabel Norris dug the slush pit again.

"You boys thought anymore about investing?" Cabel asked Lon and Sherman one day during a break.

"How much money does that sort of thing take?" Lon asked.

"Well, it depends, but if we went in together, I believe we could keep the cost down. I've been checking around a little, and there's a lot of land north of here along the New Mexico line that hasn't been leased. Folks think it's too far north, but I think they're wrong. There's a bunch of homestead farmers up there that don't know the oil business enough to push for exploration. I figure we could pretty well lease up the whole area for a song. Can you boys come up with a couple hundred now?" Cabel studied their faces intently.

"Two hundred! Hell, man what do you need us for if that's all you want." Sherman said. "You win that much in a single night's poker game!"

"You're right about that. I'd be putting up my own money too, but I'm just letting you boys in on a good thing."

"Why?" Sherman laughed.

Cabel studied him with a hard look. "Just forget I mentioned it, then." He turned to walk away.

"I've got two hundred," Lon spoke for the first time.

Cabel stopped and smiled. He looked at Sherman.

"Yeah, I'm sorry, Cabel. I didn't mean nothin'. I've got two hundred I can gamble."

"Fine! Now keep this quiet. I've got one more job this week after I finish here, and then I'm going up north on a little buying tour. I'll need your money by day after tomorrow. The money will make you partners in anything I find. Does that sound fair?"

The boys nodded.

"I'll lease up as much as I can and bring the papers back for you to sign. Do you want me to fix up a contract for us?"

Lon studied Cabel's face for a few minutes and then extended his hand. "No, a handshake will do, partner."

Cabel smiled and grasped his hand in a firm grip. "That sounds fine to me." He turned back to his mules, and Lon and Sherman watched him move away, snapping the reins.

"Old buddy, I don't know for sure what we just agreed to, but we may have just given away four hundred dollars," Sherman said in a low voice.

Lon smiled and folded his arms. "Maybe. But it might be worth it to find out what kind of fellow Cabel Norris really is."

Chapter 12

Spring came to the desert, and the warm days returned. Lon loved the life, hard hot work and all. As the drill bit ground deeper into the land he took on the look and language of the oil patch. The second well showed a little pay, but it was poor compared to the big producers. By the end of the summer they had moved the rig twice more, and Sully was showing the strain of too many wrong guesses. Rowdy was muttering that they were turning into a real "po boy" outfit, but he kept it quiet around Sully and did his job.

Lon almost lost track of Emory. Their meetings were accidental and short. Each time left Lon feeling empty for a time, but he would reason that Emory seemed happy and showed no hard feelings. There wasn't any anger between them, now, just a void that neither knew how to span.

Cabel turned up in September with a stack of leases in his pocket and some big dreams. Lon and Sherman signed where he told them and listened to his plans.

"Something's brewing up there, I tell you. All the big

companies, Humble, Kelly, they all have their people combing the area. I'm picking up the crumbs with our money but the leases are in the right spot. I figure the big strike will be northeast of here a ways. I can feel it."

"How's our money holding out?" Lon asked.

Cabel grinned. "I'm okay. Nothing a little poker game can't fix now and then. How are you boys doing?"

"We're about one dry hole away from the poor farm," Sherman said.

"No strike?"

The boys shook their heads.

"Well, you're still drawing your pay though, I guess."

"So far, but I have a feeling it will be a long time till next pay day if this well comes up a duster." Lon said. "Why, you need more money?"

"I'd take another hundred if you had it."

"We got it," Lon answered before Sherman could respond.

"Man, I don't know if you're reckless or wise." Sherman complained after they each handed over their money and Cabel was gone again.

Lon laughed and slapped him on the shoulder. "Now tell me, what better use do you have for that money than buying a piece of a dream."

In late September they set up again. This time on a off-set location to a big producer. The prospects looked good but Lon had seen enough by now to know not to get his hopes too high. He had learned that the oil business was an odd mixture of optimism and fatalism with a touch of insanity thrown in. Old timers like Sully and Rowdy had to be a little bit crazy Lon reasoned. But this time the drilling went well. The formation was loose, Charlie said. Within five weeks they were already down far enough to take a core sample.

"Here you go," Charlie directed. "Take a sniff of that and tell me what you smell."

Lon pinched out a bit of the muddy core and held it to his nose. Fumes filled his nostrils. It reminded him a lot of moonshine whiskey. He looked up at his boss.

"Oil, my boy, I think we've got a good one this time." Charlie tasted a bit of mud and quickly spit it out. "Yes sir, we'll be there by tonight, I wager." He motioned for Rowdy to come over. "Lon go tell Sherman to get to town and pick us out a control head and get a tank out here. We want to be ready. I think this baby is going to have a lot of pressure." "Let's shut down till he gets back," he told Rowdy. "No sense taking a chance of blowing this thing."

Rowdy nodded and headed back to kill the boiler. Word spread pretty fast. Sherman brought back a good collection of spectators. The land owner and investors, as well as the night crew who Sherman had alerted, came out to share in the excitement. A few town's people, who just liked to watch a well come in, turned up, too. The crowd was hushed with anticipation. Lon could hardly conceal his excitement, but he tried because the rest, Rowdy and Moses especially, seemed as calm as ever. The only clue to how they really felt was an overly businesslike manner that added drama to the whole scene.

Sully joined his crew on the derrick floor as they moved in the strange structure of valves and pipes called a christmas tree and started the drill again.

"Easy now, easy." Charlie cautioned to no one in particular as he opened the throttle on the engine drive.

Suddenly a spray of gas and oil sizzled around the control head and Lon felt a vibration start under his feet.

"Open her up slow," Charlie shouted and Sherman

twisted one of the valves and then another. Oil gushed out and spilled into the tank waiting for it. The whole mass of pipes seemed ready to leap off the derrick floor from the pressure.

"Yahoo!" Rowdy yelled and slapped Moses on the back. Moses turned and wrapped his big arms around his little friend and lifted him off the ground. The whole crew went crazy.

"It's a big one boys!" Sully yelled. "We did it. That tank is almost full already. Shut the damn thing down till we can get some real tanks in here. We don't want to spill any of this. This baby is going to pay a lot of bills for us all!"

Sully gave everyone a couple of days off to celebrate the strike. It was the first time Lon had seen the crew really cut loose. Charlie produced a jug after dinner and even Sully had a shot. After a few toasts and a few good natured lies about old times, the men went their separate ways. Lon and Sherman wound up in a dance hall, and as best he could remember later, Lon saw some of the ugliest women he had ever happened onto. But it didn't matter at the time, long as they could dance. The fun all ended around three in the morning when Sherman passed out flat of his back on a pool table, and Lon got to half carry, half drag him home.

He had no more than slung Sherman in his bed and fallen across his own, when Rowdy woke him up shouting something about Moses and a crooked cock fight. Lon tried to understand, but it was hard to stay awake.

"We've got to get down there before Moses kills one of those sons-of-bitches." Rowdy pulled Lon to his feet and slapped his hat on his head as he shoved him out the door. Charlie was waiting in the car, in little better shape than

Lon.

"Rowdy, when is that damn Indian going to learn he can't whip the whole white race in one night?" Charlie growled.

"Well, he was doing a fair job of it when I left."

"Then what does he need us for?" Lon muttered.

"He don't need us, those other bastards do!" Rowdy was almost screaming. "When Moses gets started he's hard to stop. We got to get him out of there before some real damage is done."

The tent at the edge of town was still standing when they got there, but they could see the support poles wavering and the sounds of the fight filled the night air. Inside the tent they found Moses screaming his version of a war cry and tossing his attackers left and right. The man was a blur of punches. Rowdy motioned for Lon and Charlie to follow him, but neither one moved.

"You kidding?" Charlie yelled. "I'd rather walk up on a wild cat!"

Rowdy gave them a look of disgust and started working his way through the crowd of onlookers to the side of the tent behind Moses.

The big Indian had about cleared away his assailants, and only one or two brave souls were still getting back up to throw one more punch. Moses dodged a poorly aimed desperation swing, picked the hapless attacker up lightly, and tossed him on the pile of bodies at his feet. Then he turned his drunken stare on the crowd and let out another war cry that announced he was ready for another round. Suddenly Rowdy stepped out behind him and tapped Moses smartly across the skull with a black jack, and the big man went down like a shot.

Lon and Charlie moved in quickly to gather up their

unconscious friend while Rowdy scooped up the money strewn on the pit floor. "Much obliged," he said with a tip of his hat to the crowd and the crew beat a hasty retreat.

Back in the car headed for home, Lon studied the sleeping giant. "Does this happen very often?"

"No more than the world can stand it," Charlie laughed. Old Moses is a quiet man when he's sober, but he just can't handle his liquor. See why Sully don't allow no drinking when we're working?"

Lon shook his head, "And you guys gave me a hard time for fighting."

They laughed, and Moses roused a little and smiled from ear to ear.

Chapter 13

Late the next day Lon was slumped in a booth at Claude's nursing a cup of coffee. Sherman came in, surveyed the room, and seeing Lon, made his way over. He tossed a newspaper on the table. "Look at this."

Lon took the paper and studied the headline. In large bold letters he read:

STOCK MARKET CRASH!

"What is this?"

"I don't know. That little black kid you're always talking to was peddling them and shouting as how this was something big, so I bought one." Sherman dropped into the booth across from Lon.

"By the size of the print you'd think a war was starting." Lon quickly read down the paper. "Stock market fell drastically on Wall Street again today as thousands of investors dumped sixteen million shares on the market."

"What is a stock market anyway?" Sherman asked.

"They aren't talking about livestock. I can tell that much."

"Best I can tell it's a money problem, must be bankers or something," Lon said.

"Well, professor, I figured you'd know what it was, since you read all the time," Sherman said with mock disgust. "But you done let me down."

"Wait, listen to this. It says here some men are jumping out of windows to their deaths over their losses," Lon continued to read.

"Where's all this happening?"

"New York City, it says." Lon glanced at the date. "October 29, 1929. This paper is three days old."

"Well, what did you expect. Abilene is a long way off." Sherman yawned and stretched. "Besides that, New York is a long way off. That stock market stuff can't make much difference down here."

"Guess not, but somebody must think it's important."

"Well, in the meantime, my friend, we're laying out a new site tomorrow so..." He slapped the table and jolted Lon's attention away from the newspaper. "Let's go celebrate our last night of freedom. What do you say?"

Lon groaned and shook his head. "No more dance hall lovelies tonight. I've never seen so many ugly people in my life!"

"Ok, old buddy, if you've lost your sense of adventure, let's go take in a picture show. You can sleep through it if you want."

"Now that sounds more like what I'm up to."

Lon left the paper on the table.

Chapter 14

It was a slow night at Sadie's. Emory and the crew had been there since dark but no one else had come by. Sadie was in a good mood. She wasn't pushing the girls tonight. Jeremy could charm anyone, and Sadie was no exception. He had worked out a deal to supply the house with moonshine now and then, so Sadie let her rules down for them. Besides that he was humping her himself. On the nights Jeremy brought the liquor in, he and the boys could stay around all night if they wanted, and Sadie didn't keep score as to how many times they took one of the girls up stairs.

"I'm getting hungry again," Friday announced in a loud voice. He unwound his long arms from the girl at his side, stood up and scratched his ribs. "What do you say we go get a bite to eat?"

"Rutting always makes you hungry, don't it," Jeremy said.

They were already a little drunk. Jeremy rose and slapped the cork back in his bottle. "I'll go for that, myself.

You boys coming?"

Slumped on a sofa in the corner Mason shook his head slowly and took another drink. He warned Jeremy away with a black look. Mason was in a mean mood, and the boys knew from experience to leave him alone when he got to drinking serious.

"How about you, Emory, you coming?"

"Naw, I'll stick around here. Me and Camillia here are busy." The girl's arms were draped around his neck. She turned a cool possessive look toward Jeremy and shifted her weight ever so slightly. "I ain't hungry," Emory said.

"Huh, not for food anyway." Friday winked at Jeremy.

"We'll see you boys later."

Emory snuggled closer to Camellia. Her perfume filled his nostrils.

Camellia smiled up at Emory and stretched. "I feel like dancing. Dance with me!"

Emory reluctantly let her slip out of his arms. She walked over to the Victrola and cranked the machine to start the music. As Emory watched with a drunken gaze, the girl began to move to the music motioning for him to join her, but he couldn't move.

"Come on, honey, don't make me wait." She moved her hips in a slow seductive turn.

"Don't waste your time on that piss-ant farm boy, honey." Mason suddenly came to life and reached for Camellia as she floated by. "You need a real man." He

grabbed her roughly around the waist and began to move slowly to the music. Camellia laughed softly and wrapped her arms around his neck.

Emory felt a pang of anger, but he did not move. Slowly Mason began to run his hands over the slim thighs and breasts of the girl. He whispered something in her ear, and a giggle floated across to Emory. Camellia pushed away gently and shot a quick glance toward Emory to see if he was watching. Mason pulled her roughly back to him and turned a steely stare on Emory that dared him to protest.

"You see, old Emory there. He's kinda stupid." Mas kissed the girl's neck. "He don't know how to treat a woman." His lips moved down Camellia's neck toward her breast. The girl giggled again and made a pretense of pushing him away.

"Leave her alone, Mason." Emory's voice carried over the music.

Mas lifted his head and smiled. "Well now, why don't you just come on over here and stop me, farm boy." He turned back to Camellia, who giggled and tossed her head back in an inviting way.

Emory jumped to his feet. "I said, leave her alone!" He reached for the girl's arm to pull her away.

"Stop it! You don't own me!" Camellia jerked away and rubbed her arm where Emory had touched her.

"Now, see there, farm boy. The lady don't want your help. Get back on the couch over there!"

Emory reached for Camellia again. The girl jerked away and slapped his face.

"I said, leave me alone! I'm sick of you, you hear? Leave me alone!"

Emory reeled back more from her words that from the blow.

"Why would I waste my time on a lowly piece of oil field trash like you!"

Emory stood frozen in place. The noise in the room was a deafening roar in his ears. All he could hear was Mason's laugh.

He turned and stumbled blindly out of the house into the road. He had to get away. He could hear the girl's shrill laughter behind him.

Emory started up the road toward town almost at a run. The night air filled his lungs and made the effects of the moonshine even worse.

"Oil field trash!" someone shouted. Emory looked back to see Mason following him. "She told you alright, you stupid little bastard!"

"Get away from me, Mason!"

"Oil field trash," Mason mimicked Camellia's voice.

"I said stop it, God damn you!" Emory turned on Mason with his fist clinched.

Mason stopped, and a cruel smile spread across his face. "Well now, little man, you come make me." He motioned with his hand, but Emory did not move.

"You know old Jeremy and the others are going to get a good laugh out of this. You crawling around like a whipped dog, and that whore telling you off. You dumb son-of-a-bitch"

Suddenly Emory exploded. He charged at Mason and tried to throw him to the ground, but Mason was braced for the fight. He side-stepped the lunge and watched Emory go sprawling in the dusty road. Mason started to laugh, a low guttural chuckle. Emory struggled to his feet and looked at his enemy.

"Come on in, farm boy," Mason almost whispered. Emory caught a glint of metal in Mason's hand. He was moving the knife in a slow circle as he spoke. "I'm going to teach you a lesson, farm boy. I meant to teach it to that son-of-a-bitchin' cousin of yours, but you'll do." He jabbed with the knife and moved away.

Emory broke out in a cold sweat of terror. The knife

blade danced before his eyes. Between the liquor and his fear he was almost helpless. He fought back, slugging and kicking as best he could, but Mason only shook off the blows and continued to come. The blade felt like a bee sting when it touched his skin.

"I'm going to finish you off, farm boy. You ain't the first bastard I've killed with a knife, and you won't never give nobody any trouble again" Mason was laughing as he brought the blade hard into Emory's stomach. Emory crumpled to the ground and the world went black.

Chapter 15

The crew saw the car coming in the distance, bucking through the sand hills with the motor sputtering. Everyone watched it without stopping their work, but they could tell by the way the driver forced the car on, it was bad news. When it finally slid to a stop by the derrick and the dust cleared away, Lon saw Jeremy.

"Is Lon Prather here?" Jer shouted up to Charlie. Charlie motioned with a wave of his hand.

Lon dropped the wrench he was holding and started down the ramp. Jer met him half way.

"It's Emory. We found him this morning. He's cut up pretty bad, Lon, and..."

Lon wheeled and ran back up the ramp to Charlie. "I got to go to town. My cousin's been hurt."

"Take off. We'll cover. See you tonight."

"Come on!" Lon shouted over the engine as he passed Jer going to the car.

"What happened? Did a cable snap or something?"

"No, nothing like that. He wasn't at work. This happened last night sometime. Emory got cut up in a fight."

"How bad?"

"I don't know. I found him this morning out on the road from Sadie's and got him to the doctor, but I didn't stay around. I came after you."

"Found him? You mean you weren't with him last night?"

"Yeah, at first, but we got to drinking a little heavy, and I don't..."

"Where was he when you left him?" Lon was shouting.

"Hey, man, it wasn't my fault. He won't do nothing but drink and hang around that whore house."

Lon unclenched his fist. "Who do you think did it?"

"I don't have any idea. Honest, like I said, we were all pretty far gone." Jer's voice trailed off.

The car sputtered back to town, running at its top speed, but to Lon it felt like an eternity. He should have never let him and Emory get split up. Lon always had taken care of Emory, and now he'd let this happen.

Jer stopped the car in front of a small frame building with a doctor's shingle over the door. They walked in without knocking and squinted into the dim interior.

"Close that damn door!" A voice boomed from a back room. "Who is it? What do you want?"

"My name's Prather. I'm here about Emory Campbell, the one who got cut up. I'm his cousin."

A grey headed man stepped to the doorway of the back room. He had his shirt sleeves rolled up and there was blood on his hands. He squinted over his spectacles, studying the two boys for a second. "Get in here. I need some help."

Lon and Jeremy jumped forward.

111

"Wash your hands over there real good and roll up your sleeves."

Lon stared at Emory stretched out on the table. He was unconscious and his pale face looked like a small child's.

"Move, boy!" the doctor barked. "Your cousin here needs help." Lon followed the man's orders.

"Get around over here and hold this light for me so I can sew, and you, hold that compress down tight until I can get to that cut." Lon and Jeremy did as he directed. "This boy has lost a lot of blood. It's taken me all this time on his belly wound. Where did this happen?"

Lon looked at Jer.

"I don't know. I just found him this morning. He must have tried to get home and fell."

"Well he didn't make it far like this, I can tell you." The doctor worked as he talked. "He's been slashed or stabbed about fifteen times by my counting, if we ignore all these little nicks. Somebody damn near finished him off. Here, help me hold this together while I stitch."

Lon's hand shook when he touched Emory's skin, but he followed orders. The flesh was cold and clammy to the touch.

The doctor worked quickly, and the needle flashed in and out as he closed the gash in Emory's forearm. "He must have put up a hell of a fight though. Look at his knuckles," the doctor said.

Lon looked down at Emory's hands covered with purple bruises.

"You call the law yet?" the doctor asked.

"No, I just got him over here as fast as I could," Jer repeated.

"You know anybody who would do a thing like this?"

Jer and Lon looked at one another.

"No sir," Jer said. "No one."

"Well it doesn't matter right now. All that matters is he's alive. Okay, you can move now. Let me get this last cut. I can sew him back together but the rest is up to him. I might as well tell you though, he's bad. That belly wound may have done more damage than I can fix."

Lon heard the doctor without really grasping his meaning.

"Can I stay with him?"

"Yeah, for now. I'll be in the next room. You sing out if he comes to."

Turning to Jeremy, the doctor directed. "You go get Jack Williams and tell him to get over here. If the boy wakes up maybe he can tell us who did this."

Jer and the doctor left the room but Lon was hardly aware of their leaving. He stood helplessly by Emory and watched his labored breathing. Almost an hour slipped by, and neither boy moved. Then Emory's hand moved slightly with a jerking motion, and a sound escaped his lips. Lon leaned forward and touched his hand.

"Hey, old buddy, it's me, Lon"

Emory tried to speak, but no sound came.

"Lie still, lie still," Lon said.

Emory swallowed and licked his dry lips. "Mason" The words were barely audible. "It was Mason."

Lon stiffened. Somehow he had known as soon as he heard there was a knife involved. "Why, why would he do this?"

Emory tried to lift his head, winced in pain and fell back to the pillow. Tears were in his eyes. "I'm sorry, Lon. I'm sorry. I'm no damn good. Tell Ma I'm sorry. Tell'em all."

"Lie still." Lon tightened his grip on Emory's hand.

He was still standing there when the doctor returned. The old man studied Emory's face for moment and quickly checked the belly wound again. Slowly he lifted his eyes to meet Lon's and shook his head.

"It's no use. I can't stop it. He's bleeding inside."

Lon could barely see the doctor through his tears as he shook his head in disbelief.

"Lon," Emory whispered.

Lon leaned close to hear his cousin's words, but instead Emory shivered involuntary and a stuttered breath escaped his lips.

Lon gripped his cousin's hand harder and stared wildly at the doctor, but he knew it was over.

The doctor gently took Emory's hand from Lon. Lon stepped back and stiffened his back as reality soaked in.

"Did he talk at all? Say who did it?" the doctor asked.

Lon did not respond.

"The law will be here in a minute. If he told you anything, then let's get Jack Williams, and let him go after the man."

Lon suddenly turned a wild stare on the doctor, and the hatred in his eyes answered the old man's questions.

"Don't try to settle this yourself, son. Getting yourself killed or killing somebody won't bring your cousin back."

Lon turned without replying and walked out of the room. He had an urgency in his stride. The doctor followed him to the door but made no further effort to stop him. As Lon's form disappeared into the near darkness of the street, an approaching sound turned the doctor's attention.

"Come on in, Jack. I've got another one for you." The doctor's voice was weighted with fatigue and despair.

Chapter 16

Tears blurred Lon's vision and anger pounded in his temple as he stumbled away from the doctor's office into the twilight. His jaw was clamped shut in an effort to hold back the pain.   Dead, dead, Emory....it couldn't be. He couldn't be dead. Emory's words were vivid in Lon's mind. Mason. He could see Mason's eyes burning into him at Sadie's that night last Christmas.

A sudden whir of an engine and a shout brought him out of his daze. "Hey, watch it. Out of the road!"

Lon jerked around to see the glaring lights and gleaming metal of a car swerve passed him.

Lon wiped the tears from his eyes with the back of his hand and took a deep breath of the evening air. It would be dark soon. He knew what he had to do. He was clear on that. Sadie's would be a good place to start. After a quick look up and down the road, he sat off at a slow jog toward the edge of town. His eyes were clear with purpose now.

***

115

The crew came by the doctor's office on the way into town. They expected to find Lon and hear what had happened to his cousin. Instead the car lights revealed the figures of the doctor and Jack Williams conferring in front of the doc's office. The two men turned to look, as Sully brought the car to a stop.

"Lon Prather here?"

"Not any more," the doctor responded.

"What happened?"

"I don't think you have time to hear it all now. I was just filling Jack in. The boy's cousin was killed in a knife fight, and by the way that Prather kid left, I think he knew who did it."

"You got any ideas where to look for him? Jack spoke up. "I think we better find him fast."

Sully gave Charlie a quick glance. "If it was a knife it could be that fellow that jumped Lon that night."

Charlie nodded his agreement and looked at Sherman as he answered. "Jack, we could start looking at Sadie's. That's a good guess."

"Let's go," Jack directed as he stepped on the running board of the car. He propped his shot gun on the roof and Sully sped away.

***

Lon was winded by the time he reached Sadie's but he kept moving. The lights and music loomed ahead of him as he leaned against a highline post to catch his breath and surveyed the area. Several cars were parked at the edge of the circle of lights from the door. Lon studied then carefully and recognized Mason car. His heart beat quickened, and his mind raced to decide his next move.

Laughter erupted from the building as Lon squared his shoulders and moved to the doorway. He shoved the door open and stepped inside.

The room was full. People turned to the door in surprise, their expressions registering a smile as they recognized Lon, and then confusion as they saw the anger in his eyes.

Friday Smith stepped forward. "Howdy, Lon. Come on in. If you're looking for Emory I ain't seen him or Jer all day." His voice trailed off as he turned to follow Lon's gaze to the far corner of the room. Seated on a sofa with a girl on his lap was Mason, staring back at Lon.

Lon took several steps forward before he spoke. His eyes never left Mason. "Emory's dead. He died just now." Lon was choking on the words. "But he lived long enough to tell me what happened and..."

Suddenly Mason jumped to his feet, scattering the crowd. "Come on, boy! You want me, come on." The knife blade in his hand caught the light.

Screams rang out and a scramble followed to clear out of his way. Mason moved toward Lon brandishing the knife in a slow circle. Lon crouched and braced himself to fend off the blade.

Mason chuckled, a low growling sound in his throat and stabbed at the air. Lon jumped aside as the blade grazed his ribs and Mason laughed again.

"What's the matter, farm boy? Come on in." Mas motioned with his other hand. "Come on."

He slashed again at Lon's gut catching his shirt and bringing a trickle of blood as the blade brushed Lon's skin. Mas lunged once more but this time Lon stood his ground. He stopped the thrust with one hand and brought Mason's arm down sharply across his knee with a force that sent the knife sliding across the floor. Lon heard Mason's forearm crack, and he felt his fist smash the face whose eyes turned from nameless hatred to wretched pain. Lon struck and struck again. The force of his blows turned the man to a helpless lump of blood and sweat and still he hit him. All the pain and anger and anguish of Emory's death poured out.

Suddenly someone grabbed Lon from behind and slung him aside. Before he could recover his feet, a voice boom.

"That will do, son. Stand aside. I'll take it from here." The shot gun was pointed at the pitiful form of Mason Poe on the floor.

Lon gasped to catch his breath and stared around the room. Charlie and Sully pulled him to his feet.

"Come on, let the law have him. Let's get out of here."

Lon let himself be guided out into the night. They stopped outside in the darkness.

"Emory's dead, Sully. You should have let me kill him."

"You've done all you can, son. Killing that animal won't bring your cousin back. Jack will take care of him." He pulled a bottle from his jacket pocket. "Here," Sully offered, "this will help. Down some of this and get hold of yourself. You've got to take that boy home."

Lon stared at his boss and the truth in his words burned in. He took the bottle as directed, downed a quick swallow, letting the whiskey sear its way down his throat. He wiped his mouth with the back of his hand and drew a deep breath. The two older men watched in silence. Lon squared his shoulders and handed the bottle back. He set his jaw and nodded his head. "Let's go."

Lon followed his friends to the car.

Book II
MAE
1930

Moving Bunkhouses To Winkler Co. Oil Field

In A Fevered land

Chapter 17

A line of cars and wagons edging along the sandy road followed the soft ruts cut by the lead wagon. Gusts of cold wind pushed sand swirls into the air and buffeted the procession with muffled blasts of sound as they slowly snaked their way to the gate of the cemetery and passed under the wooden arch. Lon rode in his father's car, hands limp in his lap, shoulders slightly hunched and jaw tight. The days since Emory's death had been like a long nightmare from which he could not awaken. This silent trip to the cemetery was yet another step to be taken before the dream could end. But it was not a dream, and the truth of that washed over Lon like the chilling wind outside the car. It was not a dream.

The procession rumbled to a stop, and six men lifted the casket down from the wagon bed. Slowly, with a grace that almost seemed out of place among these sunburned farmers, they carried the pine box to the grave. Family and friends, all the inhabitants of Kraly Creek, gathered around in silence and waited for the minister to speak.

Lon studied the faces around him, silent and sad. Faces

that he and Emory had known all their lives. His eyes moved to Aunt Martha, so small and fragile. She's buried other children, Lon thought, but none like this. Sickness might be something she could understand, but the violence that had taken her oldest child was beyond her understanding. Pain and disbelief were etched into her face in lines that Lon knew would never leave. Willis Campbell stood next to his wife, his arm around her thin shoulders. His face was an open scar of pain as he waited the minister's words.

Brother Randall's strong lyrical voice rolled over the crowd with the gusts of wind. "It is not for us to know the reason for God's plan. The reason he took Emory."

REASON! The word shot across Lon's mind like a lightning bolt. Reason! What reason! What a hollow, empty, stupid thing to say! Lon bowed his head to hide the anger in his eyes. Mason Poe! That was the reason, and God had nothing to do with it! Lon looked again at his aunt and uncle frozen in their grief and at the faces of their neighbors, innocent and trusting, wanting to find purpose in all this. He clenched his jaw against his pain.

The minister finished his words and stepped back as the coffin was lowered into the ground. The crowd turned away from the grave to offer their hands to the family in sympathy, but Lon stayed riveted in his place and watched the men start to fill the grave.

For a panicky second he wanted to stop them. Stop the whole thing and make it not be true, but he did not move. He only stared in silence, fists clenched, as the clods of red sand began to spatter across the wooden box. Lon felt a hand on his shoulder.

"Come on, son, let's go home," his father said.

Lon realized after they were out past the arch, that they

had not taken time to visit his mother's grave as they usually did when other funerals brought them there. Too much pain in one day, he thought as he glanced at his father.

"What about the man who did this?" Henry said as they drove along. It was the first time he had asked.

"The law had him when I left. Promised me a quick trial."

"Did Emory give him any call to do it?"

"No," Lon replied quickly. It was me he was after, not Emory, he thought, but he did not share his thoughts with his father. "There was no reason to it, no reason." Lon said instead. Then he fell silent, remembering the night Mason had attacked him at Claude's. The metallic taste of anger came back to him. That he should have killed Mason, then, was the thought tearing at Lon's gut.

They gained the main road, and Henry geared the car down to make a sliding turn in the loose sand. Lon glanced back over his shoulder at the line of cars behind. His aunt and uncle's farm house came into view across the field and his father turned into the lane.

"There are all kinds of folks in the world. That's a fact," Henry said as he brought the car to a stop by the yard-fence and turned to face his son. "Some are mean. And reason ain't got nothing to do with it."

They sat in the car for a few minutes, each lost in his own thoughts.

"You say the law has him now?" His father asked.

Lon nodded.

"Then let it be."

Lon could not look at his father, but he was saved from needing to answer as other cars pulled to a stopped next to them. Neighbors had begun to gather, carrying covered

123

dishes of food and solemn expressions. Lon felt a sickening turn in his stomach. He did not want to face them all. He looked back at his father, but Henry was already out of the car, shaking hands with several men and talking in a low tone. Lon followed his example.

The afternoon dragged by. Gradually the somber tones of the funeral gave way to quiet talk. The ladies of the community served the food, and a ritual of healing was carried out. The men, unaccustomed to the confines of a house, congregated on the porch and out across the yard in small groups and exchanged words in husky whispers. They met Lon with sturdy handshakes and uncomfortable expressions of grief. Then their conversation drifted to crops and weather.

Feeling awkward and out of place, Lon wandered away toward the barn looking for a lonely spot. In back of the house he passed his Aunt Martha's grape arbor, covered now only with twisted vines, brown and leafless in winter, and found his cousins, Emory's three younger brothers. They were involved in a solemn game of mumbly peg.

Lon nodded in greeting.

The boys did not respond at first but continued to flip their pocket knives. They glanced at one another and then back at Lon.

"Noise get too much for you in there?" Lon asked, making an attempt at conversation.

Nathan, the youngest Campbell at five years, glanced at his brothers and then spoke up, "Pa said you got a knife cut, too. Is that so?"

Lon nodded. The stitches in his upper arm twinged a little.

"Did you get the fellow that killed Emory?" Zak, the oldest, asked.

"No, the law got him, Zak."

The oldest boy looked away quickly and flipped his jack knife at the target.

James Henry, just younger than Zak, spoke. "Why didn't you get him, Lon?"

Lon studied the young faces in front of him. "I let the law handle it. I had no choice."

The boys nodded solemnly. Lon felt hollow, exposed without defense before their simple logic. He was standing here, and their brother was gone. That was the truth of it, and he could not explain it or make it right.

They returned to their game. Lon watched for a while and then moved away toward the barn. He found a spot next to the windmill tank and sat down, glad for the throbbing of the windmill to drown out the noises drifting from the house and the thoughts rattling in his mind.

He had been sitting there, legs drawn up with his elbows resting on his knees, staring across the field for some time, when a sound close by caught his attention. He turned to see two shapely legs and looked up into the face of Mae Handley. Before he could recover his composure and rise, she dropped gently to her knees at his side.

"Hi, Lon."

"Hello, Mae," he stumbled over his words. "I didn't know you were here."

"I was in the kitchen," she nodded toward the house, "but you didn't see me before. I wanted to find you. Most of the folks are leaving."

Lon looked toward the house and wondered how long he had been here by the windmill.

"I just wanted to say how sorry I was, and I hope you'll be okay."

"Oh, I'm fine," Lon said. "Emory always liked you a

lot," Lon added, and then felt silly for saying it.

A frown flickered across Mae's face and she crossed her arms quickly and looked away across the field.

"Emory used to say if it weren't for you and me, he'd still be in that blue-backed speller. Did you know that?"

Mae looked back at him and now her expression was sad. "He said that?"

Lon nodded and they both fell silent for a time.

"What are you doing now? I mean, now that you're out school?" hc asked.

"I'm not out." Mae finally smiled at the question on his face. "I'm the teacher now."

"Well that's fine. Since when?"

"Last spring. Doctor Reese paid my way to school for a year. They couldn't afford Mr. Grayson any more, times being as they are. So I took the test at Durham for my license, and they hired me for less money " Mae seemed to read his thoughts, "It's not much, but it helps out."

"Well, that sounds fine to me." Lon smiled and stared into Mae's clear blue eyes, lost for more conversation.

"Well." She patted her knees and rose. "I just wanted to say hi and tell you I'm glad your home. I'm sorry you had to come back for this reason." They were silent for a moment. "Maybe I'll see you again?"

"Yeah, I ... maybe so. I'll be around," Lon stammered and scrambled to his feet.

The girl turned and walked away. Lon watched her slim figure disappear past the arbor. Mae Handley had surely changed.

The sun was almost down. He hadn't even noticed. Lon walked back to the house, quiet now and dark. At the back door he saw his aunt and uncle seated on the screened-in porch watching his approach. He opened the screen and stepped inside.

"Boy, are you okay?" his uncle asked.

Lon nodded. He started to speak but choked on his words. "I'm sorry," he managed to get out. "Uncle Willis, I'm sorry."

His uncle reached out for his hand and Lon stumbled toward them like a small boy again. "Son, you don't have to say that."

Aunt Martha brushed the hair back from his forehead like she had done a thousand times before. "Lon, we're just thankful that the Lord let you come back to us."

Suddenly Lon was crying, silent wrenching sobs unlike any he had experienced since his mother's death. The three people clung together and shared the pain they had so carefully tried to conceal all day.

After a time Martha kissed Lon's forehead. "You better go on now. It's late and your daddy is waiting."

"Did the law get that fellow?" Uncle Willis asked.

"Yes sir."

The strain and darkness in his uncle's face made him look so old, Lon thought. The helpless sadness in his eyes would stay with him forever, he knew. His uncle's head moved slowly in a nod of resignation but no other words were spoken. Lon closed the screen behind him as he left.

Chapter 18

"**H**ow was your cotton this year?" Lon asked his father the morning following the funeral. It brought back old times sitting there in the predawn stillness with a steaming cup of coffee in his hands.

"Bout the same, I guess." Henry said. "The price still wasn't no good."

Lon pondered his words a few minutes remembering how cheated and trapped he had felt. They sat in silence for longer than normal conversation would demand. The way he and Emory had left before had not been brought up. That was a dark void between them that neither one had breached. It wasn't hostility that Lon felt from his father but more an uncertainty, caution as toward a stranger. Things were not the same as before.

"I tell you, times is bad." Henry's voice surprised Lon after the long silence. "Folks are beginning to go under. You remember Hanse Jordan over by the river bridge? Some of the best bottom land around, and I hear the bank foreclosed on him last week?"

"What will he do? He has a mess of little kids doesn't

he?"

"Four or five, I think. I don't know. He was carrying a debt his daddy got into back in the Big War and just never could catch up. That's been over ten years a ago."

"What about Mother's place," Lon asked. "Is Ratch trying to make a crop?"

Henry looked up and shook his head and then turned away. A motion that was to dismiss the subject, but Lon did not let it drop.

"Why do you put up with that, Pa? I've never understood. The man does nothing over there and..."

"He wasn't like that before the war," Henry interrupted.

Lon looked surprised, "Was Ratch in the war? I never knew that."

"He never should have gone," Henry continued. "No reason for it 'cept he just had to. He was kinda wild, you know. Adventurous." Henry cut his eyes around at his son. "Like some other boys, I know."

Lon smiled slightly. There was going to be a lecture in this conversation.

"Emory always reminded me a lot of Ratch back then. Your Uncle Willis and Ratch and me could think of all sorts of trouble." Henry laughed softly remembering. "Ratch was the crazy one, always happy, joking."

Lon tried to imagine the dark brooding bear of a man he had always known as a happy boy. He could not.

"Your mother and your Aunt Mary tamed Willis and me down pretty quick but Ratch, he was determined to stay free as long as possible."

"When did he marry?"

"Oh, not long after us. And he made an attempt to settle down with Louella, I guess. His family had the land just west of the river there, and he was a good farmer. Better than me. But he got restless."

"So he ran off to the war?"

"We were all going to, Willis and Ratch and me. We were in Durham at market when the news of the war came out. We'd been drinking a little, lettin' off steam, you know, and just decided to join right up." Henry shook his head and took a deep breath. "Just not even think about our wives, just go." He smiled at the amazed look on Lon's face.

This was not a situation Lon could imagine his father in, acting on impulse. Not the father he had always known.

"Then Willis got sick, and I had to walk him back to the wagon. By the time I got back to the saloon I was fairly sober, but Ratch had already signed his name. I argued with the recruiting agent, but it was no use. Ratch had signed. That was it." He shook his head again, as though to clear an image. "Willis and me had to come on back home and tell Louella."

"Was he in the fighting?"

"The thick of it, I understand," Henry continued, as he got up for more coffee. "He was bad wounded and gassed they called it. Some kind of poison." Henry refilled Lon's cup. "Ratch never was right after that." Henry sat silent for a few moments, remembering. "He lost his land, everything. Your mother and I set them up on her old place so that Louella and the babies would have a home." Henry shook his head.

"So you let him stay on," Lon said softly.

"He's an old friend, like family you might say, him and Louella both. I've always felt responsible for what happened. I might have stopped him from going."

Lon nodded. He understood, now. He could picture Emory, bowed up and arguing with him. He understood.

"Ratch did fairly well for a time," Henry continued, "But something just snapped in him one day. He went crazy. He's been down by the river in that little old shack ever since. Has no truck with anybody." Henry paused to cut himself a new chew of tobacco. "He hasn't planted now in seven years. Not turned a hand. But the boys are getting older. His oldest boy, Cal, is near big enough to be a fair farmer now. It'll get better."

They sat in silence for awhile.

"How are you doing?"

Henry shot his son a warning look like Lon had overstepped some boundary in asking. "I'm fine, like I said. I don't have no expenses. We've weathered hard times before, and we'll do it again."

The switch from I to we was not lost on Lon, and neither was the story about Ratch Handley. His father thought he was home to stay, Lon realized. He was the father and Lon was to step back in and be the dutiful son. Did he really believe he could just walk back in like the last years had never happened?

"I'm not back for good, Pa."

Henry studied his son's face. "I see," he responded finally. Then he rose and went out the back door.

Lon watched his father's form blend into the morning haze as he finished his coffee. It was better that he told him now. Better before his father began to plan. But that did not make it easier. Lon followed Henry out into the yard and caught up with him in the shed, harnessing the mules. He helped his father snap the traces in place and guided the animals out of the barn as he had done a thousand times before.

"Did I tell you Jeremy came by Willis's place after the funeral yesterday?" Henry said.

Lon looked back quickly from his work.

"He was looking for you, but I didn't know where you had gone to. He said he'd come by later." Henry flicked the reins expertly, and the mules moved away toward the field.

"I'll come down and spell you after a bit," Lon called after him.

"Yeah, in a while," his father responded.

As Lon went about watering and feeding the stock, Jeremy played across his mind. He had not talked to Jer since the day he came after him out at the rig to tell him about Emory. He wasn't sure he wanted to see him now. What happened wasn't Jeremy's fault, he knew, but still, in a way he blamed him as he blamed himself.

About mid morning he went down to the field to spell his father, but it gave him no satisfaction. Following the mules up and down the rows was a silent task and allowed too much time for thinking. He replayed it all in his mind and argued again and again with Emory. What if he could have talked him into changing jobs? What if he, instead of Emory, had taken the job with Jer in the beginning? What if? What if?

By mid afternoon he had covered a good bit of the field. The stubble was neatly buried to enrich the soil for another season. He was stopped at the end of the row to rest the mules and get a drink when Jer appeared, walking from the house. They studied one another as he approached.

"Howdy, Lon," Jer called when he was within earshot.

Lon nodded but did not speak.

"Your pa told me where to find you." Jer pointed back toward the house. "I got in too late for the funeral, but I came by your uncle's place ... Did your pa tell you?"

Lon nodded again.

I'm sorry, Lon. I never knew about old Mason. Honest, I... I'm sorry." Jer stopped, at a loss for something else to say.

"What happened after I left?" Lon spoke finally, "When's the trial?"

Jer's face brightened, grateful that Lon was talking. "Well, Jack Williams locked him up like he said he would and started running checks on him around the country. It turned out Mason is an escaped convict from Arkansas. He stabbed somebody else up there around Fort Benton."

Lon was silent for a long time with a blank expression Jer could not read. "So what happens now?" he said finally.

"I don't know. Maybe they'll just send him back to prison." Jer shrugged his shoulders.

Lon accepted that news in silence also, his eyes were dark with emotion.

Jer shuffled his feet and rubbed his hand across his mouth, confused by Lon's reaction, or lack of it. After a bit he added, "I . . ., I got something here for you." He fished in his back pocket for his wallet. "Emory had some money coming." He extended his hand clutching a fat fold of bills. "I figured you ought to be the one to give it to his folks."

Slowly Lon reached out for the money, and Jer took a step forward to reach him.

"It's some back wages, plus a little." He paused while Lon flipped through the roll to discover it was much more than a week or two in pay. "And then I owed him a little myself. I figure his folks can use it. There's over 300 dollars there." He paused, hoping Lon would respond in some way. "I know it don't change nothing, Lon, but..." Jer's voice faltered. "I'm sorry." Then getting no reply he turned to go.

"I'll see that Aunt Martha gets this," Lon said in a low voice.

Jer turned back quickly and smiled.

"Thanks for coming," Lon added.

"Well," Jer gave a deep sigh of relief. "I'll be obliged if you would give it to her." He hesitated, trying to think of something else to say. "You coming back to the oil field?"

Lon nodded.

"Hugh Sullivan says to tell you they're moving up north. Red is, too."

"Nothing left in Wink?"

"It's about played out, I reckon. Just about everyone is moving up on the high plains. Sully says for you to stay here until you hear from him. He'll contact you when he has a job lined up."

"How long does he think?"

"Maybe a couple of weeks."

Lon nodded and reached out to shake Jer's hand. Jer smiled as if a great weight had been lifted from his shoulders. "Well." He adjusted his hat. "I'll be going. See you in Pampa."

Lon watched Jer walk away taking long strides over the rows of plowed ground. He felt a dull emptiness like the air around him was pressing down. And the pain of that night huddled by Emory, holding his hand. It all came back to him. 'An escaped killer.' Jer reached the road and climbed through the fence. Lon squeezed the reins so tight that the mules sensed the tension and tossed their heads. 'A killer.' He should have killed the bastard when he had the chance. He clicked his tongue and flicked the reins, and the mules turned back to the field. He could see Mason's face before him, twisted and crazed as it was the night of the fight.

Chapter 19

The community of Krayly Creek looked even smaller to Lon now, if that was possible. Lon stopped his father's car outside Elmer Vernon's store. Aside from the church and school across the road and the gin down the way, the country lay flat and empty in all directions. Lon got out to fill the gas tank, pumping vigorously as the fuel bubbled inside the pump. He spoke a greeting to the collection of men scattered across the veranda of the store, farmers passing the time. A brisk dry wind cut their words and jumbled the sound as it floated to him.

Across the way noise erupted from the frame school house and a tangle of children tumbled out onto the school yard. Mae Handley appeared at the door, holding the screen against banging shut in the wind and herding the smaller students out to recess. She caught sight of Lon and waved. He smiled and waved back. Mae surely looked like a Handley, Lon thought. All seven of the kids looked like their father. Their olive skin and black hair had always been a curiosity to him. Indian blood somewhere back in the family, his father had explained years ago, but that wouldn't explain Mae's eyes. They were clear blue, Lon remembered. Clearest blue he had ever seen. As a boy in school Lon had done some pretty silly things just to get her tickled so he could watch those eyes.

The pump gurgled, and Lon realized the tank was full, almost too full. He quickly replaced the hose and capped the tank. When he looked again Mae had disappeared into the building and he felt disappointed somehow. He went into the store to pay.

"Afternoon, Lon, that'll be four bits," Elmer Vernon informed him. "You come back to stay, have you?" He asked as he took the money. Elmer was never one for minding his own business.

Lon smiled. "For a while."

"Terrible thing what happened to Emory."

"Yes sir."

"I always liked the boy, myself." Elmer continued. "You reckon the law will catch the old boy that knifed him?"

"They already have him." Lon responded.

"You don't say. Well, I'll be damned!" Elmer sounded disappointed. "Ain't that something."

"Thank you, Mr. Vernon," Lon cut the man off before he could think of another question. He nodded to the collection of men who had been listening and left the store. Outside, he noticed the children were still at recess.

He turned the car in a wide circle away from the pump. But when he reached the road, he changed his mind and crossed over to the school house. He'd just stop and say hello since he was here.

The interior of the building was dark when he first stepped in, and a familiar smell of chalk dust brought back earlier days.

"Good morning." Mae's voice pulled his attention toward the opposite end of the room. He squinted in her direction.

"I thought I'd stop over for a minute."

"Come in. It's safe. Mr. Grayson isn't here anymore." She laughed.

Lon laughed too, remembering the stern old teacher they had both had only a few years before. "Place still looks about the same," Lon commented. "Except the teacher has gotten a lot prettier."

Mae smiled and looked a little embarrassed by the remark. "I'll take that as a compliment." She paused and looked closely at him. "Going to see the banker this morning?" she asked.

Lon glanced down at his shirt and tie and laughed. "Guess the tie is a dead giveaway, isn't it? I wondered why Elmer didn't ask."

Mae smiled. "He surely would have asked if he'd had any doubt. Nothing goes on around here without Elmer's supervision."

"I guess they're all over there now discussing why I stopped at the school." Lon said.

"Probably." An awkward silence fell.

"Well, I better get going, I guess. Nice talking to you."

"Come back and visit any time. I'll stage a spell down. You can show these kids how you used to win the medal every year."

"You still do that, do you?"

"Oh, yes, big occasion." Mae rolled those blue eyes and made a graceful motion in the air with her hands. The action gave him courage.

"Say, listen," Lon spoke with sudden confidence.

"There's a moving picture show over in Durham still, isn't there?"

Mae nodded.

"How would you like to drive over this Saturday. We could find a cafe or something and..."

"Oh, no," Mae answered quickly. "I mean there's so much work to be done on Saturday. I, I..."

Lon paused, feeling foolish for his forwardness. "Yeah, I understand."

"No," Mae tried to explain, "it's just that..." Her voice faltered.

"For old times' sake?" Lon suggested hopefully.

Mae laughed softly and nodded. "Okay, I'd like that."

"Fine," Lon said. "Fine. I'll be by your place Saturday then."

"No, "Mae said quickly. "I'll be here at the school. I'll meet you here."

"Saturday?" Lon asked with a puzzled look.

"Yes, I've got some little chores. You know." Mae laughed nervously. "I'll be here. What time?"

"About five?"

Mae followed him to the door and rang the bell to call the students back.

As Lon pulled away, he glanced back at her poised by the door, one hand holding her skirt against the tug of the wind. Yes sir, Mae Handley had definitely changed. He looked across at the store as he pulled out on the road. All eyes followed him as he drove away, and he laughed out loud. Well, this little scene would give the men conversation fuel for the rest of the afternoon.

***

Mae followed his progress too. What had she done? This was a mistake. She put her hand to her throat and could feel her pulse racing. But one time, she argued with herself. What could be the harm? She so needed to be away from here if only for an hour or two. It would be okay. Lon Prather would be gone in a few days. She closed the door behind the last straggling student and began class.

Chapter 20

Lon was a little nervous when he picked Mae up on Saturday. He talked nonstop all the way to Durham. More conversation than he'd ever had with a girl in his life, he was sure, but he was anxious to have everything go well. Mae seemed tense at first. She sat very still and gripped the door handle as though she expected the vehicle to make some sudden lurch or turn.

"I'll drive careful," Lon said to reassure her.

Mae forced a frightened smile. "It just seems fast," she explained. "I've... I haven't ridden in a car much, only Dr. Reese's."

"Oh! Oh that's it." Lon laughed. "I was afraid you were having second thoughts about coming."

"No, no," Mae forced herself to let go of the door handle. "No, this is fun."

Lon relaxed and slowed the car. He could handle this. He talked on, scattered conversation about the land and weather, and Mae gradually began to relax and enjoy the landscape flowing past.

At the restaurant, his conversation continued, and her shyness began to melt away. They had been friends all their lives. He was easy to talk to. The evening progressed from reminiscing, "What ever happened to old so and so?," and "Do you remember the time?", to what it was like in the oil fields.

"I guess you were pretty lucky to fall in with your crew. They sound like a good bunch," Mae said.

"Yeah, it was luck all right," Lon agreed thinking of Emory. He grew silent.

"I'm sorry, did I say something wrong?" Mae asked after a few seconds.

"No, no, I was just thinking." Lon focused back on Mae, and almost before he was aware of it, he was telling her everything. The whole story. Only he left out the parts about Sadie's. "I just feel it was my fault. Emory never would have gone off if it weren't for me."

Mae listened intently until he had finished. Lon's voice was choked with emotion, and he looked away suddenly ashamed of his display

Mae reached out for Lon's hand and covered it with hers.

"I'm sorry," Lon blurted out, disgusted with himself. "I'm ruining everything going on like this."

"No, it's okay. I'm glad you can talk to me, Lon. It helps, you know, to talk to someone. I'm glad it's me." She smiled. "You know, you can't always control what happens in life. Not for others. Sometimes not even for yourself. You did what you could for Emory, I think. That's all you could do. He had choices to make, and he made them. I'm sure he had his own reasons for going."

They sat in silence for a few minutes.

"So." Mae spoke first. "What are your plans now?

Will you be leaving soon?

"Yeah, well, pretty soon. Sully's supposed to send for me in a week or two. And there'll be a trial. I'll go back to Wink for that." Lon's jaw tightened.. "And I want to help Pa a little. Not that I'll enjoy the farming." He raised his head and smiled. "But maybe I can help. What about you? What are your plans?"

Mae smiled, "Plans? Well, I guess those are pretty much made for me. The teaching job doesn't pay much, but it's a job. There aren't many of those around, you know. I was lucky to get it."

"I'm not so sure it was luck." Lon said. "The school board knew what they were doing."

Mae blushed a little. "Maybe, but if they had not been so desperate, I doubt they would have hired me. Doctor Reese forced them into it. As Elmer Vernon pointed out when I got the job, I'm a fill-in until they can afford a real teacher again. Meaning of course, a man."

They laughed.

"Well, either way, they made a good choice." Lon said.

"The pay comes in handy. I guess you know, mister landlord, your farm hasn't turned much profit the last few years. Daddy tries, but...well, you know."

Lon nodded.

"I don't know how Mama would make it without me," Mae continued. "Between her chickens and the garden and what I bring home we get by it. I don't see an end to it though." Mae smiled, but her eyes were sad. "I wanted very much to go on to school."

Lon nodded again, "I wanted that too. Sometimes I almost hated Mr. Grayson for telling me about it; getting my hopes up. I guess if Mama had lived she'd have insisted I go on. She always encouraged me a lot. But after she died.... Well, Pa just didn't see the sense in it."

"Yes, I know. Everyone in Krayly Creek just expects you to keep the farm going. They don't look past their own little patch of ground too far."

"That's why I had to get out!" Lon's voice was strong with emotion. "I just couldn't stay and scratch along!"

"I understand," Mae said softly and Lon suddenly felt embarrassed, realizing he had done what she longed to do but could not. They sat in silence for a few minutes. Then Mae brightened.

"Send me a post card sometime," she said.

Lon smiled, "All right, I will. I'm not too good about writing letters, but I'll sure send you a picture post card." He looked around the cafe. "You realize, of course, we talked so long that we missed the picture show."

Mae followed his gaze. "My goodness, everyone else is gone. The people must be wanting to close. How late is it anyway?"

Lon motioned toward a wall clock. "Almost ten." He grinned sheepishly. "But it feels like we've been here about ten minutes."

Mae's eyes twinkled with laughter as she answered, "I've had fun."

"Me too. But come on, we better get you back. School marms aren't supposed to keep late hours, you know."

"Right," Mae agreed with mock seriousness.

The drive went quickly. Much too fast for Lon, and when he walked Mae to the door, he kept thinking of one more thing to say to postpone the parting.

"Listen, I tell you what. Now I promised you a picture show tonight, and I didn't deliver."

"I noticed that."

"And as they say, a promise made is a debt unpaid,

right?"

"Right!"

"So, Miss Handley," Lon grinned broadly. "I think you should give me another chance. I'll come by Friday night and we'll try it again, okay? I promise not to keep the teacher out too late."

Mae hesitated. She knew it was a mistake but... "Mr. Prather, I'd be honored." Mae laughed and extended her hand. "It's a deal, but come to the school. I'll just meet you there."

Lon took her hand, so slender and soft in his. He held it in silence for a few minutes, thought about a kiss, and then decided against it. Better not press his luck. "Fine, I'll see you then."

***

Mae watched him walk back to the car as she closed the door softly, trying not to wake her family in the tiny frame house. It was safe. She gave a sign of relief when she saw no sign of her father. The hounds weren't around. He was at the river. She knew it would work out that way. Still, her heart was beating fast as she slipped into the bed with her sisters. Little Cassie squirmed restlessly on her cot at the foot of the bed. Mae watched for a moment until everyone settled down. Then she let her head fall back on the pillow. She would worry about her father later. For now, what a evening! And what could it hurt? He would be gone soon.

Chapter 21

Lon jerked awake suddenly. First light was filtering through the windows. He glanced around the room at the wallpaper, tiny flowers that his mother had chosen years ago, now faded and water stained in spots. He sat up and shook his head to clear the remnants of sleep. Pa would have been up by now. Lon stepped into his pants and work shoes quickly and pulled a shirt from a nail on the wall, not bothering to fasten anything in his haste. He looked unassembled and rumpled when he opened the door into the kitchen.

Henry was at the table over his coffee. He did not speak and his look was hard to identify. Surely he isn't angry at me for over sleeping, Lon thought.

"Why didn't you wake me up?" Lon asked as he buttoned his shirt and tucked in the tail. "I didn't hear a thing."

"You've been out late every night," Henry said in a dry tone. "You're bound to be no good in the morning after a while."

Lon laughed and sat down at the table to tie his shoes. It was true. He had spent every night the past two weeks at the Handley place, helping Mae and her mother. Mae's younger brothers and sisters seemed to enjoy having him around. Lon entertained them with stories, and they laughed in a house that did not seem to have known much laughter. Especially the youngest, Cassie, still only a toddler. She seemed to take special interest in Lon, climbing into his lap and sitting quiet and still as he talked. Lon found himself looking forward to the child's attention. She was a tiny fragile version of Mae herself in many ways. Lon had never had brothers and sisters, and he enjoyed the company. It was much like Aunt Martha's house when he and Emory were little. The family was very close he sensed, a circle drawn tighter because of the absence of their father. No wonder Ratch got no farming done. He had not come in from the river in all that time, and he was never mentioned.

Henry poured Lon a cup of coffee and pushed it across the table at him. His face still showed no expression

"Aw, now, come on, Pa. You had a girl before," Lon laughed. "You know how it is."

"Not one I figured to run off and leave I didn't," Henry muttered. He pulled a crumpled envelope from his pocket and tossed it across at his son.

Lon picked it up. "What's this?"

"Telegram," Henry said. "Fellow brought it out last night after you left."

Lon opened the envelope and read:

NEED YOU   STOP   MEET ME IN BUTLER

146

NORTH OF PAMPA   STOP   AMBASSADOR
HOTEL FEBRUARY 15   END
SULLY

Lon looked up at his father. Henry poured more coffee
in his cup. "I figured it was about your job."

Lon nodded.

"You going?"

"He says to meet him day after tomorrow," Lon said.

"What about that Handley girl you been seeing?"
Henry's voice sounded angry.

"What about it? She knows I'll be leaving."

"So you just up and run off again," Henry said. "No
thought to this place or that girl. Just go again."

Lon had never heard this tone from his father before.
The anger in his voice made it shaky and strange.

"Pa, I can't stay here. There's nothing for me here,"
Lon pleaded.

Henry grunted in disgust and stared out the window.

"What did you make last year, Pa?" Lon demanded.
"Same as the year before? You can't keep this up forever,
you know. Turning no profit year after year." Lon paused.
His palms were sweaty and his heart was pounding. He
had never talked back to his father before in his life. "That
money Emory left his folks. It'll help. Pay taxes or
something..."

"And look what it cost him!" Henry shouted. "A pile of
money don't equal a life, boy!"

Lon stopped and studied his father's lined face. So that
was it. His father was afraid for him to leave again.

"Pa, I've got money, too. And it didn't cost me my life.
I put it in the bank in Durham, 500 dollars." He paused
waiting for a response but none came. "I told the banker

that the account was open to you, anytime."

Henry shot an angry look that normally would have stopped Lon short, but not this time.

"This mess we're in, Pa. A depression they're calling it. Nobody knows what's next. Let's work together, Pa. You run the farm. Keep it going. I'll go find work, and together we'll beat this thing! You can pay the taxes, buy supplies, whatever."

"I don't need no help from you! Never have!" Henry exploded. "You go on out there and make that big money. Have it your way, but I don't need no help!"

In the silence that followed Lon could hear his own heart pounding. Finally he spoke softly. "Sully says day after tomorrow. I better get going. I'll write you where I am."

Henry did not answer. Instead he stared out across the field.

Lon stood looking at his father for a moment, but could not think of any way to change the situation. He had to leave. There was no future here. His father knew it, but he would not bend. "I'll just get my things," he said, and he was gone

***

Lon waited outside the school until the children came out for recess. Mae smiled and motioned him inside.

"Well, Mr. Prather, what have you been up to today while the rest of us poor people slaved away?" Mae asked with a mocking smile.

"Well, ma'am, I've been doing some heavy thinking."

"Oh really?"

"I got a telegram..."

"A telegram. My, I am impressed!"

"A telegram from Sully, today, saying to meet him up north in Butler by the 15th."

Mae's face went solemn and her laughter stopped. "Oh!" She lowered her head and busied herself with straightening her desk.

"I've stayed as long as I can, you know." Lon continued.

"I know." Mae struggled to keep her voice from wavering.

"But I'll be back before long."

Mae nodded.

Lon reached out and pulled her gently away from the desk and into his arms. In their two weeks together he had kissed her only twice, briefly as they parted. Mae was so shy, so nervous he had not wanted to frighten her. Now he wanted to hold her and tell her how he felt. He raised her chin with his fingers and looked into those blue eyes brimming with tears. "I love you, Mae. I want to marry you some day." The kiss was as gentle as his voice. Mae did not resist, but even as their lips touched her tears came.

Lon brushed away a tear with his thumb. "Now wait a minute. This is not exactly the reaction I was hoping for here. I know you can't come with me right now, but next time? I'll be back. I just want you to know how I feel and..."

Mae stiffened and pushed him away. "I can't. I can't leave. Don't you see? The money I make here is all that is keeping my family going. If I leave..."

"If you leave everything will go right on, that's what will happen."

"No, you don't understand. Haven't you noticed how frail Mama is? If it weren't for me, they would be all alone,

Lon. I, I can't."

Lon stared silently at her for a few minutes at a loss for what to say. "What do you plan to do? Spend the rest of your life taking care of your brothers and sisters? What about what you want to do?"

Mae's eyes were desperate as she looked up at Lon. "I'm sorry," she whispered.

"Is it just me? I mean if you don't care for me..."

The pain in Mae's look was enough to know that was not it. What then? Why had she drawn away? "Promise you'll wait for me, then. Give me time to figure something out?"

Mae nodded. She tried to smile through her tears.

"I can get a ride with Elmer Vernon into Durham if I leave now. He's waiting."

"Now?" she whispered and glanced toward the door.

"I'll write when I get settled, and I'll be back as soon as I can. It'll all work out, I promise." He kissed her forehead. "Do you believe me?"

She nodded, but she did not speak again.

"I'll be in Butler, up on the High Plains, and I'll be back in three or four months. You make some plans now, okay?"

A car horn blared outside the building. Lon kissed her again, and then he was gone. Mae mopped her eyes and tried to regain her composure. The children would be coming back in soon, and she could not let them see her like this. From the window she watched Lon climb into Elmer's car and disappear from view, and she felt more alone than she had ever felt in her life.

***

She was hardly aware of the rest of the school day. The

children sensed something was different and were quiet and restrained. Mae was glad when she could dismiss the class and loose herself in her own thoughts walking home. Her brothers and sisters walked ahead of her but kept glancing back and whispering. The mile walk passed, and Mae hardly noticed the surroundings along the road as the drabness of her world seemed to close in on her. She should have never encouraged Lon. It could never be.

The hounds came out from under the house to meet them as they approached and a stab of dread jerked Mae back to reality. Pa was back. She took a deep breath and opened the back screen. He was slumped at the kitchen table, shaggy and dirty from the hunt. Her mother was at the cupboard, cowering almost. She gave her oldest daughter a quick glance as Mae came in. The other children filed in behind Mae and tried to blend into the edges of the room, but they did not need to worry. Their father saw only Mae.

"You kids get on your chores around here," Ratch bellowed. "Your Ma needs some help."

The children scattered. Mae started across the room.

"Is that all the hello I get?" Ratch bellowed again.

Mae stopped and turned to face him. "Hello, Pa. How was the river?"

"What do you care, long as I'm there and not here?"

Mae hesitated not knowing what was expected of her.

Ratch took a drink of coffee and then motioned for his wife to refill the cup. She jumped to comply.

"Yeah, the river was fine. But I figured I was needed back here." He poured the hot coffee in his saucer and blew on it before drinking. "Boys down there tell me there's been a fellow hanging around up here."

Mae stiffened, and she could taste her fear. Ratch's

glare was fastened on her.

"I don't like folks talking about my family behind my back." His voice rose. "Talking about my daughter. You got anything to say, Missy?"

Mae started to speak, but he cut her off.

"I won't have you shaming your Mama, girl. You hear me? Boys hanging around here, day and night."

"Pa, there was nothing wrong..."

"You listen, Missy. You won't see that Prather boy no more. No more, you hear! Just cause he's the landlord around here don't mean he can have his way with my daughter." Ratch jumped to his feet. "I'll blow his Goddamn head off if he comes back nosing around."

Mae swallowed hard to control her shaking. "He won't be, Pa. He's gone," She whispered.

"Gone where?"

"Gone back to his job. He won't be back."

Ratch hesitated, considering her words. "Well, that's good." He sat down slowly, and then as an afterthought, surveyed the room. "Get on over there and help your Mama with supper.

Mae nodded and slipped out to put away her things. Her hands were still shaking when she returned to the kitchen, and she and her mother did not look at one another for a long time.

Chapter 22

Butler, Texas looked fairly civilized compared to Wink, Lon thought as he peered from the bus window. He straighten in his seat and tried to stretch the cricks from his back and neck caused by sleeping crumpled over on the bus all night.

"There'll be a thirty minute stop," the driver announced in a loud voice. "You can get breakfast in the hotel. I'll sound the horn when its time to board."

It was a wasted speech since most of the passengers seemed to be collecting their bags and getting off for good. There was definitely a hum of industry in the air, Lon thought. It was good to be back.

He found Sully in the hotel lobby, sunk deep in an arm chair reading the paper.

"Did somebody around here send me a telegram?" Lon asked.

Sully peered over his paper and smiled broadly. "So you got here." He rose and shook Lon's hand.

"Where's the rest of the crew?"

"They're already out at the site by now, I reckon." Sully consulted his pocket watch. "We fired up yesterday.

Come on, you haven't had anything to eat yet, I guess."

"Nothing but two sticks of gum since dinner last night," Lon rubbed his stomach.

"Good, let's eat and I'll fill you in." They headed for the dining room off the lobby. "Everything all right at home?"

Lon nodded. "Fair. Why'd you decide to move up here?" he said to change the subject.

"New strike up here." They found a table and ordered. "Wink was about drilled up, so we got a chance to get in early up here. You know, we want to drill'em fast and get there first."

"Jer told me his crew was coming up here."

"Yeah, most outfits did. In fact just about the whole town moved, either here or down to Pampa. That Jewish fellow, Morris, moved his store up here. It's right around the corner. And Claude's got his cafe down here about a block."

"How about that," Lon laughed.

"Morris asked about you. I told him you would probably be here within the week."

"Your telegram was pretty clear," Lon said with a laugh. "Where are you staying?"

"We've got a house west of town about a mile. I'll take you over there so you can drop off your gear. Then we'll go out to the rig."

***

They left the hotel and found Sully's car. The streets were busy but not as crowded as Wink. The town of Butler was an old oil town, built several years before in an earlier strike. The buildings along the main street were made of ornate stone and plaster that stood as a monument to good times, but as they moved away from the center of town Lon saw the tent shanties and shotgun houses that looked more like Wink. The same crowds were there, just more spread out.

"It's good to get you back. We've been short handed," Sully said.

"I'm looking forward to it. I'm here to stay except for the trial, of course. I'll have to go back to Wink for that."

Sully didn't respond, and Lon glanced around at him. "What's the word in Wink?" he asked. "When's the trial?"

Sully glanced quickly at him then back to the road. "There's been a problem there, Lon."

"Problem?"

"Mason escaped. About a week after you left, he broke out. Got clean away. You know that jail wasn't much more than tar paper anyway."

"Escaped? Where is he now?" Lon's voice was clipped with anger.

Sully shook his head. "Could be anywhere. He's broke jail before, you know."

Lon's head jerked back as though he had been hit, and he glanced quickly around at the town outside the car window.

They're still looking for him, last I heard," Sully said. "They'll get him."

Lon shot an angry glance toward him. Sully didn't sound as if he believed his own words, and Lon surely didn't.

"Don't be wasting your life looking for Mason," Sully said.

Lon looked away quickly, surprised that Sully had read

his thoughts so easily.

"A thing like your cousin's death can eat you up if you let it, Lon. You'll spend your life looking for revenge. Or you'll find him, and wind up either dead yourself, or in jail."

"So he just goes free." Lon's voice was hard and bitter. "Is that it? Just walks away."

Sully did not answer but concentrated on the road ahead. Lon fell silent and rubbed a hand across his mouth to gain control again. His hand was shaking with anger. He went back to studying the people along the street.

"Just be careful," Sully said finally.

Lon nodded and turned to stare out the window again. They let the subject drop, but Lon's mind was whirling. Mason escaped! He could be anywhere. He could be right here, right now. He had to find him. He had to finish a job he should have finished long before. He took several deep breaths to get control. He had to think.

Sully studied Lon in quick glances as he drove. After a bit he made an attempt to change the subject. "This location looks pretty good."

Lon looked around as if he had just realized Sully was in the car.

"The drilling is about the same, but the wells are deeper. It's is going to take a little longer, I imagine. The discovery well up here was a thousand feet deeper than any we sank at Wink."

"Good," Lon finally smiled. "The longer it takes, the more money I make. I've got to fill Morris's safe up again."

Sully laughed. "Son, I believe you have done become a capitalist!"

The house was an old frame farmstead stained red by years of constant sand storms. They unloaded Lon's bag and struck out for the rig.

"Look at that skyline out there." Lon pointed at the horizon as he and Sully drove along the tracks carved from the prairie. The country around them was table flat even to the eye of a native Texan like Lon, unbroken except for an occasional clump of Lebanon cedars and cottonwood trees clustered around a farm house. Above the point where earth met sky hung a reddish-black boiling mass stretching as far as the eye could see across the horizon.

"Looks like we're in for another storm today," Sully commented

"You mean that's a sand storm?"

"You got it."

"Lord, I've seen a million of those, but I've never seen anything like that."

Sully laughed. "That's a goodly part of Kansas and Oklahoma you see coming at you right there. We ought to just about make the rig before it hits. There's some strips of cloth there in the back seat. You better pick us out a couple."

"What for? Lon reached back and did as Sully directed.

"Breathing," Sully responded. "You'll need it before the day is out."

By the time they reached the well the winds were buffeting the car, and the stinging sand was swirling about them. Lon stepped out of the car with one hand on his hat and the other clutching his work jacket to keep the wind from ripping it off.

Sully began fighting the wind to tie a canvas sheet down over his car engine. Lon grabbed the corners on his side, wrestled the tarp into place, and tied it down as best he could. The sand grains underfoot rushed up to hit him in the face and hands with razor edges, and he struggled to hold his balance in the gale.

"Come on, that's good enough," Sully shouted over the wind. He started for the rig, and Lon followed him in a clumsy stride balanced against the wind. The two men struggled up the steps to the drilling floor and pulled open the door to the tool shed.

"Howdy boys, come on in here!" someone shouted. Lon rubbed the sand from his eyes as best he could and looked up into the smiling face of Charlie Brady. Behind him were the others, Rowdy, Moses and Sherman.

"Look here what I found in Butler," Sully announced.

"Well if it ain't a lost boll weevil," Rowdy shouted

"Howdy, you boys been missing me?"

Yeah," Sherman said. "They been making me do all the dirty work around here. I'm glad your back."

"How do you like the high plains so far?" Charlie gestured toward the door.

Lon laughed. "So far I'm not too impressed. Does it do this often?"

"Only about once a day," Moses put in.

"Man, I've never seen sand like this."

"There's nothing between us and North Dakota except a barbed wire fence," Rowdy said. "We can sit out here and watch five states fly by."

"By the looks of it, I'd say there can't be much dirt or sand left north of here," Sully commented. "Those folks up there have got to be down to bedrock."

Rowdy offered coffee and Lon and Sully took a cup. Charlie sat his cup down and tied his hat on with a strip of cloth. "I hate to leave good company, but we better go check on the rig. Sherman?"

"See," Sherman complained. "Since you've been gone, Prather, I get all the bad jobs around here."

The two men pulled on their coats and tied a strip of cloth across their faces like a mask.

"If we blow away out there, some of you boys come after us," Charlie called over his shoulder as he pushed out into the storm.

Outside, Lon could see it was almost black. More like night than middle of the morning. Sand drifts slithered across the derrick floor in ribbons.

"You can start out this morning helping Rowdy with the boiler," Sully directed Lon. "We won't be stringing any pipe until this lets up a little. I'll just sit this out in here. I can't get back to town anyway. I'd lose the road and wind up buried in somebody's field."

The others prepared to go outside. Rowdy took his handkerchief and wet it a little from a water jug, then tied it over his mouth and nose. Lon watched him and then followed suit. They looked like a gang of bank robbers, as they left the tool shed and scattered over the rig.

The storm continued with very little change in force for the rest of the day. Lon was exhausted from fighting the wind to stand and move, much less work. The handkerchief on his face made very little difference he found. His mouth soon filled with sand and his eyes watered and smarted. Gradually the wind gusts lessened and then suddenly they were gone. The sandy air seemed to stand still and Lon got the sensation someone suddenly turned the sun back on, it grew light so quickly. To the south he could see the storm rumbling on, but all around him the land was quiet. Sand covered everything. In some places it had drifted and stacked up like snow drifts. It was an eerie sight as he looked across the barren landscape.

"Lord a mercy, how does anybody make a living up here trying to farm," he muttered to himself.

"Mostly they don't," Sherman answered as he walked up. "These people are really hurting. Fellow told me it's even worse than this up in Oklahoma and Kansas." He kicked at a dead bird lying in a drift of sand on the derrick floor. "Look at that. Choked on sand." He pushed the lifeless body over the edge and they watched it fall without a sound into a sand drift below.

Lon thought about Kraly Creek. "If this keeps up, all Texas will be a waste land, too."

"Yeah, but according to Washington, this ain't so bad, you know," Sherman sneered.

Lon shook his head in dismay.

"My folks over in Arkansas. They haven't made a decent crop in three years

The anger in Sherman's voice cut his words. "My old man is almost dead from worry, and the goddamn government just says he's fine!" He spat off the side of the derrick floor.

Neither man spoke for a few minutes. "How's your folks doing?" Sherman asked.

"Same as yours, getting by."

"Well," Sherman slapped Lon on the shoulder, "at least we're still working, my friend. I wouldn't go back to farming for nobody."

Lon nodded his head and thought of Mae. "No, we're lucky to be here, I guess."

Sherman suddenly laughed and spread his arms out toward the land. "Here in this garden spot. Come on, the night crew is here. I want to get some of this sand out of my ears '

Chapter 23

Mae cried herself to sleep the night Lon left and many nights after that. He was wrong about things working out, she knew. He didn't understand. She could never leave. Not until Cassie was grown. Sometimes she would lie awake trying not to move and disturb her two sisters sleeping by her. The old mattress rustled and swayed with the slightest motion and the iron bedstead groaned and creaked even more. She imagined that she would just leave. Just get up one day and dress like nothing was different. Catch a ride with someone to Durham and disappear. Except, since Lon, she wouldn't disappear. She would go to him. Then one of her sisters would move, or Cassie would stir on her cot near by, and she would remember that she could never run away. In the still darkness Mae could hear her mother coughing and turning in her sleep. She was trapped. Dr. Reese had sealed her fate when her mother suffered her last bad spell.

"It's consumption, Mae. Your mother's dying." The doctor had told her when she followed him out to the car.

"There isn't much I can do. Only try to make her comfortable."

"But she seemed better last month," Mae argued.

"It's wearing her down, Mae. She's tired." The old doctor placed his hand on her shoulder. "Too many babies, too much hard work. I'm sorry, child. I'm sorry." The old man looked tired and helpless himself.

"How long does she have?" Mae choked out the words.

"Hard to say." The doctor shook his head. "If she can rest more, leave the heavy work to you and the others...," "His voice trailed off and they stood in silence for a moment. "Tell Ratch I want to talk to him." His voice was stern.

"Yes, sir, I will, he's..."

"I know where he is," the doctor cut her off. "You tell him I want to see him within the week!" Then in a hushed tone he added, "Is he leaving you all alone. No trouble?"

Mae nodded her head quickly and looked away. The doctor's strength had always maintained her through the darkest times, but she still could not easily talk about her father.

The doctor indicated he understood with a nod. "I'll be back in a few days," he announced in full voice again. He gave the starter crank a violent jerk bringing his car to life and scurried around to climb in.

That had been a month ago, and Mama was worse, weaker every day. Her racking coughs filled the house constantly while she struggled to care for her family. Mae had convinced her mother to leave the washing to her and her sisters. The iron wash pot was too heavy for her to handle anymore.

The first light of dawn slipped into the room, and Mae crawled out of bed quietly. She pulled her work dress from its nail along the wall and headed for the kitchen. Let the others sleep a while longer, she thought. She'd get breakfast before waking them. Saturday was the only time she had to get the laundry done, and it would be a day long job. Her younger brothers and sisters would help, but they would be exhausted by nightfall. She slipped out into the backyard to start the wash fire and fill the kettle from the well. That way they could get the white things boiled and hung up early. If she could finish early enough she planned to make soap. Their supply was getting low.

Chapter 24

It was the first fully clear morning Lon had seen since he had been in Butler. Charlie was taking advantage of the lull to clean and oil the machinery. He and Rowdy and Moses had the whole setup broken down and were busy dipping the parts in oil to cut the rust. Lon and Sherman stole the chance to have a smoke out past the pipe rack.

"You okay?" Sherman asked.

Lon glanced up and nodded. He was tired this morning, and he guessed it showed.

"I've been worried about you. What have you been up to at night?"

Lon's expression became guarded. "You keeping tabs on me now?

"No," Sherman said quickly, "No, it's just not like you. That's all. Out all night. Sully and Charlie are going to start noticing if you don't get some rest."

"I can handle it."

Sherman hesitated at the edge in Lon's voice. "Where you been these last few weeks, Lon. You can tell me." He paused, but Lon didn't respond. "You know, if you've got a problem, I'll help you out. You know that, don't you."

"Yeah, I know it. But this is something I have to do myself."

They sat smoking, surrounded by the throb of the rig for a bit.

"You know if your searching for Mason..."

"That's none of your affair, Sherman. Drop it!"

Sherman put his hands up and nodded. He lit another smoke and stared out across the flat landscape toward the horizon. Lon took his time rolling another smoke.

After a bit he changed the subject. "Have you seen Cabel lately? The edge was gone from his voice.

"Not since we moved up here." Sherman seemed relieved the tension was passed. "He's still convinced the next boom will be down there north of Wink on the New Mexico line. He told me to tell you he bought us some good leases. I understand he sold his mules. He's prospecting full time."

"Well, time will tell, I guess," Lon said.

"Yep, he either suckered us out of our money, or he just might make us rich, I reckon. Who can say?"

"I could sure use a little rich, all right. It wouldn't make me mad if we hit something." Lon laughed.

"Aw, we'd probably get reckless and blow it all." Sherman ground out his smoke. "Shoot if we'd had any sense we would have never given him our money in the first place." He laughed and slapped Lon on the shoulder. "Come on let's go help put this thing back together before the sand hits again."

Lon stayed seated. Sherman was right. Back there in Wink the idea of gambling with Cabel had been an adventure. But that was before Emory's death, and before

Mason's escape. Now he wished he had held on to his money tighter. He could just quit and hunt Mason full time. But he couldn't now. He had to be careful. Keep his own council. Keep his eyes open. Mason would turn up again. He was sure of that, and he'd be ready. Then he could go home. Mae's smile flashed before him. But there would be no going home any time soon. Not in any couple of months like he had said. He had to stay and finish this no matter how long it took.

"Hey, you coming or what?" Sherman said.

Lon followed him back to the rig.

***

Within the month, Lon was ready to visit Morris' safe again. Morris was glad to see him.

"You're saving for something special now, I think," the little man ventured after he saw the amount Lon had to deposit.

"Yeah, maybe," Lon answered. "So," Lon gestured toward the store around him as Morris walked him to the door. "You moved it all up here, bag and baggage."

Morris shrugged his shoulders and smiled. "You've got to go where your customers are." He opened the door to the noisy street.

"We may not be here long the way things are leaning right now," Lon said. The boom may not last long."

Morris pulled at his beard and sighed. "The wife doesn't like it here much, anyway. We may go down to Dallas. She has a brother there."

"Maybe the sand isn't so bad down there," Lon agreed

Morris shook his head and motioned toward the street. "It's not the sand. It's the times and this place she doesn't like."

A loud drum beat rumbled in the street. Lon looked down the block trying to locate the noise and then glanced back at his friend. There was a look of great sadness and worry in the little man's eyes.

"This. This is what my wife doesn't like," he almost whispered.

As the drum cadence grew louder and closer people along the street stopped to listen out of curiosity. Lon could see the procession now, a group of twenty or so men in white robes marching up the street. They marched in total silence, not glancing to the right or left, and as they passed their presence brought the crowd to a total halt. People along the sidewalks watched in silence as the group filed by. The only sound was the boom of the drum and their feet shuffling in military unison.

"They're getting braver," Morris said. "They march without their hoods today." The procession passed and disappeared around the corner a block away.

"They blame their troubles on others, those men, but hating foreigners and negroes won't get them jobs." Morris shook his head sadly. "My brother in Germany writes that there is trouble there, too." Morris adjusted his spectacles. "These are dangerous times when men band together for hatred and call it brotherhood, my friend. Dangerous for an old Jew peddler like me." Morris patted Lon's shoulder as a farewell gesture and disappeared back into his shop.

Lon walked up the street as the noise and bustle returned. People were not commenting on what they had just witnessed, he noticed. It was seemingly forgotten, swallowed up in the business of the day, but Lon could not forget the faces of the marchers, or the reaction of his friend. He turned the corner and braced himself against the wind, one hand on his hat.

He passed a barber shop with a fancy striped pole revolving in an endless stream.

"Prather!" someone called.

Lon glanced around.

"Prather, is that you?" A young black boy stepped out of the barber shop door. Lon stopped and studied the smiling face.

"Penn?" he asked.

"That's right!" the boy's grin widened and Lon recognized his friend now grown almost to his own height.

"Mercy, boy, I wouldn't have known you." Lon exclaimed and shook his hand.

"What are you doing up here?"

The boy motioned over his shoulder toward the barber shop behind him. "I'm working, giving shoe shines. Got my own business in here."

"How bout that! How's your grandpa?" Lon asked and the boy's smile faded.

"He's gone. I buried him back in Wink not long after you left." The boy was silent for a moment. "I missed you. You left so sudden. I heard about your cousin."

Lon nodded and an awkward silence engulfed them.

"So, you're doing alright now, I guess?"

"Sure, I'm doing fine. This barber here, Mr. Gage, he let me set up in his place. I do pretty good, you know. More folks up here got shoes that need a shine." He laughed and then grew serious. "I can start paying you back, now, for all those times..."

Lon shook his head, "Naw, I won't have it. That was for you and your grandpa. I don't want it back. Besides, maybe you will be able to help me out one of these days."

Penn smiled again. "Well, anyway, I can sure shine

your shoes sometime, can't I?"

"Sounds fair, I'll be around real soon."

"You do that. I'll shine'em for free, any time."

They shook hands again and Penn started to speak, then hesitated. "They catch that fellow again?"

"No, not as far as I know."

"I seen him," Penn said.

"Seen him? Where?"

"Over across the tracks, there. Black headed fellow with a purple scar?"

"Yeah, that's him. When did you see him?"

"He was with a bunch of men around a camp fire over there. I'm pretty sure it was him. About a month ago."

"Have you seen him since?"

"No, but I'm looking all the time. I want to help you. I'm looking."

"You do that, Penn, but you be careful. Stay away from him. You just come find me."

As Lon walked away his heart was pounding in his ears. Mason! He could still be here. Close. He clinched his jaw and headed for the string of beer joints out along the road. He would just take another look. The day crews would be coming in from the field.

Chapter 25

When Cabel Norris finally showed up, Lon didn't know him. The crew was eating supper at Claude's when a disheveled looking fellow came in and made straight for their table. Sherman recognized him first and rose to shake his hand. "Jesus, man, you look terrible!"

The other men spoke, and Cabel shook hands all around. He was rumpled and dirty. By the smell of him, he needed a bath, and he was sporting a scruffy beard.

Cabel smiled and pushed his hat back. "Yeah, it don't pay to look too prosperous when you're hopping freights."

"Freights! That's a good way to get your head kicked in," Sully cautioned, but Cabel waved his comment aside.

"No problem, and it sure beats buying a ticket."

Sherman glanced at Lon with a look that said, 'now we know how our partner is doing.'

"Hungry?" Lon asked.

"You buying?"

"Yeah, I'll buy. What do you want?" Lon motioned for the waitress.

"Fried steak and gravy and anything that goes with it," Cabel told her, "and coffee, lots of coffee." He looked at Lon. "I've been too busy to eat. Haven't had nothing since day before yesterday. Those damn freights are slow!" The group laughed.

"What's happening down south?" Charlie asked.

"Not much on the surface," Cabel answered. His eyes were alert and excited. "Money's drying up everywhere. Nobody can invest."

Sully nodded, "Same thing here. This well we're on now is the last one, unless I can find some backing. All the money's disappeared since the market crash. This depression is sucking us all in."

Cabel fell to the food when the waitress brought it out. The others watched in silence as he polished off every morsel and used his bread to mop his plate. When he was finally finished Cabel raised his eyes to the group and smiled. He slapped his sides in a satisfied gesture and looked at Lon. "Much obliged. I'll pay you back some day, old buddy." He glanced at Sherman. "Could I see you two fellows outside a minute?"

Cabel led them outside and around the corner away from the door. "Now, this is how it is," he spoke quickly. "The big companies are frozen. Nobody has any money to invest. I'm grabbing up every acre I can get, and it isn't taking much. The big boys are working the western corner of Texas above Wink. That's where they think the next big strike will be. I've got us up along the New Mexico line running north. There's oil down there. I can smell it!" Cabel's eyes were fierce and excited but his voice was clipped and cold. "How much money you got?" Cabel asked. "Could you give me a couple hundred?"

Sherman looked at Lon. Knowing there might be no

more job soon had made him more cautious.

"I need it now, tonight," Cabel added. "There's another freight through here at 11:05, and I want to be on it." He paused, breathing hard and studied their faces.

"What's the rush?" Sherman questioned.

"I've got a chance at leasing up the rest of the area. There's nothing down there but a scattering of homesteaders trying to make a go of it in that sand. They're hurting bad for money. I can pick up the leases for ten cents on the dollar, but I've got to move fast before someone beats me to it. I'm short and I don't have anything else to sell."

Lon studied Cabel's face in the glow of the street light and then looked at Sherman. It was a chance maybe to get the money he needed, but it was a crazy gamble. There might be no more pay checks coming in. He took a deep breath. "I'm in. Let's go see Morris."

Sherman nodded. "If Lon stays, I stay." The men shook hands and Cabel smiled for the first time, Lon realized.

"Let's go, I don't have much time." Cabel said.

***

Morris was still up. There was a light at the back of the shop. Lon tapped on the glass and stood where the light over the shop door would reveal his identity. Morris cautiously came to the window and studied the three faces carefully before he unlocked the door. "What is it?" he asked.

"Howdy, Morris, remember me?" Cabel spoke.

The little man broke into a smile of recognition. "Not like this, I don't. What are you boys doing out tonight."

172

"We need to talk a little business."

Morris locked the door behind them and motioned for them to follow him back to the back.

"What happened, you fellows lose at poker or something?" he chuckled.

"No, I've got a deal cooking down south of here," Cabel explained. "These boys are my partners."

"What kind of deal?"

"Oil leases, prime stuff. I've put in every cent I've got and I'm needing more."

Morris opened the safe and pulled out Lon's and Sherman's packets.

"You got enough to go a couple hundred?" Lon asked.

"I guess so," Sherman agreed. "Hell, it's only money, right."

They all laughed nervously. Each one handed Cabel his money and in awkward silence watched Cabel open his shirt and pull out a money belt. He carefully stashed the money in one compartment and started to strap it on again.

"These leases," Morris spoke up. "They're good, you say?"

"The best!" Cabel's voice was strong. "Ripe for the taking while times are hard."

"How much you need?"

"If I had another five hundred, I could lock up the whole area for sure," Cabel responded.

They stood in silence and waited for Morris to reply.

The little man pulled off his spectacles and cleaned them carefully on his handkerchief then set them back on his nose.

"I've got five hundred," he said softly.

"Then you've got a partner," Cabel's voice was level and hard. "I'll invest it and bring you the papers to sign like I do Lon and Sherman, here."

"Deal!" Morris grinned broadly and the men shook hands. Morris produced his own packet from the safe and carefully counted off the bills into Cabel's hand.

"We're going to be rich one day," Cabel announced as he stashed Morris' money away with the rest, "beyond your wildest imagination!"

"Within my imagination will do me nicely," Sherman laughed. "I can imagine pretty good."

Morris smiled. "Just make me an honest profit, boy. That's all I want." He walked them to the door.

"How about you, Lon? What are you wanting?" Cabel asked with a smile.

"Just don't take too long," Lon laughed. "We may be needing that money for food."

"Well, I've got to get going. That freight will be through soon." Cabel patted his middle where the money belt rested under his shirt. "I'll see you in a couple of months probably." He disappeared into the darkness with a quick stride.

"That man is either a genius or a fool," Sherman said.

Lon laughed. "So what does that make us for listening to him?"

"Time will tell," Morris said, "time will tell. Good night."

He locked up the shop behind them and disappeared into the darkness of the store. As they walked back to the cafe along the darkened street, Lon made a mental count of the money he now had in Morris's safe. Such a small amount was left, and it had taken so long to save it. Without realizing it, he gave a deep sigh.

What's the problem, sport?" Sherman slapped him on the back. "Having second thoughts?"

Lon looked at his friend and shrugged his shoulders. "Easy come, easy go," he mumbled, but his stomach did a turn as he spoke.

"You about ready to call it a night?" Sherman asked.

"Naw," Lon looked around. "I think I'll walk around a little." He glanced down the street toward the distant lights of a string of beer joints. "Maybe get a beer."

"I'll keep you company," Sherman said.

"No," Lon said quickly. "It's okay. I'll be in before long. You go on back." He walked away. "See you in the morning."

Sherman watched Lon's form disappear into the shadows of the street. 'Get a beer,' he thought. 'Like hell you are.' He shook his head in frustration. Lon was hunting again. He was always hunting, and Sherman only hoped he didn't find the man he was seeking.

Chapter 26

Into July the sand storms continued almost on a daily basis. The winds were hot and dry and the sand almost blacked out the sun at midday. At night when the winds finally died, the air and every object around still smelled of dust. Machinery clogged and choked on the sand that crept into any crevice, and the drilling equipment coughed and sputtered and often stopped. The grit of sand was ever present. In the morning Lon would shake off the sand that had settled on him as he slept. Without thinking about it, he always knew to give his coffee cup a quick rinse to remove the night's collection of sand before he filled it.

He was going through this ritual in the darkness just before dawn one morning, more asleep than awake, when a car horn sounded in front of the house.

"Hey Prather!" someone yelled.

Lon got to the door just as a heavy fist started to bang on it. He jerked the door open and found Jeremy Randell, looking wild and disheveled and reeking of whiskey.

"Howdy, old buddy!" Jeremy bellowed.

"Jeremy, what the hell are you doing here?" Lon stepped out and closed the door behind him.

Jeremy straightened and blinked his bleary eyes in an effort to compose himself. "Lon, my friend, I was in the neighborhood an' thought I'd just drop by and see how you're doing." He swallowed hard and reached out a hand to steady himself.

"Fine, I'm fine." Lon ran a hand across his face in an effort to wake up. "You look like you're doing fine yourself," he said with a smile.

Jeremy threw back his head and laughed. "Fine? Man, you don't know how fine." He grabbed Lon's arm and pulled him toward the car. "Look at this!"

It was a brand new Buick, so clean it had to be straight from the dealer. Lon stared in sleepy confusion.

Jer pulled a cigar from his pocket and jabbed it into Lon's mouth. "Have a cigar, my friend. You're looking at a wealthy man!"

"How'd you get this?" Lon motioned toward the car.

"It's all mine!" Jeremy swayed forward and patted the hood gently. "Paid cash money for it. Come on, get in, old buddy. You can drive. I'm too damn drunk to drive anyway." He pulled Lon to the car and fumbled with the door.

"No, no, I've got to leave for work here in a minute." Lon pulled away, but his eyes were still fixed on the car. "Where'd you get the money for this?"

"My friend!" Jer straightened and slapped his chest. "You are looking at the luckiest son-of-a-bitch in the whole damn world! I won all this in a poker game!"

"This car. You won a brand new car?"

Jeremy grabbed Lon's shoulder and shook him as he

spoke. "No, no, no, my friend! An oil well, man. I won an oil well!"

"A producing well?" Lon laughed in disbelief.

"No, not producing when I won it. See, this fellow I was playing had this little two-bit poor-boy rig running out here west of town. He ran out of cash so he bet that damn well against my hand, and I was holding a flush. A goddamn flush." Jeremy staggered and caught himself against the car.

So," Lon waited.

"So ..... I wasn't working right then. So ..... me and the boys went out there and drilled that damn thing in less than a week. It's flowing eight thousand barrels a day, old buddy. Eight thousand barrels. Look at this." Jeremy produced a roll of bills from his pocket and flipped through it close to Lon's face.

Well, man, that is all right," Lon grinned. "You lucky son-of-a-gun."

"Yeah, yeah," Jeremy nodded.

"So, what are you going to do now?"

"Now?" Jeremy frowned, "Man, I'm doing it. I'm going to live a little. Come on." He threw his arm around Lon's shoulder. "You don't need to work, old buddy. I've got money for us both. "Let's go celebrate!"

Lon pulled away laughing. "Naw, I can't go, Jer. That's great, but I can't. I'm still a working man. I'll see you tonight, maybe."

"Man, I can't believe it." Jer shouted. "You're going to turn me down? Lon, old friend, you are crazy, but ..." he grinned and pointed a finger in Lon's face. "I like you anyway. Here." He ripped off a hand full of bills and stuffed them into Lon's shirt pocket.

Lon tried to give the money back, but Jer pushed it into

his pocket again.

"Naw, man, let me do this, now." He grew serious. "I feel bad. I mean about Emory and all, you know. Now you take that money and .....," his voice trailed off. "Just take it."

Lon studied Jer's face for a moment and then nodded.

Jer grinned and patted Lon's arm.

"Okay, Jer, thank you. You're a good man."

Jer shook his head in a drunken gesture that caused him to stagger backward. "Naw, I ain't a good man, Lon. I'm a son-of-a-bitch, but I don't mean no harm. I'll see you around." He jerked open the car door and almost fell into the driver's seat.....""Look at this thing, Lon. This damn' thing has a self starter on it." He pointed at the floorboard. "I may just fire this thing up and drive down and see my old daddy today. Show him he was wrong. He thinks I ain't worth two bits, the crusty old bastard!"

The engine roared to life. Jer grinned and swept his hand around in a motion intended to show off the car.

Lon laughed and shook his head. "Man this car is really something. You take care now. It'll still wreck, you know, no matter how much money you've got."

"Hell, if it does I'll just buy me another one!" Jer roared away, weaving and sliding in the sandy road.

Chapter 27

Saturday night was usually busy in the barbershop. Penn could count on making a good amount since many of the town folk would be sprucing up for Sunday meeting, and even the oil field workers might be dressing out for a Saturday night on the town. Either way they might be wearing their dress shoes, and that meant shines. Penn was head down over his shine box all afternoon.

The man first caught his attention because of his shoes. They were run over bad. Old brogans, stained and scuffed, too worn out to belong to a steady working man. But when Penn looked up, he caught his breath and swallowed hard to avoid making a sound. It was the killer from Wink, that fellow Prather was looking for. The waxy purple scar was clear in the flicker of a match as he cupped his hands around the flame to light his smoke. He had only stepped inside the shop to strike the match out of the wind.

"Yes sir, can I help you?" Mr. Gage called out.

The man jerked his head up quickly at the greeting. Then he was gone. Penn went to the door and watched him disappear down the street and around the corner.

"Here you go," the man in his chair stepped down and dropped the coins in Penn's hand. Penn hardly acknowledged the payment, he was so busy following Mason Poe's route. He had to get word to Prather. He had to find out where the man was going. He had to let Prather know. "I got to step out a minute, Mr. Gage." He called over his shoulder. "I'll be right back!"

"Hey! You got customers here!"

But Penn was already gone.

"Fellow must owe that boy some money." The men in the shop all laughed.

Penn hurried along the path he had seen Mason take. He had been headed for the train yard going by where he turned. Penn turned down the alley as a shortcut. He might be able to see him again down where the railroad tramps camped out.

As he made his way through the maze of packing crates and trash cans in his path, a box fell behind him. He glanced over his shoulder, but he didn't slow his pace. Suddenly a dark shape blocked his path. Penn stopped and a spike of fear shot up his spine.

"How you doing tonight, nigger boy?" The man before him sounded almost casual.

Penn froze in his tracks.

"What are you doing down here, boy? You following me?" The man stepped closer. The smell of rotgut whiskey was almost overwhelming. "Huh, is that what you're doing? Following me?

Penn glanced quickly side to side. Boxes and crates crowded in on him.

"Speak up, boy! "I mean if I'm going to take the time to talk to a nigger, then you ought to speak back. Ain't that right, Arlo?"

Penn stiffened as he realized there was another man behind him.

The other man chuckled in a high pitched whine. "I reckon so." The laugh sounded again and then dissolved into a fit of husky coughing.

The man before him struck a match across his trouser leg and lit a cigar stub clinched in his teeth. A jagged purple scar on his cheek glistened in the light. He sucked noisily on the cigar to light it, and then flicked the match into Penn's face. Penn flinched and batted it away and the man laughed deep in his throat.

"Where you going in such a hurry tonight, boy? You got something special waiting for you over cross the tracks there, or are you following me?"

An icy sheet of fear flooded Penn's senses.

"You figuring to go tell your friend Prather where to find me, boy? Is that it?"

The man at his back laughed once more. Penn turned sideways and backed toward the wall of the alley to put a little distance between himself and his attackers.

"I been watching you, boy. You hustling around that barber shop. You're a damn good worker for a lazy no count darkie." The man spit the words at him. "I guess a light stepping nigger boy like yourself can do pretty good in there slopping spittoons and shining shoes. Is that right? Do you do pretty good? Speak up boy! I'm talking to you!"

Penn swallowed and licked his lips. His mind was racing, trying to figure an escape, but no ideas came.

"Me and Arlo here, we're mighty thirsty. So we thought maybe you could just make us a little loan tonight. Right, Arlo? Maybe just dig down in your pocket there and share a little?"

"I've got nothing for you," Penn managed to say. His throat was so tight with fear, he almost choked on the words.

"What's that, nigger? Speak up. I can't hear you." The man raised his arm and the dim light of the alley way danced on the flash of metal in his hand.

In panic, Penn swung his leg sharply and landed his knee in the soft flesh of the man's groin. The man folded over with a grunt as Penn squeezed past and broke for the opening, but he was not quick enough. The second man tackled him at the knees, and they landed hard in the muddy alley.

Penn fought with all his strength, but he could not break the man's grip. He tried to scream out but no sound came. Only the grunts and gasps of the struggle broke the night's silence. The man pulled something from his belt. Penn saw the flash of metal and grabbed at the gun as the man landed on him full force. The gun was trapped between them and Penn struggled to turn the barrel away from his gut. Then the gun fired, and both bodies ceased their struggle. Penn held his breath as the man's eyes changed from wild anger to disbelief. Blood trickled from the corner of his mouth, and he fell limp.

The other attacker had recovered his feet. He let out a savage roar and lunged at Penn in the narrow alley as he fought to lift the dead man's body off him. Penn scrambled to his knees. Run! All he could think was run. Half crawling, half running he stumbled out of the alley and across the train tracks. He crouched by a freight car to catch his breath. His heart was pounding, and he was shaking all over. Dead! That man was dead!

"Help somebody, help!" The yell came from the alley.

"Arlo's been shot! Get help!"

There was the sound of running feet.   "What happened in there? Who is that?"

Never mind me. Get that nigger son-of-a-bitch what shot him."

"Nigger, what nigger?"

"That shine boy from Gage's shop. He killed Arlo. Pulled a gun on him. He ran off that way toward the tracks."

"I'll get the law."

"Law hell! You going to let him get away with shooting a white man?"

More footsteps sounded, and the alarm was spread.

"You cover the far side of the yard and I'll go this way! There's enough of us now. We can get him."

Penn jumped to his feet. His only chance was to reach the far side of the yard and hide out until a freight came through. He made for the shed by the station house. He could lay up under the porch for a while.

"There he is!" A shout rang out.

"Where?"

"Coming your way!"

Penn never heard the shot. It was point blank to his chest.

Mason shouldered his way to the front of the crowd around Penn's body. He reached down and rifled the boy's pockets and produced a good hand full of silver.

A shot split the night air "Hold where you are! This is the law!"

The ragged clump of men froze for a second and then scattered in all directions. When the Marshall reached the body there was no one left in sight.

Mason Poe held his hand tight over the change in his

pocket to stop the jingling as he ran. The first open box car he found, he hauled himself up and disappeared into its dark recess. He felt his boot, reassuring himself he had not lost his knife in the scramble and then settled down for the night. He would count the money in the morning.

***

The next Saturday he was in town, Lon stopped by Gage's Shop, but he did not see Penn. The owner noticed him at the shine stand and came over. "Sorry. No shines for awhile until I find a new boy."

"I was looking for Penn," Lon explained. "Doesn't he work here anymore?"

"Not hardly," the man shook his head. "He got in some kind of scrape last Saturday, and somebody killed him."

The words stopped Lon short. He stared in disbelief.

"I'm surprised you didn't hear about it. He shot a man down by the rail yard there, and then somebody else got him." The man motioned toward the railroad tracks

"I can't believe that," Lon managed to say. "He, he was just a kid."

"Yeah, It was too bad. You know he was a pretty good worker. Best shine boy I'd ever had in here. Then all of a sudden he ran out of here after somebody. Just dropped everything and took off. They say he robbed a man down the alley there, but ..." Gages' voice trailed off. "Shoot, I don't know, but he's gone. Did you know him personal?"

Yeah, yeah, we were friends." Lon managed to say.

Well, I declare." The man looked astonished. "I'm sorry," he added quickly. "But you know you can't never tell about those people. You just can't never tell."

"Did you see the fellow he was following?"

No, must have been someone he knew. One minute he

was working. Next thing I knew he just lit out of here. Left a couple of customers waiting." Gage shook his head. " I just don't know."

The words hit Lon like a hard blow to the gut. Could it have been Mason?

"What happened to him?" Lon could hardly get the words out.

The barber stopped talking and looked confused. "I don't know. The sheriff had the body, I guess."

"Where could I find the sheriff?"

"Down the street there." The man pointed the way. "They already buried him, I reckon."

Lon turned and almost ran out of the shop. He stopped on the street to get control of himself. His pulse was pounding in his head. Mason! Penn was trying to help him! He fought the bile that flooded his throat. Mason had killed that kid, and nobody gave a damn!

The sheriff eyed him suspiciously when he asked about Penn.

"You say you're a friend of his?" The man sounded slightly amused at the idea.

"I knew him back in Wink," Lon explained. "He wasn't the kind to look for trouble."

"Well, he found it just the same," the sheriff drawled. "We buried him out at the colored cemetery. I can take you out there if you want."

"I'd be obliged."

They drove out in the sheriff's car. Neither Lon or the sheriff spoke. It was a futile gesture, Lon knew, but he had to see the grave. The sheriff studied him out of the corner of his eye. Lon figured the man was sizing him up wondering if there would be trouble. They bumped along the rutted road to the tiny cluster of graves and stopped by a patch of freshly turned sand.

"There you are." The sheriff pointed at the grave.

Lon stepped out of the car and stared at the plot. It was a lonely place to end up, he thought. There was not even a marker.

"Some bums down in the rail yard found him," the sheriff said. He sounded almost sad for a moment standing here staring at the grave

"Did you catch the man who killed him?" Lon asked, but he knew the answer already.

"Naw," the sheriff answered quickly. "Never had the chance. The fellow he killed was all that was left. The others ran off." He paused considering how inept he sounded as a law man. "Happens ever once in a while, you know." He added as an excuse.

"Did he have any personal belongings?"

"Naw, not a thing," the sheriff answered. "Not a damn thing."

Lon took a deep breath and turned away from the grave. "Thank you for your time."

"Aw, no trouble at all," the sheriff mumbled. "I'm sure sorry," he added as an afterthought. They drove back to town in silence.

Chapter 28

They drilled two wells that summer and fall. Both good producers, but still Sully had trouble finding investors. Money was almost nonexistent as the market crash moved through the economy like a shock wave. Sully was fortunate to have money to pay the crew. When the third well came in, it was a strong producer promising 7000 barrels a day, but the crew couldn't feel as good as the owner did. Sully had already told them they would be on their own after this one.

"There's no money. No one wants to spend another dime. Everybody's scared," he told them. "Best thing I know to do is split up and look for work. If anybody finds anything hire on as many as you can and contact the rest."

The men stood silent while Sully talked. "You got any ideas where to look?" Rowdy finally asked.

"I hear they're doing some wildcatting down in Lea County, New Mexico. You might try there, and I understand a fellow named Joiner just struck pay over in East Texas. There should be some action starting up over there."

"Moses and me will take New Mexico," Rowdy volunteered. "It's too damn wet in East Texas for us." Moses nodded in agreement

"Charlie and me are going east," Sully said. "Sherman, you and Lon can come with us. There's bound to be work there."

Sounds fine to me," Sherman agreed. "I got no place else."

"Yeah, sounds good, but I'm going home first," Lon spoke up. "I'll see you there inside two weeks.

"We're going to be damn lucky to find work, and if we do, I can't hold you a job for long," Sully cautioned

"Yeah, I know. I'll hurry."

"We'll be in Kilgore," Sully instructed him. There ought to be some kind of hotel there."

Lon drew all his money out of Morris's safe once more. He had close to eight hundred dollars between what he had saved and what Jeremy had given him.

"Where you going, now?" he asked Morris.

"Dallas." Morris shrugged his shoulders. "My wife's brother. I'll go in with him. No more boom towns." He pulled at his beard. "What about you?"

"I'm going home first, but I guess I'll try East Texas."

"What are you going to do with all this money?"

"I'm not sure. Take it home I guess."

"Well, take care," Morris wagged his finger. "Spend it carefully and don't trust the banks. That's my advice."

Lon smiled. "You don't trust banks?"

"Why do you think I have my safe?" The little man peered over his spectacles. "Banks are failing all over the country. I never did trust them. Anyway," he laughed and shrugged his shoulders, "I follow my old papa's advice.

With a history like my people, I keep up with my own."

They walked to the front of the shop. Morris glanced out into the street before he opened the door as though he were wary of the world outside. Lon gave his old friend a questioning look.

"There's been more marches," Morris explained. "Last week they tacked a warning on my door that ordered all Jew foreigners to stop stealing from the people." He grunted in disgust. " I'm not sorry to be leaving. The Klan is getting stronger."

Lon did not know what to say. Somehow he wanted to apologize, but that made no sense. He wasn't to blame.

Morris smiled and extended his hand. "Take care now, my young friend. Maybe we'll meet again."

"Yeah, I'll look you up in Dallas sometime, maybe." They shook hands and parted.

Lon looked about at the people going passed him, shoulders hunched against the wind, as he headed for the bus station. They seemed cold and expressionless. The twirling barber pole caught his attention down the street and he thought of Penn. The world was a dark and lonely place this day, and he needed to be away from here as soon as possible. He thought of Mae and home and hastened his steps.

Chapter 29

The bus stopped at every town and crossroads as it rolled south. People shuffled off and on juggling their possessions. By nightfall they had dropped off the Cap Rock on to the Lower Plains, and the scrubby mesquite outside the bus window signaled to Lon that he was closer to home. The bus wheeled into Crowell and sputtered to a stop before the only hotel in town.

"We'll be stopping here for the night," the driver announced.

"I'm having a little engine trouble, so the bus company will pay for your stay, and we'll leave first thing in the morning."

A groan went up from the crowd, and there was much mumbling and shuffling as the passengers gathered their gear and filed off.

Lon carried his satchel off with him. The bus driver and a grimy man in overalls were arguing under the bus hood.

"What you mean you can't fix it. Man, I got a bus load of folks here. You've got to get it running tonight, or the bus company will be footing the bills for this crowd for a week before I can get another bus out here."

"Look, fellow, it's a bunch of junk under here. I don't have the parts, and its been patched back together so many times now, there's nothing to fix on to."

Lon took a deep breath. It looked like he was going to waste most of his two weeks if he waited on that bus. Across the street he noticed a row of brand new Fords parked side by side on a lot. The shop next door was an insurance agency and he could see a man bent over a desk in the back corner. Lon ambled across the street and studied the cars. The shiny black paint caught the glint of the street light. Mr. Ford's favorite color, he thought to himself. He walked over to the insurance office and tapped on the window. The man stopped writing and squinted into the dark street.

"What do you want?" he called through the glass.

"You know anything about these cars out here?" Lon shouted.

The man rose from his seat and came to the front. He opened the door slightly. "Say what?"

"You know anything about these cars here?" Lon repeated.

"A little; they're mine. Want to buy one?" the man smiled and removed his wire-rimmed glasses slowly and rubbed his eyes. He had one of those open, honest faces Lon had known back home all his life. He trusted him immediately.

"Well, that depends." Lon scratched his head. "How much does one of the new ones like this cost?"

The man laughed and stepped out on the front walk and looked at the cars. "Well, they're costing me plenty right now. I bought five of them back a year ago, and then the market went bust. Nobody's buying any more. That's the last three. I was asking $700 a piece last year."

Lon frowned. "Oh well, that's a little high and to the right for me."

"But like I said, now, that was last year," the man continued. "I've had time to cool down by now." He paused waiting for Lon to respond.

"Are they gassed up and ready to roll right now?" Lon questioned.

"Ready and willing, and there's a gas station down the street there that stays open till nine thirty."

"Would you take three hundred," Lon asking expecting to be turned down.

"Cash?"

Lon nodded.

The man laughed. "Son, you just bought a car. Come on in and we'll sign the papers." He motioned Lon in. "Lovin is my name, Haskel Lovin. Just have a seat over here Mr....?"

"Prather," Lon pulled off his hat and shook the man's extended hand. He sat down by the cluttered desk and glanced around the room. The man quickly produced a contract from a pile of haphazardly stacked papers and rustled up a pen.

"Well, Mr. Prather, this here is the title," the man explained. "If you've got the money, you can sign, and the car is yours."

Lon reached in his wallet and carefully pulled out the three hundred dollars. The man stared silently as Lon counted the bills into his palm. Lon looked up, but the man was still staring at his hand. There was an awkward silence, and Lon wandered what was expected of him next.

"Son," the man spoke slowly. "I don't know who you

are, or where you got this money, but you just saved my life."

"How's that?" Lon shifted uneasily in his chair. The man's voice had the quality of prayer meeting to it.

"I haven't seen this much money in six months. I've got a wife and four kids to feed, and nobody's buying insurance or cars these days. I'm about to lose my house over back payments, and this money will keep me afloat. Are you sure you're real? I mean, I'm not dreaming, am I?"

"No," Lon laughed, "I'm real enough. Now come show me how to work this thing so I can get going."

Lovin went over the instructions and drove down to the gas station with Lon to help fill the tank and let the mechanic check under the hood.

"It's ready to roll," the man announced.

Lon extended his hand. "Well, much obliged, Mr. Lovin."

Lovin shook his hand vigorously. "No, sir, thank you. Say, you had any supper? My wife's a pretty good cook, and she isn't going to believe any of this if I don't bring you home as proof."

Lon laughed. "No thanks. I'd better be going. Maybe another time."

Lovin and the mechanic stood by the street staring after him as Lon drove out of town. The lights of town fell away behind him, and he was engulfed by the country and the ribbon of road ahead. Later as he drove through the night smelling the new car around him and touching all the knobs and controls, he chuckled to himself and tried to imagine the story as Mr. Lovin would retell it to his family.

After an hour or so he pulled off the road and studied a road map by match light. At this rate he'd be home before sundown tomorrow. Job or no job, things were certainly looking up. He pulled back onto the hard packed dirt road and continued. He was far too excited to sleep.

Chapter 30

The wind had picked up again by mid-afternoon when Lon pulled up to the gas pump at Elmer's station in Krayly Creek. No one was on the front steps of the store. Lon worked the gas pump and turned his back to the swirls of dust. Across the road he saw a crowd of cars and a few wagons gathered at the church house. That means a funeral, he thought to himself.

Inside the store it was quiet and empty. Only Elmer was there.

"Howdy, Lon, you just get in?" Elmer questioned.

"Yeah, where is everybody?"

"Over at the church there," Elmer motioned with his head. "They're burying Louella Handley today."

Lon started at the sound of the name.

"She died yesterday morning, poor thing," Elmer continued. "Been ailing for years, I guess. If wasn't for that oldest girl of hers I don't think she'd have made it this long." Then realizing who he was talking to, Elmer added, "You and Mae are..... friends, aren't you?"

"Yes, yes we are," Lon recovered his voice. "Are they all over there at the church now?"

"Yep, it ought to be breaking up pretty soon. It's been going awhile now."

Lon moved his car over by the church, but he did not go in. While he waited, despair settled around him. He could forget Mae's ever leaving with him now for sure. She would stay for her family. Hell, it didn't matter, he was out of a job anyway. Nobody in her right mind would follow him off. And there was Mason.

The church doors opened, and the crowd began to file out. The gusts of wind outside the car blew away any sound. It was a silent procession as the simple pine casket was carried from the church. Lon watched Mae with her younger brothers and sisters huddled around her come down the steps. As the processional of vehicles inched away toward the cemetery, Lon followed.

The graveside service was short. The crowd huddled together against the raw winter wind. Lon hung back at the edge of the group. He couldn't take his eyes off Mae, who sat erect and solemn through the service. Ratch Handley cried uncontrollably,pitifully, the entire time. The crowd raised their heads from the closing prayer and started to disperse. Several men recognized Lon and spoke quietly as they passed him. Finally the crowd was gone, and only a few people were left. His Aunt Martha collected the smaller Handley children and guided them away to a car. Mae watched them go without a word. Lon saw his father and Uncle Willis come forward and talk to Ratch. They gently lifted him to his feet and led him away.

"Mae," Lon spoke almost in a whisper.

She turned toward him at the sound of her name, but she made no move.

Lon almost stumbled in his haste to reach her. He gathered her in his arms and hugged her head to his chest. He wanted so much to erase the pain he saw in her eyes.

"Oh, Lon," she spoke softly and her body began to shake with silent sobs.

"It's going to be okay now, Mae. I'm here, now," Lon said. "I'm here."

Chapter 31

In the days that followed the funeral, Lon realized more and more that Mae was the force that kept the Handleys moving. Ratch Handley was certainly no help to his family. The man was almost hysterical. Lon watched him and knew that it was more guilt than grief that was tormenting him. Lon spent every waking moment at the Handley house to be near Mae and help out when he could. It was hard to hold his tongue with Mae's father. The man made no protest to Lon's presence or even acknowledged that he was there. He rarely came into the house, preferring the barn, but he hovered close and did not return to the river. When he did come in he sat mumbling to himself and crying low under his breath. He was drinking. Lon could smell it from across the room. But at least Ratch had the decency not to bring it in the house.

The children ignored him. It was easy for them. They were not use to depending on their father for anything, not even discipline. It was Mae they clung to. Lon admired her calm manner and her patient responses to her brothers and sisters. As he watched, he loved her more than ever, but also he saw that she could not leave. Except for the youngest, Cassie, her brothers and sisters were close to Mae in years but not in authority. They listened to her and heeded her directions like she was much older. And Mae seemed to shoulder the responsibility easily.

Cassie, a busy two year old now, depended on Mae completely. The child seemed to feel if Lon was there for Mae, he was there for her too, and she came to him for everything. To show him a picture she had drawn. To get a splinter out of her finger. Or just to sit in his lap and listen as he read to her. Lon spent one whole afternoon crawling under the house to help her catch a gray kitten she had seen and wanted. He was filthy and scratched all over by the time he caught it, but the child's delight in the tiny creature made him forget his labor. He had never experienced this type of protective feeling for someone. It was as though the family belonged to Mae and him, and it wasn't a bad feeling, he thought.

Lon helped the boys with the chores and made repairs around the crumbling farm house. Repairs that Ratch had so long neglected, he thought with disgust. The boys seemed to enjoy Lon's company. One afternoon Ratch came out of the barn while Lon was helping with the milking. He was staggering, and he braced himself on the shed overhang to keep from falling. His eyes were red and puffy from the liquor and the tears.

"You boys, hurry up there!" he shouted in a slurred voice. "Don't be pushing your chores off on Lon there now."

Mae's brothers hardly glanced around.

"Hear me!" Ratch shouted again. "Damn younguns, show no respect!" He ran his fingers through his matted hair. "Come on with me," he directed Lon, motioning with his hand in a move that almost threw him down. Lon looked around at the boys and then followed Ratch into the corn crib. He had to stoop low to enter and what he saw in the darkened space was Ratch on his knees clawing at the dried corn husks. Suddenly the man pulled out a jug and turned it up with a frantic motion. After a long drink he wiped his mouth and, gasping for breath, he shoved the jug toward Lon.

Lon shook his head and made a move to go, but Ratch put out his hand to stop him. "No, sit with me, boy," he pleaded. "Just sit," and he pulled the jug to his lips again.

Lon followed his request by squatting in the opposite corner.

"It's hard," Ratch mumbled. "They don't know. Them kids out there. They don't understand. I've tried, Lord knows." Ratch raked his hand through his hair again. " Lord knows ... She was a good woman, Lon, a good woman and I wanted to take care of her, give her nice things." He started to cry again.

"Mrs. Handley was a fine person," Lon responded not knowing what else to say.

Ratch wiped his eyes with the back of his hand and caught his breath. "What you hanging around my Mae for?" The anger and control in his voice surprised Lon.

"I care for her, care about her," Lon answered. "We're going to get married just as soon as...."

"Marry!" Ratch yelled. "Marry hell! You keep away from Mae, you hear? Just cause you're the high and mighty land owner around here don't mean you own me or none of mine!"

Lon stared at the man in disgust. "I never said I did, Ratch."

"Roaming around all over God knows where," the pathetic man raved on. "And show up here in your fancy new car and think you can just have your way with my girl!"

Lon's anger boiled up in his throat. "Now just a minute. You watch how you speak!"

"Oh, I see the way you've been eyeing her these last few days," Ratch snarled. "Always a staring after her like she was a hound in heat. You get! You hear me. Get on back to your big high-toned job and leave us poor folks alone." Ratch stopped to catch his breath.

Lon studied his puffy twisted face. "I won't take Mae away now. She needs to stay for the kids." Lon's voice was hard and low. "But I'll be back as soon as I can, Ratch Handley, and you can't stop me." He paused to let the force of his words sink in.

Ratch wavered, slumped in the corner like a whipped animal.

"In the meantime," Lon continued. "You quit this laying around drunk and grieving. You pull yourself together and get back to your family. They need you."

Lon rose to leave, but turned and pointed a finger at Ratch with such emotion that his hand shook. "And if I ever hear of you mistreating Mae or any of these kids. If you don't straighten up and make an effort around here, you'll answer to me. Do you understand?"

Ratch Handley stared mouth agape at the young man before him. He'd never expected such force from a boy he'd known all his life. Ratch nodded dumbly as Lon turned to leave. Then he was alone in the dark crib and he slept.

***

"So," Mae spoke in a flat emotionless tone. "What it amounts to is, I can't go, and you can't stay." They sat on the edge of the front porch catching a moment of privacy after the others were in bed. Ratch had never reappeared from the corn crib, and Mae had asked no questions. Lon stared in silence at the ground. She was right. What else could he say?

"The children, they couldn't make it on their own. I couldn't leave. Daddy can't..."

"You mean your daddy won't!"

Tears welled up in Mae's eyes.

Lon pulled her close. "I'm sorry, I'm sorry." He made an attempt to brush away her tears and gave a heavy sigh "It doesn't matter much now anyway. I can't take you with me until I have some place to go."

"Do you think you can find work in East Texas?"

Lon shrugged his shoulders. "All I can do is look. One thing is for sure. I can't stay here. My daddy is barely making it by himself. He doesn't need another mouth to feed right now.

"Hold me, Lon," Mae snuggled closer. "Just hold me."

Desire burned in the pit of his stomach. Lon could hardly bear to touch her as she leaned against his chest. Mae felt his body go tense and turned her face up to him. Lon knew at that moment she could be his without protest. He longed to move, to take her and maybe ease his pain, but he could not. He would not add to her troubles.

"I'll be leaving tomorrow," he said. His voice was tight and abrupt.

Mae did not speak.

"I know things don't look so good right now, Mae, but it's going to work out. We'll do what we have to do, and things will get better. I'll find work, and your brothers and sisters are growing up. We've got plenty of time. We'll..."

"Hush," Mae whispered softly and placed a finger to his lips. She smiled and reached up to kiss him. "I understand."

Lon gathered her in his arms and answered her kiss with all he could not put into words. Then she pulled gently away.

"Good night," she whispered as they parted. "Take care."

***

Mae slipped inside the door and watched as Lon started the car and drove away. Tears blurred her vision, and she strangled on her sobs. The desire in her body was numb now with a dull ache that could not be soothed. She closed the door and felt her way across to her bed. Her sisters stirred slightly as she lay down.

Chapter 32

Lon woke the next day to a room filled with dull light and a chill that filled his senses. His head was heavy with sleep and he felt empty and sad. And for a moment he could not think why, but then he remembered Mae. A stab of loneliness shocked him awake, knowing she was not there. He listened for sounds from the kitchen but heard nothing. His father must already be up and out for the day. Lon sat up and scrambled into his pants embarrassed that he had slept so late again. He shook his head to clear the sleep and glanced out the window toward the barn. It was then he discovered the cause of the chill and silence. It was snowing. A gentle shower of the white stuff was floating down over the yard covering everything. Pa must be in the barn, he thought. In the kitchen the coffee was still warm enough to produce a cup. Lon downed it quickly, pulled on his coat, and headed out to help. But the barn was empty. The cow in the lot made the only noise as she pawed the turf and flicked her tail while she ate. Pa had already fed her, but he was gone.

Lon walked outside and surveyed the area. He listened for sounds that would disclose where his father might be, but he heard nothing. The cold nipped at his ears. It was no weather to be outside. He blew on his hands and started back toward the house. Crossing the yard, he made one last survey around and in the distant north field he saw movement. He altered his path and walked closer. It was Pa, alright. What was he doing in the field this morning? Henry's form was stooped, busy at something. Lon started toward the field, and as he drew closer he made out the cotton sack and realized his father was picking the remains of the cotton left from the meager crop. The sack he held left a drag track through the snow in the furrow.

Henry did not hear his son approach. He was concentrating on plucking out what usable cotton he could find. Lon was beside him before he looked up.

"Pa, what in the hell are you doing out here?" Lon asked in astonishment.

Henry straightened slowly and studied Lon's face. "I'm picking cotton, boy. You haven't forgotten all this, have you?"

"Pa, it must be twenty degrees out here. You'll freeze."

Henry went back to his picking without replying. Lon followed along beside him.

"Pa, there ain't enough cotton left in this whole field to fill that sack you've got. Why are you doing this?" "What's the matter, Pa? Talk to me. Do you need money this bad?"

Henry stopped pulling at the cotton and slowly straightened up. Lon studied his father's face and waited for an answer.

"It's the taxes, Lon. They got me on the taxes. They're due by the first of the year on this place and your mother's land, and I plain don't have it."

"How much is it?"

"Two hundred and forty-seven, all totaled." Henry spoke the figure like he was dropping stones in a pond one at a time. "I asked for an extension down at the court house, but they turned me down flat. Said they couldn't make no exceptions!"

"What about the money I left you in the bank? Have you had to use all of that?"

Henry shook his head. "That money ain't mine."

"Why not? It's mine, and I left it for you."

Henry's eyes shifted away to the horizon. Lon studied his father's proud stubborn face.

"Pa, what good is it to have each other if we can't help one another out?"

Henry started to speak, but no sound came. He swallowed and looked away."I never thought it could get this bad, Lon." Henry's voice cut through the chill. "In all these years of working and getting by, I never thought this could happen to me."

"It can't, Pa. We'll go get that money, and we'll pay up. That's all. We're a team. They can't beat us together."

Henry turned and looked his son. The child who had become a man.

"Pa, when I'm away from here I know that no matter how bad it gets, I can come home. I know you're here. You told me so yourself. Now if you're here for me, let me be here for you. Let me help."

A smile broke across Henry's lips and he shook his head in that familiar way Lon knew so well. "You're right. We're a team. I forget I've got a grown man for a son."

"Well, then!" Lon clapped his hands together. Get rid of that sack, and let's go. It's cold out here!"

Henry lifted the sack strap off his shoulders and dumped its meager contents back to the earth. Lon helped him turn and shake and fold the sack so that no mildew would rot the canvas. It was a process that implied hope that the bag would be needed again next year.

Lon motioned toward the house. "Come on. I need some breakfast. My blood wasn't ready for this snow."

Henry laughed and patted the sack under his arm," Neither was my cotton." They walked back up the row toward the house.

***

Lon left that afternoon after they had drawn out enough money to cover the taxes. Henry looked like a different man to his son with the burden of his debt off his conscience. He looked younger, Lon thought, standing there in front of the house as he pulled away. As he glanced back at his form growing smaller in the distance, Lon felt a deep satisfaction with what he had been able to do. It was some amount of justification for his leaving in the first place, he guessed. And now leaving again, he felt relieved. Free. Yes, that was the truth of it. He was going, and he was glad. Even the pain of not having Mae with him was not so great that he could not feel the excitement of going. He settled into the car seat and slid his hat back on his head. He slowed down as he passed the school, but he did not stop. Another good-bye would not make leaving her any easier. Lon made one more promise to himself that he would take Mae with him before long, and things would be complete. In the meantime there was work, and there was the search. No slips, no accomplices, just him and Mason. The thought of killing Mason had become a familiar vision, but no less important to him. He would find Mason one day, and he would kill him. And an East Texas boom town was a likely hiding place. He would find him. Then he could get on with his own life. Back to Mae. Lon concentrated on the ribbon of dusty road before him, and turned his thoughts to East Texas

Irene Sandell

Book III
JEREMY
1931

Chapter 33

Lon had been on the road for two days before the countryside began to change. Instead of open plains and scattered mesquite, rolling land thick with trees and underbrush crowded in on the ribbon of road that wound through them. This was a kind of Texas Lon had never seen before, and he stopped at a pullout once to take a closer look at the great pine trees and scoop up a handful of the dirt to test. The red loamy soil ran through his fingers, and Lon noted its richness with a farmer's eye.

On down the road he found a gas station and general store. He pulled in and rolled to a stop by the pump. A thin angular man in overalls got up from a rocker by the door.

"Howdy," the man stated in a flat, all-business tone.

"Howdy," Lon answered as he stepped out of his car and stretched his arms and back.

The man worked the gas pump and looked around at Lon. "Been on the road long?"

"Couple of days."

"You from out West?"

"West of Ft. Worth," Lon responded.

"Headed for Kilgore, I guess." The man spat a stream of tobacco juice across the dirt drive.

Lon nodded.

"Just about everybody is these days. We've had forty or so cars in here today alone, I guess. You a roughneck?"

"That's right."

"I guess that oil strike over there is pretty big."

"From what I hear it is. How much farther is it?"

"About twelve miles. Ain't far."

"Is there anything going on out here?" Lon surveyed the pine forest pressed in around them.

"Just talk." The man spat again. "Old Dad Joiner come down here about two years ago and got a lot of attention talking about his ocean of oil, but we never did hear no more."

"Well, you never know. It might just happen." Lon smiled.

"Well," the man laughed. "It don't hurt to dream a little, I guess. Lots of poor-boy farmers around here could sure use a little of Joiner's oil." He replaced the pump nozzle and pulled out his handkerchief to wipe his brow. "You hungry? The wife's got some good coffee and such inside there." He motioned toward the building.

"Thanks, I believe I'll see about that."

Lon opened the screen and stepped inside the small enclosure. A tiny woman with gentle eyes looked up from the corner where she sat sewing.

"Afternoon."

"Afternoon, Ma'am," Lon removed his hat. "Your husband said you had some food?"

The woman smiled and rose. "I've got coffee and some sandwich makins' over here." She dipped up a fat sausage from a crockery jug and wiped off the excess grease on a cloth. Lon folded the sausage in the slice of bread she offered and took a big bite. The lady watched him as though waiting for some reaction. Lon smiled and nodded his satisfaction, and the woman turned back to her sewing.

"There's more there if you want it. Just help yourself."

Lon washed the bread and sausage down with a swig of coffee. Movement at the doorway caught his eye. A small girl peered in through the screen. The child's face was streaked with dirt, and her eyes seemed too large for her face. She stared blankly in at him, and Lon could not look away.

The screen door opened a little, and a man pushed the child gently aside and stepped in. He, too, removed his hat when he located the woman.

"Afternoon, Ma'am," he spoke softly. "Your husband said we could get a drink of water in here?"

The lady rose again with a smile and motioned the man forward, but he did not move. Instead he turned back to the door and signaled outside with a quick motion. The screen groaned on its spring again as four small children filed in quietly. The little girl Lon had seen was the youngest, not more than four or five, he guessed, and the other three, two boys and a girl, didn't look to be much older. Each wore the same exhausted expression, but their eyes were alert, and each carried a small knapsack.

"The woman came forward with a pitcher of water and some tin cups. Each child took a cup and waited in silence as the cups were filled. The man drank last.

"Would you like a sandwich or something?" The woman asked.

"No," the man responded quickly. "Just water, thank you, Ma'am."

215

But Lon saw the four children's quick glance at their father when food was mentioned.   The woman turned to the smallest girl and met her solemn gaze with a smile.

"I used to have a little girl about like you."

The child did not respond. She just sipped the water and gazed across the rim of her cup.

"My name's Nell Lacy," the woman continued. "What's your name?"

The little girl lowered the cup and glanced at her father who nodded for her to answer. "Addy, Ma'am."

"Addy, that's a pretty name."   The woman straightened and looked back at the table.   "You're welcome to eat if you want. No charge. It's a service for our customers." She placed a sausage between two slices of bread and held it out to the smallest child.

The little girl fastened a sharp eye on the food, but hesitated to reach for it.

"I'd be pleased if you'd help me eat it up."   The woman continued in a light tone.   "We haven't had as many customers as I expected today, and it's just going to spoil."

The man stared at the food. Lon noticed the muscle in his jar ripple as he clenched his teeth.   "Thank you, Ma'am." His voice was almost a whisper. He nodded to the children, and they all stepped eagerly toward the food.

Mrs. Lacy chatted pleasantly while she put together more sandwiches and dipped up fresh milk from a crock. The man and children fell on the food like it was their first meal in days, which it probably was, Lon considered. After every morsel was down, and every drop of milk was swallowed, the children all chorused a thank you and turned to leave.

The man wiped his mouth. "Much obliged, ma'am."

Mrs. Lacy smiled. "My pleasure. You all come back

now."

"How far is it to Waco, ma'am?" the man asked.

"It's about one hundred fifty miles, I believe," Mrs. Lacy responded. "Is that where you're headed?"

"Yes,ma'am. We've got people there. Thank you again."

The man replaced his hat and led his brood out toward the highway.

Lon and Mrs. Lacy watched them disappear past the trees in a single file down the side of the road.

"People come through here everyday like that." Mrs. Lacy's voice was shaky and her eyes moist. "It could just break your heart."

"That's a nice thing you did," Lon said.

"Well," She shook her head in a manner that meant she discounted his praise. "Ned and me decided that as long as we had a little something to eat around here, we would share it."

Lon pulled a five dollar bill out of his pocket "How much do I owe you?

"No," Mrs. Lacy raised her hands in protest. "That's not necessary.'

"Consider it a donation, then."

The woman took the money and smiled. "Well, thank you…. "You looking for work in Kilgore?

"I hope to find it."

"Well, good luck Mr...."

"Prather, Lon Prather." Lon smiled. "Maybe I can come back out here and drill a well for you."

"Now that would be nice," the woman laughed.

Lon paid for his gas and thanked the Lacys again as he pulled away.

Chapter 34

Kilgore, Texas was a flashback of Wink only with more mud. A village of two hundred had suddenly exploded into a population of ten thousand, all hell-bent on cashing in on old Dad Joiner's oil. The streets were impassable quagmires of mud and several enterprising characters were making good money standing by with mule teams to pull vehicles out.

Lon maneuvered his car as far into town as he dared. He hailed one of the mule drivers who was catching a smoke while he awaited his next hapless customer.

"Say, is there a hotel around here? Lon shouted over the street noise.

"Next block," the man motioned. "The Texas Hotel; you can't miss it."

Lon ducked into the first parking space he found and jumped from the running board to the wooden walk way. The hotel was as he expected, packed to the walls with oil men and oil talk. He worked his way through the crowd to the desk passed clouds of tobacco smoke and a patchwork of conversation that told him everybody was buying and selling leases and talking in thousands of barrels. Mixed into the throng, every lobby chair and sofa contained a body, most sleeping, hats over their eyes. Rooms were obviously scarce.

The desk clerk recognized Sully's name, alright, but he had no message for Lon.

"They'll be around directly. They're in and out of here all the time."

Lon thanked him and left a message for the crew in case their paths did not cross right away. It didn't sound like Sully and Charlie had found any work if they were around the hotel that much. He wrestled his way back across the lobby to the front walk and surveyed the street. Everyone was in a hurry and all going in different directions.

A faded blue sign that read "Club Cafe" caught his eye. Claude had made the move too. Lon laughed out loud at the familiar sight and shouldered his way in.

Over coffee, his old friend filled him in. "It's rough. There're jobs all right, but there's too many people. Trains bring'em in by the boxcar load every day. Everybody's looking for work. You boys may get on, but it'll take time."

"How did you manage to get this place next to the hotel?"

"The old boy that owned it got oil fever. He quit slinging hash and went to selling leases. I was lucky enough to be here at the right time. This oil patch just keeps getting bigger. Every time they sink a well down about thirty-eight hundred feet or so they hit oil. It's crazy!"

"Who's got it all? Are the big companies running

things?"

"Hell, no! They didn't believe there was oil down there. They've got some leases, but mostly its independent speculators, no holds barred. It's a free for all! People are moving their houses and drilling. They even moved a church about a block down here and drilled there. There's rigs everywhere. We're probably sitting on oil right now, old buddy!"

"Do you own this place?"

Not hardly! The fellow I got this from wouldn't sell one inch. He's figuring the same thing. I've picked up a few leases though, a sixteenth here and there. Never hurts to get your hand in, you know."

Claude was still talking when Sully, Charlie and Sherman showed up. They seemed glad enough to see Lon, but their mood was somber.

"So, how does it look?" Lon asked.

"Not so good." Sully pushed his hat back and sat down heavily in the booth.

"There's plenty of action, but no organization," Charlie said.

"It'll take a little time before I can put together a deal." Sully explained. "It's hard to tell who's in charge. Some of these leases have sold three and four times already. Speculations crazy."

"We've been talking," Charlie added. "You and me and Sherman had better split up and find whatever we can."

"I'll get a deal together and call you fellows in when we're ready to go," Sully said. "But it may be weeks the way things look now."

"That is, if we can find something," Sherman emphasized.

"With all this action, surely there's some loose jobs out

there," Lon said.

"Problem is," Charlie said, "Town's full of men willing to take a job at any kind of pay. As bad as times are everywhere else, this is about the only place with jobs to offer."

"The going rate is down to two or three bucks a day when you can get paid at all," Sully explained.

"Well, I've got a car now, so we can split up and start beating the bushes, I guess," Lon agreed.

"Well all right," Sully smiled.

"A car, huh. My, ain't our boll weevil stepping up in the world." Sherman reached over and flipped Lon's hat over his eyes.

"Well, you know how it is with us oil tycoons," Lon shoved his hat back and laughed.

"Yeah, and speaking of tycoons, I haven't seen or heard from Cabel. Have you?"

Lon shook his head. "He's probably still out West. He's convinced that's where the next big field will be."

"He may be right, but for now the action is under our feet." Sully pointed down, "and I'm hungry for some of it."

"I'm just plain hungry," Charlie broke in. "Claude, can we get a little food around here?"

Claude grinned, "It's about time. I was about ready to start charging you boys table rent."

***

The next morning Lon and Sherman were on the road by daylight. The hotel room the four men shared had been cramped, but they were lucky to have a room at all, Lon knew. He had slept pretty sound considering his bed roll was thin and the floor was hard.

The pine forest and undergrowth were veiled in fog rising off the moist red soil, and there was a sharp chill in the air. They followed the crude roads across the county, often little more than two red scars cut through the grass and pine needles. Any road that looked traveled by trucks might lead to a well site carved into the forest, but at rig after rig the answer was the same. They weren't hiring, maybe down the road. By nightfall Lon and Sherman were back at Claude's. They ate supper in silence, tired and discouraged.

A week went by of days just like the first. They had covered the whole county and part of the next, but the story was the same. Lon was almost broke. He calculated that he would have to watch his coins to have gas money to get home. Home. And Mae. Maybe that was the best thing to do after all. He missed her smile and her laugh. He would work with his father again. Then the memory of the farm would flood in, and he would remember why he had wanted to leave. And there was Mason. Lon pictured his dark angry face in his mind. He was probably here; leastwise, somewhere in the oil fields.

"Well," Lon took a deep breath. "Let's go give it one more shot."

The street outside was as jammed as usual. They found a walkway of planks thrown down in the mud and crossed the street by jumping from board to board. As they reached the far side Lon looked up and found himself face to face with a burly man, head down and intent on crossing in the opposite direction. A glimmer of recollection crossed Lon's mind as the man looked up and smiled.

"Well, howdy!" He stuck out his hand. "Red McGuire, McGuire Drilling out in Wink."

Lon accepted the hand shake. It was the man Emory

had worked for.

"Let's see now. I believe I know you boys."

"Yes sir, you do." Lon smiled. "Prather, Lon Prather, and this here is Sherman Caldwell." They shook hands.

"Haven't seen you since Wink, I guess."

"No sir."

Red's expression darkened. "Sorry about your cousin, Prather. He was a good hand."

Lon nodded. There was an awkward silence.

"You boys working around here?"

"We're looking, but we're not finding much,"

"Well, this just might be your lucky day," Red grinned, "Cause I just got the go ahead to drill and I'm hiring. You got a crew with you?"

"We've got four," Lon said. "Sully's trying to work a deal but it may be months before we can start."

"That's great. My crew is tied up over in Van Zandt County and won't be able to move. Come on, let's get out of this street and talk business."

They went out on the job the next day and cleared a site. Lon got introduced to the business end of a cross-cut saw much to Sherman's delight. They had to listen to long-winded stories of how fast he could bring a tree down single-handed back in Arkansas. But by the end of the first day, Sherman was as tired as the rest of them, so the stories got shorter and less frequent. The whole crew learned about clearing brush in swampland, but the complaints were superficial. They were working.

They drilled three wells for Red that spring and summer, and with all the mud and mosquitos, Lon began to miss a West Texas sand storm. He sent Mae a picture postcard showing a stand of tall pines, but for him the novelty had worn off. In the months that followed the humidity made the cooler days of fall seem colder still, and he longed to take a deep breath of dry plains air.

Chapter 35

Mae pulled the kerosene lamp closer to her across the kitchen table so the light would fall across the shirt she was mending. Her body longed for sleep, but she knew it would be a while before she could turn in. There was still more to do. Little tears had a way of becoming big ones if she didn't catch them early, and their clothes had to last a long time. The younger girls were already in bed in the next room. The boys were out on the back screened-in porch waiting for their pa. On the new moon Ratch usually came for coffee and cornmeal. It was early, but Cal had become leery. He kept watch each night as the moon changed.

"Cal," Mae called softly through the window. "You better get your brothers in soon. It's late."

"In a minute, Mae," her brother responded. His voice sounded deep and serious. Poor Cal, she thought, he feels such a weight on his shoulders. Only fifteen and three years her junior, Cal had gradually taken on the concerns of running the place as he got older. If he had not picked up the task, the farm would not have been worked at all these last few years. In fact, Mae could not remember the last time she had seen her father sober, completely sober. But when he was drunk, he usually stayed away, down by the river, off with his hounds. That made it easier. No constant fear that he was close, and worry over what he might do next. She leaned closer to the lamp and stabbed the needle back and forth through the fabric.

Outside the window the boys talked in hushed voices. There was a rustle as they rose to come in.

"I'll just sit up a bit longer," she heard Cal say. "You fellows go on in without me."

"He ain't coming tonight, Cal," Erin, one of the twins argued. "The moon is still full. He's down at Butler's Cut with the hounds." The twins came in, and Erin paused to give Mae a pleading look to help him convince Cal to give it up, but he said nothing. Abel paused with his brother.

"You boys need to get to sleep," Mae said softly. "Cal will be okay."

Erin shrugged his shoulders in resignation and followed his brother to bed. Mae listened to the sounds of the old bedstead creaking as they settled in.

It had been almost a year since Lon left, but she thought of him constantly. His postcard was tacked to the wall by the kitchen sink, and she often studied the forest scene as she washed dishes and tried to picture where he was, but it was impossible. Even when Lon described the oil towns, she couldn't get a mental picture. That made it worse somehow. If she could picture the place, she thought, then he wouldn't seem so far away. As it was, time and space seemed just to have swallowed him up when he left.

A shuffling sound came from the back step. Mae heard Cal speak but his words were cut off by a loud angry groan, almost a growl. The door flew open, and Ratch Handley filled the doorway. He held onto the doorjamb for support and shielded his eyes from the lamplight. His foul stench covered the room.

"Get me something to eat!" His eyes were feverish and wild. "You hear me girl! Get some food on the table before I learn you a lesson you won't forget!"

Mae's heart was hammering in her chest as she moved to the stove and picked up a covered plate of leftovers. She returned it to the table and stepped back.

Ratch staggered to the table and fell into a chair. He began to scoop sausage and cold biscuits into his mouth. Mae sat a cup of black coffee on the table. Ratch stopped eating and turned an angry gaze on his daughter.

"Where you been?" he growled.

"Here, Pa."

"Speak up, girl!"

"Here, Pa. I've been right here."

"You been chasing around with the high and mighty Prather?"

"No, Pa, he's not here. He's been gone almost a year. You know that."

"I don't want him around here, you hear! That sorry son-of-a-bitch, sniffing around you like a ruttin' hound dog!"

Mae opened her mouth to protest

"Don't you sass me, girl!" Ratch jumped to his feet with a threatening motion as his chair crashed to the floor. Mae flinched, but she did not back away.

Ratch swayed drunkenly. "And you, miss fancy teacher!" He spit the words out. "Down there at that school house a puttin' on airs. Acting like you're better than your Pa!"

Cal moved toward his father. "There ain't no call to talk to Mae like that Pa. She..."

"You shut your yap, boy, or I'll hide you good!" Ratch swung at Cal and almost fell. "I'll show you how to treat your old man. Standing there staring at me like that. I ought to flail you both!" He stumbled toward Mae with a hand raised to strike her. Mae backed away out of reach, but she was almost paralyzed with fear.

Ratch reached for a dog chain hanging on a peg in the wall. "Running with that Prather trash," he mumbled. "Shaming your mama's name." He raised the chain to strike.

"Stop it, Pa!" Cal screamed as he grabbed for his father's arm.

With a roar, Ratch turned on his oldest son. Cal tried to push him away without striking him, but Ratch came at him like a madman.

Mae stood helpless. She felt a touch and realized the other children were up and huddled around her. They were stiff with fear.

"Stop it, Pa, Stop!" Cal screamed as he fended off the chain. He backed into the corner of the room and slid to the floor as Ratch towered over him, bringing the chain down again and again, cursing in unintelligible phrases. Ratch raised his arm to strike once more, but as he did, Mae jumped forward, grabbing his arm with a strength she did not know she had.

Ratch froze, shocked at the grasp that held him. He dropped the chain and swung around to face his daughter. Suddenly the horror of his actions seemed to sweep over him, and he went limp, almost falling. He stared wildly around the room at his children, their eyes wide with fear. Then he shoved Mae aside and bolted from the house. The screen door slapped shut with a hollow crack behind him.

Trembling, Mae stooped to help Cal up from the floor and wiped blood from the chain marks on his cheek. His shirt had bloody tears in several places where the blows had landed. The younger children huddled close to Mae and Cal.

"There now," Mae struggled to sound calm. "We're safe now."

Outside she could hear her father stumbling around the yard and cursing at the hounds who were howling and whining to be off on a chase. The noise moved away into the night, and the knot of fear in her stomach subsided.

It's all right now," she whispered. "He's gone, now. Let's get to bed, all of you."

The children moved away without protest. Mae got the salve from the cupboard and applied it carefully to Cal's wounds. Neither of them spoke. There were no words for their pain. Mae helped Cal up and out to his bed on the porch. Then returned to her own bed, but she was too exhausted to sleep. It was almost dawn before she closed her eyes, and the dogs had not returned.

***

The next day, Mae and the younger children went about their school day like zombies. As in the past, they shared a common shame at their father's conduct, and they kept their own council. All day Mae worried about Cal and Sarah left at home to tend the farm and care for Cassie and by the look in the other's eyes, she could see they also feared that their father would return. They walked home quickly at the end of the day, staying close together. The boys did not run ahead as usual.

As they neared the grey weathered house Mae strained to see Cal. He was there. She could see him at the windmill tank. Mae exhaled in relief not realizing she had been holding her breath. The children rushed ahead to their brother. He's not here, Mae thought, not sure whether she was relieved or worried by the fact. Then she sighted the dogs.

"The dogs came in about an hour ago," Cal said as she reached him. "Old Blue was first."

The statement struck hard. Old Blue was Ratch's lead hound. She never got lost like the others. She always found Ratch again after the chase. Something must be wrong if Old Blue came in without her master.

Mae looked out across the fields toward the river bottom.

"Maybe we better go look for him?" Erin suggested.

"I was just waiting for you all to get in," Cal replied. "Me and Erin will go find him. The rest of you stay here at the house."

Mae nodded.

"You all see to the chickens, and Abel you milk. We'll probably be back by supper time," Cal directed in a confident tone.

The two boys struck out across the field toward the line of cottonwoods and mesquites that marked the river.

Sarah met her at the back door holding Cassie in her arms. Mae sent the others about their chores and watched her brothers' forms grow smaller in the distance. She surveyed the tree line once more as though she expected to see Ratch coming , before she went in to get supper started.

Dark settled over the farm. One by one the Handley children finished their chores and came to the kitchen. Mae kept up a steady chatter about the school day and anything else that crossed her mind, but the children were quiet, waiting.

Suddenly running steps were heard and Erin, winded and sobbing, burst through the door. "Mae, we've got to get the doctor. We found Pa. He's...He fell off the bluff at the point.. Cal's with him but he's..." Erin's voice cracked between gasps for air.

Is he alive?" Mae asked in a trembling voice."

Erin shook his head. "I, I don't know. I couldn't tell. Cal just yelled for me to get the doctor. It's bad, Mae, it's bad."

"Sarah," Mae sprang into action. "Get Old Josey and ride over to Mr. Prather's. Tell him we need the doctor. He's got a car."

Sarah headed out the door to the barn. Mae whispered a silent prayer that the mule would go without protest.

"I've got to go back," Erin said. "Cal said bring a lantern and a wagon sheet. When the doc comes, send him out to the point. He'll know the way. Tell him to hail us, and we'll show him a way down."

Mae nodded that she understood. Erin took the supplies she offered and disappeared into the night. Cassie snuggled close and clutched at her knee. Mae smoothed the child's hair and stared out into the darkness.

Within the hour, a crowd was gathering. Word spread quickly through the community, and the men folk came to offer their help. Doc Reese and Henry Prather organized the group and struck off across the plowed field.

Willis and Mary Campbell came, and Mary immediately went to work getting the younger ones ready for bed. Her soft voice chatted on about little things to take their minds off the disaster around them, and in no time at all, they were asleep. Mary returned to the kitchen to find the two oldest girls standing at the window staring into the darkness. Mary placed her arms around each girl and pulled them to her. Mae turned toward the older woman and suddenly she was crying. Mary hugged them both without speaking.

Several hours passed before they heard the men returning. The door opened, and Doc Reese came in. "We brought him in, Mae, but there was nothing I could do. He must have stumbled and fallen over the bluff last night. I think he was probably dead instantly. He struck some rocks and his neck was broken."

Mae sat silent for a moment, absorbing the words.

"Are Cal and Erin alright?"

The doctor nodded. "They'll be in shortly. I don't think you should see him, Mae. There's no reason, and he had a bad fall. I'll take him on with me now, and we'll get him ready for burial."

"What does Cal say?" Mae asked.

"He agrees with me, I'm sure."

Mae nodded. She was tired, so tired of holding up and making decisions. It was good to have someone to take charge.

Dr. Reese reached in his bag and pulled out a bottle of medicine. "I'll leave this here for Cal, Mae. You can see to his cuts. He must have fallen himself trying to get down to your Pa. You don't want him to get blood poisoning."

Mae took the bottle and nodded her understanding. The old doctor paused as if he had more to say and then changed his mind. He reached out and touched her shoulder gently. "It's over, Mae. It's over."

And crying softly, Mae buried her face into his shoulder.

"I'll take Ratch on now," he said after a moment.

Mae straightened and brushed at her tears.

"I'll stay the night," Mary Campbell broke in. "I'll see the girls to bed."

"Try and sleep," the doctor said. He stepped out into the cool night and spoke to Henry Prather. "You and Willis follow me home. I'll lay him out in my office. There's nothing more to do here. Mary said she would stay the night."

Mae stared out into the blackness as the men's steps and the sounds of the cars died away into the night. Then she went back to the table to wait. Mary settled the others in bed. Cal and Erin came in within the hour. Mae heard them approach and met them at the door. She gathered them into her arms.

"We couldn't help him," Cal whispered. "I..."

"Shh," Mae said. "You did the best you could. None of us could help him. It's over." The boys nodded solemnly. "It's over," she repeated.

Chapter 36

Lon turned the collar up on his coat and checked the steam gauge before him. The mist from his breath fogged the glass. He rubbed it off and leaned close to check the numbers. They were steady. He turned and squinted his eyes against the glare of the rig lights out into the dusk that was settling over the town. Firing boilers wasn't a half-bad job on a cold night. The rest of the crew moved silently about their duties. The deal for Sullivan Drilling had never jelled, but Sully had found them all a job working night crew for this outfit. Sully seemed almost glad to be back on the drilling floor again. He and Charlie worked together like a pair of matched mules.

Sherman came back to the boiler shed rubbing his gloved hands together. "Man, it's cold tonight, old buddy." he shouted over the throb of the engine. "You wouldn't want to trade places for a while and go move that line while I watch these gauges for you?

Lon just grinned.

"Naw, didn't think so," Sherman held his hands up to the heat radiating off the boiler.

"I'm sorry, Sherman, It's a tough job back here in all this heat, but somebody's got to do it, you know." Lon shrugged his shoulders.

Sherman grinned and started back to his post.

Lon looked across to the neighboring rig. No more that a few feet separated the derrick floors, and the bases of the rig towers touched or overlapped. A man could get a running start and go a good city block length jumping from derrick to derrick without ever touching the ground. The glare of the rig lights blotted out the surroundings, but Lon knew that they were wedged in between houses and stores in the heart of Kilgore, every rig drilling as fast as possible to reach the pay below.

Just outside the ring of light at the platform edge, a movement caught his eye. It was about that time he guessed. A sweat-stained hat appeared and under it a man's pinched face drawn down into his shoulders, the collar of his flimsy jacket turned up to fend off the night chill. His hands, red and raw, clutched a rolled newspaper.

"Say, mister," he shouted over the engine. "Okay if I sleep by the boiler tonight?"

"Fine with me," Lon shouted, "but no smokes.

"No sir, sure thing." The man disappeared again. Lon walked to the edge of the platform and watched the man's progress as he selected a dry spot near the boiler tank, spread his newspaper over his shoulders and appeared to fall asleep instantly. Another man waved to catch Lon's attention from the ground below. He pointed toward the boiler and held up his newspaper. Lon waved back. He pointed to a No Smoking sign tacked to the rig and the man nodded. Then he moved to choose a place inside the ring of warm dry ground. It was the same every night. By morning Lon knew the ground would be covered with them, twenty or thirty men, maybe more, oil field tramps down on their luck.

Charlie walked up and looked over the scene beside Lon. "I tell you what, I don't care how many times I see it, it still gets to me."

Lon smiled slightly. "And the scary part is the only thing between them and us is this damn job."

"Yep, we sure as hell ain't getting paid, are we? How about a cup of coffee? You got any made back here?" They walked to the tool shed.

"You heard anything about our pay?"

Charlie smiled. "Nope, I doubt if I will very soon. We're drilling this thing on a promise. Our boss promises us, we promise Claude down at the cafe and the man at the hotel. They promise all their creditors and on like that."

Lon laughed. "Well, if they didn't take credit they wouldn't have any business."

"One of these days somebody's going to show up in this town with real money and blow the whole economy." Charlie filled his cup.

"Well, as long as everybody keeps on running on credit, we're okay, I guess."

"Yeah, we're up here, and they're down there." Charlie was suddenly serious again. "But I still can't get used to it." He drained his cup and headed back to the drilling floor.

Lon stepped back out into the cold with his cup still in his hand.

"Say mister, could you spare a little of that coffee?"

Lon looked up quickly at the unexpected voice. He could barely see another tramp huddled at the top of the stairs, his red hair bare to the cold. Lon looked closer.

"Jeremy? Jeremy is that you?"

The man squinted his eyes against the light and coughed. Lon moved closer. "Jeremy, it's me, Lon." He caught the man's arm and pulled him the rest of the way on to the derrick floor.

"Lon?" Jeremy muttered. Recognition spread across his face. "Well, I'll be damned! How you doing, boy?" He coughed again and wiped the back of his hand across his mouth. The smell of whiskey hung over him like a veil.

"How am I doing? Hell, man, what about you. Get in here." Lon pulled Jeremy into the tool shed and poured him a cup of coffee. Jer's hands were shaking so he could hardly hold the cup. The thin cotton jacket he wore gave no protection.

Lon watched his old friend gulp down the hot liquid. He refilled the cup and Jeremy's shivers began to subside. He sniffed, wiped his nose against the back of his sleeve and stared at Lon through red- rimmed eyes.

"So, how's it going?" Jer straightened a little and brushed his hand through his hair.

Lon smiled, "Well, better than a poke in the eye with a sharp stick, I guess. How bout you?"

"Well," Jer laughed and took a deep breath that brought on a fit of coughing. "I've damn sure seen better!" He said after he caught his breath.

"Man, the last time I saw you, you were..."

"I was on a roll, wasn't I?" Jer laughed and sounded like himself again. "Boy, Lon, you should have come with me that day. I did have me some fine times."

"Well, what in hell happened, man. You had an oil well in your pocket and a brand new Buick, I..."

"Fast women and slow horses, my friend. But I tell you, old buddy, what a way to go."

"You lost it all?"

"The whole damned shooting match." Jer turned his palms up. "The last clear day I remember I was in Tulsa,

Oklahoma in a high stakes crap game. Lost the well on a bad roll, and next thing I knew, I woke up in a whorehouse down by Oklahoma City without a dime to my name. Woman out there told me I sold my car to some old boy for five hundred dollars and then turned around and blew the whole roll. But I don't know. I don't remember a thing."

"How did you get here?"

"Hopped a freight. Man, those cars are cold! If it hadn't been so damn crowded I think I'd have froze." Jer stuck his empty cup out and Lon refilled it. "Have you seen Red? I hear he's down here somewhere?"

"Yeah, he's here. We worked for him back in the summer. Drilled a few wells just north of here toward Longview."

"I was hoping he was hiring. I need a job, I reckon."

"Yeah, well, first you need a meal and a bath. I've smelled better in a cow lot."

"I need a drink is what I need," Jer declared, "but I don't suppose you choir boys have anything around here, do you?"

"Sure do," Lon grinned. "I have a little more coffee."

Jer smiled and downed his cup.

"There's a cot back there," Lon pointed to the back of the shed. "Go on back there and lay down awhile." He took the empty cup and turned Jer around.

Jeremy made no protest to the idea. He fell face first on the cot and seemed to be out immediately. Lon pulled an old work jacket off a peg and spread it over Jer's shoulders. Hollow eyed and stubble-faced, Jer looked like every other panhandler Lon had seen in the oil fields begging for handouts. He shook his head and went back to check the boiler pressure. He would see about cleaning Jer up tomorrow. But when Lon checked back in on Jeremy just before sun-up the cot was empty. He noticed that the work jacket was gone, too. Lon gazed around out into the grey dawn and shook his head. No telling where he would go from here. Probably to locate a bootlegger first if he had any money left

He kept his eye out for Jeremy for several weeks after that but never saw him. Jeremy had disappeared into the mob. When Lon ran across Red McGuire, he learned that Red had seen Jer back in February right after he had shown up at the tool house.

"I hired him on for a while, but I had to let him go. He's drinking pretty bad," Red told him.

As the months went by Lon added Jeremy to his search.

Chapter 37

Red Bluff Gambling House was a busy place. The flimsy structure, half wood, half canvas was bulging with people crowded in shoulder to shoulder around the tables. Sweat and smoke hung heavy in the humid air, but the crowd didn't seem to notice. Their attention was drawn to the center table where some guy had a run going, and the bets were high on how long he could keep it up. Jeremy Randall blew on the dice and rattled them next to his ear. He hesitated a second and glanced around the crap table at the sweaty faces and intense expressions.

Come on , buddy! Throw the damn dice!" someone shouted and other voices mumbled in agreement.

Jeremy threw back his head and laughed in delight as the dice clattered down the table and struck the far bank. "Come on six," he shouted and like magic the dice followed his bidding. The close-packed crowd erupted in a burst of noise. The winners laughed and reached out to slap Jeremy on the back, and the losers grumbled at his luck.

Stand back, boys. I'm on a roll!" Jeremy shouted as he scooped up the dice the dealer passed back to him. "I'm going to break this damn outfit tonight! Come on baby, sing for me!" The dice rolled another six and the crowd roared again. Jeremy's pile of winnings grew once more. "Let it ride," he directed. The crowd buzzed as the word was passed. He's letting the whole bundle ride.

"Let me in on this, someone shouted. And a dozen hands moved to cover Jeremy's wager. A man on a roll like this came along only once in a great while. The dice rattled again, and Jeremy shouted in delight. Ten straight passes, and he was still alive. The last year was mainly a blur to him, just a series of gin mills and a job now and then. But he'd been sober for several days now, out of money and out of hooch. He had sold his last valuable possession, a gold pocket watch, to some guy on the street. How he had hung on to it all this time was a mystery. For that matter how he had gotten it in the first place was a mystery. But, however, he used the money to get into this game, and look at me now, he thought. Jeremy, old boy, your luck is back! He grabbed up a bottle next to his pile of winnings and downed a stiff shot of whiskey, wiped the back of his hand across his lips and scooped up the dice again.

A hand reached out and clutched his arm. Jeremy tried to jerk away and looked around at his intruder.

"You better lighten that pile of winnings a little, don't you think?" The man was a small wiry guy in a snow white suit and Panama hat. Jeremy stared down at the dandy who was restraining his arm. "You could lose, you know," the little man spoke in a whisper out of the corner of his mouth. "Why lose it all on one toss. Pull some of that out and stay ahead of the game."

"What the hell to you care what happens?" Jeremy sneered.

The man smiled exposing a gold front tooth and released Jeremy's arm. "Just thought you ought to think about it." He shrugged. "All these dumb bastards are waiting for you to crap out. They could care less if you blow it."

"And you do?" Jeremy laughed. "You care?"

"I just hate to see stupidity get lucky, that's all."

Jeremy studied the little man for a moment. "Okay, pretty boy, I'll do it your way," he said as he scrapped a pile of bills back from the board.

A groan went up from the crowd. They wanted blood, not caution. "Come on, hot-shot, throw the damn dice."

Jeremy let the dice fly, and again he watched his point settle to the table. "Well, at least you didn't break my luck, pretty boy," Jeremy shouted over the confusion.

"Ricco, the name's Ricco, and I saved your greasy neck!" The little man scrapped off more of the winnings. "Now roll'em again!"

The game continued, and Jeremy lost track of the passes. He drained one bottle of red-eye and was well into the next when the magic stopped.

Above the noise of the gamblers a deep voice boomed. "Texas Rangers! Stand where you are!"

The crowd went silent, and Jeremy struggled to focus his eyes toward the sound. A tall man in a wide brimmed Stetson filled the doorway. Behind him were several men with sawed-off shotguns.

"This won't take long, folks," the ranger drawled. "If you'll just line up and file past my deputies here so we can get a look at you." He motioned toward the men at the door.

The crowd erupted in confusion again. Jeremy scrambled to pick up his winnings, jamming handfuls of money in his pockets and down his shirt. He realized Ricco was grabbing too, but he did not have time to protest. The little man grinned up at him once more and then dove under the table and disappeared. Jeremy peered around confused until he saw a big deputy with a shotgun over his arm was pointing for him to get in line. He followed orders.

At the door, the people passed between two more deputies who studied them for a few moments and then let them pass.

"What's going on up there?" Jeremy whispered to the man in front of him.

"They're looking for outlaws," the man whispered back. "Just show'em your hands and you'll be fine."

"My hands?"

"They don't bother a working man. They're looking for folks that don't show no signs of an honest day's work." The man sized Jeremy up. "You'll pass, I think." Then after a pause. "Ain't you the guy...?"

"Yeah, yeah, now shut up and move on."

As they moved closer to the door, Jeremy mimicked the man in front of him and held out his hands. The oil stains in the creases of his knuckles and under his nails were faded some since he had not worked lately but they were enough. The deputy only studied him for a moment before waving him on without comment. Jeremy stepped out into the sultry night air and joined a small crowd of men who had passed through the door themselves and were now watching the others with relief and amusement. Jer watched the door for the white suit, but he did not appear. He squinted his eyes into the surrounding darkness and wondered if the little guy had some how escaped, then dismissed the idea and settled in to wait. That little shit had some of his money.

"Hey, what's going on here? What did I do?" a voice carried over the crowd.

Jer stood on his toes and strained to see. The wiry little man in the fancy suit was standing in the doorway.

"Caught this little fellow trying to squeeze under the tent canvas, boss," the deputy drawled.

"If you'll step over there, we'd like to ask you a few questions." the ranger ordered.

"Hell, no, I ain't going. Who do you cowboys think you are?" The man jerked away and adjusted his jacket.

"I'm the man who's telling you to step over there," the Ranger said in a hard, even voice.

Hey, you got nothing on me. I'm not sticking around for this bullshit," the little man tried to push past into the yard.

As Jer and the others watched a great hand reached though the doorway and grabbed the man by his collar. The ranger lifted the man off the ground. He dangled there momentarily with a puzzled look before he realized who had him. "Get in the truck!" the Ranger snapped and with a twist of the man's collar, spun him around and out of his jacket. Then with a shove of his boot he sent the man sailing into the open truck bed.

The crowd murmured, but the lawmen seemed unaware of their audience. All in all it was quite a sideshow, and Jeremy enjoyed it right along with the rest, but he kept one eye on the white jacket. The place emptied out, and the rangers prepared to leave with their collection of passengers. One deputy closed the back on the truck and hopped on the running board as the driver started up. Jeremy watched Ricco and his money disappear into the darkness. Most of the crowd started to drift away. Jer caught sight of the man he had talked to in line.

"Where they taking them, you reckon?"

"Church house in Kilgore most likely."

"The hell you say!"

The man laughed at Jer's reaction. "Yeah, that's what I heard. The building has been abandoned. Somebody broke in and stole everything. The rangers ran a log chain down the center, and they're chaining people on it while they check them out against wanted posters."

"Where you headed?" Jer asked.

The man looked back. "I'm going home to bed. I had enough excitement for one night." The men with him chuckled in agreement.

"Which way is that?" Jer asked.

"Kilgore. You need a lift?"

"Yeah."

The man nodded and walked toward a Model T truck. Jeremy climbed in the back with two other men.

"You the fellow that was having all that luck tonight?" one of the men asked.

I was till that little bastard on the truck there ran off with my money."

The men laughed. "Man, I never have seen anything like that run you made!"

Jeremy smiled. "Me neither."

The noise of the truck drowned out any opportunity for further conversation. Jer sat silent and enjoyed the breeze whipped up by their motion. As the night air began to sober him up, he started to wonder how much money he had stuffed in his shirt and then worry that the two men riding with him were wondering the same thing. They were in the edge of Kilgore by the time Jer decided he might be in danger if these guys were to get any more curious, so at the first stop sign he jumped off the truck and hurried away into the night.

Under a street light in the center of town, he pulled out a handful of crumpled bills and made a quick count. He came up with fifty dollars, and that was only a little dab of the stuff rustling around inside his shirt and pants pockets. He grinned broadly, realizing what he had done, and then crammed the money quickly back into his pocket. There was more to attend to. He had to find that church.

He picked his way along the roadside, trying to avoid the deep mud ruts. The town was fairly quiet for a Saturday night. The only real activity was down the street where a truck was backing up to the doorway of a small frame building. The place was crawling with armed deputies all sporting shotguns. Jer stood at the edge of the circle of light streaming from the church door and watched the truck from Red Bluff unload. Ricco came out quietly and filed into the building.

What's your business, mister?" a deep voice called from the shadows.

Jeremy jumped at the sound. He hadn't seen the man approach. "I, I need to talk to one of your prisoners in there."

"Not tonight," was the short reply.

"When will you be releasing those folks?"

The man chuckled softly. "That depends on who we're talking about. A fellow's got no warrants out on him, he'll be out pretty quick. On the other hand, if somebody's looking for him..."

Jeremy nodded his understanding.

"If I was you," the guard continued, "I believe I'd forget about visiting and get out of here. Understand?"

"Yes sir, I surely do." Jer backed away from the circle of light. "Much obliged," he added as he turned to walk away. Shit! That greasy looking little bastard is probably wanted in five states. He would never see his money again. He crammed his hands in to his pants pockets in disgust, but when he felt the wad of crumpled bills his mood changed. Hell, so what if that little guy got a hand-full of his winnings. He was still flush.

***

By the next day Jer was a new man. A hot bath, a little sleep in a real bed, and a new suit of clothes transformed him from an oil field bum who had hopped a freight into town to a fair copy of a prosperous man. Jer stood on the walk outside a café picking his teeth with a toothpick and savoring the steak dinner he had just consumed. And the best part was, he still had a roll of bills in his pocket. Not even counting the money that little low-life Ricco took, Jer figured he had a stake that just might set him on a winning hand again. He had won one oil well, Jer smiled to himself. He could do it again. All he had to do was find the right game.

The crowd on the sidewalk around him milled by in its usual stream. Jer started working his way along the walkway. Maybe he'd look old Lon up and let him know he was on top again. Maybe he'd find a bootlegger with some decent hooch. He was open to anything.

On the muddy street beside him the scream of grinding gears caught his attention. A truck loaded down with day laborers was struggling to push through a mud hole that had gotten almost big enough to swallow it up. Jer stopped to watch as the driver ranted and cursed as his tires spun, spitting up mud for ten feet behind. Some loud voice boomed out ordering the men standing in the truck bed to jump down and push. Jer laughed at their misfortune as the workmen landed in mire over their boot tops.

The men laid their shoulders to the truck and tried to shield their faces from the mud spitting from the spinning tires. Poor bastards, Jer laughed. Not today. It wouldn't be him today. The truck broke free, and the men scrambled back on as the driver pulled away. He watched the men spitting mud and wiping their faces in a hopeless effort. One face caught his attention and Jer looked closer. It was Mason Poe. He was trying to gouge mud from his eye with a muddy knuckle and the scar on his cheek showed up clear as could be. Mason Poe! The truck disappeared around a corner but Jer stared transfixed after it. He had figured Mason was dead by now; hoped he was. He never expected to see him again, and least ways anywhere near where Lon Prather was. Jer started walking with new purpose. He had to find Lon.

Chapter 38

Several days later the search paid off. Jer found the Club Cafe and recognized the sign. Claude told him Lon would probably be in that night.

"Looks like you been doing all right for yourself," Claude said.

"Off and on," Jeremy agreed. "You wouldn't know of a good game around here, would you?"

"Maybe," Claude surveyed the room. "But the stakes are pretty high.

"I can stand it. Set me up for tonight, would you."

"Will do."

Jer spotted Lon at the door. "And keep it to yourself, okay?"

Lon and Sherman took notice of Jeremy's new clothes first. Jer grinned and flashed his roll of bills.

Sherman gave a long, low whistle. "My friend, where did you get that?"

"You boys should have been with me. It was my

night!"

"I'd say so." Lon laughed. "The last time I saw you, you looked like a down heeled tramp and now..."

"Crap table, my friend."

"How about that, now." Sherman slapped Jer on the shoulder. "We were just about to eat. What say you buy us dinner and tell us all about it. Right, Lon?"

"Sounds good."

"You're on," Jer agreed.

Jer ordered steaks, and he produced a bottle from under his jacket that he had been saving. "Try a little of this in your water glass." He snapped the seal and unscrewed the cap.

"Where did you get that stuff?" Sherman exclaimed. "That's the first real whiskey I've seen in years."

"Oh, boys, you got to know where to go." Jer laughed. He handed the bottle around, and they filled their glass. "Now," Jer wiped the back of his hand across his lips. He was here to tell Lon about Mason. But now facing him, Jer was not so sure. He could still remember the anger in Lon's eyes when he talked about Mason. Jer searched for the right words, but nothing came to him. Looking at Lon's smiling face, he could not blurt out his news. Lon would go after Mason. He was sure of it. Maybe get himself killed this time. No, he couldn't tell him just like that.

"What's the matter?" Lon asked. "What are you staring at?"

"Hmm, oh, nothing." Jer took another drink. Hell, he reasoned, Mason will probably be gone in a day or two, and he sure as hell won't be looking for anyone who can recognize him. Better leave Lon out of it. "So, how's it going? You boys working?"

"Every damn day," Sherman laughed. "What about

you?"

Jer laughed. "Not any more, my friend." He patted his pocket. "I'm going to find me a high stakes game and turn this roll into a fortune."

Lon and Sherman laughed along with him.

"You don't believe me?"

Yeah, I believe you, Jer," Lon said. "If anyone can do it, you can."

Jer caught sight of Claude signaling from the counter. "I've got to go take care of business, but it's been nice talking to you boys. Enjoy you dinner."

"Much obliged. You come back and tell us how you make out."

Jer conferred with Claude at the counter and then waved once more to his friends and walked out. Lon watched Jer disappear out into the night.

"What you bet he'll be flat busted inside a week." Lon ventured.

Sherman laughed and shook his head. They concentrated on their steaks.

Chapter 39

The oil field workers ambling along the sidewalk in the early evening twilight did not take notice of the dark shape in the alley. Head down and hands jammed in his pockets, Mason Poe looked like a hundred other tramps along the street trying to hide away, blend into the surroundings. But Mason was different from the others who only thought about their next drink. He had a purpose in his vigil. He peered out from under the edge of his hat brim and studied the faces of the men passing. His eyes darted quickly to cover the crowd as it passed his field of vision. Prather would come along sooner or later Mason knew. He had stumbled on to the Club Cafe accidentally and recognized Hugh Sullivan talking to the owner. And if Sullivan was here, Mason reasoned, his crew had to be around, too. It had taken a week of watching, rushing over here after work on the road crew each day, but it had paid off. Prather and his running mate showed up just as he had figured, all bluster and smiles. He would have gotten him that first night if Prather had left the cafe alone, but he walked out with three other fellows. Bad odds. It didn't matter though. He could wait. Mason had been waiting this long. He smiled to himself as he lit a smoke. He would just bide his time, and Prather would never know what hit him.

The cafe door opened and closed signaling someone's approach. Mason heard a laugh he recognized, and a spike of hatred struck his spine. He stiffened and peered out toward the sound. Prather and his friends were stopped, talking to a newspaper boy.

"It's a fact," the boy said as he handed over the paper. "That new president, Roosevelt, has closed them all. See the head line there?

ALL BANKS CLOSED"

"Let me see that," Lon said as he handed the boy change.

"I don't know why you are worried, Prather, you've got to have money in a bank before you can lose it," one of the men with him said, and the group laughed.

The men gathered around Lon and read over his shoulder.

"That's sure what it says here," Lon said. "Closed for inspection and they will reopen if they are sound."

"Come on, "one of the men directed. "You can read that back at the room. Let's get out of the street."

Mason listened as the voices faded away into the night. The bastard had turned the other way! He was walking away from Mason's hiding place, disappearing into the dark again.

A near growl escaped Mason's lips, and he spat on the ground. Not tonight. He took a deep breath and glanced both directions before stepping back on to the sidewalk. Next time. Next time he would be ready, and Prather would go down. Next time Prather would pay for that beating back in Wink. Mason jammed his hands deep into his pockets and walked quickly away. He would get that son-of-a-bitch next time.

Chapter 40

By Spring Sully had his deal together. "It's about twelve miles west of here." He pointed in the general direction. "We'll have to cut a road and clear the site. It's in virgin timber but not far off the road." The men all groaned. "Well, look at it this way, boys. We're getting good at swamp work."

"Who does the land belong to?" Charlie asked.

"A fellow by the name of Lacy," Sully answered. He saw recognition flicker across Lon's face. "You know him?"

"Met him once," Lon responded. "Him and his wife."

"Course, they're not the only ones in it." Sully went on. "Claude, here, has a piece, and several other people here in town own some. Our big money is out of Dallas."

"Speaking of money," Sherman added, and all the men laughed.

"Well..." Sully pulled at his ear. "It's the same as before boys. They're talking regular pay, but we'll see. It may be like the last one, you know. We may not see a dime until we're done." The group was silent. "But," Sully shook his head, "All I can say is, we'll be working, and when I see any money, you'll all see it, too."

"One thing about this deal," Lon spoke. "We won't go hungry. Claude has to keep feeding us to protect his investment."

Claude laughed in reply. "That's a fact, boys. If I've got something to cook, you've got a meal, but," he winked. "I'm going to be keeping very close books on you all, so you can settle up later."

"Hell, man," Charlie put in. "By then you'll be rich, and you won't even need the aggravation."

***

The crew cut the large pines and snaked them out with log chains. Then they stacked the underbrush that the tractor pushed over and burned it. The thick smoke from the green brush fires hung close to the ground in the swampy humid air, filling their lungs and burning their eyes. The closeness of the forest around the cleared area kept out any chance of a breeze to relieve the heat and smoke. It would be the same with the drilling gases when they started the well. There would be no smoking on this job from start to finish. The danger of fire was too great with the gasses close to the ground and no cross wind to push them out.

They set the rig about four hundred yards off the highway almost directly behind the Lacy's station. Lon stopped in to visit several times. Mr. Lacy still ran the pumps, and Mrs. Lacy still dispensed her food and goodwill to the world that flowed by along the road. The neighboring farmers dropped by regularly to check on the well, and the crew came to be on first name basis with many of them. Just small farmers, lean and hungry looking, but decent folk, Lon thought.

"This well means a lot to these people," Nell Lacy explained one morning when Lon and Sherman stopped by the store. "If you find oil here, then they know they all have a chance, too. No wells have been drilled out our way before, you know. It's all been over East and south of here."

"Well, you've got a good chance here, I think. You need to be thinking about what you're going to do with the money," Sherman teased.

The Lacys both laughed. Ned scratched his head and took a deep breath. "Well, I tell you one thing for sure." He slapped his thigh. "I'm getting us clean out of debt to everybody! Everybody," he repeated. "Then..." his voice trail off.

"Now, Ned, don't go banking on this too much," Nell cautioned. "It isn't sure, you know, and it's not good to get your hopes up."

"Well," Lon sat his coffee cup down. "We better get on. It's time for our shift to start."

They left the store and followed the crude road to the rig.

"Truth is," Lon said after they were in the car. "None of these folks can even imagine the money they will be making if they do strike oil."

"Yeah," Sherman agreed. "I know how much money we're talking about, and I can't ever imagine it either. It can do some strange things to folks." He laughed. "You remember that old boy out at Wink who lived in that little tarpaper shack of a place with his wife and six kids, and all he bought with new money was a big old Buick automobile?"

"Yeah, that and plenty of rot-gut. Those poor little kids were barefoot in December, and he just bought that damn car."

"Well, maybe he's gotten smarter by now, "Sherman reasoned. "Or broke."

They rolled into the clearing.

"Looks like the Dallas boys are here today," Sherman announced.

"Good. Maybe we'll get paid," Lon answered in a dry tone and Sherman smiled and shrugged his shoulders.

The steamy air pressed in on them as they stepped from the car. The well was silent, and the forest sounds of birds and insects had returned. Sully and Charlie were in deep conversation with two men in business suits and clean grey Stetson hats. Sully motioned to Lon and Sherman to join the group. "These here are my other two boys," Sully introduced them. "These gentlemen are out of Dallas, boys. We've been talking a little business this morning."

Then to the two men Sully said. "If you'll excuse us here a minute, fellows, I need to talk to my crew." The two men nodded and walked back to their car. Sully motioned with his head toward the derrick floor and then lead the way up the ramp. He pointed toward a bucket of fresh cuttings on the drilling floor. Charlie reached down, broke off a piece and passed it around. The smell was unmistakable. "Charlie thinks we cut the Woodbine last night, and I agree." Sully explained. "I figure we're close to bringing this thing in, and it looks good."

The cutting felt grainy and oil saturated in Lon's fingers.

"The boys out there came down here with no money and more excuses this morning." Sully gestured toward the men waiting by their car, arms folded.

"Sully and me have been talking," Charlie said. "We could tell them we won't finish the well until we see our money."

The group was silent.

"We've got to understand, though," Sully cautioned. "They may just say "fine" and go get another crew to come out here. The question is, are we ready to back our words and hold our ground?"

The men all looked at one another.

"Hell, let's do it. I've never gone on strike before. This is as good a time as any," Sherman spoke. The others laughed nervously and nodded agreement.

"Fine," Sully nodded. "I'll go tell'em and see what they do."

He lumbered down the ramp to the ground below and confronted the men. The crew stood silent and watched from the derrick floor. Sully talked with his hands, Lon noted, as he explained their side of the deal. The two men listened in silence and then walked back toward their car to confer. Sully stood with his arms folded across his chest, and his legs slightly spread apart like he was ready for anything.

The men broke off their conference and made a move to leave. "We'll be back in about an hour," one of them called across the forest clearing. Then they were gone.

Sully turned back to the derrick. "Well, boys. we've done it now," he laughed. "We're either going to get paid or we're going to get to fight a new crew, one or the other."

The men all laughed uneasily. It was going to be a long hour.

"You ever done anything like this before, Charlie?" Lon asked. He squatted on his heels next to Charlie, who was sitting by the tool shed looking out across the forest that ringed the well site.

"Naw, but I've heard of it."

"How did it work out?"

"Well," Charlie took a deep breath. "Several ways. One time the boys got their money. Another time they got arrested, and then one I heard about, a new crew got brought in, and they had a hell of a fight."

Lon listened without comment.

"This old boy I knew got his head bashed in by a length of casing, and then they all got arrested."

Lon stood up and looked around the area. It would be easy to pick up a group of out-of-work well hands that would be glad to take over the job, fight and all. It might do to locate a weapon, he thought, just in case.

The time droned on with only the buzz of insects and the hum of cars on the road to break the silence. Finally, about noon a car turned off the highway and bumped its way to the rig. There was no second crew, only the two men from Dallas. Sully met the car as they stopped, and the crew watched from the rig as the man on the passenger side got out and produced a canvas pouch. He counted a fistful of bills into Sully's hand and then broke into a wide grin. Laughter floated up to break the silence. Sully shook hands and turned back to the crew.

"Fire her up, boys!" he shouted.

"Well, I'll be damned!" Charlie said with a laugh. "Okay, boys, let's go,"

The crew sprang to action. The boilers were fired, and the well came to life.

Within the hour word had spread through the neighboring farms, and a crowd began to gather. Solemn-faced farmers stood in small clumps at the edge of the clearing. Their wives came too and perched on the hoods of their cars holding babies and shouting warning and instructions to older children who played in the dirt close by or collected pine cones into small piles. Two enterprising young boys showed up with soft drinks from Lacy's store and made a good profit off the crowd, who needed something to do to justify the time.

The sun was hanging low over the trees as the crew made ready to test the well. Ned and Nell Lacy closed the station and walked down. As the drill stem carrying the test piece disappeared into the well a hush fell over the crowd. All sensed that something important was about to happen. Suddenly the derrick floor began to vibrate slightly. Lon felt it through the soles of his shoes. He glanced across the derrick floor to Charlie who was standing with his hand lightly on the drilling pipe. A thin smile spread across his lips. A gurgle rumbled up from below and gas belched up and filled the air. Then there was silence. For a few seconds everyone stood frozen in place. Charlie's smile faded and was replaced by a questioning frown. The crowd began to mumble and gaze around in confusion. Was it over? Was it dry?

Suddenly the rig groaned and began to rattle visibly. Charlie signaled for Sherman to reverse the engine and back the drill bit out of the well, but as he did the drill cable above their heads buckled in a strange 's' curve. The crew watched it curiously for a few seconds before it dawned on them what it meant. Then almost at the same instant they scrambled back away from the well-head just as the rig floor seemed to explode. Up out of the ground came mud and oil with a great belch of gas. Casing began to rise out of the hole and fall to the side of the tower like soda straws. The crowd screamed and drew back but they were too mesmerized to take their eyes off the sight before them. The oil sprayed down in a steady shower covering the people. Lon watched Sherman's face disappear under a thick black coating and began to laugh. He wiped the oil out of his own eyes and slapped Sherman on the back as Sherman let out a wild yell and tossed his hat in the air.

Shocked out their daze by the oil shower, the people began to scream or cry or laugh. The ground turned to an oily bog and farmers slipped and fell and rolled in delight. And still the well gushed.

The men from Dallas were shaking hands and slapping backs, their grey Stetsons now black with their new wealth. Lon caught sight of the Lacys through the crowd. Ned was going crazy, dancing a wild jig. Nell stood with her arms wrapped across her chest in an embrace of delight and smiled. He could see her clean white teeth against the oily film on her face and hands. Their neighbors rushed to congratulate them, and in their excitement was an unspoken message that they could be next. It was a gusher

***

"50,000 barrels a day!" Sully shouted across the crowd at Claude's. "50,000 barrels," he repeated. "Bringing in this well proves that the field runs west, as well as north and east. And there's plenty more where this came from!"

"Say, Claude," Charlie shouted, "What is one sixteenth of 50,000 barrels, I wonder?" The group laughed as Claude turned his palms up and grinned from ear to ear.

"Well, I tell you, folks," Claude surveyed the room. "I don't know exactly to the dollar, but whatever my share is it's enough for a celebration. As of now the cash register is closed for the night and food and drinks are on me!"

The crowd went crazy.

"Man, you're going to have the entire town of Kilgore in here inside of an hour!" Charlie warned.

"Hell, I don't care," Claude shouted. "Find me some whiskey, and I might even tear up my I.O.U. box tonight."

***

The Lacy #2 was as rich as the first well. By fall the acreage behind Lacy's store sported six iron derricks standing guard over six strong producing wells. Across the tree tops other derricks sprouted. Other companies had moved in to test the area, and the neighboring farmers were reaping the rewards.

Work was steady again for Lon and Sherman, although the pay was still low. Even the biggest oil strike in the United States could not absorb all the jobless in the country. But a little would buy a lot Lon found. His life was good. He was saving again, planning a future with Mae. He wrote her often. His letters were short, about the Lacy's or his work. But he wanted her to know he had not forgotten her, so he wrote something. Then Mae sent back word of her father's death, and Lon's hopes dwindled. She was the oldest. Would she ever leave Krayly Creek now?

Chapter 41

The population of Kilgore could only be guessed. There were the people on the streets, in the shops and houses, oil workers in the field, or those searching for work, who could be counted in the light. There were the night people who filled the gin joints, dance halls and gambling halls when the sun went down. But down away from the lights, hidden in ragged patches by the railroad tracks or makeshift shanties at the edge of town was another group, the bums scratching for space among their own kind, saturated with cheap gin when they could get it, sleeping off their last spree.

Jeremy Randall was no stranger to this underbelly of the oil field, so he was not surprised when he awoke there next to what had been a tiny fire, now only ashes. He lay still for a moment after he opened his eyes and surveyed the area before he realized the reason he had awakened. His arm was pinned back at an awkward angle and he could not move it. The feeling was gone from his hand, but a knife sharp pain was drilling into his shoulder, and his efforts to shift his position had brought him to consciousness. He struggled to turn his head toward his problem and found his face pressed into an oily, ragged jacket worn by some equally drunken fellow. Jer jerked away and sat up unsteadily. His arm flopped forward and the feeling began to rush painfully back. He rubbed his hand and arm, studying his situation.

Well, old buddy, you did it again," he muttered under his breath.

Shaggy lumps of ragged clothing were scattered here and there. One man stirred at Jer's activity, but the rest lay like death.

Jer's hand moved to his lips. They were cracked and dry between a stubble of beard. His hands, feeling restored, began to tremble. He patted his pockets but found no bottle, and he groaned involuntarily. All his energy became focused on the search of the ground around him. He stumbled to his knees and crawled forward. The glint of a glass bottle neck sticking out of the pocket of the man sprawled across from him caught his eye. Jer slipped the bottle out deftly, considering his trembling, and waited for a reaction from his victim, but the man never moved.

He doesn't need it, Jer reasoned as he unscrewed the cap and threw down a shot. The liquid had no effect. He tossed down a second, and it began to burn through the coating of his mouth and throat. Finally a third shot hit the mark. He gasped to get his breath and shook his head like a great dog shaking off water. Ahh, that was better. He staggered to his feet and stretched his back. Time to move on

It was twilight, he judged, but what day? How long had he been here, and where before that? He remembered... Jer took another drink from the bottle. He remembered a card game, high stakes. Hell, he must have lost. Jeremy patted his pockets again. Crumbled in his pants he found a dollar bill. "Shit," he whispered. That's it, he thought. I must have lost the rest. He took a deep breath and started making his way through the bodies.

He was behind some sort of warehouse, as best he could tell, in a ravine by the railroad tracks. He scrambled up the embankment and dusted off his hands as if that small act would wipe him clean and made for the road he judged to be ahead in front of the warehouse. The ground around him was strewn with metal pieces, some sort of earth moving equipment, he guessed. Bright headlights swung across him, and he flinched at the intrusion. Several large trucks turned into the yard by the warehouse and their brakes squealed to a stop.

"Okay, men," a man shouted. "Stand down and draw your pay."

It was a group of day laborers coming in. Probably a road crew, Jer thought. Been clearing pine and filling swamps all day for a lousy two dollars. Then he remember Mason and the truck he had seen. How long ago? He had lost track. Jeremy stood at the edge of the light from the trucks and watched the men unload and file past for their money. Sure enough, there he was. He was tired and ragged looking and had a hat pulled down low over his eyes, but the scar on his cheek still showed. It was Mason Poe alright. The little man took his money and walked away quickly without looking back.

"Be here at sun-up tomorrow if you want work," the boss shouted out over the group as the men dispersed.

Jeremy watched Mason leave the yard and then hurried to follow. He had no plan, just a thought that someone should do something. The murdering bastard was getting away again. No one noticed him as he followed. He had to run at times. Mason was making toward town at a good clip. He had purpose in his stride.

I'll see where he goes and then tell Lon, Jeremy thought. *No, I'll just see where he goes.* He hurried on, keeping a distance back, but it would not have mattered. Mason was not interested in who followed. He hurried toward the town lights, back to where businesses were still open, and turned down the main street by the Texas Hotel.

Jer rounded the corner and stopped short because his prey had halted. Mason was peering in the window of a cafe and then apparently finding what he sought, he stepped to the edge of the window and slumped his back against the wall.

Jer smiled to himself. Waiting for his bootlegger probably, he thought. He took a nip from his own bottle and checked its contents against the light. Almost empty. He had to conserve. He might be here awhile.

Mason lit a smoke. Jer could make out the flare of the cigarette when he took an occasional drag. Ever so often Mas quickly peered over his shoulder into the cafe, his profile silhouetted against the light from inside. Jer settled himself against the corner of the building across the street. This was good. Mason the watcher would not be expecting to be watched himself.

A hour passed. A few customers came to the front of the cafe and paid out. Jer could see them through the gold letters on the window that read Club Cafe. Mason would always glance around, but then he would turn away as the people came out the door. Jer studied the faces too, wondering who Mason was waiting on. Club Cafe. The words sank in. This was Claude's place, Lon's hangout, and a cold shiver went up Jer's spine. He jerked to attention, and all haziness of the liquor was gone. Mas was waiting for Lon! And as if on cue, he saw him. Sherman was with him as the walked to the register to pay. He paused to talk with the girl at the counter.

Mason saw them too, and Jer watched him straighten and step back around the corner into the dark alley. He disappeared into the shadow as Lon came out the door and stopped to light a smoke as he waited for Sherman.

Jeremy's eyes were riveted on his friend as he raced across the street. He saw Mason crouch and lunge at Lon's back, his face twisted in hatred, his eyes on his target. Jer hit him blind side, and sent Mason sprawling back into the dark alley.

Lon started at the flurry of activity behind him. He turned and stared into the darkness, trying to grasp what was happening. But in the dim light he could not identify the two men entangled on the ground before him.

Mason hit the dirt with a loud grunt as his attacker landed full weight in his midsection. He gasped for breath and struggled to push away. He had managed to hold on to his knife as he fell, but his arm was pinned by the man who had tackled him. He grunted and thrashed about with his free arm, but he could not break loose. The man coiled his arm and struck him hard with a tight fist, again and again. Mason gouged at his eyes with his free hand and tried to turn his knife into him, but instead his grasp on the knife slackened, and though he struggled to hold it, it slipped down his palm leaving a thin trickle of blood in its path. The hold on his arm was stronger, much stronger. Mason struggled and rolled to free himself but it was useless. He tore at the eyes and ears of his attacker, but the man could not be stopped. Then Mason felt the burn of the blade rip into his stomach. He screamed, and the man lifted his head. In the dim light Mason could see his face. "Jeremy!" Mason's breath came short and heavy and his hands closed around the knife in his gut. "Jer," he repeated in astonishment, "Son-of-a-bitch!" Blood trickled from the corner of his mouth and Mason's head fell back in the dirt.

"Jeremy?" Lon called out.

Sherman emerged from the cafe. "What the hell...?" He helped Lon pull the man to his feet. Jer was shaking uncontrollably, his body still rigid with the fury of the attack.

"Jer, what...?" But then Lon saw Mason, and his questions were answered.

"He was laying for you," Jer struggled to say between breaths. "He's.." but he could not finish. He stumbled against Lon and went limp.

"Let's get out of here!" Sherman urged. They were back in the alley at the edge of the light from the street. No one else seemed to have seen the struggle. Lon nodded, and the two of them took Jeremy by either arm and half dragged, half carried him down the alley and out the other side. They stopped under a light and considered their options. Jeremy was out cold. He was filthy, Lon noted, and smelled of rotgut. If Mason had not called out Jer's name, Lon would not have recognized him.

"Let's get him back to our room and clean him up a little." Lon whispered. Then we can tell how bad he is."

"Do you think he's cut?" Sherman asked.

Lon felt Jer's midsection but found no blood. He shook his head. "He's just passed out, I think."

"Was Mason dead? Could you tell for sure?"

Lon shook his head. It had happened too fast. He wasn't sure of anything, except that Jer had probably saved his life.

"Let's get out of here before someone finds the body!" he whispered. They hitched up their hold on Jer and made for their hotel.

The night clerk was asleep. They slipped Jer past and up the stairs with as little noise as possible.

"God, he stinks!" Sherman whispered when they had made the landing. "We got to clean him up or we won't be able to stand to be in the same room."

"In here," Lon directed toward the community bath. Sherman fumbled for the light chain while Lon held Jer up. Then working as quietly as possible, they stripped off Jer's clothes and checked for cuts, but they found none.

"Not a scratch," Lon whispered. "Here, let's get him in the tub." They stuffed him in and turned on the water. "Go get some black coffee while I keep his head up so he won't drown." He slapped Jeremy's face lightly, and Jer responded by fluttering his eyelids, but nothing more."

"Reminds me of scalding hogs," Lon whispered.

Sherman laughed softly and disappeared out the door. Lon looked at the pitiful man before him naked and shaggy. "What the hell did you do tonight, old buddy?" The vision of Mason lying in that alley with his own knife in his ribs was clear. Sweet justice, Lon thought, sweet justice at last. A feeling of relief from a burden long carried washed over him. Mason was dead. Emory's death was avenged, but better than that, a black rot had been stricken from the world. And who had accomplished it? Who could he thank for releasing him from his quest, as well as saving his life? Lon shook his head in wonder and dismay at the twists fate had dealt them and bent to his work of reviving Jeremy.

***

It was late the next day before Jer was fully conscious. Lon sat by the bed and waited for him to awaken.

"How long has it been since you ate?" he asked when Jeremy finally roused. Lon began spooning broth into Jeremy's mouth as Jer struggled to control his trembling. His skin was pale, and his eyes were deep set and red-rimmed.

"Where'd I get these clothes?" Jer asked.

"Sherman bought them this morning. We burned your others."

"Did they find the body yet?"

"Yeah, I understand the sheriff found him about sun-up."

Jer took in Lon's words without further comment, but Lon could read the question in his eyes.

"Just another dead body in an alley," Lon added. "They won't be looking for anyone." It was a common thing, Lon knew, to find a body on the street in any boom town, whether it was Kilgore or Butler or Wink. And Jer knew it, too. There would be no questions asked. The town was full of drifters. And even if there were, if the law could identify Mason, they would find he was an escaped prisoner. It was over.

"You saved my life," Lon said.

Jer blinked his eyes and smiled slightly. He was fighting hard to control his trembling.

"How did you find him?" Lon asked. "How did you know?"

Jer managed a grin. "I'm a lucky son-of-a-bitch. You know that. Just lucky."

"Lucky for me, this time." Lon said. He worked at getting the rest of the soup down Jeremy. The activity seemed to take all of Jer's strength. He sank back on the pillow.

"If you could get me a little something stronger, I'd be fine," Jeremy said. He clasped his hands together to stop the shaking.

"No, old buddy, I can't do that. Just get some sleep. We'll talk later. You've been mistreating yourself pretty bad lately. It's time to rest."

Jer fell back to the pillow and closed his eyes. He shivered under the thin sheet, and Lon pulled a blanket over him and stared down at his friend. Jeremy's eyelids were twitching and the trembling of his body didn't stop. Lon leaned back in his chair and tried to get comfortable. He had to go back to work tomorrow.

***

They worked steady for the next few months. Sully took Jeremy on as a roustabout against his better judgement after Lon's promise to watch over him. Jer made a good hand once he got his strength back. He was quiet and subdued for once. Kept his head down and stayed busy. Lon collected his pay for him and doled it out to him as he needed it, saving the rest. Jeremy didn't complain. He knew if he got loose with any cash at all he'd probably find a bootlegger, and he'd be gone again. The days went fairly well. He was eating healthy again, but only Sherman and Lon who shared their room with him knew about the nights. How he woke up in cold sweats yelling about the knife and vomiting up all that he had eaten that day.

"You're asking for trouble taking this guy on your conscience," Sherman counseled.

"So, what would you do?" Lon cut his eyes around at

his friend

Sherman laughed, "Well, I guess I'd do the same, but don't go getting any ideas about saving that bastard. He doesn't want to be saved."

"He's trying," Lon said defensively, but he knew that Sherman spoke the truth. Jer had to be watched like a child, but he could not just cut him loose. He had to try.

Chapter 42

The changes wrought by the Lacy oil strike did not stop at the field itself. Ned and Nell leased out the station and built a house closer into town in a new section populated with other newly oil rich families. They threw a big party as a house warming, and the crew from the first well was invited. The men splurged a little and bought some dress clothes. It was the first suits Sherman or Lon had ever owned.

"I tell you, boy. I was born to be rich," Sherman exclaimed standing in front of the mirror.

Lon pushed him playfully out of the way and adjusted his tie. "Pretty slick," he declared at his own image.

Jeremy slapped himself laughing. "You boys look like bankers on a holiday."

"You going to be alright without us tonight? Sure you don't want to come?" Lon asked.

Jer waved him off. "Lord, no! I'm not dressing up like that for nobody, not even a French whore! You boys go right on. I'll just hang around here."

The large colonial brick house was thrown open for the

evening. They could see people crowded in every room when they drove up out front.

Lon studied the house with a wary eye. "I haven't ever even seen a house this big, much less been invited in."

"Well, just try not to embarrass me," Sherman said with a grin as he pulled at his collar. Sully and Charlie looked equally uncomfortable and nervous in their new clothes.

"Come on, we don't want to miss anything," Sully said, making an attempt at humor.

Ned met them at the door. He was greeting everyone that came in with more vigor and style than Lon would have ever thought possible of the little man back at the service station.

"Come on in here, boys," Ned directed. "These here fellows are the ones that made this all possible," he announced in a loud voice to the people within ear shot. "Now I want you boys to have a good time tonight. Mama has just outdone herself on this party. Go on in there and let her know you're here."

Lon and Sherman found Nell in the living room in a circle of friends. Aside from the expensive clothes and surroundings, she had changed little, Lon thought. Her eyes were still as kind and her voice as soft.

"Lon, I'm so glad you boys could come. Have you found the food yet?"

"No, ma'am."

She led them out back where tables had been set up, and a crew of caterers were busily serving up barbecue turning on a spit. "This is called a patio," Nell Lacy waved her hand around at the area and her eyes twinkled in amusement. "Isn't this something? I spent more on these fancy little tables and chairs and plants than Ned and I spent on our whole place out at the station."

"Well, you can afford it now. Why not have it?" Lon responded.

"That's what Ned keeps saying," Nell sighed. "But it's just about too much for me. Not that I'm complaining, you understand," she laughed softly. "Now you boys eat up." She pushed them toward the crowd at the buffet table. "I've got to get back to my other guests."

A catering company out of Dallas was handling the dinner. As he went through the serving line, Lon recognized many of the faces in the crowd as the Lacy's neighbors. But they weren't lean and hungry farmers tonight. Proving out the Lacy lease had started a run on the surrounding farms. Now most of the people had their own wells, and more were being drilled.

They drifted back into the house as the evening wore on and found Ned Lacy and a group of men in deep conversation. Claude, Sully and Charlie were near the center of the circle.

"Proration, hell!" Ned growled. "That's just another way the big boys are trying to keep us from bringing up the oil."

"They're madder than hell that they didn't see this coming and lease everything up, so now they want to try and cut themselves in," Claude said. The cafe owner was another one who had fared well on this strike.

"Well, I don't want the government telling me what to do," another man said. "As far as I'm concerned 'rule of capture' is the law." The group mumbled in agreement.

"But what they're saying is that by pumping it out so fast, you're actually losing oil," Sully spoke up.

"That just don't make no sense to me," Ned said.

"I'm surprised at you, Sully," Claude said. "You've been around wells for a long time, and I figure you know your business. I never saw you stopping once you struck oil. You drilled'em and pumped'em as fast as you could."

"That's true," Sully agreed, "And I've watched a lot of fields go dry. That field the big companies have over in Van Zandt County is still pumping strong, and it has been three years now. All those wells are prorated to pump only so much oil a day, and the pressure is still strong. I've seen big fields, bigger than that one go dry in less than three years. Maybe these geologist fellows are on to something." The group erupted in mumbles again.

"Geologists!" Another man spoke up. "Them smart college boys don't know a thing about oil wells from where I stand!"

"No, maybe not, but they know about oil and where to find it. We may be sorry we didn't listen to them one of these days," Sully said.

Claude laughed. "Well, I doubt that. I've made more money in the last six months than I ever dreamed existed, and no amount of proration is going to take that away."

"That goes for me, too," Ned said.

"The price of oil keeps dropping. You're making less money every day." Sully reminded the group. "It's down to ten cents a barrel now."

"Hell, that ain't no problem. We'll just drill more wells."

"All I know," Charlie spoke up, "Is that all these fields are the same. They all go dry some day."

"And I'm going to get my oil up before somebody else gets to it!" Ned announced. "Right, boys?" Most of the group nodded in agreement.

"And I'm for sending somebody down to the state capital to see to it that the big companies don't pull this on us. They're threatening martial law if we don't slow our production down."

"Hell, let'em try it," one of the men said, and the group erupted in confusion again.

Lon and Sherman moved away from the group. "All that talk, and the working man's still pulling only two dollars an hour!" Sherman muttered under his breath.

"You boys ready to get out of here?" Sully broke in as he and Charlie walked up behind them. "I've had about all of this rarified air I can breath for one night."

"Let's go find us a drink someplace where everybody ain't so damn rich," Charlie muttered.

The lights and noise from the house spilled out across the lawn as they walked to the car. "What do you think about going back out West?" Sully asked when they reached a quiet distance.

"You got something in mind?" Sherman asked.

"This mess around here is too crowded. Just about every damn fool in the country is down here scratching. I got a cablegram from Rowdy yesterday. He and Moses are working out north of Wink. They say there's more work if we're interested."

"Well, I'm for anything that would get me out of these damn swamps!" Charlie said.

"The law is fixing to shut this whole field down," Sully added for emphasis.

"You think the governor will really do it?"

"He just about has to. These crazy fools around here are spilling almost as much as they're producing, and none it is worth the price of pipe line to carry it."

When do we leave?" Lon asked.

"The sooner the better," Sully said. "We've got another two to three weeks on this job, and then we can pull up stakes."

They drove back to the hotel in silence, each thinking ahead to the move.

***

When Lon opened the door to their room, he knew something was wrong. Jeremy was gone, but more than that, the dresser drawers had been rifled through. He had found the money Lon had hidden away for him, and he was gone. Lon and Sherman looked at one another, then back at the mess.

"Well, old buddy, you tried," Sherman said softly.

"Where do you figure he went?" Lon said as he checked his hiding place. Jer's money was gone alright, better than forty dollars.

"Hell, who knows! You can't keep running him down," Sherman said. "If he wants to go, he can go."

Lon sank down on his bed. Sherman was right. He could not hold Jer forever. No more than he could have changed Emory's mind. He threw the empty money pouch hard against the wall and fell back on the bed.

"Good night," Sherman called as he turned off the light.

"Good night!" Lon lay awake most of the night staring at the light patterns on the wall from the hotel sign outside. This mess with Jer was just one more screw-up on his part, he thought. Why couldn't anything ever work out smooth? Like with Emory. He should have been able to talk some sense into him. Lon's stomach knotted up again as he thought about his cousin. It was always the same. And Mae. Lon saw her face clear in his mind. When would he ever be able to offer her any kind of a future? His body ached with loneliness at the thought of her. When would he ever get anything right?

Chapter 43

Jer did not turn up the next day or next week. Lon and Sherman went on working and avoided the subject. The well was progressing on schedule. Sully went ahead with their plans to leave when it was completed. Lon was glad. He had seen all the swamps and trees he ever wanted to see again, and worrying about Jeremy put him in a black mood. The dumb son-of-a-bitch could go on and kill himself if he wanted. But that didn't stop Lon from looking for him. He went back to prowling the bars at night, now hunting his friend.

***

But Jer did not want to be found. Forty dollars bought a lot of booze. He doled it out carefully, two dollars a bottle. He made sure no one saw where he stashed the money inside his sock and was fortunate not to be robbed while he was passed out. He had not intended to be gone so long. He was only looking for enough money for a drink that night when he stumbled on to Lon's hiding place. Then one drink lead to another, and he realized he could not go back drunk. He would sober up a little first. Then he got thirsty again, and that's the way it went.

He woke up in an alley, slumped against a wall, his chin on his chest. He was vomiting, and as he wiped the back of his hand across his mouth he saw blood streaking his arm. He staggered to his feet and tried to make it to the street. His stomach was heaving and he gasped for breath. He fell forward on the sidewalk and was aware of a scream and people swirling around him.

"Somebody get a doctor!" a voice yelled.

***

Lon took his hat off as he entered the sanitarium. The whiteness of the place made him squint his eyes against the glare. He asked directions at the desk and followed the nurse's instructions to the right room. Jer was asleep when he entered. He looked pale and drawn again. But they had cleaned him up and given him a close shave. Lon stood looking at his old friend, studying the lines and blotches in his face. He looked old for only twenty-five, older by far. A rustling sound behind him turned his attention.

"You Prather?" a man in a white doctor's coat ask. Lon nodded "He told us to call you when he came to. He's been here five days, but he only regained consciousness yesterday. You a relative?"

"No, just from the same home place."

The doctor nodded. "Well, we patched him back together this time, but if you want to help him, you got to keep him off the liquor. A belly full of rot gut and no food will do any man in, and this fellow has been too long with both."

"Was he poisoned?"

The doctor nodded, "But not just from one bad batch. It's all the garbage he's been drinking for years. It's eaten the lining out of his stomach. He was vomiting blood when he came in. Probably had been drunk for about a week. Something finally gave way in there. If he does it again, he's a goner. Can you help him?"

"Did you tell him this?"

The doctor nodded. "But in my experience these men don't listen. I've seen too many. If you can keep him off the sauce for good, he can make it. Even improve. But one more spree like the last one, and he's a dead man."

"When can he get out of here?"

"I'd say in a couple of days. Does he have any way to pay the bill?"

"I'll stand for it."

The doctor nodded and extended his hand. "Good luck," he said matter-of-factly and walked away.

Lon sat down, expecting a long wait, but Jer must have sensed someone was there. He opened his eyes, blinked, and smiled weakly.

"Say, old buddy," Lon said.

"Thanks for coming," Jer whispered. Tears welled up in his eyes, and he attempted to raise his hand.

"You've got to sleep and get your strength up," Lon said. "We're moving back out west in about a week."

"I can't go home like this," Jer protested. He tried to raise his head.

"No, not home," Lon explained. "We've got work in Odessa."

Jer relaxed and fell back on his pillow. "Man, you don't need me tagging along."

"You just get better." Lon said. "We're going back out to God's country, out of these damn trees." Jer smiled "I'll be back tomorrow." Lon backed away to leave.

Jer roused a little. "I'm sorry," he whispered.

Lon waved him off. "Tomorrow." He responded.

***

In a week they were finished. One more producer for the Lacy's, and the last well allowable on the original tract. Sully passed out the pay in cash.

"Make it last boys."

Lon collected Jer from the hospital the next morning after he and Sherman had checked out of the hotel. The fog was rising off the lowlands as they headed west. By noon they were out of the big trees and the flat horizon in the distance was a welcome sight. Lon pushed the car forward and thought of Mae. It had been too long since he had seen her.

Chapter 44

It was three in the morning when they reached Krayly Creek. Sherman and Jeremy were both slumped in the car seat deep in slumber. Lon glanced at them as he turned off the main road. Probably they would never wake up if he was lucky, but he had to at least see Mae for a moment. He stopped by the front gate and eased out of the car. Sherman and Jer both shifted positions some, but neither woke.

The house looked bleak in the moonlight, and the porch still sagged. Little had changed, Lon thought. His boots crunched the gravel on the path.

"Hold it right there!" a voice spiky with fear yelled.

Lon stopped cold. "Cal, is that you?" Lon called. "It's me, Lon." He caught a glint of moonlight on gunmetal at the corner of the house and squinted to see more.

"Lon?" The boy stepped around the corner in his long-johns, and Lon heard the click as Cal let the hammer down easy on his rifle. "What are you doing here?"

Lon started to respond, but before he could speak, the front door opened, and she was there. Mae rushed forward and threw herself into his arms. He felt her cool skin against his cheek and the soft curves of her body through her gown.

"You're here, you're finally here," she whispered between kisses.

Lon could only laugh softly and kiss her again. He was at peace.

Mae looked toward the car. "Can you stay? Are you back to stay?" she asked.

"No," Lon answered, "We're moving back West. I've got a couple of boys with me now. You remember Jeremy? He's out there sleeping."

"Oh," she whispered and paused to hide her disappointment. "I'm glad you stopped," she added.

Lon kissed her again, "Are you okay? I mean, the farm and all? Do you need anything?"

"No, no, we're fine." They sat down on the edge of the porch. "Cal is doing a good job with the farm, and the twins are getting old enough to be more help to him."

"I got your letter. I'm sorry about your Pa."

"Don't be," Mae said. "He was a tortured man, Lon. He's better off." She looked up into his eyes. "He's better off, and so are we." Her voice was strong and determined.

"How's my father" Have you seen him?"

Mae nodded, "He's well. He's holding on. They plowed the cotton under. Did you hear?"

Lon shook his head.

"The government is paying the farmers to do it. "The government man says getting rid of the surplus will save the market and drive prices up," Mae explained. "I don't know, but your father signed, I hear. It was worthless in the field."

Lon looked out across the dark expanse toward home.

"I better go see him," he said to himself as much as to Mae. Then he looked back down at her hugged close to his side. "We've got work in Odessa. Sully is already there. We have to be there by tomorrow, or we lose the job."

Mae nodded her understanding, but the sadness in her eyes tore at his heart. He could not leave her behind again. "Come with me, Mae," Lon said suddenly. "Come now. I don't know when I'll be back, and I want you with me. We can get married in Odessa tomorrow. I'll be making good money again. It will be fine." He was talking fast, trying to say so much in so little time.

Mae pulled slowly away. Her head was down, and he could not see her eyes.

"Lon, I just can't leave. The kids..."

"The kids you're talking about are only a couple of years younger than you, except for Cassie," Lon protested. "Sarah is grown. She can run the house for a while."

"Sarah's gone," Mae said softly. "She married Zak Campbell last month."

Lon stopped short and studied her face. "See, she didn't let any of this stop her. She's got what she wants. Now it's your turn."

"But Cassie..." Mae protested.

"Cassie is Sarah's sister, too. Same as the others. She can take over." Lon stopped, breathless. His heart was pounding as he looked down at Mae, but she only looked away and blinked back her tears.

"I can't go with you, Lon. I can't"

"You mean you won't! If you love me, you would go. There's nothing holding you here but you!" He placed his hands on her shoulders and turned her to him. "Hell, Mae, we can come back. We will come back. But you have to decide. Do you love me or not?"

She was trembling. "You don't understand, Lon." she whispered. "I'm sorry, but I can't leave."

"Mae, I can't stay! You know that! I've got a job there. I have nothing here, and neither do you. I've got to go, and if you wanted, you could go. That I understand."

Mae reached up to touch his cheek with a trembling hand, but he jerked away. For a moment he froze there, then he turned and walked quickly to the car.

Sherman and Jeremy had hardly moved. He started the car and sped away into the night. He was numb with pain and anger at her, at himself. To hell with her and the rest of them too!

The car tore through the night following the lane around the fields to his father's house. Sherman roused up on one of the sharp turns Lon made, sliding in the sand drifts.

"Where the hell are we?" he muttered.

"Go back to sleep," Lon growled. "I've got a stop to make."

"We've got to be..."

"I know! We'll make it." Lon shouted. "Just shut up and leave me alone."

Sherman shrugged his shoulders and slumped back down in the seat. This was no time for questions, he figured.

Lon slid to a stop in front of the house and stepped out of the car. "Pa!" he yelled. He knew better than to step up on the porch without hailing his father. "Pa, it's me, wake up!" he called again.

"Back here, boy!" a gruff voice answered.

Lon walked to the side of the house and looked into the screened-in porch at the back. In the thin moonlight he could see his father sitting in a rocker. Lon walked closer.

"You up, Pa?" I figured I'd be waking you."

"Naw." Henry's speech was slow and strange. "No sleep for me tonight."

"You okay?" Lon opened the screen door. His father wore only his hat and his long-johns. Lon noticed a empty whiskey bottle tipped over on the floor by his chair. In all his years, Lon had never seen his father touch hard liquor.

"I was just sitting here thinking," Henry stared out into the night. "This farm is dead right now. Not a thing in the field." He stared at his son with sad, vacant eyes. "It woke me up from a sound sleep," he said.

"I heard about the cotton," Lon answered.

"Hardest thing I ever did," Henry continued. "Excepting burying your mother."

Lon squatted down beside his father's chair.

"Will this help, you think?" Lon asked.

"I don't know. Don't know a damn thing anymore," Henry muttered and then fell silent.

"I'm on my way West," Lon said. "We've got a job at good pay again." He stopped and waited for a reaction from his father, but none came. "I have to go on tonight, or they'll give the job to someone else." He hesitated. "I can't stay." He followed his father's gaze out into the night for a few moments. "Did the bank reopen?" Lon asked finally.

"The bank?" Henry said. "Naw, it's gone. Did you have much in there?"

"No," Lon answered. "A couple hundred maybe. I haven't been drawing much pay."

"Well, it's gone now," Henry rubbed his eyes and looked at Lon like he was seeing him for the first time. "Where'd you say you were going this time?"

"Back West. Odessa," Lon replied.

Henry nodded and then added, "Don't worry about me,

son. "I'll be fine by morning." He motioned toward the empty bottle. "Things will get better. I'll plant again." His voice trailed off.

"I know," Lon said.

"You know." Henry paused and studied his son's face for a moment. "You were right to go.'"

Lon started to speak, but Henry continued. "I was wrong to try and hold you here. It was a man's choice you made, son. And you were right. I wanted you to know that."

Lon nodded, and they both stared away toward the river. Some how those words from his father made a difference.

"I've got to go, Pa," Lon whispered after a time, but Henry made no reply. Lon hesitated a moment, and then before he gave it conscious thought, he grabbed his father in an embrace like he had not done since he was a small child. Henry lifted his arms up slowly and returned the rough clumsy hug.

"I'll be fine, son. You go along." He patted Lon soundly on the back. "I'll be fine."

Lon straightened and pushed the screen door back. "I'll write when I'm settled."

"Take care," Henry called after him.

In A Fevered land

Book IV
Cabel
1934

Chapter 45

Cabel Norris looked out of place in the law office conference room. Dressed in worn khaki work clothes and brogan boots, he stood out among the business suits and ties. But the oil company officials and lawyers around him were there because of him. He knew it, and so did they. Cabel read the contract through carefully. Let'em wait, he thought. And they did. The room was silent except for a scattered cough once or twice.

Harold Briggs, the chairman of the board of Cloverleaf Oil Corporation, second largest company in the United States, sat at the end of the conference table and studied the young man across from him with grudging respect. He had out guessed them all, Norris had. It galled Briggs mightily to admit it, but this young pup had gotten in on some prime country while Cloverleaf and the rest of the big operations were sitting on their butts in Wink. But the game wasn't up yet. A smile curled slightly on his lips as he puffed on his pipe. Briggs had seen more than one hungry bastard try to cut in on the big money, and he's watched most of them fail. Let Norris enjoy his spot for now. Briggs took a deep breath through his nose and relit his pipe. He could wait. It was all clear in the contract, and he knew the young man would sign. He was getting everything he asked for and more.

Cabel looked up and indicated he wanted a pen. Several were offered. He chose one and signed without further ceremony, then sat back and smiled.

"Welcome to Cloverleaf Oil, Mr. Norris," Briggs said. "Our men will start preparations tomorrow. We'll have our first derrick up inside a week." He stood up to indicate the meeting was over, and Cabel shook hands all around. Harold Briggs walked around the table to extend his hand. "And when you are ready to talk a deal on your leases along the New Mexico line, you let us know."

Cabel smiled. "Not likely. I'm using the money you're paying me to finance my own drilling company. I'm going to be your new competition."

Briggs laughed. "Well, you aren't the first to try that, son. There's been plenty of others before you." They walked out together. "And I wish you luck. But if you run into trouble, give us first shot at those sandhill leases. Deal?"

"Deal!" Cabel shook his hand again. Not a chance, old man, he thought. I didn't come this far to give up. This is only the beginning. He walked out of the building without glancing back.

Briggs and his aides watched from behind the office window. "I give him six months," one of the company men muttered.

"See to it!" Briggs snapped. He turned on his heels and walked away.

***

Standing there before the Cloverleaf building, Cabel felt like shouting his news to the world. He had done it! He had collected the leases and named his price. There was cause for celebration today. But he didn't shout. He didn't even smile. Instead, he took a deep breath of the dry desert air and walked away. There would be time to celebrate later. For now there was still a lot of work to be done.

The last six years had not changed Cabel Norris much. He showed little wear from the freights he had hopped or the meals he had skipped. Lean and tanned, he still had the same boundless energy that kept him going almost without sleep. Work was his tonic and a gamble his relaxation, whether on an oil lease or a poker hand. He had left home at the age of twelve, fleeing poverty on a Tennessee hill farm, and he had never looked back from his goal. He would be a millionaire before he reached thirty, he had decided, and now his plan was close to reality. He had just signed a contract that could bring him that million within a year. All he had to do was wait for the wells to be drilled. He was sure the oil was there.

Midland was a booming oil town just down the tracks from Odessa. Cabel liked the place, and he intended to make it his town, although he had shared that fact with no one yet. He had made a promise that Cabel Norris Oil Company would dominate the whole region before he was through.

Out on the street he looked like every other oil field worker on his way to a job site, down to the sweat-stained band on his hat. Cabel smiled to himself as he walked along, knowing of his new conquest, a major interest in what was about to be the biggest oil strike of the century.

Out on the highway running west to Odessa, he flagged down a truck. According to rumor, Hugh Sullivan was back working in West Texas. That meant Lon and Sherman would probably be there before long. It was time to fill his partners in and get a firm contract signed.

A Cloverleaf Oil truck hauling casings ground to a stop. "Where you headed?" the driver shouted over the engine noise.

"Can I get a hitch over to Odessa?" Cabel shouted back.

"Sure thing, get in."

Cabel settled himself in the cab.

"Looking for work?" the driver asked as he pulled out.

"Yeah," Cabel replied. Let the man think what he pleases.

"I know one or two fellows out here, but I don't think they need men right now."

"That's how it's been all over," Cabel said.

"I hear the big boys are talking about a new field west of here. You hear anything?"

"Yeah, I heard that, but you never know. Could be nothing."

"If you can hold out a little longer, there's bound to be some jobs in that," the driver said.

"Yeah, I'll probably come back over here in a day or two. Right now I've got to see some folks in Odessa."

The driver nodded his understanding. "I was out of work for a year before I landed this job. Hope you won't have to wait that long."

"No, I hope not."

The man rambled on about his family and his past. Cabel nodded at the right times and made a few comments that sounded like he was listening, but his mind was busy on other things. Plans for his company, plans for expansion.

All those years across a poker table had prepared him well. The truck driver never noticed his indifference or guessed the real business of his passenger.

"I'll get off anywhere along here," Cabel directed as they reached the edge of Odessa.

"Tell you what," the driver said. "I got a little lucky in a crap game last night." He pulled a five dollar bill out of his pocket and extended it to Cabel. "I get paid today, and all I'll do is end up drinking this extra money. Let me loan you a little until you find a job."

"Naw," Cabel shook his head. He was caught off guard by the gesture from a stranger. "I'll find something, I'm sure."

"Well, until you do," the man insisted. "I've been in your spot before. Might be again. You can pay me back double one of these days, if you want."

Cabel took the money. "What's you name?"

Brace Whitman," the man said with a smile. "Look me up when you find a job."

The driver stopped the truck by the side of the road, and Cabel climbed out.

"Much obliged," he called.

"Good luck!" the trucker answered.

Cabel looked at the bill in his hand and smiled. He pulled out his shiny new Cloverleaf pen and wrote something across one end, folded it neatly, and placed it in his wallet.

Across the road the huddled buildings of Odessa shimmered in the heat. Cabel checked the traffic on the dusty roadway and headed into town.

Chapter 46

As far as Lon could tell, Odessa was another sandy bog along the railroad track. No different than Wink really, except the train close by made transportation easier. The people looked the same. The place was crowded with men seeking work, and con men seeking loose money. Sherman and Jeremy roused up and shook themselves awake. It had been a long tiring trip since Krayly Creek with Lon angry and silent behind the wheel.

Lon drove through the crowded streets trying to remember Sully's directions. When he spotted Charlie at the well site, he pulled the car over and rolled to a stop. Rowdy and Moses were with Charlie. The sight of them was a lift to his spirits. Sherman jumped out of the car and gave a greeting yell that could be heard over in Midland probably.

"Glad to see you boys had the good sense to come back West," Rowdy greeted them when they all shook hands. "Me and Moses were getting tired of one another's lies. We need some fresh material."

"I'm surprised to see you boys have stayed out of jail this long," Sherman said.

"Who says we have?" Moses said with a grin.

"Sully will be here tomorrow," Charlie explained. "He's signing papers today with Kary Oil."

They were laying out pipe and stringing cables within two hours of their arrival. Charlie told them with some ceremony that theirs was to be the first job drilled inside the town limits. Lon and Sherman climbed up the derrick to help rig the crown block. The land in all directions was as flat as the ocean might be.

"Now that's what I call a view," Sherman announced.

Lon looked up from his work and surveyed the area. "No damn trees in the way; that's for sure."

"I haven't seen a good sunrise since we left Butler," Sherman joked, trying to get a response out of his friend.

"Well, you'll get your chance tomorrow," Lon answered back in a flat tone, and just kept on working.

Sherman puzzled over Lon's foul mood. He had said little since they stopped off in Krayly Creek, and he didn't seem in any hurry to cheer up. It must have something to do with that stop they made, but he'd probably never know for sure. Lon kept his own counsel. Sherman shook his head and went on with his work.

They found an oil shack to rent that night. It was a shotgun house of tar paper and wood that had been moved in by the oil company. They were plunked down in rows creating an entire neighborhood of fragile looking shanties. The people flocked in and were settled in a day. Men with families could have a house to themselves.

Lon thought of Mae. He was angry at himself for forcing the issue, angry at her for not coming. Mainly he was hurt. Why? He kept asking. He had been so sure she truly loved him. Why would she not come? Or was he wrong about her? Was he wrong about everything?

"What the hell's the matter with you," Sherman asked when he walked up on Lon staring off across the country side."

Lon jerked around and gave him a black look. "Nothing!"

"Well, snap out of it, man. We've got money in our pockets and all this time on our hands. We could be raising some hell around here, and all you want to do is sit."

Lon stared into the distance and sighed. Then he looked back at Sherman and smiled slightly. "You're right, partner. We've got things to do. Right?"

"Right! There's bound to be a dance hall somewhere in this godforsaken hole. Let's go find it."

"You're on. Get Jeremy and..."

"He's not feeling too chipper, he says. Let's leave him. Moses and Rowdy are in there."

Lon looked toward the house.

"Come on," Sherman motioned. "He'll be fine. I swear, boy, you're part mother hen, I do believe."

Lon followed along. Sherman was right. To hell with all of it. He needed a little relaxation.

They found the music easily and the liquor even easier. Sherman danced himself down to exhaustion while Lon sat solemnly in the corner and got blind drunk thinking about clear blue eyes. It was the most satisfying self pity he had ever gone through. Rowdy and Moses came looking for them by two in the morning and began pouring coffee down them. By sun-up they were standing without help and ready to report to Sully.

Lon had never felt worse and somehow it helped. They were a sad lot when they faced their boss the next morning, but Sully asked no questions.

We're getting paid in company scrip," he announced. "They aren't using money with most of the banks gone bust, so Kary Oil is printing its own. Rowdy here tells me it'll buy you anything you need at the stores here, pay your rent, whatever. Does that sound fair?"

The men nodded.

"The pay is six dollars a day, and you work an eight hour shift."

A mumble of surprise and approval rose from the crew.

"Hot damn! I never figured to see that much again."

"It's government doing," Sully explained. "Something called the National Recovery Act. It's making shorter hours so that more workers can be hired. The way I see it you boys' biggest problem is going to be staying out of trouble with all that free time."

They all laughed.

"With a little luck," he continued, "We'll be able to stay here for a while. I figure this is going to be a big field, and we're in on the ground floor. So let's go to work."

The group began to scatter, and Jeremy followed Lon and Sherman toward the rig.

"All right!" Sherman slapped Lon on the shoulder as they started to walk away, and then both of them winced in pain. Their hangovers still had a few hours to go. "What do you say to that, partner?"

"I say things are looking up," Lon answered, but he was not smiling.

Sully called after them. "Lon, you and Sherman. Could we see you a minute?"

"Oh shit, here it comes." Sherman mumbled.

They turned back to see Charlie and Sully waiting for them.

"I'll wait over here," Jer said and kept on going. He was still keeping a low profile around Sully.

Lon considered how he was going to defend his actions of the night before, but could think of nothing. He waited for Sully to speak first.

"How bout your friend there. Will he stay sober this time? Sully asked.

"He's trying, Sully. That's all I know." Lon said, and he was conscious of Sherman giving him a sidelong glance.

"Well, we'll give him another chance. He can help Rowdy fire the boilers, but he better understand my rules. No drinking."

"I've talked to him. He knows how it is," Lon said.

Sully nodded. "Okay then, we've got a six well contract here if this first one is a producer. We're going to start several wells at the same time, and we'll be needing more drillers. Charlie and me think you boys can do the job. What do you think?" He studied them with a poker-faced expression.

"Well, I think I'd sure appreciate the chance to try it!" Lon responded, and Sherman nodded in agreement.

Sully and Charlie broke into wide grins.

"The pay will be better," Charlie put in.

"That sure won't hurt," Sherman said.

They shook hands. "Keep this under your hat for now." Sully said. "But I want you boys to work along side Charlie here step by step so you'll be ready. I figure this well will come in strong."

When they joined Jeremy, he was slumped against the platform with his hat down over his eyes. He straightened as they walked up. "What did he say? Am I working?"

"He said we're all going to be rich sons-of-bitches, my friend," Sherman said.

"Alright! Let's celebrate!" Jeremy said, then caught himself. "I mean, let's get to work!"

Lon laughed as he pulled on his work gloves. It was the first time he had really smiled in days.

Chapter 47

It took two days to locate Lon and Sherman. Cabel found them at a boarding house. Mrs. Murphy's Home Cooking, the sign on the porch proclaimed. The dining room was filled with hungry roughnecks crowded around a large dining table. Several ladies were busily sitting out huge bowls of vegetables, meat and gravy, while the diners found their chairs and tucked their napkins in their collars. The lady in charge greeted him with a big Irish smile and a dinner plate.

"Have a seat and help yourself."

Cabel followed her orders and found an empty spot across from Lon and Sherman. When Lon looked up, Cabel was already dishing out a heaping pile of potatoes.

"How you boys doing these days?" Cabel said with a big smile.

"Well, if it isn't the wandering dreamer," Lon said.

Sherman looked up from his plate and smiled. "How is it you always show up a eating time?"

"I heard you boys were out here. You timed it perfect."

He leaned closed and whispered. "I got the leases in my pocket, and Cloverleaf Oil is calling me Mr. Norris."

"How many of those leases have our name on them?" Sherman asked with a grin.

"Enough to keep you counting your money for a while when one of the wells comes in." Cabel answered as he helped himself from every bowl that was passed.

"You already have a contract?" Lon asked.

Cabel patted his pocket. "Right here next to my heart. I'll show you after we eat."

"Yeah, mister, after we eat." A gruff voiced roughneck beside him growled. "Pass them beans down here and quit your talking."

Cabel handed the bowl over and turned his attention to the food. They ate their fill and got up to leave. Mrs. Murphy swooped down to remove their dishes, and four other hungry diners took their seats.

Lon introduced Jeremy to Cabel as they walked outside. Cabel shook his hand, then looked at Lon and Sherman. "Can we talk a little business?"

"I'll be out at the car." Jer said quickly.

Cabel waited until Jer had walked some distance away before he reached into his pocket and produced the papers. "It says right here, gentlemen, that the Cabel Norris Oil company has a contract with Cloverleaf Oil for one-eighth the royalty on any well produced on the following leases." He turned the paper where they could see the list of properties and waited for a reaction.

"You mean we hold all that?" Sherman said in a whisper.

Cabel nodded his head slowly.

"One-eighth?" Lon asked.

"They're due to start drilling the test well next week,

and I'm going to be there on the front row, I can tell you."

The Lon and Sherman laughed nervously.

"All we need is a couple of good producers, and we'll be set for life," Cabel added.

"What's the percentage that we hold in this deal?" Lon asked.

"Well, I figure I've done all the leg work on this. It's my show. But you boys believed in me when you had no reason to, right? So I'm saying you two and Morris hold fifteen percent each. Docs that sound fair?"

"Fifteen percent? Of the whole shootin' match?" Lon asked in surprise.

"If you agree."

Lon and Sherman laughed nervously again and glanced at one another.

"I've got a contract here in my pocket, if you want to sign it. It'll make it all official." Cabel produced the paper.

Lon read over it quickly and nodded to Sherman. It looked clear enough to him.

"I've got to warn you, though," Cabel added. "You aren't going to see much profit right away when these wells start coming in. As holder of fifty-five percent of the company, I'm going to use any income we get to start our own drilling operation. If you don't want that, I'll by you out flat, but if you stay in, you are in for the whole show."

"You want to start drilling your own wells?" Lon asked.

"I want to drill it, pipe it, refine it, ship it, and pump it."

Lon laughed again and took a deep breath. "Can you do all that?"

Cabel nodded. "What do you say?"

"I say go for it." Lon looked to Sherman for a reaction.

"You got a pen on you?" Sherman asked.

Cabel produced the Cloverleaf pen from his pocket.

"Picked this one out special for this occasion."

Lon and Sherman both signed, holding the paper on their knee.

"One of these days I'll build a bronze statue of us signing this contract on the street corner like this." Cabel said.

"You know, Cabel, right now..." Sherman handed the pen back. "I believe you will do just that."

"I'm going to Dallas to find Morris this afternoon. Then, I'll be back out here before they spud in the first well. I'll keep you posted about the field. Soon as I know something, you'll know." Cabel folded the contract and stuck it in his pocket. "See you around." And he walked away fast, like he had a thousand things waiting for him to do.

Lon and Sherman watched him disappear down the street dodging trucks and pedestrians. Then they looked at one another for a second, trying to take in all that Cabel had just dropped on them, but it was just too much at once.

"Come on, we better get back to work."

"What are you guys so quiet about?" Jer asked as they drove back to the rig.

"You probably wouldn't believe it even if we could explain it to you," Sherman said.

Lon laughed. "When we believe it, we'll let you know."

That night when all was quiet save for Sherman's and Jer's gentle snoring, Lon considered the news Cabel had brought and all the possibilities. The thought of being rich was mighty pleasant. But he had seen too many dreams lost. He wouldn't get his hopes up too much. Maybe it would be better to sell. Cabel said he would buy him out. It could be the money he needed to be set up for the future.

He rolled over and punched at his pillow in frustration. What future! Without Mae he didn't particularly give a damn!

***

Sully was right. The sand formation was easy drilling. The well came in at 40,000 barrels a day within three weeks, and the town folk went crazy. They were heroes. The town tract became a maze of derricks, and Lon and Sherman stepped into their new jobs with a show of outward confidence. They hired more crew and started the process of breaking in a new team. Lon put Jeremy on firing boilers. He was still pretty frail looking, but he was staying sober.

"Course he is now," Sherman said. "Every time he tries to eat or drink anything, he pukes up his guts. But he'll heal up, and then you'll have to watch him every minute."

Lon knew it was probably the truth, but he had to try and help. What else could he do? Jer was very docile these days. All the bluster and big talk were gone. He was down, and he knew it, Lon thought, and he needed a break.

Jeremy was happy to be working again. Even if he was little more than day labor, at least he was not on the dole. But God he was thirsty! His mouth and tongue felt numb and dry. There wasn't an hour he didn't crave a drink. At times he hated Lon Prather for being so damn right all the time! All those years Jeremy had been the leader, the man with the world in his pocket. And Lon and Emory had followed him. Hung on his every word. It was hard to admit that the tables were turned. Now he was the weaker one, and Prather was his guide. But all the while Jer remembered East Texas and how scared he had been lying in that alley belching blood. If it hadn't been for Lon... So he tried. He fought the trembling and the thirst, and he kept his mouth shut. Lon agreed to hold his pay again so Jer wouldn't be able to give in to the urge for a drink. And Jer promised not to take the money like last time. This time he would make it.

It was mid-summer before the drilling slacked off at all. The derricks kept going up, and the wells kept blowing in. Sullivan Drilling had never had it so good. Sully bought a new Packard, and he and Charlie took to smoking nickel cigars. Lon and Sherman got a real kick out of watching their mentors riding 'high on the hog'. Moses and Rowdy invested in a fighting cock. It was like the men were realizing all their dreams after a long wait. Lon and Sherman got accustomed to having money in their pocket, even if it was company script. It spent the same. And all the time the anticipation of Cabel's promise hung in the future. Life was good. Only one dark spot spoiled Lon's vision. Mae was ever on his mind.

Cabel was on the drilling floor when the well came in. If he had told any one how sure he was that the well was a gusher, they would have never believed him. But he knew. "Thirty thousand barrels," the driller shouted over to him, and Cabel just smiled and nodded. He had known all along. So now he was on his way. Just a little more patience, and it would all come true. As soon as he had the capital to get started, he would start developing his own leases, and those were all his, no one-eighth anything. That afternoon he drove into Midland and ordered the first Cabel Norris Oil Company sign to be painted. Green background and gold letters. He had carried the design in his mind for years. He got telegrams off to Lon and Sherman, and one to Morris in Dallas. It wouldn't be long now.

In the offices of Cloverleaf Oil, Harold Briggs took the news of the strike in stride. It was business as usual for him, but Cabel Norris crossed his mind. He envied the young bastard, he had to admit. Even respected his guts and grit. Norris had it in him to be a big man in the oil business. But he would nail him, regardless of how he felt personally. This was business, and if that young buck thought he could outsmart Cloverleaf Oil and lock up the whole New Mexico line using Cloverleaf money to do it, he had a few lessons to learn. They would give young Mr. Norris just enough rope to hang himself, and then they would take what they wanted.

Chapter 48

By the following fall Lon and Sherman were both feeling fairly comfortable in their new jobs. The drilling had been easy, and they learned what to expect. They were on off-setting sites just west of town, and it was the first time since the high plains they had been out in open country away from towns or trees, or both. Sherman's rig was shut down for the afternoon waiting for a test crew to come out. He left a skeleton crew at the well site and drove over to Lon's rig, the Ranger #1. He had a new telegram from Cabel to show him. Two more wells had come in, and Cabel was reporting on their success. Sherman still didn't quite believe that he was getting as rich as Cabel said, but he was starting to adjust to the idea. He smiled to himself thinking of what his folks were going to say when he came home a millionaire. Then again, he couldn't imagine what they would say, or what he would say either. It took some getting used to.

He stopped the car next to Sully's green Packard parked about fifty yards from the rig. Sully and Charlie were sitting in the car having a smoke.

"What's going on?" Sherman asked.

"They ran into a tight formation," Sully answered. "Lon's getting some on the job training right now. The pressure control crew showed up short some men, so Lon and his crew are helping them out."

Sherman started toward the rig.

"You going up there?"

"Why not?" Sherman asked over his shoulder. He could see Lon standing on the drilling floor watching the proceedings. He only needed to talk to him a minute.

Lon saw him coming and waved a greeting. They met at the head of the ramp, and Sherman handed over the telegram.

"What's going on over here?" he asked.

"We've hit some high pressure gas down there. These boys are helping us run some pipe," Lon said as he started reading the message. "This looks good," he said after a few minutes. "Guess we're going to be rich in spite of ourselves." They both laughed softly

"Mind if I look this over? I've never seen this done before," Sherman said.

"Go right ahead. They're shut down right now, fixing a leak in the second pressure valve. Jer is over there helping them. Just don't get in their way."

Sherman nodded and walked closer to the drilling table.

"I'm going to go catch a smoke right quick," Lon called after him, and Sherman waved that he understood.

High above the derrick floor, Moses guided the pipe into position out of the way as the men below worked on their equipment. From his high perch he saw Lon walk down the ramp and Sherman move over closer where he could see what was going on. Jeremy and the two men from the pressure crew were bent over the drill table adjusting the valves.

In the next instant Moses saw fire boil up the casing and explode over the men like a flood of flames. Saw it rushing up through the derrick frame at him. He watched, paralyzed in disbelief for a moment, and then in a flash of human instinct to survive, he scrambled out of the platform cage and grabbed one of the guy wires that anchored the tower to the ground. As he slid to safety the wire cut through his heavy leather gloves and into his hands like a razor's edge, but when he reached the ground he was well away from the fire. Moses looked back to see the tower topple slowly over like a melted candle. The entire rig was buried in an orange ball of fire.

Lon didn't hear the first explosion. All he felt was a blow from behind like a sledge hammer had struck. It knocked him the rest of the way down the ramp, head over heels. He slammed the ground flat on his back, and when he opened his eyes he saw only fire. The air was a boil of flame above and all around him. He stumbled to his feet. His only thought was to run, and the fire followed. He could feel the heat like a searing hand pushing him along. Holding his breath in panic, he hurled himself forward, and as he burst out of the fire into the open desert, he tripped and rolled into the waiting arms of Sully and Charlie.

The two men smothered the flames on Lon's arms and back, and eased Lon to the ground. Sully shouted something, but Lon could not understand him over the roar of the fire. He tried to rise clumsily, but Charlie held him back.

The well was screaming like a raging beast. The men watched in horror, helpless to act, but they could see nothing but flames where moments before there had been a derrick. The fire from the drill table spurted out like a blow torch in all directions, eight feet off the ground. Sully and Charlie dragged Lon back from the heat and waited. Then motion caught their eye. Two forms scrambled out hugging the ground, pulling and dragging one another to safety. Rowdy and one of the special crew men who had been on the ground under the platform were safe. The fire had only blistered them as it blew out above their heads.

An apparition wrapped in flames stumbled out of the fire. Rowdy and Charlie tackled the form and rolled it on the ground. The man who emerged was more dead than alive, all clothing and skin seared away. He coughed and choked and gasped for air, but they were powerless to help him.

Trucks from a neighboring well roared up, and men came running to help. Lon and the nameless man from the pressure crew were lifted into a truck bed and Charlie jumped up beside them.

"Get going!" Sully screamed and the truck roared away.

Hugh Sullivan and Rowdy turned helplessly back to the fire. They squinted their eyes and shielded their faces from the searing heat.

"Moses?" Rowdy shouted.

"He was in the tower!" Sully answered. They looked to where the tower had been.

"Help me!" someone shouted. Rowdy's head snapped around at the familiar voice to see his old friend stumbling toward them tripping over loose sand and tufts of grass. His shirt and pants were covered in blood, and he held his hands out in a helpless offering.

The two men scrambled to his side as Moses collapsed, his knees buckling under him. Rowdy pulled off a glove to find deep gurgling gashes in Moses' palm. The sickening white of bone showed through, and one finger was almost severed, but he was alive! Rowdy quickly ripped his shirt and began to wrap the hand while Sully worked on the other one. A secondary explosion shook the ground under them, and the three men looked up at the fire, now burning even wilder. They waited in silence while more workmen from nearby wells rushed up to help, but no more men stumbled out of the inferno.

***

Lon could see nothing but the sky rushing over him as they bounced and jolted to the main road. Charlie cradled Lon's head in his lap and stared straight ahead.

The truck carrying the men careened on to the main road. In his daze Lon wasn't sure what had happened to him. His burns were so deep he could feel nothing, but his nostrils were filled with a sickening sweet smell, and he was thirsty, so thirsty.

Charlie hovered over him and the other man, but he did not touch them. There was nothing he could do. Lon could not recognize the man beside him. He was a black smear of blisters and ragged flesh, and in his shock, Lon never considered that he looked the same. The man was delirious, crying for water and calling out names. Lon lay quiet. The truck slid to a stop at a gas station, and Charlie grabbed a water hose and held it out for them to drink. They gulped the water in gasping breaths. Lon could not get enough.

"That's it. Go!" Charlie shouted. He tossed the hose back and the truck shot away.

Lon did not pass out. With Charlie's help, he walked into the hospital in a semi-conscious fog and stood meekly against the wall while the truck driver carried the other man in. "I need a smoke, Charlie," he whispered.   Charlie lit one and held it out.   Only when Lon reached out to take it, did he realize the skin from his forearm and hand was hanging loose like torn sleeves at his elbows.   He stared transfixed at the sight, confused.

A nurse gently touch his shoulder, but he felt nothing.

Charlie and two attendants lifted him on to a table where a nurse began to cut away his charred clothing.   The sickening smell washed over him again.   Then everything went black.

***

When he awoke he was aware only of the pain, an all engulfing pain.   He heard a groan gurgle from his own lips like a sound from far off and caught a flutter of white at his side, but he could not turn his head.

"He's conscious," a female voice said.   "Get the doctor."   And the sound of quick footsteps faded into the distance.

The nurse slipped a needle into his hip, and a flood of relief swept over him.   He tried to focus on the person at his side, but she stepped out of his line of vision.

"Mr. Prather?" a deep voice spoke.

"Where am I?" He tried to ask, but his voice came only in a crackling mutter.

"You're in Baylor Hospital in Dallas, Mr. Prather. I'm Dr. Gaines.   You were severely burned in an oil field explosion. Do you remember?"

Lon blinked his eyes.

"You've been unconscious for some time, Mr. Prather. We've been waiting for you to come around."   Dr. Gaines gave directions to his nurses in a low voice and then spoke to Lon again. "Did the shot help?" he asked.

Lon tried to nod.

"Just lie still, now," the doctor directed. "You're going to make it, Mr. Prather. You've come this far."

Lon drifted off to sleep only to be awakened again in a few hours by the searing pain. Time passed. Hours? Days" He did not know. His life was measured by the morphine they gave him.

***

Doc Reese and Mae Handley walked quickly down the hospital corridor. Their footsteps echoed along the deserted hall and at the nurse's station Nurse Finnely looked up at the sound. "This wing is restricted," she said softly.

"I'm Dr. Reese. Doctor Gaines was to notify you."

"Oh, yes, Doctor. Doctor Gaines called."

"Is he conscious?"

"He drifts in and out. I'm afraid he won't be able to talk to you," She paused. "He shouldn't really be disturbed."

Mae stiffened at the words. The fear that had gripped her from the moment Doctor Reese came to tell her of the accident seemed to clutch her throat. Unconsciously, she gasped softly, and the nurse and doctor looked at her.

Dr. Reese put his arm around her shoulders in a protective motion. "We only want to see him for a moment. Could we...?"

Nurse Finnely studied the face of the pale girl and considered the possibility of having to revive her. She looked near collapse.

Realizing what the nurse might be thinking, Doc Reese tightened his grip on Mae's shoulder. "She'll be fine.

We're just very concerned. If we could just see him for a minute."

After a moment Nurse Finnely nodded and led the way down the corridor, but she gave no encouragement. "His father was here two days ago," she said. Mr. Prather never woke up."

"We'll only stay a moment," Doc Reese repeated.

The hall was dark, barely illuminated by light from a shaded window at the end of the hall. The door the nurse opened bore a NO ADMITTANCE warning. She turned the latch and pushed the heavy door back without a sound

Mae hesitated at the threshold. She was so frightened. Her heart pounded in her chest, and she could feel herself trembling inside, but she had to see him. No matter how terrible, she had to know. Doc Reese gently guided her into the room.

All that was visible by the low light aimed toward the wall was a high hospital bed piled with white gaze. Mae stared for a few seconds before she made out Lon's face, barely visible among the bandages. He was totally swathed in the gauze except for his eyes, nose, and mouth. His eyes were closed, and his face was swollen. His lips were blistered and distorted.

"How are his vital signs?" Doc Reese asked the nurse in a professional tone.

"Stable, doctor. He's awake from time to time, but only for a few minutes."

While they talked in hushed tones, Mae walked timidly forward to stand by the bed, so close she could have reached out and touched Lon's face. Tears welled up to blur her vision. Oh, Lon, she thought. What has happened to you? You have to live. I love you so.

Doc Reese came to stand behind her. "The chart looks

good," he whispered. "He's doing as well as can be expected."

"Is he in pain?"

"No, no. They're giving him morphine. He's going to make it."

"We need to go now," the nurse said.

Doctor Reese took Mae's arm and lead her from the room.

"Thank you," Mae whispered to the nurse when they got back to her hall station.

The nurse smiled. "We'll take good care of him," she said. "He's going to make it, I think." She felt she needed to say something to this frail young woman. Something to relieve some of the pain she say in her eyes.

"Thank you," Mae said again.

Nurse Finnely watched the doctor lead Mae down the hall to the elevator. Her heart went out to them, and she had wanted to say something to help, but it was so hard. So many times she had to talk to people like this. People who wanted so desperately to hear there was a chance their loved one would recover. And so often their hopes came to nothing. The new patient was critical. Burn victims were so fragile. So many things could go wrong. Taking a deep breath, she walked back down the hall to make her rounds

***

Mae and Doctor Reese left the hospital and stopped on the front walk. Mae looked up in confusion at her surroundings. She had hardly been aware of the ride down on the elevator or the other people around them. Now she had no idea where to go next.

Doc Reese gently took her arm. "Do you feel like

eating something? Maybe a soda water, or something?"

Mae shook her head. She took a deep breath and gazed around trying to think clearly.

"I need a cup of coffee before we start back," Doc Reese said. "Come on." And he guided her across the street to a coffee shop.

Mae was aware now of the traffic and the street noise. It was as strange as the hospital had been.

"Too many people around here," the old doctor muttered sensing Mae's apprehension.

She smiled slightly and nodded. Mae had never been in so large a city before.

They settled themselves in a booth, and he ordered coffee. Mae stared down at her hands.

"This is the best place Lon could be," Doc Reese said. "He's getting good care."

Mae did not respond, but the tears came again, and he rushed to offer her his handkerchief. This fragile woman child before him was like his own daughter. He had seen her through so much hardship in her short years, and the old doctor admired her strength and goodness. Now he fumbled for something to say that would give her hope, but nothing came. The boy was bad. He had never seen so severe a burn before and even his attempts to cover his concern with professional questions did not stop his hands from shaking, and his heart from aching. Lon Prather was like one of his own children, also. He had delivered him in the back room of his daddy's farm house and spanked the breath of life into his lungs. He had watched him grow into a fine young man with a questioning mind and great promise. This was not fair. The boy should not come to this. And most of all, Mae loved him. This child he so prayed would find happiness and escape her past, longed for Lon Prather to recover. It was not fair that these two should suffer.

Mae tried to dry her eyes and looked up at the doctor. "Do you think he has a chance?" she whispered.

Doc Reese nodded solemnly. "Lon is strong. He has a chance."

"He looks so helpless."

"We'll come back when he's awake," the doctor said. "You'll see. He's going to make it. He's made it this far."

Mae shook her head. "No, I can't come back." She wiped at her tears again with a trembling hand. "It's no use. I can't marry him. You know that. It's useless to come."

"No! I don't know that." Doc Reese's voice was urgent. "Don't say that, Mae. It's wrong!"

"But you know it's true," Mae whispered. "I sent him away because I can't tell him the truth and now it's too late. I only pray he'll survive."

They sat in silence while the old doctor finished his coffee.

"Come on, child. I've got to get back."

Mae cried softly as they drove along. Doc Reese watched her from the corner of his eye, but by the time he had maneuvered his car through the unfamiliar city streets back out on the highway toward home where he felt more secure, she was asleep.

The doctor eased down into a comfortable slump behind the wheel. It was a six hour drive back to Krayly Creek, and it would be night before they got there.

Chapter 49

Cabel Norris hovered over the cutting the driller offered. He did not like what he saw, but his expression did not reveal it.

"It's a duster, Mr. Norris," the man said. "I'm sorry, but we've got ourselves another dry hole."

"Well!" Cabel straightened. "Nothing to do but try again! How soon can you move this rig up that draw there?"

The man dropped the cutting back into the bucket and dusted his hands. "Now, that depends on the color of your money, I guess, Mr. Norris."

"My money's plenty green," Cabel answered. "You just move the rig and spud in again."

The driller lifted his hat and scratched his head as he followed Cabel's gaze up the draw he indicated. "You figure this third time is charm, do you?"

Cabel did not answer. He just nodded. He had been in enough poker games to know how to bluff.

The driller bit off a tobacco plug and motioned for his

men to begin the task of plugging the hole. He had done this many times before and would do it many more, he knew. These wildcatters never give up, he knew. They're all the same. Dead sure the next hole will be a gusher.

Cabel walked away down the ramp. No need to worry. He had just picked the wrong spot again. The income from his other leases was coming in. He could afford a few dry holes now. But it worried him. He had not figured on the breakdowns and delays they had run into in drilling. Everything that could possibly go wrong had happened. Bits shorn off and boiler trouble. The time delay was eating away his cash reserve. And he had been so sure about this location. It was a gut feeling, nothing more, but he was used to being right, God damn it! He studied the lay of the land as he reached the ground below the derrick floor. Looking for what, he thought. He laughed to himself and shook his head. Hell, it could be anywhere. But it was here! He was sure of that, and he would find it, if it took every cent he could raise. The oil was down there! He cranked up the old truck he had borrowed and headed back to Midland. The fellow he had borrowed it from would be wanting the rest of his money.

***

The day Lon knew he was going to live had nothing to do with how he felt. By that measure he would never have given himself a chance in hell. His choices were either excruciating pain when the morphine's effect wore off, or the senses-numbing oblivion that the drug brought. The day he knew he was going to live was the day Nurse Finnely tickled his foot as she passed his bed. His right foot was the only part of his body that was not swathed in a bandage. In his drugged haze he stared at those toes poking out of the covers a lot. That tickle cheered him more than any words of encouragement he had gotten from the doctor because he figured there was no way that nurse would be tickling a dying man.

Out his room window the Flying Red Horse of the Magnolia Building turned in an endless circle. It was the only thing he could see from where he lay. The slow turn of the sign was like a dancer without music floating in the night sky, and it gave him something to fix his eyes on, something to do. Sometimes when he watched it, he would hear Mae's voice, and he thought he must be delirious again. It was only a dream. He knew that. She had not come. Mae had not come to see him at all.

***

You've got visitors today," Nurse Finnely told him one morning just as the sun's first rays were dimming the red neon of the Magnolia sign.

Lon cut his eyes around as far as he could. "Are you sure?"

"Doctor Gaines says it's okay. You think you're up to it?"

Lon shook his head. "I don't know ." He was suddenly afraid to face anyone. "Who is it?"

Well, there's a couple of people, but we're going to let them in only one at a time. They can only stay for a few minutes."

Lon looked toward the door and saw his father slip into the room, hat in hand.

They neither one spoke at first. Henry just stood by the bed and looked at the stranger that was his son.

324

"Hey, Pa," Lon whispered. "I guess I messed up this time, huh?"

"How you doing?" Henry managed to say and then added. "Hugh Sullivan brought me up here."

"I'm going to make it, I believe," Lon replied. "Is Sully out there, now?"

His father nodded. "We've been up here to Dallas a couple of times before but you never knew we were here."

Lon looked confused at the idea that he had been unconscious so long.

"They told me I couldn't stay but a few minutes," Henry said. He glanced around the room. "They treating you pretty good, are they?"

"Can't complain."

"Willis and your Aunt Mary said to say they were thinking of you," Henry look uncomfortable. He shuffled his feet and started to sit down on the window ledge, but changed his mind and straightened back up.

Lon searched for something to say. Too much had happened. He couldn't begin to explain. "Has the weather been good?" He finally asked.

"Yep. Cotton's up about knee high."

It's summer, Lon thought to himself. "Prices looking better, you think?"

Henry nodded. "I figure to sell some this year, leastwise."

They both fell silent. Lon shifted his weight as best he could. The pain was returning. He would need another shot before long.

"Doctor says you'll be able to get out of here soon," Henry added.

Lon nodded.

"Come on out to the place and rest up. You hear?"

"I'm looking forward to it, Pa."

The nurse stuck her head in the door.

"I guess I have to go now," Henry said, "but I'll be back." his voice cracked with emotion.

Lon made an effort to lift his hand, and his father gripped his fingers gently.

"I'll see you later." Lon said softly, and his father nodded.

Henry Prather left the room, and another head popped around the door.

"Sully! Come on over here."

"How's it going?" Sully approached the bed carefully as if he were afraid his movement might cause Lon some pain.

"How are the rest of the boys?" Lon asked. "Charlie, is he here?"

"No, he didn't come, but he says hello," Sully replied. "Rowdy and Moses, too."

"Sherman?" Lon asked. "Is he okay?" He had been afraid to ask anyone until now.

Sully shook his head and looked down at his feet. "He didn't make it, Lon."

What about Jeremy?"

Sully shook his head again.

"You never found them?"

"No..., no we didn't..., but Moses and Rowdy got out okay."

"Moses was in the tower," Lon remembered.

Sully nodded. "Cut his hands up a little on the guy wire, but he got out quick."

Lon fell silent.

"I'm sorry," Sully added and then fumbled for something else to say.

"They never made it at all?" Lon asked again.

Sully shook his head. "There was nothing left to find, Lon. Not even a belt buckle. Nothing!" The sadness and disbelief in his words caused his voice to crack.

Lon blinked his eyes and recalled Sherman standing there on the derrick floor waving at him just before the explosion. His face was clear in Lon's memory. Lon's hands began to tremble more and his guts cramped up. He needed a shot. He needed it bad.

"There was another fellow on the floor there, too," Sully continued. "One of high pressure crew. He never got out either. And then that fellow that went to the hospital with you. He died that afternoon. They were all standing right over the hole when it blew." He stared at the young man before him; a mass of bandages and angry scars, and thought of the boy he had hired back in Wink. This was hard to take. Lon and Sherman were like sons to him. "We put up some crosses out there for them," he added. "Out at the site. That's the only marker they'll have, I reckon."

Lon remembered the flat lonesome terrain around the well site and tried to picture the crosses.

"Did they get the fire out?" Lon swallowed several times. He was dry. His mouth was like cotton. He needed a shot.

"Yeah. Took'em nine days and three tries, but they blew it out with 140 quarts of nitro."

Lon shook his head in reply, but he could not speak. He was fighting too hard to control his trembling.

"It's the biggest fire that part of the country has ever seen," Sully continued. "They've got a barbed wire wall around it. You can't go near it for fear a spark will set it off again. They drilled an off-set slanted well to let off the gas pressure." He studied Lon's face. "You want me to get the nurse in here?"

Lon nodded unsteadily.

"I'll be back tomorrow. We'll be around for a day or two." Sully quickly backed out of the room, and Nurse Finnely popped in.

"I need a shot," Lon managed to say, but she had the needle in her hand. She slipped into his hip quickly and a rush of relief surged through his body. Jer and Sherman, Lon thought as he drifted off. Why not me, too?

Chapter 50

In the days following the visit from Sully and his father, Lon did a lot of thinking. He was not critical anymore, and he began to think of living. And as the hours passed, Lon felt more hope, but a new worry. He began to worry about the morphine.

"I don't know why you folks are going to all this trouble to save me," Lon told the nurse once when she came in with his shot. "I'll just be a dope head when I get out of here."

"You worry about the healing, and we'll worry about the shots," the nurse said cheerfully.

So he tried, and it was enough to keep him busy. The skin grafts were begun, and without the morphine, he surely could not have survived.

"We can control the pain to some extent," the doctor explained, "but you will have to handle the rest. We'll work until you can't stand it anymore, then we'll stop. Days and nights blended into a horror of endurance. For hours after a session Lon would shake uncontrollably, his nervous system so badly overloaded it could not absorb all the pain.

"We are experimenting on you, Lon," the doctor explained in a gentle voice. "I'm sorry, but we're doing all we can to help you. You know that."

Lon nodded. He was shaking again, like a severe chill, and his shot of morphine was doing little to cut his discomfort.

"We're going to make it, though," the doctor added. "You're strong, and I'm stubborn." He smiled slightly. "Now we'll work until you say stop." And he continued the tedious process of grafting skin from Lon's hip to his back in tiny particles.

But then one day it was done. Almost suddenly, Lon felt, because he had grown so accustomed to the routine. And the long vigil of healing and guarding against infection began. As the nerve endings in his arms and back began to heal the feeling returned and with the feeling came more pain. It washed over him in sheets like a continuous flood rippling over his skin. Although he fought it as best he could, Lon called for the morphine more and more often. And without question, the nurses brought what he asked. The shot would bring blessed relief for a short time and along with it a clear enough head to realize what he had become. Then the realization that he was an addict would haunt his short period of relief from physical pain, and he would worry about the future. How much of his pain was from the burn and how much from the addiction he could not say, but as the morphine began to wear off and the shaking and cramping and searing flashes of heat and cold returned, Lon knew he would ask for another shot. He had no concept of time anymore. How long he had been lying in the hospital; how long since the fire; he could not even guess.

"You're getting better," Nurse Finnely told him one day. "You're starting to ask questions."

***

Within the month Lon was able to move around. The skin grafts were healing. His back and arms were a mass of angry scars, and the new skin was sensitive to the slightest touch. Often it would tear and bleed at his joints when he moved. He started a rehabilitation program to rebuild his muscles, but he was as weak as a child. He fought needing the shots. It seemed like hours, but he knew it was probably only minutes that he struggled against the cramps and the sweating and chills. It was no use, however. In the end, he would call for the nurse, and she would bring the needle. He hated himself for it. He was weak. Even Jer had been able to fight off his craving for liquor at the last. Lon remembered watching Jeremy day after day trembling and sweating. And the nights he had listened to him tossing in half slumber, crying out to his own private demons. And he had licked his addiction. If Jer could do it, why couldn't he? It was best that Mae was not here after all. He would not want her to see him like this. Mae, he thought, and the pain pressed down harder.

"I've got to get off this stuff," he said through clenched teeth as he watched the needle slide into his hip.

Then stop calling for the shot," Nurse Finnely said. She smiled broadly, and Lon hated her for her cheerfulness.

"Yeah, right!"

"I'm serious," the nurse said. "This is in your mind anyway. Did the shot help?"Lon nodded. His trembling was slowing.

"It's sterile water," the nurse held up the needle.

331

"Dr. Gaines decided you didn't need the morphine several weeks ago. We've been cutting the doses with every shot."

Lon stared at her in disbelief. "But the pain."

"In you mind the shots help." The nurse filled his water glass and handed it to him. "Your body has been in pain so long it expects it, I guess, but you've been standing it on your own for some time. You're one tough cookie, you know."

Lon smiled slightly at his own ignorance. He was bewildered. He was elated. "Then I'm not an addict?

"Not any more."

"Well, I'll be damned!"

"The doctor will be in soon," she continued as she straightened the covers and adjusted the curtains. "He's threatening to send you home, I think, but we're trying to talk him out of it."

Lon laughed, shaken out of his confusion over what the nurse had told him. "You've got be ready to get rid of me!"

The nurse laughed and left the room. Her quick efficient steps echoed softly down the hall.

Lon lay back and stared at his Flying Red Horse, and for the first time, started to plan his future.

Chapter 51

Well number three and four came up dry also. The driller didn't have to say a word this time. Cabel was getting good at reading the cuttings himself. "What do you want to do now?" he asked instead.

Cabel straightened and took a deep breath. "Move up the ridge there, and let's try again."

"It's your money," the little man said.

"You let me worry about the money. I'll get it."

"You'll get it?" The driller's head snapped around. "What in hell does that mean?" This ain't a charity outfit here. Do you have the money or not?"

"You move the rig. I'll go get the cash. How's that?" Cabel's face was expressionless. He couldn't let the man know he had no money left. Every last dime Norris Oil had collected from the Cloverleaf leases was gone. Swallowed up in promissory notes on the four dry holes. Such a run of bad luck shouldn't happen to a dog. Every piece of equipment, it seemed, had broken down at least once. Every time Cabel talked to the driller, it was another delay.

He had never figured on this much cost in the beginning.

The little man studied Cabel through squinted eyes while he bit off a fresh chew. "I tell you what," he drawled. "You go get the money, and I'll wait right here. We ain't moving nothing till we see a need to."

"Right!" Cabel agreed. He turned to leave.

"But if you ain't back by tomorrow, we'll be gone!" the man shouted after him.

Cabel cranked the engine on the truck and climbed in pretending not to hear the man's parting threat. He would get the money somehow.

The driller spat off the side of the derrick platform and watched Cabel drive away bucking up the sandy ridge. *Stupid bastard! He doesn't suspect a thing. Well, what the* hell. *Money was money, and he'd take his pay where he could get it. Besides that, half the breakdowns hadn't been his doing at all. And he couldn't have stopped the oil if it had truly been down there. That gave him some satisfaction. That bastard Briggs and his Cloverleaf crowd were paying for more work than he was actually having to do.*

***

There's someone here to see you today," Nurse Finnely said while she was helping Lon back to bed after his therapy session.

He was exhausted and helpless to pull himself straight on his pillow. "Who is it?"

"A Mr. Morris Steinman, I believe."

Lon looked puzzled.

"He's says he knows you," she added. "He came once before while you were still unconscious. He owns a big department store downtown, I understand. I'm impressed!" She added with a smile.

The next face at the door was Morris. He slipped into the room and smiled up at Lon in the high hospital bed.

"Morris, get in here!"

"Sully looked me up when he was here and told me about you. I wanted to come to let you know that I'm thinking about you."

"How are Sully and the boys doing? Have you heard from them lately?"

Morris shook his head slowly. "Not good, I'm afraid. The fire took everything Sully had, you know."

"No, I didn't," Lon replied.

"Kary Oil went under also, I hear. The cost was incredible. Cloverleaf bought them out. I don't know if Sully is working again."

They fell silent for a moment. "Sully didn't say a word," Lon said after a time.

"He'll get going again, I expect." Morris said finally. "You know the oil business."

Lon nodded in agreement. "I guess he will."

"It's good that you are making such progress," Morris changed the subject.

Lon shrugged. "It's hard to call it progress some days."

"It will come, you'll see. It will come."

"So! It's been a long time," Lon brightened. "How are you doing here in Dallas?"

"Fine," the little man smiled. "I'm in business with my brother-in-law, and the store is good. My wife likes it here."

"I didn't recognize the name. Steinman?"

Morris smiled and waved his hand. "My wife said we needed two names now, and my real name is so long. Not good to remember for business. I have a new one."

"And your store? I understand it's big."

"The biggest in town," Morris beamed. "You'll have to come in soon." Morris pulled up a chair and sat down.

"Have you heard from Cabel?" Lon asked.

Morris nodded. "That fellow never lets down. He's got big dreams."

Did the Cloverleaf field prove out?"

"Seven producers so far."

Lon raised his eyebrows in surprise. One-eighth of seven wells, he thought quickly.

"Don't count your money yet, though," Morris cautioned. "Cabel is using the royalty money to develop Norris Oil."

Lon nodded. "He said he would."

"I understand his first two wells were dry. I haven't heard anything lately."

There was a long silence while each of them considered the loss. Lon knew the disappointment of a dry hole and the cost.

"But, we may be rich yet." Morris smiled and smoothed his moustache with his index finger. "What are your plans?"

"I'm going home soon, they tell me." Lon said. "After that, I don't know."

"What about your young lady? The girl you were saving all that money for?"

Lon shook his head quickly. "No, that didn't work out."

"Oh." Morris looked disappointed. "Well, maybe things will change. You never can tell."

Lon smiled slightly, but he didn't respond. Morris could not know how often he had lain here thinking of Mae and wondering why she did not love him. And now that he was going home, part of him still hoped that some change would come. But it was an empty dream. He was recovering, but there was no guarantee that he would not be a cripple for life. If she did not want him as a whole man, she would surely not want the weakling he had become. The ugly scars on his arms and back were not going to disappear and as to his future, he did not know what he would be able to do.

"I better be going," Morris said. "Don't want to over do, you know."

'Thanks for coming to see me."

"You need to come see my store."

"I'll do it." Lon smiled. "When they ever let me out of here."

Chapter 52

The banks were no help this time, and Cabel had nothing left to sell. Nothing but his New Mexico leases, and that he would not do.

"I'm sorry, Mr. Norris," the bank officer said. "Money's tight. We're not speculating right now."

"Hell, man, where would you be without wildcatters? What do you mean, you don't speculate?"

"My hands are tied, Mr. Norris," the man said defensively. "Go see Harold Briggs over at Cloverleaf Oil. They're the only people out here with the capital to risk on unproven leases."

"Hell, yes. They know a deal with they see one. But I don't want to sell. I want to drill!"

"I'm sorry. That's just the way it is."

Cabel stormed out of the bank, brushing customers aside. He was out of business. Nobody would bankroll him now, he knew. He surveyed the street wondering what to do next. The Cloverleaf Oil Company sign across the way jumped out at him. Briggs would love to get hold of his remaining leases. Cabel knew that for a fact. But he wasn't ready to roll over yet, was he? Cabel remembered how sure he had been when he started that first hole. He knew the oil was there. Hell, even now he was sure! But he was busted. So what could he do? Give up? Not yet!

He considered his options for a few minutes and then cut out through the cars. He'd just go see what Brigg's deal was. It wouldn't hurt to give it a try.

The secretary remembered him. He felt sweaty and sand covered; out of place in the fancy office setting, but he didn't care, and she didn't seem to mind. She showed him right in to Briggs' office. Briggs came around the desk to meet him. His handshake was hearty. The old man smells blood, Cabel thought quickly.

"So, Cabel, how's my newest competition doing out there in the sand hills?"

"You know damn well how," Cabel shot back. He looked around for a chair and sat down without waiting to be asked.

Briggs took time to light his pipe, eyeing Cabel over his pipe stem as he did. "Yes," he said finally as he shook out his match. "I hear you've had a run of bad luck out there. How many dry holes is that now...four?"

"Five."

Briggs sat on the edge of his desk and studied the young man before him. "And what brings you here today?"

"I'm out of money," Cabel announced flatly. "And the bank won't finance me."

"Times are shaky."

"Would you be interested in buying up some of my royalty on the wells you hold?"

"You mean you'd sell a sure thing for another dry

hole?" Briggs asked in amazement.

"What do you say?"

"If you don't mind a little advice, wouldn't it be smarter to just sell me the sandhill leases and take a one-eighth like you did on the other land? Why risk losing everything?

"Because I'm not looking just to be a percentage of someone else's company," Cabel shot back. "I want my own business."

"And if you're wrong? If there is no oil in the sand hills?"

"The oil is there."

Harold Briggs laughed softly and shook his head. The boy has guts, he thought. But that is all. He'd seen it before, time and again. Wildcat fever had gobbled up more men than bootleg whiskey.

"What about your partners?" Briggs asked.

"We have an agreement. I make the decisions!"

"I see." Briggs drew on his pipe and studied Cabel for a few minutes. "I can't consider only part of your royalties. My stockholders wouldn't hear of it. It would have to be all or nothing."

Cabel considered his words. Briggs had the upper hand, and he knew it. There would be no other offers. This was it. Take it or leave it. He had figured as much. It was a buyer's market. "That's fine with me. Only from there on I name my own terms."

Briggs nodded. "Very well. What do you want?"

"Stake me to three more wells, no strings attached. I'll pick the spots. I'll sign over my one-eighth interest in your field, but not my New Mexico leases. The sand hills aren't included."

"I'll have the lawyers get the papers ready." Briggs stuck out his hand. "I admire your style. You're either going to be an oil field legend or the biggest sucker in the Permian Basin."

"Just get the money out," Cabel said.

***

You can go home now, but only to rest," Dr. Gaines directed Lon as he dismissed him. "I don't want one of my major successes to get out there and over do it too soon." He smiled as he checked over the healing scars on Lon's back and arms. "You were very fortunate, Lon, that your face escaped the flames. Give yourself a little more healing time, and a long sleeve shirt will be all the protection your skin needs."

"When will I be able to work again?"

"That's up to you, I'd say." Doctor Gaines paused in his examination. "You'll probably never be able to do much heavy physical labor again, Lon. The burns were too extensive."

He lifted Lon's arm level with his shoulder, as high as it could be moved before the folds of scar tissue stopped it. "At this point I just can't say how much use you will have in your arms."

Lon winced in pain. His arms had been bandaged to his sides during the slow process of healing, and he still could not lift them easily. Trying had been the hardest part of his rehabilitation so far and had shown the least results.

"You need an indoor job, out of the heat with minimal physical exertion," Doctor Gaines continued.

"And what would that be?" Lon asked with an edge to his voice. "All I know is drilling oil wells and farming cotton."

Dr. Gaines looked Lon square in the eye. "I don't

know, Lon. It's up to you, but after what I've seen you go through this last year, I have no doubt that you'll find your way. I'm marking you down as one of my personal medical successes. You can't let me down."

That afternoon, after sixteen months, Lon walked out of the hospital under his own power.

Chapter 53

The holes were dry. It was surprising how quickly they were drilled, one after the other in rapid succession. Cable stayed at the site, slept under the pipe rack, but he could not will the oil in. A dry hole was a dry hole.

He sat on the side of a ravine and watched the men dismantle the rig and haul it away. He was a legend, all right. Eight dry holes and he had lost everything. Harold Briggs must be laughing his ass off over this one. Cloverleaf wins again.

A car stuttered up over the ridge and slid down the sandy slope to the well site. Cabel made out the driver. It was Hugh Sullivan. He hadn't seen him in over two years. Rumor had it that Sullivan Drilling went bust after the oil well fire. Lost everything he had was the word Cabel had gotten. The car stopped on hard ground, and Sully got out, slapping dust from his clothes. He ignored Cabel at first and watched the men loading the drilling equipment. After a bit, he sauntered over close to Cabel and stood silently, watching the workers.

"Tough luck," he said after time.

"Yep," Cabel responded.

"What are you figuring to do now?" Sully looked squarely at Cabel for the first time.

"Well," Cabel gave a dry laugh. "I guess I'd better figure out a way to explain this to my business partners." He looked around at Sully. "Then I've got to figure out how to finance my next rig. You got any suggestions?"

"Well," Sully drawled. "You might go cut a deal with Cloverleaf for these leases and sit back and let him hunt for a while."

Cabel smiled and shook his head. "I doubt I could bring that off again after eight dry holes. Harold Briggs would see me coming. He wouldn't want any part of this."

"The hell you say!" Sully shot back. "He'd jump at the chance. Why else would he go to so much trouble to keep you from bringing in a well?"

"I don't follow you?"

"Hell, boy, haven't you figured it out? Briggs has been betting against you all along. He's probably paying your driller to see to it you fail."

The words were like a hard slap. Suddenly it was clear. The delays, the cost overruns. How could he be so stupid? "That son-of-a-bitching little driller! I'll tear his hide off one inch at a time!" Cabel started to storm away.

"Hold up, now!" Sully called, and Cabel stopped, frozen by his anger. "There's plenty of time to settle that debt. Briggs is your real enemy. That's who you need to get."

"I'll blow his damn' head off! That's what I'll do!" Cabel was talking through clenched teeth.

"And what will that get you?"

Cabel paused to hear Sully out.

"You're playing in the big leagues now, son. This ain't no little poker game here. Harold Briggs has been chasing these oil patches around Texas most of his life. You think he's going to let some young buck waltz in here and corner the last good field out here? Hell, no! He's going to fight you. So he pays your driller to slow you up, that's all. Gobble up your cash and force you to over extent. It happens all the time. You don't fight that with a gun. You fight it with your wits!"

"And I reckon you have an idea how to do that?"

"I might." Sully rolled a smoke and offered his sack of makings.

Cabel waved him off. "Never picked up the habit." He laughed again. "Too expensive. I always figured to save that money and invest it." He looked back at his rig site, now no more than a ragged bald patch in the desert floor. In a few days, he thought, you'll never know anything was here. "As you can see, I'd have been better off to have taken up smoking. I ended up wasting the money anyway."

"You still got this lease here, don't you?"

"Yeah, it's mine." Cabel waved his arm out toward the horizon in disgust. "Ever last sand dune."

"You ever seen a cable tool rig?" Sully went on.

"Yeah, once or twice."

"I used to run one of them things for almost nothing. Hooked it up to the rear axle of my car, and me and Charlie could drill a hole all by ourselves."

Cabel perked up. "Is that right?"

"I was thinking. If you had a mind to, you could pretty near drill your own well out here with a cable rig. The formation is pretty loose."

Cabel broke into a grin. "You wouldn't happen to know of one of those cable rigs, would you?"

"I've got one stored over at Wink. Never had the heart to get rid of it." Sully smiled slightly. "It's the only thing the lawyers didn't take after the fire. It's worthless to most folks, I guess."

"So you figure, I..., we could hook this thing up and do some drilling?"

Sully nodded slowly.

"And what would you take for your trouble?"

"One-eighth of every well I drill, and the satisfaction of seeing Cloverleaf Oil squirm a little."

"You got a beef of your own?"

"Cloverleaf bought up my leases at auction after the fire. Walked off with every well I had for almost nothing." Sully ground out his smoke. "I just hate to see all the aces go to the same player every time."

"What if I'm wrong? What if the oil isn't here?"

"It's here all right." Sully said softly. "We both know it, and so does Briggs. He never would have gone to this much trouble to break you if he wasn't sure."

Cabel surveyed the barren land around them with new enthusiasm.

"So. How about it?" Sully asked. "We find the oil first. Then we settle with Briggs later. Deal?"

Cabel stuck out his hand. "Well, what are we waiting for, partner?"

Chapter 54

Lon untied the bucket and slowly began to lower it into the well; hand over hand, each motion a forced movement that tore at his stiff muscles and tender skin. He gritted his teeth and gripped the rope tightly. Then as he heard the bucket hit the water below he began to haul on the rope with all his strength. The pain flooded over his arms and shoulders as he strained to lift his arms above his head. Sweat broke out on his forehead, and he groaned involuntarily with his effort. When he had first begun, he had often had to drop his hold on the rope and let the bucket fall back into the water. But after weeks of trying, he could now bring the bucket all the way to the surface before he lowered it again. The scar tissue on his arms would crack and bleed from time to time, and his arms would tremble and ache for hours after his efforts, but he was regaining use of his arms bit by bit. To hell with what Dr. Gaines had said. Back here at his father's place in Krayly Creek he had begun to mend in a way that could never have happened cooped up in that hospital. He would have a lot to show the doctor when he went back for his check up. He started to lower the bucket again.

The sound of an approaching car caught his attention. Doc Reese pulled up in his Model A Roadster and hailed him from the road. Lon waved back but continued his exercise.

"So, you're still at it, I see," the doctor called as he walked over.

"I'm getting downright good at this, Doc."

The doctor had been dropping by once a week to check him over, and Lon enjoyed surprising him with his progress.

Doc sat down on a bench by the well and pulled off his hat.

"Delivered Zak and Sarah Campbell's firstborn this morning. Sarah is doing fine." He rubbed his tired eyes. He had been up all night again. "Mae came over there to help her sister, so I left. Thought I'd look in on you on the way home."

Lon concentrated on the rope and bucket. He did not want to hear about Mae's sister and her new family. Not when he and Mae had no chance for their own. "I guess Aunt Mary is happy," he said after a bit.

"Yeah, she was over there beaming like it was all her idea." Doc laughed and dipped up a drink from the bucket Lon offered. "I delivered all the children in this place. Now I'm on the grandchildren."

Lon laughed as he took a drink himself.

"When's it going to be your turn?" Doc said.

"My turn at what?"

"Having a family?"

Lon shot the doctor a sharp look. "Well, I don't see the ladies lining up out here. So if you are waiting on me for more business, you might look around for other prospects."

"You look strong enough to me. You've got nothing to keep you from it."

Lon turned his attention back to the rope.

"So," Doc continued. "What's stopping you?"

"From what?"

"From marrying Mae Handley. You want to, don't you?"

"Now, Doc, that's not rightly any of your business..."

"My business. Hell boy! Don't tell me my business. I brought you into this world, and I'll damn sure tell you my mind if I please. And I'm telling you not to let her get away. What's holding you back?"

Lon stopped short and studied the old man for a moment. "Look at me," he said flatly. "Look at these arms. Would any woman in her right mind want to touch me, do you think?"

"If she loves you that won't matter a whit!"

"Well, she doesn't! She doesn't give a damn about me. I've already asked her to marry me. Twice! And she turned me down flat! He started to haul on the rope again with renewed strength.

"Well, maybe loving you is not the problem," Doc said.

"What are you saying? That she does love me? I wouldn't put money it. All this time and she's never come to see me. Not once!"

"Hell, boy, what you don't know would fill a book!" Doc slapped his hat on his head and rose to leave. "I brought her to Dallas myself to see you when you were still out cold. She cried all the way up there and all the way back."

Lon stopped and let the bucket splash into the well. "Why didn't she come back when I was awake?"

"She'll have to tell you that herself, I guess." The old man paused as if he were arguing with himself, deciding what to say. "Sometimes, boy, folks have scars that just don't show. You're worrying about scars." He motioned at Lon's arms. "But some things can be worse than that. Some people carry their wounds inside."

Lon stared at his old friend, puzzled by his words.

"I'm a doctor, son. I can't tell all I know. But you go see Mae. You go ask her why she thinks she can't leave here. You ask her if she still loves you, and then you marry that girl. She's as fine a person as God ever made, and she deserves some happiness!"

Doc turned on his heels and stomped away to his car. Lon stood dumfounded by the old man's outburst. He watched him drive away trailing a plume of dust.

Chapter 55

The men were excited about drilling. It had been a long time since they hooked up a cable rig. It was simple, much simpler than the rotaries they had been operating for the last few years. Rowdy and Moses felt like craftsmen again as they nailed the derrick frame into place and rigged the lines.

"You sure about this thing?" Cabel asked with a grin, once it was up."

It was a spindly looking sight to say the least. Charlie rigged a drive belt to the rear axle of Sully's green Packard, and they were set to start.

"This baby can find the oil if it's down there; just the same as a rotary," Sully assured Cabel. "Believe me, I've done it before."

Cabel smiled and raised his hands in a sign of resignation. "I'm in no spot to question. Let's give her a try."

It went slow. The steady pounding of the tool into the ground moved down by fractions of inches, but the crew was content. Charlie and Sully, Rowdy and Moses slipped back into a familiar routine. The rig hummed night and day, and their main cost was only the gasoline Sully kept pouring into his Packard.

Cabel was anxious. He stayed on the rig almost night and day, but the others seemed fulfilled just to be working the old rig again.

"How did you come to pick this here spot?" Rowdy asked one morning as he sat on an overturned bucket sharpening a drilling wedge with a rasp.

Cabel looked around at the land. "It was just one I hadn't tried before, I guess." He smiled slightly. The guessing game for a drill site was a sore point with him. "You think it was a bad choice?"

Rowdy kept working. Tool sharpening was a never ending job. "It's a likely enough spot, I guess."

Cabel nodded, reassured somehow by this grizzled old oil man's words.

"If it don't pan out though," Rowdy continued, "Moses thinks you ought to try that uplift over there to the north."

Cabel followed Rowdy's gaze. "What uplift? All I see is a sand dune."

Rowdy smiled and studied his handiwork on the cutting tool. "Well, that's your problem, Sonny. You don't know an uplift from your ass. But it's there.

"And that's where the oil is, you think?"

"We'll see," Rowdy answered. "Here, help me haul that line up, and let's try a new blade on there."

***

Within two weeks Sully broached the idea of giving up on the well and moving the rig. "Charlie figures we're down plenty deep to be showing pay and the cuttings aren't right. I think we missed the oil sand."

"Rowdy says we should try north," Cabel suggested. He says Moses thinks there's an uplift out there."

Sully studied the horizon. "They might be right."

"Well, there's nothing to do but move up there and try, I guess." Cabel shrugged his shoulders. It was getting harder and harder to keep believing in all this.

"We'll break her down tomorrow," Sully said. "I've got to go to town for supplies. Come on and help me unhitch the car, and you can go with me. It'll do you good to get away from here."

Cabel did as Sully said. It was the first time he had been into Midland since he made his deal with Briggs. In town it seemed every truck and building had a Cloverleaf sign on it.

"Briggs is still doing alright, I see," Sully observed.

Cabel studied the signs in disgust. He didn't know whether he was madder at Briggs for his underhandedness, or himself for being so stupid. They pulled in across the street from the Cloverleaf building, and Cabel studied the windows of the second floor office. *One of these days*, he consoled himself.

***

Harold Briggs stood at the window and surveyed his town. It was his town, he thought confidently, right down to the people in the street. If they didn't work directly for Cloverleaf, they were dependent on Cloverleaf people to buy their products. The competition was all but dead. He had outsmarted them all.

Down below he watched a dust covered green Packard

pull up and saw Hugh Sullivan and that young Norris kid get out. His men had told him those two were working together, but he had heard no more of them. Briggs smiled to himself. Those leases he had picked up at auction when Sullivan went under had proven quite profitable. And he never could have gotten them if he had not been on the bank board that called in Sullivan's note.

Briggs moved his gaze to Norris, standing by the car, arrogant as ever. Well young man, you've learned a lesson or two this year. Wonder if you're ready to talk a deal yet? Briggs motioned behind him for one of his aides.

***

They got the supplies they needed on Sully's credit at the general store. Cabel carried one of the boxes out to the car and waited. It was humiliating to be this broke, on the take from Sully.

"How's it going out in the sand hills?" a voice interrupted his thoughts. Cabel turned to see one of Briggs' aides smiling at him. "We hear you're trying to use a cable rig out there."

"The hell you say," Cabel mumbled.

"Mr. Briggs would still like to talk to you about your land, Norris."

"You tell Briggs I'll see him in hell first."

"You'd be wise to take him up on his offer before you kill yourself out there."

"You tell him to stay the hell away from me, or I'll be around to settle up with him some day when he least expects it."

"Are you threatening Mr. Briggs, Norris? Because, if you are..."

"Stand clear!" Sully bellowed as he shoved the last box in the window of his car. The man jumped back. Sully climbed in the car and gunned the engine. Cabel got in and Sully pulled away with enough speed to leave the man coughing in their dust.

"It won't do you no good to fight him now." Sully advised. "He's too powerful. But if we make a strike out there..." He left Cabel alone with his thoughts.

***

Sully rented a truck to haul the rig, and they began the work of breaking it all down the next morning. Cabel was feeling low. This many failures had sapped his confidence. The horror of being trapped out here in the sandhills drilling dry holes one after another for the rest of his life was too much to consider. If Sully and the others had not been so damn philosophical about it, he would have chucked the whole mess and walked off. Anything but sit here and broil or freeze watching the holes come up dry. But he didn't say it out loud. The men around didn't seem to see his lack of interest. In fact, he made little difference to them at all. They were content doing what they were doing. Running that old rig, nursing it along. They loaded the whole setup on the borrowed truck and set off up the draw.

"I think that far ridge looks favorable," Rowdy pronounced, and Moses nodded agreement.

"Then the ridge it is," Sully shouted over the engine. He ground the gears on the old truck and made a sputtering start. Charlie and Moses rode with the equipment and Rowdy and Cabel followed in the Packard. It was a sad looking parade bumping through the sage and sand. The truck engine whined as Sully angled the heavy load up the ridge. Halfway up, the crusty top layer of sand began to slip away from the tires, and the old truck skidded sideways along the slope. Sully raced the engine but the truck's tires only spun in the sand, and slowly, as the men watched helplessly, the truck bed tilted, and the derrick sills and rig machinery began to slide off the side. Charlie and Moses leaped off the truck bed to save being crushed by the shifting load. As the truck sank to its axles, the whole load toppled off in a jumbled pile in the sand.

No one spoke. Sully struggled out of the truck cab where it sat buried up to the running boards. Charlie and Moses dusted themselves off after their jump and joined Rowdy and Cabel by the car. They all stared for several minutes at the mess as the last pieces of casing rolled off the truck bed and bounced down the slope.

"Well," Sully drawled finally, "I guess this looks like a good spot. What do you say, Charlie?"

Then Cabel started to laugh. Slow at first, sort of a sputtering chuckle. Sully joined in, and then Charlie. Rowdy broke into a wide grin and slapped Moses on the back. Moses winced from the unexpected blow, and they both joined the laughter. Rowdy laughed so hard he had to sit down and wipe his eyes. Suddenly Cabel had never felt so good in his whole life. It was the perfect spot for this poor-boy operation. One by one, the men regained their composure and started sifting through the jumbled pile. By dark they had set the derrick stand and untangled the lines. They could be drilling by tomorrow night.

Chapter 56

It was several weeks before Lon got up the courage to go see Mae. He had made up his mind. She was going to have to tell him she didn't love him to his face. Then maybe he could move on. But Doc Reese was right. He had to know.

The circle of trees around the old house looked like an island marooned in a sea of cotton fields as he drove up. Cal Handley had the land looking pretty good again, he observed. His father had been right. Things were getting better.

Lon got out of the car and started up the path. Cassie saw him first. She was out in the garden. She came running toward the car out of curiosity, but stopped at the corner of the house and stared timidly at him.

"Hello, Cassie. Do you remember me?" Lon squatted down on his haunches to be at the child's eye level. "I'm Lon. Remember?"

Cassie smiled sweetly. "I'm watering my flowers. See?" She pointed toward the garden plot. "Mae helped me plant them. Come and see."

Lon followed her up the gravel path. He had forgotten the feeling Cassie caused in him. She was as full of life and gentleness as Mae. The child huddled proudly over the tiny patch of flowers, a mixture of bright summer zinnias. "See?" She said.

Lon knelt down on one knee beside her to admire her garden.

"This is mighty fine, Cassie," he declared, and the child giggled in delight.

A sound caught his ear, and he turned to see Mae watching them from behind the screen door. He felt a churn in his stomach at the sight of her. She was beautiful.

"Hello, Mae," he said softly. He stood up and faced her, his hat in his hands. "Can I come in?"

She smiled slightly and touched her hair. "I didn't expect company." Mae's voice faltered.

Lon glanced down. She did not want to see him. And for a moment he almost turned and fled. He shouldn't have come. He locked his jaw and took a deep breath to steady his nerve. And then look quickly back into her eyes. He couldn't let this moment pass. "Could we just sit and talk for a minute?" He motioned toward some chairs on the porch.

Cassie lost interest in the flowers and ran off to an old rope swing at the edge of the yard.

Mae hesitated only a moment before she stepped out, closing the door quietly behind her. Lon backed toward the chairs, reluctant to take his eyes off of her for fear she would change her mind and go back inside.

"How are you?" Mae asked. "You look well." Her voice quivered slightly, and Lon sensed that she was frightened.

"Better, I'm..." He paused and looked down at the khaki

sleeves covering his arms. "I'm doing fine. And you?" His tone was gentle. He did not want to scare her.

"Well, I..., I'm a mess." She touched her hair again. "I've been at Sarah's helping her with the baby."

"She doing okay?"

"They're both fine."

He motioned for her to sit and she did. Lon leaned against the porch rail before her. For a moment they just sat, fighting an inner battle, looking at each other, then quickly looking away. The only sound was the bluster of the wind carrying Cassie's voice toward them as she sang some children's song. Lon watch without seeing as she stretched her toes out in delight and pulled the swing higher and higher.

"Why didn't you come back to see me after I woke up?" he asked suddenly. He was too upset to make small talk. He had to know.

"I..., I didn't think you would want to see me," Mae whispered. "I only came because I had to know you were alive."

"But you came."

Mae nodded, her eyes suddenly shiny with tears.

They fell silent again, each struggling with what to say next. A southwest wind whistled around the corner of the porch, tugging gently at their hair and clothing.

"Tell me why you can't leave here." Lon asked.

Mae jumped at the question, but she didn't look away.

"What did Doc tell you?" she whispered.

"Nothing. Only that I should ask you."

Mae looked down at her hands and said nothing.

"Tell me, Mae. I don't understand. Doc says there's a reason."

Mae raised her eyes and took a deep breath. "Cassie's

not my sister," she whispered.

She paused, and Lon waited for her to continue. He did not understand.

Mae raised her chin as though gathering courage and looked him directly in the eye. "The reason..." Her voice faltered, and she took another deep breath before she continued. "I can never leave her...She's my daughter."

Lon held his breath, stunned by what he heard. He had not known what to expect after what the doctor had said. He had puzzled over his words again and again, but no answer had come. Never this. He stared with a blank expression at Mae unable to comprehend what she was saying. "I know you feel responsible for Cassie. I understand..."

"No," Mae cut him off. "No, Lon, you don't. Cassie is my daughter. Not my sister."

Lon stopped short, lost for words, flooded with questions. He realized Mae was speaking again. Her voice was calm now.

"I don't remember much." She paused struggling for words, but she continued. "Mama was very sick. My father would be gone for days. And when he was home, he was drunk."

Lon stared dumbly at her. What was she talking about? Why was she telling him about her father?"

"I had to go in the night for Mary Campbell, Mama said. She was scared, I guess. She had a bad spell. But when I got to the house, everyone was gone."

Lon's mind whirled. Ratch! What was she saying! His stomach turned at the sickness of it. His first instinct was to bolt. He had to move. He jumped up from the railing and walked to the far end of the porch. He gripped the porch rail and stared away toward the river, his back ramrod straight, thoughts boiling in his brain. Cassie's singing drifted around him.

Mae's voice came to him through the roar of thoughts in his head. "Did Emory ever talk about me?" she was asking. "Mention me at all?"

Lon forced himself to listen. "What? Emory? No...,no, what's he...."

"I didn't think so. He probably tried to pretend it never happened."

"What are you talking about?" Lon was choking on his words. She made no sense.

"Everyone was gone that night, like I said. Everyone but Emory. He came out from the barn when he heard me at the house. I was glad to see him at first, but as I walked over to him, he looked strange. Wild eyed and unsteady on his feet. He was drunk."

The roar in Lon's head stopped, and suddenly his thoughts were clear, painfully clear. He remembered.

Mae walked toward him at the railing. Her hands were shaking, but her voice was hushed and clear. "He grabbed at me and missed. I turned to run, but he grabbed again." Silent tears streamed down her face. "He raped me, Lon. I tried to fight, but...," She fell silent.

Mae straightened and wiped her eyes with a trembling hand. "So..." She took a deep breath. "That was it. He was sick afterward. I think he was as horrified as I was. I just ran. I ran home and told my mother. She was terrified that word would get out. The neighbors, she said. They would blame me. Never Emory. Never the man." Mae reached out to balance herself against the porch rail with a trembling hand. "And then you and Emory were gone. He was so drunk, maybe..." She paused. "He was gone, disappeared with you."

Lon's mind was churning. Emory? So this is why he was so eager to run away. So eager to leave when he had always been against the idea before. Emory's dying words rang in his ears again.

"I'm no damn good, Lon. Tell them I'm sorry."

"I, I know it's hard to believe, Lon." Mae was saying. "It's hard for me sometimes. It seems so long ago now. Doc tells me it's the mind's way of dealing with something too painful to bear." She struggled with what else to say. She needed him to understand. Regardless of his reaction, it was better that he know. Doc Reese was right. He was always right.

"I stayed at home at first, hidden away." Her voice faltered, remembering. "If it hadn't been for Mama and Doctor Reese..."

Lon raised his hand to stop her words. He did not want to hear more. But he knew she could not stop now.

"It was simple, really. People don't see what they choose to ignore," she said as to herself as to Lon. "Cal and the others were too young to know what was happening really."

"He never said a word." Lon's voice was only a whisper.

"So, you see. It's not you. It's me. I can't leave Cassie, and I'm not exactly who you've believed I am."

"He never told me," Lon repeated. "Emory never said a word."

Mae smiled slightly. Her eyes seemed weary. She looked down for a moment, and then she continued. "When Doc Reese came out Mama swore him to secrecy. He lied for me. I'm not sure why. I would have died from the shame of it if Doc hadn't been there. He took me to a home in Abilene. I registered under another name. Mama spread the word she was expecting again, and no one questioned it. Not even my father. Doc took care of everything." Mae turned to look up at Lon. "But what would these people have done to me, thought of me, if they had known the truth?"

She was right, he knew. Mae's mother and Doc were right. Their way had saved her from added pain.

"I'm sorry, Lon. I told you once that people often have little control over their future." She paused as though she were searching for the right words. "I wanted to tell you when you were feeling so burdened by Emory's death. Thinking you were responsible for taking him away. Emory had his own reasons for leaving. It wasn't your fault."

"No more than all this was yours."

Cassie's voice floated toward them on the wind. Emory's child. Lon watched her progress, dark curls blowing in the wake of the swing.

"And this is why you wouldn't marry me?"

Mae nodded and bowed her head again. "I couldn't lie to you."

"But I love you, Mae. Nothing can change that. Do you love me?"

Mae raised her head. Her blue eyes were brimming with tears as she nodded.

"Then that's all that matters." Lon straightened his shoulders and spoke in a voice that was no longer confused. "Something that happened so long ago can't hurt us now. The only thing that can hurt us is if you send me away." He studied her face for an answer. "We should be together. That's what is important. You and I and Cassie." Lon reached out and gathered her into his arms.

Mae pressed her face against his chest. "Yes," she

whispered. Lon kissed her forehead and held her close, and he was content again for the first time in a long while.

"It will all work out, Mae. I'm getting stronger every day. We'll be together, and it will work out. I promise."

"I can help," Mae said quickly. "You have to rest and recover.

Lon hushed her with a kiss.

Chapter 57

Cabel Norris rented the entire second floor over the Permian National Bank building. It was his first extravagance. The kelly-green sign with gold letters was raised to the roof of the building, and the town of Midland got a look at its newest tycoon.

The field was big, just as Cabel said it would be. The biggest yet, and for every barrel produced, one-eighth went to Sullivan Drilling, one-eighth to the land owner, and the rest to Norris Oil. He hired accountants to keep score. Even in a town where many fortunes had been made overnight, Cabel Norris turned some heads. He was young and smart and lucky, a combination to be respected.

And he was eccentric. That's what the people loved best. Stories began to circulate within a few weeks of his antics, and the grizzled old oil field workers laughed and passed them on.

"He drilled nine dry holes before he struck, is what I heard!"

"I heard it was nineteen!"

"He's never owned a suit of clothes in his life, but last week he needed a suit for a meeting, so he sent out and bought everything the Men's Store had in his size."

"I hear he and Hugh Sullivan are suing Cloverleaf Oil for three million dollars, and they stand a good chance of winning."

"Old Briggs is squirming in the light."

Cabel Norris was the stuff oil field legends were made of.

"I figure there's a need for a good trucking line out here," Cabel explained to Sully. "What do you think?" They were slumped in their chairs with their feet propped on the desk. Cabel had his hands behind his head, his favorite thinking position.

"Cloverleaf Oil has the only fleet of trucks working now," Sully agreed.

"We'll be needing them soon, and there's plenty of independents who would use us, if we could provide the trucks," Cabel added.

He suddenly sat forward and pulled his wallet out. "Get on the phone to Dallas and order us up a fleet of trucks," he called to his secretary. Cabel opened his wallet and pulled out a creased five dollar bill and looked at it.

He smiled slightly and handed the bill over to the girl. as she came to his desk.

"And send someone over to Cloverleaf Oil and find this fellow here." He pointed out the writing on the bill. "Tell Brace Whitman that the man he loaned five dollars to wants to make him the head of a new trucking line."

"Yes, sir," the girl said. She was growing accustomed to Mr. Norris' strange orders and was quick to follow through.

Sully watched the scene with interest. Cabel waited for

his comment. "I tell you, son. I do believe you're going to be good at this high roller life." They both laughed.

"Morris Steinman called from Dallas this morning." Cabel said. "That law firm he suggested will file suit on Harold Briggs and Cloverleaf Oil by the end of the month."

"I want to be here to see that," Sully chuckled.

Cabel turned to other matters. He pulled a note pad off the desk and started writing, scribbling in quick strokes. This was the last order of business for the day.

"Let me get this message off to Lon, and I'll be ready to go eat. When did the boys say they'd be in?"

"Charlie said sundown. Rowdy and Moses will be hungry by then."

Cabel finished the message and handed it over to Sully to read

TO: LON PRATHER

THE FIELD IS BIG   STOP   NEED AN OPERATIONS DIRECTOR   STOP   GET   HERE   AS   SOON   AS POSSIBLE   STOP   NEED HELP SPENDING ALL THIS MONEY   END
        CABEL NORRIS OIL CO.

—THE END—

About the Author

Irene Sandell

Irene Sandell is a native Texan with family roots that go back 5 generations. Born in West Texas and raised in the Central Texas town of Hamilton, she developed a love of the unique history of the Lone Star State and its people. *In A Fevered Land* is her first novel.

Other Books by Irene Sandell

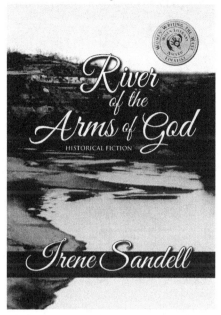

River of the Arms of God

Kate Walters believes she is escaping her controlling father for the life of her dreams when she hastily marries Colby Walters and moves to his ranching empire, Pantera. But she soon finds that the wide open lands of West Texas have a host of their own secrets that hold her captive. Only when she is shown the strength to stand on her own by Sarah Graham, a young woman who lived along the Butterfield Stage Route and walked the same ground 100 years before, does Kate find true freedom. The life lessons that both women learn lead them on journeys that reach across the years and span the continent.

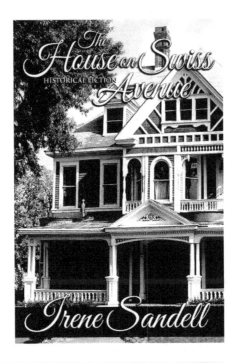

The House on Swiss Avenue

Robyn Merrill hopes that starting a new life in a new place will help to heal her broken heart, but the path she chooses and the people she encounters are not what she expected. Secluded in her family mansion, Adeline Sinclair has spent a lifetime devoted to memories and to the history of her family, only to question her choices in her twilight years. Her house on Swiss Avenue brings the two women together to unlock secrets that alter each of their lives, and help them make peace with the past and welcome the future.

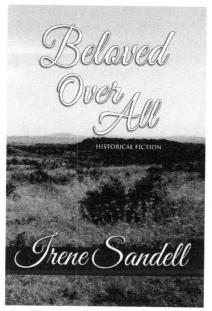

Beloved Over All

Stella Carter and her husband left the racial strife of Kentucky searching for a safe haven in Texas. Benjamin Walters came west seeking to escape the violent secrets of his past in Missouri. Henry Prescott was one step ahead of the law when he left Arkansas for the cattle range of the Southwest.

Unimagined hardships, Indian wars, captivity, and outlaws await these pioneers in the maelstrom of events that engulf the Texas frontier following the Civil War, but they also find daring, courage, and the strength of a mother's love in their quest. The lives of buffalo hunters, Indians, soldiers, cowboys and settlers intertwine in the struggle to find their place in this beloved land. Based on true characters and events, this novel weaves an action-packed saga of the American frontier.

Made in the USA
Middletown, DE
19 February 2019